ALAMUT

A Foundation Book
Doubleday
New York   London   Toronto   Sydney   Auckland

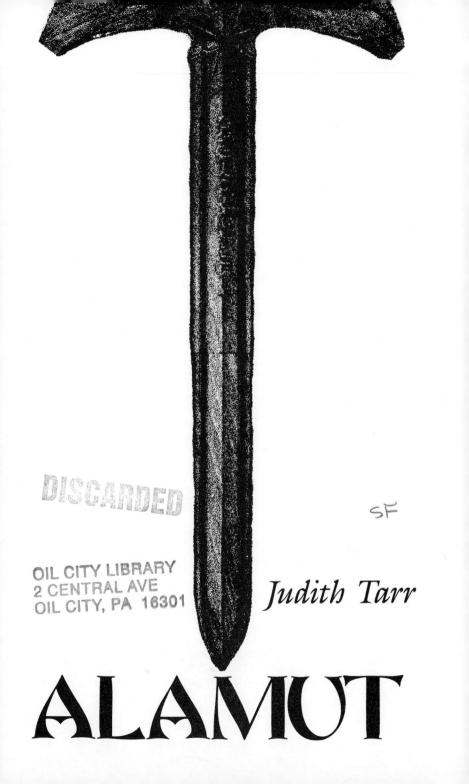

Judith Tarr

ALAMUT

A FOUNDATION BOOK
Published by Doubleday,
a division of Bantam Doubleday Dell Publishing Group, Inc.
666 Fifth Avenue, New York, New York 10103

FOUNDATION, DOUBLEDAY, and the portrayal of the letter F are
trademarks of Doubleday, a division of Bantam Doubleday Dell
Publishing Group, Inc.

Library of Congress Cataloging-in-Publication Data

Tarr, Judith.
　Alamut / by Judith Tarr.
　　p.　cm.
　"A Foundation book."
　ISBN 0-385-26435-6 : —ISBN 0-385-26435-6 (pbk.) : $7.95
　I. Title.
PS3570.A655A79　1989
813'.54—dc20　　　　　　　　　　　　　　89-35225
　　　　　　　　　　　　　　　　　　　　　　CIP

FIRST EDITION

To
Jim Frenkel
who wanted a Big Book

With thanks

ACKNOWLEDGMENTS

This book could not have been what it is without the help of a number of people. Douglas Chester was in at the inception, with extensive and invaluable information on "Damascus" steel, and some hands-on experience thereof—giving me, indirectly, an entire subplot and a good portion of my cast of characters. I owe a particular debt to Anatoly Belilovsky, M.D., for aid and advice in matters medical; any errors or infelicities in that regard are entirely my own. Susan Shwartz, in buying a short story called "Defender of the Faith" for her anthology, *Moonsinger's Friends,* provided the impetus for what eventually became this novel. Sandra Miesel has been invaluable in guiding me through the complexities of medieval Islamic history and scholarship. My agent, Jane Butler, kept the idea alive for more years than either of us can easily count, on the principle that one should sell no book before its time. To all the people who kept my spirits up in the face of a killer deadline, particularly Esther Friesner, Harry and Laura Turtledove (for the Alamut Saloon), and all the Susans, thanks and a weary grin. And last but far from least, thanks to Lou Aronica and Amy Stout of Bantam Doubleday Dell, whose enthusiasm for an outline and a pair of sample chapters turned the whole unwieldy object into an honest-to-goodness book.

I

AQUA BELLA

I

The sun was gentle in the first hour of its rising. It lay lightly upon the hills of Jerusalem; it washed with gold the walls of Aqua Bella castle, and the village huddled beneath them, and the green that was the great wealth of the demesne: the oaks that were holy, the olives that were more than holy, and the glorious tangle that traced the track of the stream. Women were washing in it, singing sweet and high, with here and there a ripple of laughter.

He came by the road that led to the sea, riding all alone, all his armor and his weapons borne on a dove-grey mule. His destrier was a fine blood bay, and he a fine high-spirited creature himself, his grey cloak flung back from a flame of scarlet, and gold about his brows, and a ruby in the pommel of his sword. He sang as he rode, setting the charger's pace.

> *Chevalier, mult estes guariz,*
> *Quant Dieu a vus fait sa clamur*
> *Des Turs e des Amoraviz,*
> *Ki li unt fait tels deshenors. . . .*

The women's singing faltered and died. Safe in their veils of greenery, they stared out at the wonder: a knight in gold and splendor, unguarded, unattended. He was a mad one, surely, or one of God's protected.

His voice was both deep and clear, free and glad and fearless, calling the air to arms for a battle thirty years won.

> *Ki ore irat od Loovis*
> *Ja mar d'enfern avrat pouur,*
> *Char s'alme en iert en pareïs*
> *Od les angles nostre Segnor.*

3

No fear of hell had ever troubled him, nor any fear of mortal steel. His stallion danced, shying from the flutter of a veil; he laughed and bowed to the eyes staring wide or shy or brightly fascinated from the thicket, and never lost the rhythm of his song.

Alum conquère Moïsès,
Ki gist el munt de Sinaï;
A Saragins nel laisum mais,
Ne la verge dunt il partid
La Roge Mer tut ad un fais,
Quant le grant pople le seguit;
E pharaon revint après:
El e li suon furent perit.

His eyes asked no pardon of Saracen women, nor ever thought to need it. Among the leaves a smile flashed, or two, or three. The charger snorted. Its rider bowed again and wheeled about, cantering up the road to the castle. The women watched him go. One by one, slowly, they went back to their washing. In a little while they were singing again. A new song: of morning and of sunlight, and of a spirit of fire on a Frankish charger, singing the conquest of their people.

The road and the song ended together. The knight hailed the guard at Aqua Bella's gate, light and glad, offering his lone and splendid and most assuredly Christian self to a stare both narrow and wary. The wariness was Outremer, embattled kingdom that it was, with the Saracen snapping at its throat; and people always stared at him. "Tell your lord," he said, "that his kinsman comes to greet him."

The eyes narrowed to slits. The bay charger stamped, tasting darkness under the morning's splendor. The knight shivered in the sun. His gladness was gone, all at once, irretrievably.

"Brychant!" Young, that voice within, but breaking with

more than youth, though it tried to be steady. "Brychant, who comes?"

No one, the guard was going to answer. The knight watched the thought take shape. Now was no time for guesting fools, fresh off the boat from the look of this one, white as a lily in this sun-tormented country, riding alone and all begauded like a lure to every bandit in the east.

The guard's mouth was open, the words coming quick and harsh. But the speaker within had come up beside him. A boy, slender, dark as a Saracen, with eyes like a wounded fawn. They took in the stranger, once, quickly, and again more slowly, going impossibly wide. "Prince?" the boy whispered. "Prince Aidan?" He gathered himself with an effort that shook his narrow body, and bowed, all courtesy. "Your highness, you honor us. You must pardon Brychant, we are all amiss, we—"

Prince Aidan was out of the saddle, Brychant still glowering, suspicious, but bellowing for lads to tend the stallion and the mule. The prince spared no thought for anything but the child who was so perfect a courtier, and who struggled so fiercely against the flooding tears. "Thibaut," said Aidan, taking him by the shoulders. "You would be Thibaut." He was shaking. Aidan stroked calm into him. "What has happened?"

The tears burst free, and knowledge with them. "No," said Aidan very softly. "Oh, no."

The boy was past hearing. The guard and the servants were nothing and no one. Aidan's arms gathered the child; his mind followed where the darkness led.

They had laid him out in the hall. A priest muttered over him. People hovered. They were not, Aidan noticed, either milling or keening. Their grief smote him, but their fear was stronger. It choked him.

He thrust through it. Somewhere he disposed of the boy. His arms were empty as he stood over the bier: a table in truth, with a silken cloth on it, and another over the one who lay there. A man no longer young but not yet old, sun-dyed as they all were here, but fair under it, bone-pallid now; black hair early going grey, long nose carved to match the long chin, the face that had always been so mobile gone suddenly and hideously still.

"Who killed him?" Aidan heard himself say it; he shivered to hear it. So soft, and so calm, and so very deadly. "Who cut him down?"

"Who are you to ask?"

He spun. Others flinched. This woman did not. He hardly saw the shape that held the soul. Here was fire to match his fire, grief to rival his own, and a will as implacable as all heaven. His body thought for him. It lowered him to one knee, bowed his head. "My lady."

"Who are you?"

She knew. But she needed to hear him say it. "He was my sister's son." He looked up, into dark eyes. "Who has done this thing?"

"If you are what he said you are," she said, "you do not need to ask."

She was not afraid of him. Even when he stood, tall even for a westerner, with all the names on him that Gereint had told her of. He went back to the bier, bent over it, laid his hand on the cold cheek. "Child," he said in the tongue of their own people, richer and darker than the rattle of the *langue d'oeil*. He stroked the silvered hair. "Gereint, child, what was it that could not wait for me?" His hand slid from the head to the stiff shoulder to the silenced heart. Ten years. So little a time. The boy had gone because he must. As Aidan had lingered, because he must. Cares; a kingdom; a little matter of wars and embassies. Gereint had wanted glory, and Jerusalem.

He had had both. And a lady of the kingdom beyond the sea, and a demesne scant hours' march from the Holy City, and death in the morning when at last his kinsman came to fulfill the promise made before he went away.

Under the pall they had robed him in eastern silks. But Aidan was what he was. He saw the narrow wound, so thin to be so terrible, through which the blade had pierced the heart. Gereint had never waked to feel it. Asleep beside his lady, he died, and she slept on oblivious, and woke to find him dead. And on the pillow between them, a cake. Round, savory, warm yet from the baking. Such cakes were not made in that house, nor in any save one.

Hashishayun. Aidan had heard of them, as a legend, a tale to frighten children. Assassins. Infidels, madmen, fanatics out of Alamut in the black heart of Persia. They came like spirits in the night, killed as their masters commanded them to kill, vanished into air. If by God's grace a man could catch one, the murderer turned his weapon on himself and died in a madness of joy, singing the praises of his unholy god.

Aidan's head came up. He was smiling. Hands flickered. Someone had crossed herself. His smile widened. Alamut was mighty, so they all said. Alamut was invincible. But this, he was willing to wager. It had never had to face the like of the Prince Aidan of Rhiyana.

He turned to the woman. Margaret de Hautecourt, he named her in his mind. Gereint's lady, with whom he had confessed himself quite besotted, laughing even through the formal phrases of his letters. No great beauty, she. A little round dumpling of a woman, older than her husband and showing it, and no sign in her of her Frankish father. She could have been full sister to the women by the stream. Infidel. Saracen. *Pullana* as they would call her here, half-blood, powerful and yet despised.

His head shook once, invisible. Not despised. Not she. She knew what he was, and she understood what it meant, and she had no fear of him at all.

He spoke to her, measuring each word. "For what they have done," he said, "they shall pay. By my name I swear it."

She startled him. She touched his hand; she said, "No. This is my doing. I will not drag you in the mire of it."

"He was more than kin to me. He was my sister-son. I was with him when he was born."

More signs of the cross. Margaret turned. Her voice never rose, but the oglers scattered. The castle woke, shaking off its shock, becoming again a strong holding.

And all for a few soft words. Aidan let them rule him. He accepted servants, service, a bath of eastern length and luxury. The clothing spread for him was stark, black and white, and rich in its plainness: Arabian silk, and something softer than linen, finer, miraculously cool. "Cotton," said the man who waited on him, a Saracen himself, bearded and turbaned and exquisitely courteous. He offered food, wine. He provided escort to the solar, where the lady sat with one lone, drowsing attendant for propriety's sake, ruling Aqua Bella with a firm hand.

And ruling herself. For an hour she had forgotten everything but death. Now she remembered who she was. She greeted Aidan as a great lady should greet an outland prince, veiling grief with courtliness. "I regret that we must meet under such a shadow," she said in that soft voice which made him think of silk over steel. "Gereint was like a boy, waiting for you to come. Every morning he would say, 'Today. Maybe it will be today.' And laugh, because he was a man grown and a baron of the High Court of the Kingdom of Jerusalem, and he was eager as a child to see his beloved kinsman again."

"And before I passed your gate, you grew most heartily sick of me."

She laughed, startling herself. "I did wonder that any man could be such a paragon. Greatest knight in the west of the world, and sweetest singer, and fairest and most courtly of men, and—"

"Lady, stop! I cry you mercy!" He was laughing, through tears, as she did. "Where Gereint loved, he loved immeasurably. I have some little fame, and of fortune enough, but I am a man like any other."

"Not quite," said Margaret, soft again and steady.

8

He looked at his hands. Long hands, too slender for their strength, too white and too smooth and too young. He raised his eyes. Margaret was looking for truth. He gave it. She did not flinch from it. "My father was mortal," he said.

"Your mother was not."

"Her daughter was."

"And her daughter's son." There was no bitterness in Margaret's voice. "Gereint was proud of his lineage, though the magic had passed him by. He was the kin of white enchanters; he carried splendor in his blood. And yet, he said, he was glad to be mortal. He was not made to bear the greater burdens. The beauty, or the deathlessness."

"We can die," said Aidan. "If the blade be keen enough. If the heart be torn, or the spine severed. We can be slain."

"As easily as he was slain?"

His head came up. "It was a mortal man who killed him." His throat closed. He was cold, suddenly. "Tell me why."

He thought that she would not. Her face had gone stark.

She fixed him with eyes that were beautiful in the round plain face. There was no softness in them. Such eyes had faced him across bared steel, and at the council table, and in the courts of kings. They were, at least, human. His own were not.

"Tell me," he said.

"It was none of his doing." She did not wring her hands like a weak woman. They were fists in her lap; she studied them as if they fascinated her. "Did he tell you all that I am? Hautecourt of Aqua Bella, yes. Baroness born in Outremer. But born also on the other side of the wall. My mother was a daughter of the House of Ibrahim. In the west that is nothing: a merchant house, and infidel besides. But in Aleppo it is as close to nobility as makes no matter. Among the kingdoms of trade, my mother was a princess, the daughter of a queen. The House of Ibrahim is known wherever caravans go; it has kin and allies and servants from London to Samarkand, from Genoa to Byzantium, from Rus to Nubia. The silk roads, the

9

spice roads, the roads of gold and salt and furs—it has power over them all.

"And power, as you who are a king's son know, begets jealousy. Children of the House have always traveled far to seal alliances, and sometimes have forsaken the Faith of the Prophet for the House's sake, as long ago they forsook the faith of Moses. So did my mother do.

"I was her only child. She raised me in two worlds; and my father allowed it. He was an odd man, my father. Much older than his lady, and a rough soldier to look at, a famous fighter, and yet he had been a monk. Not even a fighting monk; a Cluniac, a cloistered ascetic. He left, none of us ever knew why; came Crusading; served the King of Jerusalem, won his demesne, took a wife from the House of Ibrahim. People said he had gone infidel. I think it was only that, at heart, he was a civilized man." She looked at her guest, new come from the wildest west, and shook her head once, sharply, as if to clear it. When she began again, she seemed to be speaking of something else altogether. "What do you know of the *Hashishayun?*"

She said the word calmly, without the hiss of hate and fear that Aidan had always heard in it. As if it were only a name.

It was sublimer than contempt. Aidan gave it what tribute he could muster. "They are the Assassins. Madmen, drugged or possessed, trained to kill in utmost silence and with utmost dispatch. They believe that murder is their path to Paradise. They obey a mad king, or kings. There is some doubt that they are human."

"They are quite human," said Margaret with only the barest hint of irony. "They are schismatics, heretics as Christians would say, fanatic followers of one whom they call the Lost Imam. Their heart and center is in Aluh Amut, Alamut, the Nest of Eagles in Persia; but they are strong through the lands of Islam. They are very strong in Aleppo, where is the House of Ibrahim. And they are strongest in Masyaf in Syria, so that some are calling that fortress Alamut the lesser, or simply Alamut.

"Their faith is simple enough. They wait for the return of their Imam who was lost long ago. They live by strictest laws. All other faiths are false, and false believers are their prey. They work their will through terror; murder is, indeed, their road to salvation. They have slain caliphs and sultans, lords of Islam and of Christendom, priests and mullahs and ascetics: any who has set himself against their mission or their lord.

"The greatest of their chieftains in Syria is the lord of Masyaf. Sinan is his name. Sinan ibn Salman ibn Muhammad, who calls himself Rashid al-Din; whom others call Sheikh al-Jabal, the Old Man of the Mountain. He professes loyalty to the lord in Alamut, and yet it is an open secret that he serves himself foremost. The Assassins of Syria pay lip service to Alamut and do the bidding of Masyaf. In Aleppo they do not even trouble to bow to Alamut.

"You know what power is," said Margaret. "Never too sweet, and never enough. Sinan bids fair to command all his sect, and through it to sway most of Syria and Outremer to his will. But *most* is not *all*. He would have more. In order to win it, he needs eyes and ears in every city; he needs allies, servants, slaves. He thinks," said Margaret, "that he needs the House of Ibrahim."

While Margaret spoke, Aidan left his chair and began to prowl. It was his way; he could sit still, if he must, but stillness robbed him of his wits. In the silence he spun on his heel, facing the lady, waiting.

She smiled very faintly at a memory. Gereint, warning her: "He can never sit for long, except in the saddle. He can't help it. He was born restless. God's mistake. His brother got all the quiet; he got all the fire."

"That's not strictly true," Aidan said. Suddenly he grinned. "But true enough." His head tilted. "Sinan wants a web of loyal spies. I can understand that. Why precisely your mother's family?"

"It is the greatest," Margaret answered. "And it has something which he wants." She met his eyes. Sea-grey, Gereint had said, like his own: northern seas and northern stone. They put her in mind of fine steel. When he shifted, the strangeness flared at her, cat-green. "I was a widow when Gereint came here," she said, "a ruling lady with two young children, and men enough to defend me, and Aqua Bella mine by right. My husband had been a vassal of the Prince of Antioch; he left other sons than Thibaut to inherit his lands. It had not mattered to me. I had Aqua Bella. And I had my share in the House of Ibrahim.

"Sinan asked for me. For me, not for one of my cousins, because I was both Frank and Saracen. My Christianity was no impediment. I am, after all, a woman, and a woman is what her man commands her to be. He wanted my House and my place in the Kingdom of Jerusalem. Perhaps, a little, he wanted me. I was not so ill to look at when I was young.

"I refused him," she said. "He persisted. He could not understand that I was my own woman. I had taken one husband for duty and to please my father. I chose the other to please myself. Then, I thought, Sinan would let me be; and I wedded my daughter to a baron in Acre, lest he turn his mind to her.

"But Sinan is of the people of Alamut. He accepts no will but the will of his master, and since he reckons himself master, that will is solely his own. He granted me some little peace. Then he commanded me. I would set aside my Frankish boy; I would accept his suit. My answer had no words. Only laughter. I was proud of it. I was a very perfect idiot.

"I grew more perfect with time's passing. Sinan, having commanded, turned to threats. He slew my best hunting hound; he slew the mare I had raised from a foal. I gave him only defiance. Then he let me be. I thought that I had won. I lowered my guard. And when the new message came, I defied it. *Yield,* it said, *or truly I resort to force.*

"I defied it," she said, "and for a long while again no blow fell. I was wise, I thought. I took great care to guard myself. I thought that he would abduct me; I took every precaution against it.

"But he is an Assassin. His force is deadly force. He did not take me. He took my lord."

Aidan was still. A quivering stillness, like a flame where there is no wind.

"So you see," said Margaret, "it is all my doing. I will not surrender the House of Ibrahim into that man's hands."

"Indeed you shall not."

His face and his voice between them brought her to her feet. "You have no part in this."

"Your enemy has made certain that I do."

"Then you had best slay me, for I have been your kinsman's death."

Aidan considered the logic of it. He could do that, even in the white heat of rage. His teeth bared. It was not meant to be a smile. "You know what your folly has won you. That is revenge enough. No, my lady; your suitor owes me a blood debt. He will pay it in his own person, if I have to pull down Alamut stone by stone."

"Masyaf," she corrected him, cool and fearless.

"Masyaf, and Alamut, and every hut and hovel which owes fealty to the *Hashishayun*, if need commands it."

"All for a single human life?"

"He was my sister's son."

She touched him as if she thought that he would burn. Her hand was cool and steady. He caught it. It did not try to escape, even when his grip woke pain. "So strong," she said. Observing only, interested. "Do you truly mourn for him? Or are you glad to have found so mighty a battle?"

He could kill her. Easily. One effortless blow. Or he could break her mind. She was a mortal woman. She was nothing before his power.

She knew it. She cared not at all. She could do naught but

what she did; she would yield for no man, nor ever for a white he-witch whom grief had driven to folly.

He let her go. "I will do what I will do," he said.

She bowed. It was not submission. "Will you see your kinsman laid in his tomb?"

"I have time," he answered her.

"Indeed," she said, "you do." She sat again, called for her women.

He was dismissed. That was novel enough, and he was bemused enough, that he let her have her will. Later she would pay its price. If he chose to ask it.

2

The baby was teething, and fretful with it. Whatever he wanted, it was not what anyone could give. When his grandmother rocked him, he wailed for a sugar tit; when the aunts tempted him with a sugar tit, he howled for his mother's breast; when she gave him the breast he struck it hard enough to bruise, and screamed in earnest. His mother was tempted to scream with him, if only to drown him out.

"A proper little prince, he is," said Laila, who resented him. She had been the most junior wife until he was born, but at least she had had Sayyida to be superior to: a mere daughter of the house, youngest and last to be married, and that to a fatherless nobody. But Sayyida had done what Laila had never been able to do. Given her husband a son, and so become a person of note within the limits of their world.

"A prince," Laila repeated, hands pressed prettily to her ears. "His whim is our law. Why, I've hardly slept since—"

Sayyida set her teeth before she said something regrettable. Her breast throbbed. She ventured to dance Hasan on her knee. His screams modulated to a hiccoughing roar.

"Here," said someone new. "What is this?" She swept Hasan into her arms.

The silence was so abrupt that Sayyida reeled. For a long moment she simply sat and luxuriated in it. Then she opened her eyes and stared.

Hasan had met his match. His fists were tangled in the most wonderful hair in the world. He had, improbably, begun to laugh.

Laila loosed a little shriek. Stout comfortable Fahimah had the wits to go in search of food and drink as the laws of hospitality demanded, but she would not look directly at their guest. Mother—to Sayyida she was always and irrevocably that —sat very erect and very still. She would not go so far as to express dislike, but her disapproval was cold enough to burn.

Sayyida did not care for any of them. "Morgiana!" She flung herself upon her guest, baby and all. Hasan did not even frown. He was quietly and blissfully fascinated. "Morgiana!" his mother cried. "O miraculous! Would you care to adopt a son?"

Morgiana smiled and shook her head. She was as indulgent with Sayyida's exuberance as with Hasan's fierce tugging at her hair. "Peace be with you," she said, "and with all this house."

That put Sayyida in mind of her manners. She bowed as politely as she could when she wanted to dance with delight. "May the peace of Allah be with you, with your coming and your going; and may that going be late and blessed." She sucked in her breath. *"Morgiana!* When did you come? Where have you been? How long can you stay? Did you know about Hasan? Have you—"

Morgiana laughed. "In order, O impetuous: I came just now, I have been where I have been, I can stay until the evening prayer, and yes, I knew both about Maimoun and about this handsome son of his."

Laila made a sign against the evil eye. It was not directed entirely at Morgiana's boldness in trumpeting Hasan's virtues to every demon that could hear. "This worthless girlchild," she said, "has been driving us to distraction."

Morgiana hardly glanced at her. Sayyida swallowed a grin. Laila not only knew that she was pretty; she made sure that no one else remained unaware of it. But beside Morgiana she shrank to insignificance. Morgiana was wonderfully, outrageously, exhilaratingly beautiful. Her skin was ivory. Her eyes were the clear green of emeralds; or, Laila had said more than once, spitefully, of a cat's. Her hair was rich enough to kill for: beautiful, improbable, the color of the dark sweet wine which no good Muslim should touch, pouring to her knees. She glowed as she sat on a cushion in the worn familiar room, amid the clutter of four women and a baby; even in plain respectable clothes, she looked as if she belonged in gold and silk.

Fahimah came back with the maid and a small feast. Mother disapproved in silence. Laila sniffed, and frowned. *"Zirbajah?* Fahimah, we were saving it for—"

Mother looked at her. It sufficed. She sulked, but she was silent.

Morgiana nibbled bread, salt, a little halwah; she dipped a fingerful from the bowl of *zirbajah,* savoring the rice with its pungency of garlic and spices. Hasan snatched, greedy. She placated him with halwah, with which he was well content.

A miracle. No, Sayyida thought. Morgiana. The others, even Laila, were wary of her, almost afraid. She was the family legend, and the family secret. A very solid secret, savoring *zirbajah,* sipping thick sweet kaffé from the silver cup that only came out for a guest of high note.

When she had tasted everything and complimented it duly —gaining from Fahimah the name of the new pastry cook in the bazaar, who had apprenticed in the sultan's own kitchens —she settled to an age of uncomfortable chatter.

Sayyida had trained herself to see the necessity. She had never been able to train herself to be patient. Morgiana never told her best tales in front of the older women. To them she was an infamous eccentric, endured because their lord and master had bidden them endure her, and accorded hospitality because the Prophet enjoined it upon them. To Sayyida she was simply and most complexly Morgiana. And that was wonder and splendor, and tales that had no equal, because they were the truth.

But she did not tell them to everyone, nor would she cut short the rites of courtesy. Sayyida sat at her feet and tried to remember a matron's dignity, and struggled not to fidget. Surely Mother knew. She followed Morgiana on every step of every furlong of the pilgrimage to Mecca; questioned her minutely regarding her every companion; counted every stone of every holy place in that holiest of cities.

Laila, of all people, came to the rescue of Sayyida's sanity. She yawned delicately, like a kitten, and stretched in the manner best suited to the multiplicity of her curves. "I beg our guest's gracious pardon," she said, "but my lord husband is coming to me tonight, and I must rest, or I shall hardly be fit to please him."

Sayyida bit her lip. Mother was above jealousy. Fahimah was oblivious to it. But they were reminded of duties that could not wait. Morgiana would not have them abandon necessity for her sake; no more would she spoil it by naming Sayyida's name. "I am quite content," she said, "to wait upon the little prince. If his mother should wish for an hour's respite . . ."

"Of course she should not," Mother said tartly. "Go on, girl. Take the lady to the garden. And mind you bridle your chatter. She has no need to hear the foolishness that passes in you for conversation."

Sayyida hugged herself and danced round the rose arbor that was Fahimah's greatest pride. "O brilliant! O wonderful!" She plucked a blossom and buried her nose in it until she sneezed. Morgiana watched with glinting eyes. Sayyida claimed Hasan, who was hungry, and sat on the grass to feed him. Her grin was anything but matronly. "You planned the whole of it, didn't you? Even Laila."

"Laila needs no plotting but her own." Morgiana shook rose petals upon Sayyida's head. Hasan laughed at the breast. Morgiana brushed a hand through his curls, light and quick and oddly tender. Odd, because Morgiana was not a gentle creature. She tossed aside her veils and her dark voluminous robe, uncovering what Mother would have been appalled and Laila much interested to see: the dress of a young man of Damascus.

"Is it safe?" Sayyida asked. Foolishly, but she could not help herself.

Morgiana folded her lithe slimness on the grass and plaited her hair with flying fingers, binding it with a bit of green silk, tossing it over her shoulder. Her smile was a white fierce thing. It was not womanly at all, and yet it was utterly female. Very much like the rest of her. "It," she said, "is quite safe. Ask rather, am I?"

Sayyida thought about it, carefully, with Hasan tugging lustily where she was most tender. She bent her head over him. "I would die for him," she said almost to herself. She looked up. "And so," she said, "would you."

Morgiana's smile vanished. She leaped up. Sayyida, startled, raised her arm to shield her son. She lowered it without apology. Morgiana expected none. She spun into a sudden wild dance, sun to Sayyida's awkward shadow, graceful as the panther's spring, and as passionate, and as deadly.

But not to Hasan. Morgiana dropped down in front of them both. "You trust me too much," she said.

Sayyida shook her head.

"Obstinate."

Sayyida smiled.

Morgiana sighed. "Chit of a child. Do you know what your husband knows of me? A rich man of this city, I; rather too fanatic in my piety; and rather too fond of good Damascus blades, for blade of flesh, alas, I have none. He would pity me, if he despised me less."

"Ah," said Sayyida, undismayed. "He's a man, and newly come to proof of it. Of course he's insufferable."

"Does he make you happy?"

It was not an idle question, however idle its asking. Sayyida shivered slightly. For Hasan she had no fear at all. For his father . . .

She gave Morgiana the truth. "I am twenty-one years old. All my sisters were given to husbands as soon as they began their women's courses. I was the youngest, the last bitter disappointment before Allah took pity on our family and granted it a son, the daughter whom against all duty and propriety my father condescended to love. He let me grow as you've seen me grow, happier than I had any right to be. But the truth is the truth. *For a woman there is but marriage or the tomb.* He asked me. He never commanded me. He offered Maimoun, and I took him."

"But are you happy?"

"You've seen Maimoun." Morgiana's eyes were narrowing, which was dangerous. Sayyida met them steadily. "He has made me happy."

Morgiana closed her eyes. Sayyida swayed, freed from the force of them. It was true, her heart said, beating hard beneath Hasan's cheek. Maimoun was nothing like perfection. He was too young to be wise, he was brilliant and he knew it, he was male. But he was Maimoun. Set on his wedding night before his wife, looking for the first time at her unveiled face, he had not been appalled. His face had not even fallen. "Not pretty," he said to her later, judicious, a little drunk. "Not ugly, either. Just exactly right for me."

"Tell me," Sayyida said to her guest, "where you've been since I saw you last. Aside from Mecca," she added dryly.

"What! Have you no piety?"

Sayyida bowed as best she could with Hasan to think of. "Verily, O Hajjin, this Sunni heretic pretends to a modicum of devotion. But not to the turning of every stone between Damascus and the Qaabah."

Morgiana laughed: a rarity, and glorious. Hasan left the breast to stare at her, laughing with her; nor would he rest until he had regained possession of her lap. Sayyida covered herself demurely and leaned forward. "Now," she commanded, "tell."

"I hear and I obey," said Morgiana.

Morgiana had been everywhere. Had done, Sayyida was certain, everything. Things that no woman would dream of doing, and some that even a man could not encompass. When Sayyida was small she had taken every word of every tale for purest truth. When she was older she had dismissed it all as tales and folly. Now she believed it again. Morgiana was Morgiana. She did not need to spin lies.

She had a gift: a fruit of surpassing strangeness, brown-furred without, green and glistening and tart-sweet within. It came from a country even stranger than itself, farther away than Sayyida could conceive of. "As far as stars?" she asked.

"Not quite so far," said Morgiana, "nor as far as I have gone. There are worlds within the world, away over the seas. And people . . ." She rocked Hasan, eyes vivid with wonders. "Men the color of earth, who worship the sun. Black men who dwell in deserts that would slay the grimmest Bedouin; and they dwell there naked, clothed only in their pride, and all the world to them is but a shadow in the dreamtime. They were not afraid of me. They found me gentle, for a spirit of the air."

Sayyida nibbled the last of the fruit. She had Morgiana's knife to cut it with, a beautiful thing, and new. She turned it in her fingers. "Another of Father's?"

"Maimoun's."

Sayyida's brows went up. "Not, I hope, for my sake."

"His work is good," Morgiana said, "whatever he may think of me."

"He doesn't know the truth."

"Do you not trust him?"

"Father hasn't seen fit to tell him. How can I?"

"Your father never saw fit to tell you."

"He didn't need to," Sayyida said. "He still wishes I'd never learned it for myself. But he's wise enough, letting Maimoun have his peace. Maimoun is much too insistent that I be sheltered from all the ills of the world."

"Even childbirth?"

Their eyes met in perfect understanding. Sayyida sighed, shrugged. "It gave me Hasan, didn't it? He is worth anything. Even teething."

Morgiana considered him as he drowsed in her arms. "I killed a Christian this morning," she said.

Sayyida stilled. She was not thinking of Hasan, or even of Maimoun. Her eyes were level on Morgiana.

"It was very simple," said Morgiana. "One thrust, precisely where it mattered most. His wife never stirred. He forges a good blade, does your father."

"I hope you told him so."

Morgiana went back to her rocking of Hasan. She looked like a girl, a child, hardly yet a woman. Then she turned her head, and her face had no humanity in it.

Sayyida shivered. It was hard sometimes to remember what Morgiana was. Not a woman. Not even human. She feigned humanity so very well; and then it would strike, all at once, in a word or a gesture, or a flare of light in those great cat-eyes. "Ifritah." Sayyida barely said it aloud. "Spirit of fire."

Morgiana blurred into motion, swifter than a mortal could move; laid Hasan with all gentleness in his mother's arms; and stilled, utterly, as nothing human could. She sat on her heels as a servant might, but she had never done more than play at servility. As she played at being a woman.

"I do not play at killing," she said.

Sayyida started. "I wish you wouldn't do that!" She bit her tongue.

"Do you know," said Morgiana, "I can say to no one else

what I say to you. Not in all my years. No one else has ever known what I truly am. What is it, do you think? Do I grow soft in my dotage?"

"You're not old."

"Not to look at." Morgiana's hands went to her cheeks, as if she searched for signs of the age that would never beset her. Sayyida did not know how old she was. But Sayyida's father had inherited her, like his old and honored name, like the trade which had begotten it, like the house in which he had been born. Her blades had always come from that one forge. Her name and her guise had changed with each appearance, but the smiths had always known the truth of her. None, Sayyida was assured, had thought of her for more than a moment as a woman. She was a demon in woman's shape, a servant of the Angel of Death, the Slave of Alamut.

"Masyaf, now," said Morgiana. "Alamut is no longer what it was." She laughed, soft and bitter. "When my putative master revealed the resurrection of the Lost Imam—that being his unworthy and quite unbalanced self—and declared the Millennium, I left him. There was no place in his new world for the Slave of Alamut. But Sinan the crafty had carved himself a kingdom in Syria. He could make good use of an immortal murderer, who cannot be seen, who cannot be caught, who cannot count the legions of souls whom she has sent to Iblis in the name of the Faith." She lowered her hands from her face, turned them, examining them. "Strange. The blood never shows." Her eyes flashed up. "Is that why you let me touch your son?"

"You would never hurt him."

Morgiana snatched Hasan from his mother's arms. Sayyida could not even tighten her grip before he was gone. He woke at the movement, screwed up his face to protest, saw Morgiana and crowed. She buried her face in his swaddlings.

When she raised it, her cheeks were only slightly damp. She looked angry. Hasan's brows knit; he patted her chin, which was as high as he could reach. She fixed him with a hard stare.

He ventured a smile. She bit her lips until they bled. "I feast on children," she said to him. "I build castles of their bones. My own master calls me the deadliest weapon in the world. He commands me with my name and with the Name of Allah and with the Seal of Suleiman, and with an oath I swore when I was young and mad; but if I do not obey, he dares not punish me. He thinks that he desires me. He does not know how very much he fears me. He whom all men fear: Sinan the wise, the Sheikh al-Jabal, the Old Man of the Mountain.

"And you," she said, "O innocent, find me enchanting."

"You are," said Sayyida.

Morgiana snarled horribly. Hasan whooped with delight, and snatched. He won her plait; it found its way promptly to his mouth. She did not try to rob him of it. "I could harm him," she said. "Never doubt that. But whether I would . . . there lies the limit of Sinan's power over me. He has learned it. He bade me slay a man whom perhaps you know. Salah al-Din, he calls himself."

"Saladin?" Sayyida was proud that she knew the Frankish corruption of his title. "He's our sultan now. Father made a sword for him once, when he was still only Yusuf the Kurd, Ayyub's son. You haven't killed him yet, have you? He's warring near here somewhere. Father and Maimoun and the rest have been run ragged, keeping the emirs in weapons."

"Indeed he has been warring round about," said Morgiana. "Making himself sultan of Egypt and Syria. I have not killed him. I will not. I am done with murder."

"And yet you killed a Christian."

Morgiana's face darkened. "I swore an oath. My folly; Sinan's desperation. That far and no further he may bind me. At least," she said, "he was not a Muslim. Even a Sunni heretic."

"I am a Sunni heretic," said Sayyida.

"You are a woman, and therefore possessed of neither faith nor reason." Morgiana's lightness was the lightness of the sword in battle. "And I am less than a woman: an ifritah, of those children of Iblis who have embraced the True Faith. Three orders of beings are set above me: men, women, and males of my kind. I am a slave of slaves of the slaves of Allah.

"Or so it is said," said Morgiana. "I know that there is no one like me in this world. If there are afarit, they shun me. I am stronger than any man, and swifter; I have magics beyond human conception. I begin to suspect that I am no one's slave. Except, of course, Allah's."

"God is great," said Sayyida, bowing to the Name. "If you grow so weary of killing, why do you stay? Go away from Masyaf. Leave the Assassins to their knives and their terror. You've done their bidding for years out of count. Haven't you done enough?"

"Perhaps," said Morgiana. "Perhaps not. Suppose that I could elude my oath; suppose that I left. Where would I go?"

"Anywhere. You have the whole world to be free in; and even the terrible Assassins won't find you who were the most terrible of them all. Why," Sayyida said, "you could even stay here. Father wouldn't say anything. Maimoun can think that we've a cousin visiting. Hasan would be delighted. And I," she said, "would have some peace while he teethes."

Morgiana smiled and shook her head. "The tigress cannot hide herself among gazelles, however fond of them she may be. And to leave Sinan . . . it has been too long. Or not long enough. I am not his tame dagger; I will take no more Muslim souls. But there are Franks enough to cleanse the world of, and a nest of them in particular, with which I have hardly begun. Apostates; children of one who repudiated the Faith. They have mocked our Mission. I must see to it that they pay."

"I'm not sure I like you when you talk like that."

Morgiana set a newly drowsy Hasan in Sayyida's lap and kissed her lightly on the forehead, startling her speechless. "Honesty," said the ifritah. "That is what it is. May I darken your door again?"

"Do you have to go?"

Morgiana nodded.

"Come back quickly," said Sayyida. "And when you've had your fill of Christian blood, remember. You have a place to go. If you need one. We—I've always thought that I could use another sister."

"Such a sister," Morgiana said wryly. "I will come back. I give you my word."

"Go with God," said Sayyida. As always, Morgiana was not there to hear her. She had winked out like a candle's flame. As swift as that, and as silent, and as absolute.

3

Aqua Bella had two towers. One, newer and by far the more massive, was a straightforward affair, square and solid; from its battlements one could see Jerusalem. The other was far older and narrower, like a minaret, anchoring a corner of the wall but serving no purpose beyond that. Its lower levels housed the oxen that drove the olive press, and, now, a horse or two belonging to the crowd of mourners who had gathered to see Gereint to his tomb. The upper reaches were empty of aught but spiders, and long forbidden to the castle's children, for its stair was treacherous.

They, of course, had found ways round lock and bar; but dust and spiders soon palled, and the stair was merely crumbling stone, easy enough to climb if one were careful. There had been owls in the tower, to swoop and hoot and be deliciously terrifying, but the last had flown away years since and not come back. The children had found other diversions, and left the old tower in peace.

Thibaut needed to be alone. He had been doing his best to be a man, to honor Gereint's memory, but a day and a night of it had worn him down. The keep was full of people come to pay their respects and, no doubt, to eye the new and wealthy widow. Their voices grated on Thibaut's ears; their looks of pity made him want to hit them. What did they know of grief? What did they know of anything but greed and lies and vulgar curiosity?

He had heard them talking when they thought him out of earshot. "Convenient for the young one, this. He'd not like to share his inheritance with his stepfather's get, however fond they all pretended to be."

Remembering that, even on the dim crumbling stair Thibaut had to stop and drive his fist against the wall. It made him feel no better. He was wept dry. His father had died when he was too young to remember. Gereint had been less a father than an elder brother: at first in Jerusalem where a young knight from the west found time to spare for a very young *pullani* with an enormous stock of questions, and later in Aqua Bella when the knight had become the lady's husband. People had always acted as if Thibaut should mind seeing his mother happy. As if he could have done anything but loved Gereint, who always seemed to be laughing or singing, who treated his lady's children as his own, who even in a temper had always been careful to be just.

Thibaut's throat would not stop aching. He picked his way up the last few lengths, grimly, trying not to think at all.

There was someone up there.

For a moment Thibaut's mind was empty indeed. Then it filled, with rage. This was his place. No man in the world had a right to be there, and only one woman; and she was in Acre, being a baroness and maybe not even yet aware that Gereint was dead.

Then Thibaut saw who it was, and his rage died.

He seemed unaware of Thibaut's coming. He had folded his long body into the curve of the parapet, cheek against the stone, eyes staring away not eastward to Jerusalem as Thibaut might have expected, but north. The sun was full on him, and yet it had not even warmed that impossibly white skin. He should have been flayed alive. He looked as impervious as marble, and as still.

Thibaut's heart was beating hard. This was legend, sitting there in Thibaut's place, as Thibaut himself so often had sat, looking barely older than Thibaut. But much taller. Thibaut, as his peers of the pure blood were never loth to remind him, was a perfect little Saracen.

Gereint had never minded. "You'll never win a battle by weight or length of arm," he had said on the training field. "But you have grace and speed, and a good seat on a horse. You'll hold your own."

The prince looked like Gereint as a marble image looks like a man. The same long limbs. The same fierce arch of nose. The same black hair, thick and not quite straight. Even the same long pointed chin, though Gereint had been no beauty, and this was beauty to stop the heart.

He never seemed so alien when he was with people. He pretended. Maybe he cast a glamour, a semblance of human solidity. Alone, he was himself, and that was not a man.

Then he moved, and he blurred a little. The keenness blunted. The beauty shrank to handsomeness. The light on him was only sunlight, though powerless still to stain his pallor.

Thibaut tensed to bolt, found himself picking his way across the narrow space. Aidan had left him Joanna's place, the crenel that framed the winding of the eastward road. He settled in it. Riders were coming, more vultures at the feast.

"Templars," said Aidan, "and a Hospitaller riding with them. Is that a prodigy?"

It was not impossibly hard to match that light, easy tone. "It's unusual. The Military Orders must be speaking to one another this week."

"They honor our kinsman."

Thibaut almost choked. *Our.* He had said that. But no, it was a manner of speaking. He was royalty, after all.

Aidan was watching the riders. Thibaut had not seen him

move, and yet he was very close. Close enough to see the veins glimmering blue under the moon-white skin; close enough to see what the sun did to his eyes.

Thibaut could not even be afraid. They had grown up with the tales, he and Joanna. This was real, that was all.

It retreated slightly. It laid a hand on Thibaut's shoulder, warm and solid. "Yes," said Aidan. "I'm flesh and blood. Were you expecting living fire?"

Thibaut did not like to be mocked. "I was expecting dignity."

Aidan laughed. "From me? Oh, come! Dignity is my royal brother. Dignity is a synod of bishops, each more constipated than the last. I'm a hellion from my cradle."

"You want—" Thibaut was having trouble getting it out. "You want to seem . . . not ordinary. But—less than you are. Somehow."

The grey eyes rolled like any ordinary man's. But there was a stillness behind them. "Oh, to be a legend! Youngling, I'm quite as solid as the next man. If only half as human."

Thibaut's head shook. He did not know where his words were coming from, but they would not stop coming. "You have to shrink and hide, to be safe. But then you hide it again: you dress it in gold and scarlet and act outrageous, and everyone is afraid of you, but it's a useful fear. It keeps them from thinking. That you are—what you really are."

"And what, O sage, is that?"

Mockery again. Thibaut's fault, for being so small for his age, and his voice just broken, his cheeks still as smooth as a girl's. He glared at the prince, but he answered coolly enough. "I think you must be an ifrit. Not a jinni, they are of earth, and you are air and fire."

"Empty wind," said Aidan, leaning back against the parapet and grinning. His teeth were white and sharp. "I'll tell you what I am. I am king's son and king's brother of a kingdom in the west of the world. Half an hour sooner from the womb, and I would have been king, for which blessing I thank God at every day's rising. My father was good solid mortal stock, clear back to Ambrosius. My mother was . . . what she was. She raised my brother to be king. She raised me to be whatever I wanted to be. Both of us were meant to live in our father's world. There was no other for us, she said. Though even then we knew that we were like her, as our sister was like our father."

He did not sound sad, or angry, or afraid. This was an old tale he was telling, and all its grief was worn away.

"You never asked her why?" asked Thibaut.

"She would never tell us. She was very old, though she looked like a young maid. She had been alone for years beyond count. She was a little mad, I think. She loved our father quite beyond reason. Enough to refuse to be his wife, and to bear and raise us apart from him and his people and his Church that hates our kind. But when he was crowned king and it was noted that he had neither wife nor doxy, and never a bastard to prove his virility, her selflessness found its limits. She could not bear to lose him to any mortal woman. She came to him in his court, and she brought us with him, a pair of yearling whelps with his face. 'These are yours,' she said, 'as am I. If you will have us.'"

"And he said he did," said Thibaut, enthralled.

"It was a great scandal," Aidan said. "But it was also a marvelous tale, and she was supremely beautiful, and she was prompt to give him a daughter with human eyes. And, to the priests' disgust, she was quite unmoved by either holy things or cold iron. She would never let them baptize her, but us she sent coolly to the font, and it was no worse than water ought to be in March after a long winter. Even when they sent us to a cloister to be educated, she ventured never a protest. 'A king's sons should have learning,' she said, 'in all that they may.' My brother took to it. I," said Aidan, "was less tractable."

"In what? The cloister or the learning?"

"The cloister," Aidan admitted after a pause. "The learning

was interesting, if sometimes more edifying than I liked. But the walls I was locked in . . . I thought I would go mad."

Even yet the memory could dampen his brow. He tried to laugh it away. "You see. I'm no legend. I'm merely very odd."

"Wonderful," said Thibaut. He would never dare to touch, but he could hug his knees and stare with all his heart. "You came here alone," he said. "Did you lose your servants?"

"I had none."

Thibaut was incredulous.

Aidan looked down, shrugging. "Well. I had a few when I began. Some I sent back. Some I set free. I wanted to see this country bare, with no crowds tugging at me."

"But now you're here," said Thibaut, "and it's not fitting. You are a prince. You should have an entourage."

The prince's eyes glittered. "I should? And who are you to say so?"

"Your station says it," Thibaut said with barely a tremor, "and the dignity you won't admit. You can't demean yourself like a hedge-knight from a Frankish byre. You have a name to uphold."

For a moment Thibaut knew he would be smitten where he sat. But Aidan's glare turned to laughter. "God's bones! What a priest you would make."

"I can't," said Thibaut. "I'm heir to Aqua Bella."

There was no regret in that, but no horror at the prospect of priesthood, either. Thibaut had thought once that he might like to be a Templar, and ride about with a red cross on his breast, and be looked on with holy awe. But he was three parts a Frank and one a Saracen, and that one was enough. He was no longer bitter about it. He did not fancy sleeping in a stone barn with a hundred other men, and never bathing, and growing his beard to his knees. When he had a beard to grow, which did not look to be soon.

Aidan, like Gereint, seemed to know by nature what a bath was for. And he did not seem to care that Thibaut's mother was half a Saracen. His own was all an ifritah; or whatever they called her in her own country.

"I want to be your squire," said Thibaut.

Aidan's brows went up.

"I'm old enough," Thibaut said. "I'm trained. I was Gereint's, before—" He swallowed, steadied. "I have to be someone's. It's expected. I need it. And since you are a prince, and alone, and the best knight in the world—"

"No," said Aidan.

Thibaut had not heard it. Would not hear it. "You need me. Your rank demands me. *I* need *you*. How will I ever make a knight, with my face and my puniness, unless you teach me?"

"You did well enough before I came."

"That was before," said Thibaut. "Now I'll never be satisfied with less."

"Has it ever occurred to you that that is impudence?"

Thibaut blushed, but faintly. "It's true." After a moment he added, "My lord."

Aidan smiled. For him, that was restraint. He laid his hands on Thibaut's shoulders and looked him in the eyes. Thibaut stared, fascinated. Aidan shook him with a whisper of his true strength; even that was enough to rattle Thibaut's bones. "Listen to me, Thibaut. Listen well. I am honored that you think me worthy of your service. I would be honored to accept it. But I cannot."

"Why?"

Aidan's breath hissed. He seemed as much amused as angry. But through it he was somber, and that somberness quelled Thibaut utterly. "Because, Thibaut. Yesterday I swore an oath, and that oath binds me. I cannot—dare not—allow another to share it." He paused, as if he waited for Thibaut to ask, but Thibaut could not. "I swore to exact payment for Gereint's death. I swore to exact it from the Lord of the Assassins himself, in his own person, and to stop at nothing until I should have done it."

His hands tightened on Thibaut's shoulders. Thibaut

gasped, but he was strong. He did not cry out. "Now do you understand?" Aidan demanded of him. "Now do you comprehend why I must be alone?"

"No," said Thibaut.

Aidan let him go so suddenly that he fell against the parapet. He righted himself, shaking, but trying to hide it. His voice came out as a squeak, until it steadied somewhere between alto and high tenor. "He was never of my blood, but he was my kin. He was all the father I ever knew. It is my right to share in taking his blood-price."

Aidan looked at him. Thibaut knew what he saw.

The prince's face twisted. "You'll make a man," he said, as if to himself. But then: "No, Thibaut. I have defenses against Assassins. You have none. And they will strike you. Believe me, Thibaut. They will."

"That's so whether I stay with you or no. Mother won't tell me, but I know. I'm marked. They'll come against me next. At least, with you, I'll have a little hope. Of defending myself. Of taking revenge for Gereint."

"You should have been a scholar," said Aidan. "You argue like one." He rose abruptly. "Your mother will have my hide."

And Thibaut's. But Thibaut was too rapt in bliss to care. He had what he had wanted since he was old enough to understand Gereint's stories.

He did not want to be alone any longer. He smiled at the prince's black scowl, and knelt there in the sun on the broken tower. He laid his hands on Aidan's knees; he said the words that made him the liege man of the Prince of Caer Gwent. The Prince of Caer Gwent accepted them. He did it roughly, without pleasure, but he did it. "And on your head be it," he said.

It was true, Thibaut saw to his own satisfaction. Aidan looked different when he was by himself, or with people who knew what he was. In hall, among strangers, he seemed remarkable still, but humanly remarkable: a tall young man with a strikingly handsome face. Even his pallor was dimmed, though that would never be anything but startling in a country where every man was burned either black or scarlet by the sun.

"He's as white as a maid," someone said in Thibaut's hearing.

"God knows, he doesn't fight like one," said someone else.

"Why, have you seen him?"

"Seen him? He's knocked me clean over the crupper." The man sounded anything but ashamed to confess it. "Here, I forget—you've been mewed up in court. We had a bit of tourney in Acre, a sennight back. Nothing of consequence, merely a handful of challengers and a few wagers made. There'd been the usual crop of tyros on the boat from Saint Mark, cocky as they always are, and stinking to high heaven. But that one was as fresh as a girl, and someone remarked on it as you did, and someone else took it up, and one way and another we were all hot to muss his pretty curls for him.

"We had pity on his innocence. We matched the weakest of us with him. You can imagine what happened."

The other apparently could not. His eyes were on the slender figure in black, bending over a lady's hand, dwarfed beside her great blond-bearded consort.

"It was," said the knight from Acre, "surprising, if not incontestable. Yet. It could have been blind luck. He was holding back, we found out soon enough. And he kept on doing it. I dared to think I had him, till I found myself flat on my back, staring at the sky.

"Then he lost his temper. I don't know precisely what set him off: I was still taking inventory of my bones. I think someone accused him of mocking us, and challenged him to show us what he could do.

"Now, mind, we were limping and groaning and sweating from the heat, but he was as fresh and cool as a flower in a lady's garden. He'd changed horses twice, taking offers of mounts more used to the climate than the one he'd brought from the west. They were good horses, not nags or rogues: we were fools, but we were honest fools. I remember, he had Riquier's big grey, and Riquier rides him on a bit-shank a span long, but our lad had the reins on the beast's neck and was guiding him with his shins. He rode down the lists with his lance in rest, and though he had his helm on we knew he was glaring at us. Then he lowered his lance at the one who'd armed to keep us company, but who'd never meant to fight, and no one was minded to challenge him."

"Balian, of course," said the other.

"Balian," the knight agreed. "Of course. We've all done our share of listening to troubadours. So, obviously, had the boy from the west. Of course we tried to talk the young fool out of it. Balian is a man in his full strength, Balian is seasoned, Balian is the unconquered champion of Outremer."

" 'Therefore,' said the westerner, 'I will fight with him.' "

"He meant it. Lances first, then if neither would yield, swords, until one either yielded or was hurt too badly to go on. Balian was hardly willing. He's a gentle enough soul, when he's not breaking lances. But a challenge is a challenge, and Balian understands a young man's hunger for honor. He could give that even with defeat.

"You know how it goes in any tourney. The knights take their places at the ends of the lists. The destriers champ and snort and shake the ground with their pawing. The world holds its breath. Then the lord raises his hand. The lances come down. The shields come up. The horses lumber into motion. It's dream-slow; then it's blurringly fast.

"Even before the lances met, we knew what we were seeing. God knows, there are no knights in the world to compare with ours in Outremer; and often we've seen it proven, with every ship that comes out of the west, and every sunstruck cockerel who fancies himself a champion.

"This one was cockerel enough, but he could ride a joust. He broke his lance on Balian's shield, and Balian broke his on the westerner's, and neither even swayed in the saddle. They'd been testing, we could see. Neither said a word that we could hear, but they stopped in the same instant, dismounted, and set to with swords.

"Now, Balian can ride, but it's with the sword that he excels, and it's with the sword that he's held his title so long. His arm is made of iron and his wind is unbreakable, and he has an eye like a Cairene cutpurse. There are men who'd swear that he sees a stroke coming before his opponent has even thought of it.

"And here he'd met his match. Soon enough they had their helms off, and they were grinning like boys on a lark, but going at it with all they had. Or Balian was. The other was still —still!—holding back. Till Balian saw, and his grin went wild, and he struck in grim earnest. Struck, if the other slipped the merest degree, to kill.

"And the other saw, and his smile never wavered, but I saw the glitter in his eye. He turned that stroke, and he sent the sword spinning out of Balian's hands, and he laid his point against Balian's throat, gentle as a mother's kiss. 'You'll make a swordsman,' he said."

There was a long pause, with breaths drawn sharply in it. Then: "By the Cross! Did Balian kill him for it?"

"Balian? Balian cursed him in three languages, and then asked him if he'd mind taking on a pupil."

Thibaut grinned to himself. The tale had won an audience, and they were all trying not to goggle. No one was suggesting, Thibaut noticed, that the young cockerel was not as young as he seemed. Rhiyana was small and very far away, and played little part in western wars and none in those of the east. No one here knew what its king was. As for his brother . . .

People would believe what they wanted to believe. That had always been Gereint's wisdom and his safety. His lineage was not a thing to speak of where a stranger could hear it. He had been a little afraid, sometimes, when he talked of his uncle's coming, though he laughed at himself. "He's older than I, and wiser, and he's long learned to seem, if not ordinary, at least human. And yet . . . he is what he is. He never lies about it. If someone asks him direct . . ."

So far, no one had. Thibaut intended to keep it so. Though it meant coming within reach of his mother's eye, he stationed himself in Aidan's shadow, armed with a bland stare and an air of squirely watchfulness.

They laid Gereint in his tomb under the chapel of Aqua Bella, and although he might have had a bishop to sing him to his rest, his lady would have none but her own humble chaplain. Old and all but blind, he still had a sweet voice, and his wits did not wander overmuch, although he forgot once and called Gereint by the name of Margaret's father.

It was as Gereint would have wished it.

"He was blessed in the end," said Margaret when it was over. "He died without pain, in the prime of his life. He had nothing to regret."

Hall and solar were full of people who would need, soon, to think that their presence comforted her. But for this little while, in the cool dimness of the crypt, they let her be. Thibaut did not want to be there, but he could not make himself go elsewhere. Under dust and incense and old stone, he thought he smelled death. Foolish. His grandfather's tomb held naught by now but old bones, dry and clean under the effigy. Gereint was sealed tight in the niche that would have been Margaret's, embalmed in spices and wrapped in lead and laid under a slab that had needed four strong men-at-arms to shift it. Later his effigy would lie there, all in armor, with the cross of Crusade on its breast.

Aidan knelt by the niche. If he prayed, it was a warrior's prayer, a fierce intensity. A saint might look like that as he labored to raise the dead.

Thibaut shivered. That, he already knew, was beyond Aidan's power.

Margaret moved slowly through the crypt. Her shadow was huge in the light of the lamp over her father's tomb. She paused by Gereint's, and laid her hand on its lid. A tremor rocked her. Thibaut looked at her in something very like horror. Margaret was the strongest person in the world. Margaret never lost her temper, or her composure, or her wits. Margaret never wept.

It was as if the castle itself had begun to crumble and fall. Thibaut was frozen in shock, helpless. Aidan moved as if he had never been rapt in prayer, rising, touching her. And she let him. She came to him as to a haven. He sank down, cradling her as if she had been a child, rocking her, saying nothing. His face was deathly still. His cheeks were wet.

Thibaut did not know what he did until he had done it. He crept close to them, and huddled by them. There was room for him, and warmth and strength to spare. They held at bay the cold of death. They began, slowly, to heal him.

4

For Aidan there would be no healing while Gereint's assassin lived unpunished. He worked, ate, spoke, even laughed, but the memory never left him, nor the grief. *Even an hour,* his heart mourned. *Even an hour sooner . . .*

But beneath that, infinitely darker, infinitely more terrible: *I never knew. I in all my power, in my pride, in my certainty that the world was mine to do with as I chose—I was as blind as any mortal worm.*

Gereint had died, and Aidan had had not the slightest suspicion. He had been all joy, looking to the road's end, knowing how Gereint would be when Aidan came: trying to be a man, to remember his dignity, but damning it all and whooping like a boy. He was dead before he knew it, gone, taken away where mortal men went; where Aidan could never go.

The hall of Aqua Bella saw a prince at the lady's table, eating little, but calm, composed. Behind the mask, he wept and raged.

The Assassin had left no trace, no memory of presence. The cake was gone, cast away in fear. Gereint was in his tomb.

But Aidan knew where to hunt. Masyaf had sent the murderer out; to Masyaf, inevitably, the murderer must return. Aidan would be waiting for him.

Aidan stopped pretending to eat. His kind needed little sustenance, and even that, now, was more than he could stomach. The guests were quiet as befit a funeral, but they seemed hungry enough, and thirsty for the wine that came out of Bethlehem. At the high table, Margaret ate and drank sparingly but calmly. Thibaut, who was young enough to find healing in tears and a strong embrace, was eating as if he had had nothing for days. Maybe he had not. He did not often glance at Aidan, but his awareness was palpable, like a hand on Aidan's shoulder.

Gereint had been like that. It was not adoration; nothing so foolish. It was kinship, deeper even than blood.

It was a gift. Aidan did not want it; it did not fill the place that was empty. Yet he could no more refuse it than he had refused Gereint.

The air was stifling. So many human bodies, so many human minds, pressing on him. He rose, not too ungracefully, murmuring something. The Lady Margaret inclined her head. Her eyes saw too clearly by far. She endured this because she must. So must he, if he would be courteous, but courtesy was beyond him. He bowed low to her and fled.

The garderobe was a brief refuge, but its air was too thick for his senses. He found a courtyard to pace in, not caring what it was, or where, or who saw. Only the thinnest veneer of sanity kept him from launching himself into the sky.

Watchers did not linger long. Perhaps he frightened them. But one stood in shade, as still as he was restless, and slowly that stillness touched him. A monk, he thought: a Benedictine, swathed in black. But under the habit was mail; on the breast was a cross, not large, of simple shape, stark white against the robe.

The Hospitaller. Gilles, his name was. He was not what Aidan had been led to expect. He was fastidiously clean, his hair cropped short round the tonsure, his beard long but well kept. It aged him, as perhaps he intended: under it he could not have been much past thirty.

His eyes widened a little as Aidan halted in front of him. The glamour had lost itself, baring the truth of what Aidan was; he cared neither to restore it nor to befuddle the man's mind, churchman or no. Gilles had Saracens enough to hunt. This one lone witch-man was no prey of his.

"So," said the Hospitaller without greeting or pretense. "It's true, the tale I've heard."

Aidan bared teeth longer and sharper than a man's. "What tale might that be, Brother?"

"I think you need not ask, my prince," said the Hospitaller. He leaned against the wall and folded his arms, at ease, half smiling. "They say the king your brother is your very image, as like as man and mirror."

"How not? We're twinborn. That's a power in itself, the old wives say."

"Are you both left-handed?"

Aidan laughed, startled, beginning to like this soldier-monk. "Both of us. How did you know?"

The blue eyes glinted. "No magic, my lord. I watched you in hall. You should learn to eat with your right hand if you intend to go among the infidels. They take very unkindly to a man who does not."

"Why is that?"

"A teaching of their Prophet. He ordained every smallest action. The right hand, he decreed, shall be for eating and for cleanly things. The left is for wiping oneself, and for giving the devil his due."

"Do they all fight left-handed, then?"

"Oh, no," said the Hospitaller. "War is holy, as holy as prayer. The blood of infidels is their Eucharist."

"What makes you think that I should care for an infidel's mummery? I came to kill them, not to dine with them."

The Hospitaller's eye rested on the cross that Aidan wore, blood-red on black: the Crusader's sign and seal. "A most devout sentiment. You'd make a fine Templar."

"Would they take me?"

"The Poor Knights of the Temple of Solomon will take any who hungers after Saracen blood."

He did not, Aidan noticed, say any man. "You of the Hospital, no doubt, are more discriminating."

"Less zealous, perhaps. Our concern is not only with war but with its aftermath. We tend the sick and the wounded; we do what we may to bring the infidels to the light of the true faith."

Aidan began to pace again. The Hospitaller followed, shorter by a little but long-legged enough, though he walked lame.

"A wound?" Aidan asked him.

He shrugged, deprecating it. "A small one, inconveniently placed. I mend."

"There's been fighting, then?"

"There's always fighting. Syria has a new sultan. We pacted with him for a truce, but—"

"You pacted with a Saracen sultan?"

Gilles laughed, not quite in mockery. "So shocked, prince? Did you think it was all holy war without respite? The kings of Jerusalem themselves have done more than swear truce with their enemies; they've been known to enter into active alliances, pitting Saracen against Saracen and taking the side of the stronger."

Aidan shook it off, enormity though it should have seemed to an innocent from the farthest west. "Kings, yes. Kings do whatever they must. But the Church is the Church, and Saracens are unbelievers."

"They are also men, and they surround us. We do as we must. We hold the Holy Sepulcher. We will do anything—anything at all, short of mortal sin—to continue to hold it."

Aidan nodded slowly. That, he could understand.

"And you," said the Hospitaller. "Have you come for the holiness, or for the fighting?"

"Both," Aidan said. "And for my kinsman who went before me."

"You loved him."

That was presumptuous, from a stranger. "He was my kin."

There was a silence. Aidan paced in it, but slower now, calmer.

"Masyaf," said Gilles, "abuts, and some would say is part of, a fief of the Hospitallers."

Aidan whipped about.

Gilles backed a step, but he went on steadily enough. "It stands near the demesne of our fortress of Krak. Its master has, on occasion, been persuaded to acknowledge our dominion."

"What are you telling me?"

The Hospitaller had paled, as well he might. "The Sheikh al-Jabal is not a vassal of our Order. He pays us no tribute, as the Templars have forced him to do, and thereby won his enmity. Yet there may be somewhat that we may do, to win reparation for this murder."

"Why? Are you responsible for it?"

"God knows," said Gilles, "that we are not. Our way is the clean way, in battle, against proven enemies. And Lord Gereint was in all ways a friend of the Knights of the Hospital of St. John of Jerusalem."

Aidan eased by an effort of will: not the feat some might have taken it for, who knew him only by reputation. He could understand goodwill, however much it might owe to expedience. He could not smile, but he could nod, bowing his head to courtesy. "I shall remember," he said.

Gilles looked like a man granted reprieve from hanging. He

knew it; he laughed at himself, though his words were somber. "Yes; remember us." He paused. His tone changed. "And you, sir? What will you be doing here in our country beyond the sea?"

Avenging Gereint. Aidan did not say it. He answered as he had answered every other inquirer, though more warmly to this one than to some. "I came to fight the infidel. It has been in my mind to journey to Jerusalem, to look on its king, and if he will have me"—*and if I will have him*—"to be his liege man. What higher lord can there be, than the holder of the throne of David?"

"A worthy ambition," said the Hospitaller. "You've never considered any other of our princes?"

Aidan knew a test when he scented one. He shook it from his shoulders. "Raymond of Tripoli, perhaps: there is a great lord and gentleman. But he is a count, and I am royal born. I should look first to a king."

"Such a king," said Gilles, sighing. There was no irony in it. "Young, little more than a child, and yet a great warrior, a gifted general, a scholar of no small accomplishment, a paragon of grace and courtesy. And for all of that—" His voice caught. "For all of that, God has exacted a price of surpassing cruelty. He has seen fit to make our lord a leper."

"Yet he is king," said Aidan. "No one has ever contested his right to the crown."

"No one is so great a fool. He *is* king. He was meant for it from his birth. Even when he was grown to boyhood and his malady was known, he was our king who would be."

"He inspires remarkable devotion."

Gilles shook his head and smiled wryly. "Am I so transparent? So, then: you will go to Jerusalem. I think you will find our lord worthy of your service. He will be most glad of you. Every knight is precious here on the sword's edge between Christendom and the House of Islam. A knight of your proven skill is thrice and four times welcome."

Aidan shrugged. He was not modest; he had never seen the

use in it. But he had other purposes that this man could not see. They came clear as he stood there: a bitter clarity.

Its embodiment came toward him across the sunstruck courtyard, slight and dark and fixed on him as a moth on a candle's flame. Thibaut had proper reverence for the soldier of God, but for the Prince of Caer Gwent he had his whole heart and soul.

It was not in Aidan to refuse such a gift. The pain was its price. He held out his hand to the boy and smiled, and that smile was the beginning of acceptance.

II

JERUSALEM

5

No city had ever been more holy. Holiness breathed through the very stones; quivered in the air; dizzied Aidan's senses that were keener than a man's. The hand of God was on this place, this loom of walls and towers by the mount of Sion, this City of Peace.

It did not matter what the eyes saw. Bare stony plain rolling into the hills of Judea; bleak dun rock, dust and thorns, the fierce light of the desert. On the hill, a grey wall, and towers in it, and their king above them all, David's great square Tower frowning westward. Grey-green to the north: outriders of the Mount of Olives. Deeper green to the south: terraces planted, said the Lady Margaret's sergeant, with figs. Nowhere a glimmer of water, and never a moat to ward the city, only the great empty fosse and the steepness of its walls. Water here was a precious thing, rich and secret, hoarded in cisterns and in caverns, or held in guarded wells. Stone was lord; and sun; and sanctity.

They rode to David's Gate in somber splendor: the lady under her banner of black ram on silver, her women in black, her servants, her men-at-arms, her son in black and silver beside the knight all in black. His scarlet and gold lay in the armory of Aqua Bella, forsaken until his vow was fulfilled. His mail was black, his stallion's trappings black with no adornment but the silver of bit and buckle, his helm at his saddlebow all black, his lances on the sumpter mule, his shield without device save the palm-wide, blood-red cross of Crusade. In one respect only he had yielded to eastern sense, and that was in the surcoat over his mail, long and loose and belted with black, but the heavy silk was white, with the cross on its shoulder.

He was growing accustomed to it; schooling himself not to

yearn, shamefully, toward scarlet and blue and gold. Gereint's life deserved no lesser sacrifice.

He resisted the urge to rub his chin, where the new beard was growing, thicker and faster than he might have expected, and fully as fierce in its itching. Vanity, it was not, nor heedlessness of it, either. If he would ride into Saracen lands, it might be wise to seem a Saracen.

He had told no one why he did it. They thought it a tribute to grief, and it was that, also. The men-at-arms had a wager on how soon he would exchange his red cross for a white one, and turn Hospitaller; or else let the red cross grow to span his breast in the fashion of the Templars.

Margaret watched him and said nothing. She was wise enough to take issue with nothing that he did. Thibaut still walked softly round her, but she had not taken him to task for affixing himself to Aidan's side. While the prince was content to remain near her, she could see as well as know that her son was safe from harm.

What it cost her to keep from clinging to the boy, Aidan well knew. He did not know that there was liking between them, but of respect there was much, and a certain wary acceptance of what was. Gereint, and now Thibaut, bound them; made them kin.

His stallion came up beside her grey gelding. She glanced at him, unsmiling, yet the air about her was almost light. "Does it disappoint you?" she asked, tilting her head toward Jerusalem.

Here, so close to the gate, the road was choked with people, their progress slowed to a crawl. Other parties rose out of it, armed and mounted, escorting lords, ladies riding in litters, a merchant with his veiled and jeweled wife. Lesser luminaries rode in smaller companies: poor knights fresh from Francia by the raw look of them, their mail worn bare, without the surcoat to keep the sun at bay; squires who lacked the means or the will to win their spurs; mounted sergeants with their men marching behind them. A great press of people on foot jostled and babbled under the horses' hoofs, pilgrims in sackcloth with mantle and scrip and staff, hats jangling with tokens from every shrine in Christendom, but seeking now the palm of Jericho that was most sacred of all; laborers bent double under the weight of their burdens; slaves and captives in chains with the overseers' whips cracking over them. The lame and the halt and the sick dragging their slow way into the Holy City. Beggars wailing for alms, pi-dogs yapping, lepers crouched on the dunghills in their rags and their hideousness, or cutting a swath through the crowd with bell and clapper. Caravans coming to Jerusalem, caravans going out of it, in a roaring of camels and a shouting of drivers and a clashing of the arms of their escorts.

Over the gate flew a white banner, the golden crosses gleaming on it, sigil of the Kingdom of Jerusalem. Aidan breathed deep of sun and dust and humanity, dung, herbs, horses and heated steel, and shook his head. "Disappoint me, lady? Never. This is Jerusalem."

A smile flickered, astonishing, for it made her young again. Then it was gone. The gate was before them, dark after the glare of the plain. Guards idled in its shade, paying little heed to all who passed.

No more did the city care. Holy, high Jerusalem: it embraced any who came to it. Even his kind; even his power, which was the merest feeble glimmer before its great flame of sanctity. Yet it did not diminish him. He burned the brighter here for that he was so small a thing. He drew a breath, half glad, half deliciously afraid, and plunged into the heart of it.

There was no reasoning with stone. Joanna could weep, rage, storm; Ranulf would sit immovable, ignoring her, seeing nothing but what he had set his mind on. When on rare occasions he was inclined to speak, it was to dismiss her with a word. "Women," he would say, heaving himself up and leaving her to her raving.

He had taken her son away from her. Aimery would be

fostered where it would best serve his father's advantage, and that was not at his mother's breast. Ranulf did not see why she should object. She had maids and pages of her own to train, and he expected her to produce another heir to his house in as short order as God would allow. Was that not what she was born for? Was that not why he had taken a wife at all?

He had come to do his duty. She was aching in body from so long in the saddle, all the way from Acre to Jerusalem after a hard and housebound pregnancy and a difficult birthing, and aching in soul for Aimery and for the news that had greeted her when she came to the city. Gereint dead at an Assassin's hand, dead and buried: shock enough to fell her when she heard. It stunned her; she could not even weep.

And Ranulf was there, driving out her maid and her page, not even troubling to take off his shirt. He had not bathed in a month; even across the room she could smell him. He dropped his hose and his braies, sparing her not even a glance. She had learned how little good it did to clutch the coverlet and protest.

When they were married, she had thought him a handsome man. His features were heavy but well-formed; his hair was thinning a little, but it curled still, and it was the rare, true Frankish gold. His body was thick with muscle, kept strong at the hunt and on the field. And he had an honored name and a substantial property won with his valor in the wars, and no heirs but those which she would give him. It had been considered an excellent match.

His weight rocked the bed. He still had not looked at her. He had made it clear long since that he did not find her beautiful. With her belly still slack from bearing and her breasts still swollen with milk after an unconscionable while, she would be even less to his taste.

He was not brutal. That much, she could say for him. "If this one is a daughter," he said as he parted her legs, "I'll let you keep her."

She struck him backhanded, with all her strength. "Get out of my bed!" she screamed at him. "Get *out!*"

He did not even give her the satisfaction of rape. His shrug was perfectly indifferent. "Tomorrow, then," he said.

When he had taken himself away, she wept a little, and battered her pillow, and felt no better for it. Her servants had not come back. She lay and stared at the whitewashed ceiling. The smell of him lingered. She gagged on it.

If he would argue with her, reprimand her, even strike her —but no. He left her to her moods, and came back when she was calm, and wore her down by sheer force of indifference. He did not care what she did, if only she kept out of sight and provided him with the offspring he wanted.

Which then he took from her and gave to strangers, and left her empty, womb and heart.

She staggered up. With shaking hands she drew out the first garments that came to her, and put them on. She had to rest between the shift and the gown. Her hair was too much for her. She let it hang. In a voice that, if not loud, at least was steady, she called for her maid.

No one tried to stop her. She took very little: only a single bundle and her chestnut mare, and mute Dura who never questioned her mistress' will. Ranulf was gone. He had women in the city, Joanna knew that. No doubt one of them was accepting with pleasure what Joanna had spurned.

Joanna wished her joy of it.

For Joanna there would be no more of it. Her refuge was waiting, and it welcomed her with unfeigned gladness, even in mourning. Her chamber was as she had left it, Cook had dainties for her, Godefroi the house-steward gave her the word she hoped for. "Tomorrow," he said, "they come."

She did not try to think beyond the moment. She prayed for Gereint's soul, and then she wept for him, cleanly, in her own narrow bed. Then, cleansed, she slept.

*   *   *

She was ready when they came. She could do little for lank hair or shadowed eyes, but what she could do, she had done. Her gown was fresh; its somber blue suited her not too badly. She had found that she could eat, and drink a little wine. She was still sipping it as she sat on the roof, leaning on its ledge, shaded by the lemon tree that grew in a great basin in the angle of the wall. The street below was its narrow, quiet self. When she looked up she could see the great grey dome of the Church of the Holy Sepulcher.

They came from the other way, from the Tower of David. Her eyes leaped to their head: the small round figure on the grey horse. There was a young man just behind her: Thibaut, it had to be. He had grown. He had not lost his habit of riding with a hand on his hip, which he thought elegant. It suited him better now that he was almost old enough to carry it off.

There they all were, the servants, the soldiers, dour Brychant in his old scale armor that he had taken from a Saracen. And there was—

There was a knight in black on a blood-bay horse, and he was not Gereint. He could not be. That long lean body, so light in the saddle; that sharp hawk-face; that turn of the head as Thibaut said something—it was not a dead man riding.

And if it was not, there was only one thing it could be.

Her fingers clamped on the balustrade. Grimly she pried them free. Her heart was beating hard.

He was not so like his kinsman as he came closer. A family resemblance, that was all. He was certainly much prettier; and yet she was disappointed. Handsome, yes. But where was the beauty that cut like a sword?

He looked up, and she gasped. Oh, indeed, a sword: straight to the heart.

Her mother asked no questions. Thibaut did, but only with his eyes. Prince Aidan, who could not have known that there was anything to ask, was courtesy purely. Warm fingers lifting her cold ones; the brush of a courtly kiss. She did not think that anyone saw how she trembled.

His voice was deeper than she had expected, yet clearer, its western lilt stronger even than Gereint's had been. It made her think of far green places, and of water falling.

It was witchery. She knew it, and she did not care. Thibaut was far gone in it, she could see. Margaret seemed impervious, but Margaret was Margaret. She wore her widowhood as she did all else, with quiet competence.

With greetings disposed of, Thibaut took the guest in hand. Joanna stayed with Margaret, which meant a detailed inspection of house and servants, and the overseeing of the baggage, and the disposal of a caller or two. Joanna fell into her old place a step or two behind her mother, like a young wolf-hound in the wake of a small, rotund, and very busy lapdog.

But she was not the child she had been. She had to sit down, rather abruptly, in the middle of her mother's still-room.

Margaret did not seem to hurry, but she was there very quickly, kneeling on the floor beside Joanna. Her hand was cool on Joanna's brow; her arm was firm. She took no notice of the flutter of servants, except to dismiss them. "Tell me," she said.

Joanna shook her head hard. "You have grief enough."

"Let me judge that," said Margaret.

Joanna's teeth set. The dizziness was passing. She almost wished that it would not. To run away—that was as simple as taking her horse and riding to her mother's house. To tell her mother why . . . that was harder. Margaret would not have done it. She would have found a way to rise above it.

It came out tail first. "He took Aimery," Joanna said. She surprised herself with how quietly she said it. "He never asked my leave. In the night, while I slept, they took him away. When I woke he was gone." Her hands were fists. She could not make them unclench. Her heart had been clenched since that bleak waking. "When I asked why—I tried to be calm;

oh, God, I tried—Ranulf said, 'Does it matter?' And when I asked why he had never consulted me, he said, 'Why should I have consulted you? He's my son.' As if I had never carried him in my body; as if I had never nursed him at my breast. As if I were nothing at all."

"It might have been better," said Margaret coolly, "if you had not insisted on nursing him yourself."

Joanna gasped as if she had been struck.

"But," her mother went on, "to take him without your knowledge—that was ill done."

"It was unspeakable."

Margaret frowned slightly. "Perhaps he meant to spare you pain. A clean cut, all at once—a man would think so, if he were young and rough-mannered and unaccustomed to women."

"He doesn't care enough to spare me anything. I'm no more to him than the mare in his stable. He doesn't consult her, either, when he takes her foal away from her."

"He comes from Francia," said Margaret, "and not from a wealthy house. He knows no better."

"I hate him," gritted Joanna.

Her mother's frown deepened. "What has he done to you, apart from this one misjudgment? Has he beaten you? Dishonored you?"

"He has women."

"Men do," Margaret said. "Islam at least admits the truth, and allows concubines: a great wisdom. But beyond that? Has he mistreated you? Has he shamed you before court or people?"

"He hardly knows I exist."

"I doubt that," said Margaret. She held Joanna's eyes with her level dark ones. "What do you want of me? I have no power to make you a child again."

Joanna flushed. That was exactly what she had wanted. To unmake it all. To take refuge behind her mother's skirts, and forget that she had ever been a woman.

"I won't go back," she said. "I've given him what he wanted. I owe him nothing."

"Except honor."

"What has he given me? He took my baby."

Margaret sighed. "See how God has tested me. That child of mine who seems a very son of Islam, is as perfect in forgiveness as any Christian could wish to be. But that one who seems all a Frank . . . she neither forgets nor, ever, forgives."

Joanna's chin came up; her back stiffened. "Are you telling me to go?"

"No," said Margaret. She rose, smoothing her skirts. "I am telling you to go to bed. You insisted, I suppose, on riding from Acre?"

"You know what a litter does to me."

"I know what the saddle does to a woman new risen from childbed. Now, go."

Joanna had wanted to be a child again, and to forget that she was a mother. It was not as blissful as she had thought, to have what she had wished for. But Margaret was not to be gainsaid. Joanna went where she was bidden, and did as she was told. There was an odd, rebellious pleasure in it. She was safe here. No one would lie to her, or betray her, or be indifferent to her. She had come home.

"Joanna is always angry at something," said Thibaut.

Aidan opened an eye. The eastern habit of drowsing through the heat of midday had struck him at first as sheerest sloth, but he was learning to see the use in it. Here, in a cool tiled room, with a servant snoring softly as he swayed a great water-dampened fan, and a scent of roses drifting from the window on the courtyard, it was utter luxury. He who seldom slept had slid into a doze, until Thibaut's voice startled him awake.

The boy perched at the end of the couch, clasping his

knees. His brows were knit. "She's run away from Ranulf, I can tell. I'm surprised she didn't do it sooner."

"Your sister doesn't look to me like a coward," Aidan said.

"Did I say she was? She doesn't run away because she's afraid. She runs away because she's angry. She'd kill, else."

Aidan raised a brow.

"She would," said Thibaut. "She should have been a man. She has too much temper for a woman."

"Or too much spirit?"

Thibaut nodded. "Mother says she's the purest Norman in Outremer. She should have been born a hundred years ago; she'd have come on Crusade and carved herself a kingdom."

Aidan could imagine it. She was nothing like her mother or her brother: head and shoulders taller than Thibaut, and robust with it, her brown hair doing its best to curl out of its braids, her eyes more grey than blue, a color that made him think of thunder. Or perhaps that was only their expression. Angry, yes, and hurt. The world was not going as she would have it; and she was not one to forgive.

"What is her husband like?" Aidan asked, giving up sleep for lost, and rising to prowl. He was aware of Thibaut's amusement; he flashed teeth, at which the boy laughed.

But Thibaut's answer was sober enough. "His name is Ranulf; he comes from Normandy. He's a younger son, as most of them are, but he's done well here. He holds a fief near Acre; he's rich in spoils from the wars. He's not bad to look at, either. Women like him."

"Your sister doesn't."

"She was happy enough when she married him. He's not much for airs and graces, but he's never minded that her blood isn't pure. She's strong, he says, and she'll give him strong sons; and her property is quite enough to satisfy him."

"I see," said Aidan. It was all very good sense. He doubted that that would matter to the sullen child who had greeted them with such a mingling of joy and defiance. Who was, he realized, ill in body as in mind. He was no healer; that was his brother's gift. But he could see a body gone awry. She had given her lord a son, it seemed, but she was not as strong as he had hoped. Or as she had expected to be. She would not forgive herself that, either.

"I think," said Thibaut, not easily, but as if he could not keep from saying it, "I think it wasn't good for her—what Mother and Gereint had. That, and listening to songs, and dreaming about love. Love isn't something a woman should be thinking of when she marries."

"Maybe not the first time," Aidan said.

"That's what Mother always told her. She said she believed it. But Joanna always wants to have everything all at once."

Aidan paused by the window. In the courtyard below, a fountain played, cooling the air. He breathed in roses, water, sunlight. If he willed it, he could stretch out more than hands, see with more than eyes, hear with more than ears.

They were all here, the three whom Gereint had taken for wife and children. Whom the Master of the Assassins had marked, and whom he meant to have, whether in life or in death.

Therefore Aidan was here, and not on the road to Masyaf. Sinan would surely strike again, and surely it would be soon: too soon for Aidan to dare to leave the house unguarded. The High Court was gathering for the Feast of the Conquest, that high and holy day on which Jerusalem had fallen to the armies of Crusade. Margaret must come before it to proclaim formally the death of the lord of Aqua Bella, and to beg the king's favor in naming a new lord. It would, inevitably, be Thibaut, but he lacked a year and more of his majority. She would stand regent again as she had in his infancy. "And," she had said, "it may keep him safer than if I named him lord. Sinan would kill him surely then."

Aidan stretched his more-than-senses. The city beat upon them. He made of them a shield, and raised them, and set them on guard. They marked who should be in that house, who meant well and who meant ill, who passed and who tarried.

It was awkward at first, that warding, like new armor: stiff, unwieldy, flexing strangely against his skin. But slowly, with use, it fitted itself to him. Not even armor now, but another skin, a body that encompassed all within that house.

He leaned against the windowframe, battling the weakness that always struck in the wake of power. It passed slowly; he straightened.

Thibaut had neither noticed nor understood. He was intent on his own troubles. Yet those ran disconcertingly close to the currents of Aidan's own. "It's as well she's come, isn't it? Then if she's attacked, we'll be here to defend her."

Aidan liked that *we*. He grinned at the boy and went in search of his cotte. "Well, sir. Shall we see if anyone else is awake?"

6

Ranulf did not even care enough to send a man to fetch his wayward wife. Nor, at first, could she care that he did not. With her mother's presence, something in her gave way. Her body, drawn taut for so long in resistance, said of its own will, *Enough.*

She slept as she had not slept even when she was a child, and ate as she had not eaten since Aimery was conceived. She was let be, and let mend, as much as she might in the grief that was on that house. Even grief was part of her healing. It let her forget what she could not escape: that no word had come from her husband. No pursuit. Not even a rumor of his anger.

She had given him what he wanted. It seemed that he wanted no more of her.

For once, it seemed, they had agreed on something. She told herself that she was glad. She forced her mind away from him. He had refused her right to her own child. So would she refuse to be wife as well as mother. She was Hautecourt again, and Hautecourt only. She had forgotten his name.

She swore it to herself, alone, sitting on the fountain's rim in the inner court. It was early yet, barely past dawn; the air was cool, the spray cold on her cheek. The bright fish swirled under her hand, seeking the crumbs she cast for them.

Odd how one could feel a presence, even without sun to cast a shadow, even without sound of step on stone. She stiffened, but she would not turn. In the three days since he came, she had not seen him. He had been elsewhere, riding out in the city; she had been in her bed or moving slowly about the house, taking her meals alone or, once, with her brother. Who had been full of him, and worthless for talking about anything else.

She willed him to go away. She did not want him to see her as she was now: pallid, lank-haired, shapeless with childbearing; used and discarded, and sworn not to care. When she was young and full of Gereint's tales, she had dreamed it all otherwise: she high and proud, a great lady like her mother, and he princely as westerners almost never were, bowing over her hand. He had bowed when he met her, but she had blushed and stammered and been a perfect idiot.

Great lady, indeed. She had acknowledged long since that she had no beauty. She had no greatness, either. Only obstinacy. With that, she was most richly gifted.

It fixed her eyes on the fish. Even when a hand filled itself from her bowl, and cast as she had cast, rousing them to a new dance. For him they leaped high, even into the air, as if they would fill his hands with their living gold. Even they knew what he was.

Still she would not look at him, except in glances. He wore all black now, for Gereint. But he was clever: he kept a little scarlet still, in the cross sewn on the shoulder of his cotte. No doubt he knew what the starkness did to his pallor. He looked no more canny than the cat that purred and wove about his ankles.

He gathered it up, meeting its steady, predator's stare. They had the same eyes.

"Your familiar?" she asked. It was easy, if she did not look at him.

"My distant kin," he answered, lightly, taking no offense that she could perceive.

"She wants you to bewitch a fish into her claws."

"So she does," he said. "But not these. I'm not one to betray a trust."

The cat yawned its opinion of honor among two-legged folk, but it went on purring, content to be held and stroked and promised other, more licit prey. Joanna watched the long white fingers trace that sleek, striped length. She had never seen fingers so long, so delicate and yet so strong. They looked cold. How warm they were, she well remembered.

"Joanna!"

She looked up, startled; and angry. It was an old trick. And she a fool, for falling to it.

She had known what would happen. Once she looked, she lost all power to look away.

Sometimes a man was too beautiful. It was absurd; it was faintly repellent. It made the eye dart, hunting for flaws.

This went beyond it. There was nothing pretty in it. Nothing comforting, to sneer at. Nothing human.

He had been smiling. He was no longer.

"You shouldn't have done that," she said, light now and heedless, because she had lost her battle.

His lips thinned. She needed no magic to know what he was thinking. Mortals were always easy prey for his kind. Too easy. It was the beauty and the strangeness, and the spark of fear.

She looked straight into his eyes, not caring if she drowned there. They were clear grey, with no blue in them; level, a little blank, like a cat's, and a green flare in the back of them. They would hunt best by night, his kind. Like Assassins.

"The sun is no friend to you," she said.

His head shook, a flicker, barely to be seen. "We have an accommodation. It lets me be. I accord it due respect."

"That could be your downfall, here. You should cast a deeper glamour."

He was not surprised that she knew. She wondered if he was ever truly surprised at anything. "I choose not to," he answered her.

"Why?"

"Because I choose."

Stubbornness. She could understand that. And vanity. There was another glamour he could cast, that would spare him insult and suspicion and deadly certainty; but that would raddle his beauty and grey his hair, and give him the proper count of his years.

"Would you like that?" he asked, reading her without shame.

"What would you do if I said I would?"

She gasped. He laughed aloud, out of the face he should have worn. Even mortal, even lined and greyed, he would never have lost his wickedness.

Or his beauty.

"Well?" He had changed even his voice. It was thicker; it had lost its edge of clarity. "Shall I stay so?"

"Would you?"

He turned his hands, knotted as they were, gnarled, seamed with old scars. There was another on his cheek, under the iron-grey beard. "Goddess. I had forgotten those." He did not seem to notice what he had sworn by, he with the cross on his shoulder. He flexed it; winced.

"It's as complete as that?"

"To convince, I must convince myself."

"Then, if it went on long enough, would you . . . die?"

The word was as hard to hear as to say, but he seemed

unmoved, preoccupied. "I don't know. Perhaps. Which would mean, when I go beyond the mortal span—" He shivered. "Do you remember Tithonus?"

Joanna nodded, shivering herself. "The pagan. He had immortality, but forgot to ask that it be immortal youth. He withered. He never stopped withering. And he would never die."

Aidan was on his feet. The magic dropped from him like dust and darkness. His hand was strong and smooth and young, pulling her up. She was tall enough to meet him eye to eye. That startled him a little; then he laughed. "See how we maunder! Come, show me your city."

As if Thibaut had not shown him every inch of it already. But his eagerness was irresistible; even when she knew what he was running from. Not death, but deathlessness.

She looked at her rag of a dress; touched her hair. "Like this?" she had asked before she thought.

No mere man, he. He understood. "Go on, then. But be quick."

As quick as she and Dura between them could be. She put on the blue dress again; a light mantle over it; a veil for her hair. No jewels but her silver cross, since she was in mourning. Severity did not suit her, but it suited propriety.

She did not stoop to ask how she could walk far, who had been ill so long. He had not troubled to. Her mare was saddled for her, and the tall gelding that had been Gereint's, and a mule for Dura. His manner declared that he, a knight and a prince, did not intend to walk where he could ride. He set her lightly in her saddle, his touch as cool as Gereint's had been, like a brother's, or a father's. Of course it would be. They were kin. And she was a married woman.

She gathered the reins. Her mare was restive, in season. Wise of him to choose the gelding over his stallion. Dura shied away from him, clambering onto the mule by herself, watching him with great wary eyes. It was fear, but clean, as of a storm in the desert: something to be feared and evaded, but never hated. Hatred was beneath it.

No doubt he was as accustomed to that as to a silly girl's vaporings. He mounted with that grace of his that was more beast than human, and rode ahead of them into the street.

Aidan had not thought, before he dragged Joanna out with him. It was impulse, which he was given to, and not wisely, either. She had been ill and was still not as strong as she should have been. But her pleasure was warm; her anger had sunk down deep. There was color in her cheeks. She was—not pretty, no. God's whim had kept that for her brother. But handsome, certainly, and when she smiled, which she almost never did, she blazed into beauty.

He was blinking in the light of it, barely noticing where they were, until his nose told him. The street named, wittily enough, the Street of the Bad Cooks. Pilgrims found their sustenance here, at ruinous prices, and saints alone knew what cost to their stomachs. His own heaved gently, once, and subsided.

They had left the horses at the crossing, and paid a boy to look after them. Joanna's choice. The boy would not abscond with the merchandise: Aidan's doing. He did not need to be told how it was, here. The Temple was a den of thieves still, after a thousand years.

Joanna, who knew this city as he knew his own sea-scented Caer Gwent, led him with the silent maid down a passage that might have been a cavern for all the light there was in it. Cities were like this in the east: covered over against the sun, often vaulted as was this into which they entered, lit like churches through louvers above and with lamps below, airy and astonishingly cool. Here the stink of human habitation was overlaid with sweetness, herbs and fruits and flowers; and clamor enough to set him reeling. Fiercely he damped his senses. How the cats in the gutters bore it, he would never know.

"Born to it," said Joanna. He had spoken aloud without

intending to: sure sign of his confusion. She eyed him. "You haven't been out before."

He glared. She did not have the grace to be abashed. "Only to the gate and the plain," he admitted, snapping it, because she would stare until he did. "To get out. To ride where the wind is free. I don't . . . do well in cities. This . . ." His brow was damp. Damn it.

"Do you want to go home?"

"No!"

She barely flinched. His weakness seemed to make her stronger. She did not presume to take his hand, but she said, "You must have found Acre appalling."

"And Saint Mark. And Rome. And Marseilles. And Paris." Naming them exorcised them, a little. "Acre was worse. After the sea; and so large. Jaffa I could almost bear. This is merely uncomfortable." If she reckoned that a lie, she did not say so. "Are you hungry?"

He had caught her off guard. She recovered quickly, which he could admire. He had discovered a passion for the fruits of the east: oranges, lemons, yellow apples of paradise. With these, and cheese from the market beyond, and wine from a tavern in the shadow of Holy Sepulcher, they made a feast. Joanna forgot, or at least chose not to remember, that her legend was a coward within the walls of a city.

Some of his acquaintance might have confined that to this city: to the holiness that lay on it like its mantle of dust. He might almost have been fool enough to credit it, restive as he was, trapped in the center of so much humanity.

He looked up at the dome as they approached it. It had no such blazing beauty as that other in the Temple's heart, the Dome of the Rock that rose like a sun out of the east of Jerusalem. This was a blunter grandeur; the center of every vow of every man who had taken the cross. From it the King of Jerusalem took his title, and every knight who rode under his banner: Defender of the Holy Sepulcher.

Here.

Mortal stone, first. A simple tomb, bare and unadorned, empty. Three days only had it held a body, and then that body was gone.

Piety had built the shrine over it. Zeal had raised up the basilica in all its splendor, with its satellites about it: the lesser churches, the palace of the Patriarch, the cloister, the priory, the houses of monks and pilgrims and defenders. Chanting echoed out of it, and prayer, and the cries of the vendors who even here could ply their trade without heed to the holiness of the place.

They ascended the steep hill and passed the gate with its columns from Byzantium, all three pressed together in the flood of pilgrims. Aidan perceived anew Joanna's height, a bare hand-width less than his own, and a solidity that astonished him. Her limbs were long, but her shoulders were wide, and her hips; her breast was deep and full.

She was not aware of him, except as a presence at her side. With an impatient mutter she broke free of the press, pausing in the court. Her veil had slipped. Even severely bound, her hair had a fancy to curl, to meet the sun with red lights and gold, and the rich red brown of cherrywood.

The maid covered it with laudable, and annoying, alacrity. Joanna hardly noticed. "See," she said. "There."

Two portals; and a third, rightward, that led to the chapel of Calvary. Leftward, high and square, the bell tower, silent now, domed as everything seemed to be where Islam or Byzantium had been. Behind it, the high strange roof of the Sepulcher, and the dome that was new and holy, and a little farther from them all, the lantern and the little dome of St. Helena's chapel. There was a glitter on it all, and not all of it was holiness. They had made it rich, all they who worshipped here at the Navel of the World.

For all the crush of people, the weight of sun and sanctity, the city-sickness that had beset him since he entered David's Gate, he was steadier here than anywhere but under open sky.

He would have liked to shout it aloud. *See! Is there any holier place than this? See how it welcomes me!*

Joanna did not ask him what he wanted. She took a place in the line of pilgrims, and he took his own behind her. She was barely tiring, seeing all this familiarity with eyes made new because he was new to it. The pavement under their feet. The columns that held up the roof. The circle of pillars that rounded the Sepulcher, and over them the rotunda open to the sky. And all about that splendor of God, the splendor of man in mosaicwork: the Virgin; the Angel of the Annunciation; the apostles; the Emperor of the Romans, Constantine in his glory; Saint Michael of the sword; the prophets; Saint Helena bearing the True Cross; and focus of them all, the child Jesus for whom it had all been made.

But the tomb was hidden. In all that loftiness, it lay beneath a stone, a low lintel over it, and a priest on guard, directing each pilgrim downward to his heart's desire. King or commoner, knight or monk, slave or free, here it was all the same. Even human, or not.

He could have fled. If the priest had known what descended under his brusque and tireless hand . . . a flicker of thought as it touched: *Half an hour more, and Marbod to relieve me, and, God's bones, if he stands a moment longer between me and the privy*— He did not even see the unmasked face, the eyes opened wide to dimness, the green cat-flare of the lamplight in them. Aidan bent them down and crossed himself, and descended into stone-cool darkness. Empty; and for that, they worshipped it. He laid his brow against the stone. Empty. Even prayer was silent here. It simply was.

He spoke his vow in silence, as he was bound to do. To defend this place with sword, tongue, life. But first, the other. One word escaped him, a whisper in the gloom. *"Alamut."*

"Come," said the priest, sharp, shattering vow and sanctity. "Time's up. Out."

And if he rose up in a tower of flame, what would this earthbound idiot do?

He came quietly, head bowed, meek as any proper pilgrim. Joanna was waiting. Her smile flickered. Her hand slid into his, simple as a child's. She was thinking of wine lately drunk, and of a privy.

She would never understand why he laughed. Softly; but heads turned. He met glares with a cloying show of humility and a devout sign of the cross.

Thibaut was furious. "You went out without me. You went into the city, and you didn't tell me. I went half mad, looking for you."

Aidan refused to be contrite. Joanna was disgustingly smug. "So," she said. "Next time, don't lie abed so late. It's your own fault for being so lazy."

If Aidan had not been there, Thibaut would have leaped at her. Not that he could ever have won a fistfight—damn her, she was still stronger than he was, and had the reach of him besides—but he was more than half mad, and she was smiling. Simpering. Daring him to do it.

Therefore, by God's bones, he would not. He folded his arms till they hurt, and lifted his chin. "I may be lazy, but *I'm* ready to go to court. You won't even have time for a bath. You smell," he said, "like a horse. On a dunghill. In a garlic field."

She had no scruples about audiences. She screeched and sprang.

Aidan pulled them apart with appalling ease. He did not even try to stifle his laughter. Thibaut was embarrassed. Joanna, he was delighted to see, was mortified. She beat a rapid, and seething, retreat.

There was in fact time for a bath, and Aidan took it. It was shocking decadence, good westerners declared, to bathe in hot water, all over, every week. He could happily have done it every day; and did, here where he found indulgence in his madness. Like his cousin the cat, he was fastidious.

Court dress was at least as complicated here as in Francia,

and in the latest fashion besides. But even a prince there might not boast garments of silk so costly as these. Margaret's gift, and she would not be gainsaid. Black, he was sworn to, and black it was, but black on black in brocade that would not have shamed an emperor. And under a cotte cut brief as all the dandies were wearing it in Paris, a shirt as fine as a spider's weaving, as white as his own skin; and hose cut exactly to his measure; and shoes of—doeskin?

"Gazelle," said Thibaut.

The cloak was the best of all: watered silk, black and glossy as his hair, but its lining was his own beloved scarlet, and its brooch was ruby and gold. "I can't—" he began, with tearing reluctance.

"You shall," said Margaret.

He turned to face her. She granted herself no such dispensation as her will forced upon him. She was all severity, swathed and coifed as relentlessly as a nun. She had trammeled all that was left of her beauty. But for a moment, as she looked at him, it glimmered in her eyes.

It was that to which he yielded, and not her soft command. It gave her joy to see him: a pure joy, as in a fine horse or a rare jewel. And yet to her he was neither beast nor oddity, but simply himself.

He bowed low and kissed her hand. "As my lady wishes."

Joanna did not, after all, come with them. She pleaded weariness after her morning in the city. True enough; but Aidan knew that it was more than that. She was no more healed of her wounds than he, and less practiced in ignoring them. *Later,* he told his memory of her, hardly knowing what he promised.

It was a very little distance to the palace, but they rode it, because they were what they were. A lady of the High Court must show her pride, even in mourning. She led her men-at-arms, her ladies, her son and her guest, as she had led them from Aqua Bella. Under the stark grey wall, in the shadow of

the carven gate, Aidan lifted her down from the saddle. She
was calm, unruffled by the clamor of the courtyard, where
every lord's retainer in Outremer seemed to jostle for precedence. On Aidan's arm, with Thibaut a respectful step behind,
she found her path cleared, the clamor muted. People whispered, as they must. A widow in this kingdom, ruler by right
of her own demesne, was a valuable commodity. A widow on
the arm of a handsome young stranger was fascinating, and
more than faintly scandalous.

Aidan was not precisely born to courts: he had not even
known what a city was until he was old enough to be a page.
Yet it was in his blood, and in a lifetime of being son and
brother to kings. As he entered the wide glittering halls,
strange with their eastern carpets and their scents of musk and
sandalwood, he felt as if he had come—not home. But to a
world which was, at its center, his own. These sun-stained
people shimmering in silk, these dark-eyed women, these men
with their air of mingled languor and ferocity, were courtiers;
and courtiers, he knew. The dart of eyes, the whispers, the
eddyings about power that was or power that wished to be,
woke senses which the months of pilgrimage had lulled to
sleep. It was like battle, but subtle. And, though his reputation would have died the death had he admitted it, in its way
it exhilarated him.

Lady Margaret drew an eddy of her own, of a size to raise
his brows. She was not, in strength of arms or in size of
holding, by any means one of the great ones of the kingdom.
Yet she had power: the power of her presence, and the power
of her empire of trade. The Constable of the Kingdom himself
bowed over her hand, and the Marshal had condolences
which seemed sincere. More to the point, the ladies accorded
her respect, without open sneers at her breeding. Others were
not so fortunate. They kept to themselves; veiled, some of
them, in Saracen fashion, with dark eyes and plump ivory fingers fretting jewels as rich as any there.

Thibaut was as tense as a hound in a new kennel, and carried himself the haughtier for it. There was, Aidan noticed, a certain division among the young as among their elders: tall and fair by tall and fair, and dark and small lingering side by languid silken side.

The *pullani* were hardly infidels. Most were Syrian-bred, or Armenian: Christian on both sides. Thibaut was the odd one. *His* blood was true Saracen, and they all knew it. His mother they did not touch. But in quiet places away from elders, in the courtyards among the oranges and the pomegranates, he was fair prey.

Aidan laid a hand on his shoulder, saying something, it did not matter what, and bared a gleam of teeth. Let them touch him now. It would be a pleasure to teach them tolerance.

Thibaut's wits were quick: he knew what Aidan was up to. He scowled. "Here, my lord. Don't. It's not fair."

"Are they?"

"They're beneath you. Look, you've better quarry waiting, like those knights in Acre."

That was true, and the boy wanted to fly on his own wings. Aidan was a falconer: he pulled him briefly close, and let him go.

Names and faces blurred past. Later, when Aidan needed them, they would come clear. Today he was the lady's shadow. That was accepted. They had had his name and his titles at his entrance, in the herald's strong voice; they could see in his face that he had been kin to the lord who was gone. It was a little disappointing that he was not, after all, a scandal; but worse that though he was a royal prince and thus a rarity, he was a prince without an army. He could at least, he heard someone mutter, have brought a man-at-arms or two.

Thibaut's sentiments, almost to a word. Aidan smiled and glanced about. The boy had wandered, freed, and found a companion or three who seemed disinclined to tan his infidel hide for him. The eddies had altered again. Margaret seemed quite content to discuss needlework with a cluster of ladies, matrons all and not remarkably interested in her pretty shadow.

He was not unduly dismayed. The glamour was its own defense. He leaned back against a wall hung with a carpet like a field of jeweled flowers, and watched the currents of the court.

There were, he took note, a goodly number of women both handsome and more than handsome. These had their attendants: young, most of those, and much given to the fashion for silken indolence. And, his nose told him, for perfumed curls. Henna seemed much the rage for the darker gentlemen; the fairer, perhaps, assisted nature in their quest for perfect gold.

He was a fine peacock for Rhiyana, but scent was past his limit. Curls . . . He shook a not-quite-straight, most unabashedly black lock out of his eyes, and smoothed his new beard. Very new, alas, and grievously out of fashion.

His eye crossed another. Dark, that one, and buried deep in admirers. The lady well deserved them: she was young, slender and tall, and very beautiful. And, from the set of her full and lovely mouth, very discontented. Something about her made him think of Joanna.

Joanna would not have looked well in the cloth of gold that so splendidly adorned this lady, but the cut of the gown would suit her. Aidan smiled, thinking of it. The lady returned his smile.

That had not been wise. Aidan shrugged under his mantle. What was wisdom, in a court? He sketched a bow. The lady's eyes began to dance. Without her edge of discontent, she was breathtaking.

And bold. Her lips pursed, miming a kiss. Her finger crooked, which was brazen. If no one yet had seen what passed, and with whom, he soon would.

Aidan left the wall, wandering with apparent aimlessness, keeping his quarry at the edge of his eye. She knew what he did, and was amused. It gave her time to watch him.

An elegant personage in an archdeacon's gown gave him her name. "Sybilla," the man said. "Princess Sybilla. The king's sister." The elegant personage had a disconcertingly keen eye and a ready tongue. "Poor child, it's not an easy life she has, with her brother so grievously afflicted, and no heir possible but through her. She must marry, and marry supremely well, for the kingdom's sake. But the first man chosen for her proved a fool and a libertine, and shamed her beyond swift healing. Now the envoys quest through Francia, seeking another fit, if God ordains, to be our king."

"But your king lives," Aidan said.

"And for how long?" Grief shadowed the archdeacon's eyes, deep and lasting. "He has been a leper since he was nine years old. It worsens as he grows out of boyhood. If he lives to be a man, he'll not live much longer than that. And our kingdom needs a king to follow him without delay, a strong one, or surely it will fall."

"It's fragile, this realm of yours."

The archdeacon nodded. "This is the sword's edge. All Islam waits beyond us, crouched to spring. Saladin has sworn to drive us into the sea; to hound us to our lairs in the west, and scour us from the earth. Let him settle his differences with his own kind, and let us lose the strength of our crown, and surely he will keep his vow."

Aidan drew a breath. It was sweet, that tang of danger, that bright edge of fear. He smiled. "I think he may have to wait a while. It's not so weak, this blade you've forged."

"God willing," said the archdeacon. "I come from Tyre, which held even against Alexander. Our king is not remarkably less than he. Maybe he'll live as long."

"You know him well," said Aidan.

The archdeacon shrugged. "I've been his tutor. I was the first to know that he was ill, and how. He played, you see, with the boys of his age, and you know how they are. They'll test one another. One day they tested courage, pinching to see who would howl first with the pain. Our Baldwin had his arm pinched till the blood sprang, and he never made a sound, nor even flinched. That was rare fortitude, I thought, and fittingly royal.

"But," the archdeacon said, his eyes filling though he must have told this tale a thousand times in the years since it began, "he denied that it was courage. 'I don't feel anything,' he said with perfect innocence. 'Truly, I don't.' And truly he did not. His arm and hand were dead to any torment I dared inflict.

"Of course I knew. We all knew. We tried to prove it false. We summoned every doctor east of the sea. We subjected him to tortures, to make him whole. Useless, all of them. God has made him what he is; God has no intention of letting him go."

And Sybilla, sulking amid her sycophants for that her new admirer had let himself be waylaid by her brother's tutor, was God's instrument for the continuance of the dynasty. "God's ways are a mystery," Aidan said. "I understand you've found a candidate for the lady."

The archdeacon was taken aback; then he eased. "Ah. Of course. You're new from the west. Was he on your ship, our messenger?"

"On one that came in just after it: and joyous he was, too. Not that he breathed a word," Aidan said, "but rumors flew, as they will. He didn't deny them."

The archdeacon shrugged slightly. "What can a messenger do?"

"Lie," said Aidan.

The other laughed. Suddenly he looked much younger. "No, there's no doubting it: you are a prince."

"You weren't convinced?"

"There are princes," said that most worldly churchman, "and there are princes. You'll do well here."

Aidan bowed an ironic degree. "You flatter me."

"I give you your due." The archdeacon paused. His voice changed subtly. "Since your knowledge is so complete and your wisdom so evident, I forbear to ask your indulgence in the matter of the lady. She is young; she has been raised, if I dare say it, somewhat less than wisely. She—"

"She is headstrong, and willful, and not excessively inclined to reflection." Aidan smiled at the archdeacon, who could not in propriety do other than look affronted. "I had a mare like that. She'd been let run wild, except when she was bred. Her foals were splendid, but they needed a strong hand. We were always most careful which stallion we chose for her."

It was hard for the poor man, to hear the truth so, and to be unable to rebuke the one who uttered it. Aidan was almost abashed. It was his tongue: it ran on if he let it, and its edge was cruel. He spoke a little softer, with rather more care. "There, I overstep my bounds. She's a fair lady; I pray her new lord is good to her. Under a wise hand, she'll grow into wisdom."

The archdeacon accepted the apology for what it was. For that, Aidan not only liked him; he admired him.

They understood one another. Aidan moved a little, away from the lady. The archdeacon cast eyes on a man with whom he needed to speak. But paused, first, as if at last he had made up his mind to it, and said, "I heard you sing in Carcassonne, twenty years agone. I saw your temper then. I see it now."

"Headstrong, and willful, and not excessively inclined to reflection."

"So you would have us think. Be gentle with the child, prince. She's no match for you."

"May I sing for her?"

"At her wedding," said the archdeacon, "with my blessing."

"Then, if I can, I shall."

The archdeacon bowed and sketched a sign of the cross. Aidan bent his head. Their eyes met briefly, before the archdeacon turned away.

Aidan shivered a little. It was not so terrible, to be known here. This one neither hated nor, unduly, feared him. And in that last glance had been a bargain. For the princess' safety, the archdeacon's silence. Not from Archdeacon William of

Tyre would Outremer discover that the prince had been a troubadour in Carcassonne, somewhat before he could, from the evidence of his face, have been old enough to sing.

A thread of melody wound through his head. *Domna, pouois ne me no · us chal* . . . "Lady, since you care not for me, and cast me away . . ." His own, that one. Someone else was claiming it of late; he was welcome to it. Aidan did not cling to his mind's children, once they had grown and gone away.

The lady was unhappy, now that he seemed to have forgotten her. The faithful would suffer for her pique. But Aidan had struck a bargain. He let himself be drawn toward the safer harbor of a circle of young knights. One had been at Acre, and one or two were new in Outremer. Those looked rough and raw and sun-scorched, and slightly stunned by the wonder of it all. "Here," they greeted him, eyeing his elegance. "How do you do it? You look like a *pullani* born."

If it was an insult, he did not intend to notice. "First," he replied, "a bath." They looked appalled. "Do you know what they have here? Soap! Scented, by Our Lady's sweet white breast, and soft as her kiss. With a dusky maiden to administer it, and another to wield the sponge, and . . ."

"His Majesty, Baldwin, fourth of that exalted name, King of Jerusalem, Heir to the Throne of David, Defender of the Holy Sepulcher!"

The herald's voice had gone rough with crying the name of every lord and lady and lordly scion of the High Court. But now it rang forth with its fullest vigor, in spreading silence.

Aidan, taller than many and somewhat nearer the door than most, saw clearly the one who stood framed there. He did not like it, to be singled out so: that was as clear to Aidan's senses as if he had uttered it aloud. To human senses . . .

He was a little older than Thibaut, just at his majority. He was tall already, but slender, reed-frail in his richness of silk, robes that seemed less Frankish than Saracen. He wore the long cotte of the older fashion, and jeweled gloves such as a

king might choose to wear; but it was the headdress which
gave him that air of foreignness. Aidan had seen it on
tribesmen in the desert east of Jaffa: the *kaffiyah,* the headcloth with the coronet binding it about the brows, drawn like
a veil over the face, baring only a glitter of eyes. This one was
silk, and royal purple; its circlet was gold. The eyes were dark
within it, yet clear, with a shadow on them, of weariness, of
long suffering.

Only the rawest newcomers stared. The rest went down in
obeisance.

The king gestured without speaking. They straightened;
they began again, slowly, their dance of power and favor. He
paused, scanning their faces. Aidan felt the touch of his eyes as
if a flame had passed, too swift to burn.

The king stirred, descending. His walk was slow, not lame,
not quite, but careful, as if he did not trust his feet. The
sickness was in them, as in his hands: the left that seemed
strong enough in its glove, the right that was withered, held
or bound close against his side. And his face, veiled, that no
one had seen in a year and more. It had been handsome, the
whispers said, like his father's, with a fine arch of nose, and a
strong clean line of brow and cheek and chin. What it was
now, only rumor knew.

And yet he did not invite pity. He held himself erect, his
head at a high and kingly angle. His voice was soft and low,
with a hint of a stammer; he did not use it overmuch as he
circled the hall, but listened to those who approached him,
his clear eyes fixed on their faces. Most of them, Aidan noticed, found ways to avoid kissing his hand. Some were rather
ingenious. The king was aware of it: Aidan saw it in the flicker
of his glance. The wound was an old one. He had taught
himself to be amused by it, and to admire the more clever
expedients, ranking them like knights in a joust.

Margaret neither shrank nor evaded. The king's eyes smiled
at her, but saddened quickly, filling with tears. "I . . . re-

gret . . ." he said, his stammer deepening for a little, until he mastered it. "I'm sorry. He was a good man."

"Yes, highness," said Margaret steadily. "My thanks to you."

The king shook his head, a quick gesture, almost sharp. "If there is anything—if you need aid, comfort—"

"I shall remember, majesty," Margaret said.

"Do that," said the king. "I order it. Now, or later, after the court has met on the matter—ask, and you shall have whatever you need."

She bowed low.

There was a silence. She was not inclined to fill it. The king was reluctant to go, although others waited with veiled impatience: in that much, he betrayed his youth. His glance found Aidan, who had come up while they spoke, cat-quiet as he could be when he wanted to be. The fair brows went up under the *kaffiyah*. "Why—why, sir! You look just like him."

Aidan bowed over the gloved hand: the leather dyed crimson, the jewels sewn with gold wire, the foul-sweet scent of sickness beneath. He was being ranked high, for setting lips to it, for neither trembling nor radiating saintliness. But it was nothing to be proud of. He was not a mortal man. He could not fall prey to mortal sickness.

"My lord's kinsman," Margaret was saying. "Aidan, Prince Royal of Rhiyana, new come from the west."

Baldwin knew him, as Thibaut knew, as Gereint had known: in wonder and in high delight. His eyes shone. "My lord! Well met. Oh, well met!"

"Even without an army?" Aidan asked him wryly.

"Oh," said Baldwin, dismissing it. "Have they been at you, then, for coming alone? More fools they. You are quite enough in yourself." He held up his hand. A ring glowed there, gold set with a great emerald. "I had your king's gifts, when I was crowned—isn't it a wonder that he knew, all the way from the west of Francia? See, I wear the ring, and I read the book whenever I may, and it comforts me. Is he a kinsman of yours, that great scholar who wrote it and called it the *Gloria Dei?*"

"Not that I know, sire," said Aidan, taking note that the boy spoke readily enough, once he was into it. "Most likely not. He's a monk in Anglia, very saintly they say, and quite shut away from the world. But it's a remarkable book, isn't it?"

"Wonderful," Baldwin said. "We'll read it together soon, you and I." He paused. "You are here for that? To be my knight?"

Such surety: only a king could know it, and only a young one could carry it off. Aidan smiled into the wide brown eyes. "To serve you, my lord, as best I may. Only . . ."

"Only?" Baldwin asked, when Aidan did not go on.

Aidan dropped to one knee, taking the king's hand in his. It was bone-thin beneath the silk. "My lord, I will pledge to you, but first there is a thing which I must do. When it is done, I will come, and if you will have me, I will be your liege man until death shall part us."

Listeners were awed, or fascinated, or shocked at his temerity. The king met his eyes, and nodded slowly. No child, this, however brief his count of years. "What will you do, prince?"

"My sister's son is dead," Aidan said. "I have sworn to take revenge on him who ordered that death."

Baldwin nodded again: bowed his head, raised it. "I . . . see."

He did. For that, Aidan would never regret what he had said, or the impulse that had made him say it. "I'll come back, my lord. Even if my body falls. I'll serve you with all my power."

Baldwin's hand trembled. That was no small promise, and no little gift. But Aidan sensed no fear in him, no horror of what had come to serve him. "Come back whole," he said, "and come back strong. We need you, we of Jerusalem."

7

Joanna would not, adamantly would not, ask. And for a maddening while, no one would tell her. They were all full of what the king had said to the prince, and what the prince had said to the king. It was burgeoning into a legend already.

"All they *did* was put off swearing the oath of fealty!"

Thibaut blinked at her vehemence. "But that's not what matters. It's how they did it. Like something out of a song. They looked at one another, and we could all see: they belonged together."

"You make them sound like a pair of lovers."

Her voice caught on that. Thibaut did not notice. "Of course they're not. They're a king and a man whom God meant to stand beside him."

"Why not? Witchkind can't get sick."

Thibaut went away in disgust, and there was no one else whom Joanna could ask. Except, of course, that she would not. It was nothing to her whether Ranulf had been in the High Court, or whether he had spoken to anyone of his wife.

"He didn't."

She jumped. Aidan sat beside her on the roof. He had a frosted cup, which he gave her. She took it blindly, sipped. Sherbet.

He sat back at his ease, stretching out his long legs. "He wasn't there," he said. "No one seemed perturbed. It wasn't a formal session, after all."

Her cheeks burned. She gulped cold sour-sweetness, lemon and sugar iced with snow from Mount Hermon.

When she choked, he pounded her back, forbearing mightily to laugh at her. She cursed him, but silently, glaring under her brows. He went back to his panther-sprawl. He was out of his finery, in a shirt as plain as a commoner's, and plain rough hose. The shirt was unlaced. She refused to look.

"I don't think he's going to denounce you," said that damnable, lilting voice, "or repudiate you in public. As far as anyone knows, you've come to be with your mother in her grief, and he is allowing it."

"How magnanimous of him."

"Isn't it?"

Her eyes blazed on him. He smiled, lazy, yawning like a cat in the sun. "Your face," he observed, "is a remarkable shade of crimson."

She hit him.

He was not there; and then, unstruck, he was. His hand had caught her wrist. She barely felt it, but all her strength did not suffice to break her free.

She swung left-handed. Again she struck only air. Again he caught her, and held her with effortless ease. She kicked him, hard. His eyes widened. He was still laughing, but she had made a mark. Her knee came up, threatening. "Let me go," she said.

He obeyed. He did not move off to a prudent distance, or try to protect his jewels.

Her flare of rage had faded. She sank down in a huddle of skirts. All at once, she began to cry.

He folded his arms about her and held her. At first she shrank within herself. He neither moved nor spoke. Little by little she uncoiled. Her arms crept up, circling his neck. She buried her face in his shoulder and wept herself dry.

She lay against him at last, spent. Somewhere in the long siege, he had begun to stroke her hair, slowly, steadily. Now his hand moved down her back, seeking the knots, loosening them one by one. His heart beat slow and strong, slower than a man's. It was—she stiffened. It was on the wrong side. His fingers kneaded the stiffness, softening it, smoothing it away.

It was no worse than the rest of him. His scent, or the lack of it. Even the cleanest man still smelled of man. He smelled of nothing but the salt of her tears and the linen of his shirt and the faint rose-sweetness of the bath. But he was solid against her, beast-warm, a flow and slide of muscles under her hands, the surprising softness of his hair. Even his beard—it barely pricked, soft and downy-thick against her palm.

With sudden violence she pulled away. He did not try to hold her. His eyes had gone dark, the color of rain. He was old enough to be her grandfather. He was her kin in forbidden degree. He was not even human.

If he mocked her, she knew that she would die.

He touched her, the barest whisper of a touch, tracing the line of her cheek.

She recoiled. His hand fell. He half turned, half shrugged. It was her salvation, that shrug. She hated him for it.

She scrambled herself up. "I have to go," she said.

If he heard her, he gave no sign.

Yes, she said in her head. *Be like that. See if I care.*

He did not hear that, either. She spun on her heel and stalked away from him.

He drew up his knees, laid his head on them, sighed from the bottom of his lungs. *Dear God,* he thought. *Dear unmerciful God.*

The first woman in twenty years whom he had even wanted to look at, and of course it must be this one. A child. With a temper. And a husband. And an Assassin on her track.

She wanted him. They usually did. Sometimes they hardly knew it. She knew; but she had not named it, yet. She had not seen its echo in his eyes.

God willing, she would not. She had pain enough. Her idiot of a husband, her son, the shadow of death over this house. She was wise when her youth and her spirit would let her be. She would see that she was only falling to his accursed, alien seduction, and she would resist it. He would be as cold as he could ever be, oblivious, neither man nor mortal to care that a mortal woman yearned for him.

He laughed, sharp and bitter. He would pretend that she was the Princess Sybilla. That one, he could stalk for plain cat-pleasure, if he had not made his bargain with her brother's tutor—chancellor as the man was, in truth, and a power in the realm. She was nothing to him. She was prey.

His mother had warned him long ago. "Never let a human touch your heart. That way lies only grief."

Truly. Even Gereint, who had been blood kin—he had died, and dealt a wound which would not heal. They were all so. It was their nature.

And what was his? He should be cold; he should be soulless. He should be the cat, the beast that walks alone, the hunter in the night. But he was half human, and although perhaps he had no soul, he had a heart; and he had never learned to harden it.

He raised his head. The sun had sunk low. Jerusalem was all gold, a city washed in light.

He watched the light spread wide and fade, and the stars bloom one by one. The others came up in the cool of the dusk, and servants with them, bringing the daymeal. Aidan felt the wards draw in about them. Joanna sat as far from him as she could. It seemed to be her best defense, to pretend that he did not exist. He had rather less strength of will; but the eyes of the mind were not so easily averted as the eyes of the body.

She ate quickly; she fled. He did not linger long.

Thibaut followed him down to his chamber. It was, of course, the boy's place, to attend him as he retired, to ease him out of his clothes, to ready his bed for him. He did not want to be followed. Or waited on. Or, by God, touched. Touch pierced every shield, laid the mind bare in all its aimless, shapeless, maddening humanity.

It did no good to evade him. He pursued, innocently persistent. To Thibaut, even temper was admirable: the famous fire, the flame out of the west. When Aidan snapped at him, he took no offense at all. His lord, he would tell the squires in the High Court, was a hot-tempered man. But bold and high-hearted, and generous with his favor. Altogether a perfect prince.

Aidan thrust him reeling back. "Will you stop that? Will you just stop?"

Thibaut stared, surprised. It had never gone this far before. *"Stop thinking at me!"*

The boy stood still where Aidan's arm had cast him, back to the wall, all eyes and astonishment. Aidan made a sound, half growl, half moan. He flung himself down upon the bed. All his shields reared up and locked.

Quiet. Blessed peace. Himself, alone.

His skin knew how Thibaut crept about, doing all his duties, shirking not one. The last was the lamp-cluster, diminished to a single flame. He lay on his pallet across the door. To all appearances, he went directly to sleep.

Muscle by muscle Aidan unknotted. Shame pricked. All this child had ever given him was devotion; and he repaid it with hard words and the back of his hand.

Thibaut was a huddle of sheet, a tousle of black curls, a soft sighing of breath. No weeping there; no hurt that would last the night.

None that passed the walls. Aidan left them, high as they were, and impregnable. This one night, by God's bright blood, he would have peace.

Silence; stillness. They slept, all of them, even the dog in its kennel. The lady curled like a cat in half of the great curtained bed, and her maid snored beside her where once her husband had been. The daughter slept alone, her tossing stilled, her cheek streaked salt with the track of a tear. The son . . .

That was not he in the chamber of the crimson tiles, flung naked across the coverlet. He was a brown child, slight and small. This was tall and pale, and a man grown—that, most certainly. He had no blemish on him, save, to Muslim eyes, one: he was not circumcised.

Morgiana shaped herself out of air, standing over him, enchanted. There was no moon tonight, and yet he glowed with its cool pale light. No whiter skin had ever been. Except—her breath caught—her own. Shadow hid his face. Hair, nightblack, thick and long.

He stirred, tossing a little. She caught at darkness, to conceal herself, but paused. His hair had fallen back.

Oh, no Frank, not this. Eagle's face, keen as the dagger's blade, without softness, without flaw. He had not even marred it with that ghastly Frankish fashion, the shaving of the beard that was a man's beauty and his pride.

Her hand reached of its own accord, but did not, dared not, touch. Joy welled up in her, and sudden, piercing terror. He was like her. Now that she knew what to see, she saw the light, the sheen of his magic, the power that was of air and fire.

But after joy, after terror, crushing certainty. This house had been barred to her, walled and guarded beyond the world as in it. Tonight, the walls had fallen. He had raised them. He, for what reason she could not know, had cast them down. He was the enemy. He was the lady's demon, as she was her master's.

"No," she said behind her gritted teeth. He was ifrit, spirit of air. Her kind. Hers.

If one could profess Islam, why not that other faith?

Almost, in pain, she laughed. She had come to kill. She had found—not a brother. No. Most certainly not a brother, if Allah indeed was merciful.

Their eyes met. His were blurred, full of sleep. Grey eyes, like rain. Green flare where the light struck. He frowned a very little; yet, at the same time, marveling, he smiled. The word he spoke was none she knew, and yet she knew it. "Beautiful," he said. "So beautiful."

The terror rose up and drowned her. It raised the power; it smote him all unwitting, deep into sleep.

She had come to kill. There by the door, laid across it as if any mortal child could guard against this horror that she was, slept the one to whom she had been sent. Small, slight, dark. A child, but almost a man.

Her hand struck of its own will, swift and clean. The heart throbbed against the blade: struggling, protesting. She thrust the dagger home.

He was dead before he knew that he had died. The last of his dream fled past her. Light, a snatch of song, a keen eagle-face. Love that touched the edge of worship; joy; pride. *I am his. He is my lord.* A flicker of shadow. *Even when he thinks he does not want me.*

It drove her to her knees. *Out,* her mind clamored at her. *Out, go!*

Always before, implacable as the Angel of Death, she had come, killed, vanished. Remorse came after, and the dark thoughts, and the horror of her bloodied hands. Not now. Not in the house of the enemy. With power behind her, working free of its bonds; the dead before her, cooling slowly, lying as if he slept. A boy. A child. An innocent. And she had murdered him.

A great cry swelled in her, filling her, till surely she must burst asunder. It swept her up. It cast her into the night.

Aidan started awake. He had been dreaming. A wailing like wind in empty places; terrible, heart-searing grief, grief like madness, sweeping him down into the dark.

It was quiet. Memory swam through the darkness. Behind the dream, another. Faint, indefinable sweetness. A shimmer of light. A face. A white, wild beauty; hair that could only be a dream, rivers of it, red as wine. Eyes—

Eyes like his own, fixed on him as if they would devour him.

His manhood was heavy on his belly, stiff and aching. Wise fool, he mocked himself. Run cowering from a human woman, dream one of his own kind. And not even the one he knew, his brother's slender ivory queen. Ah, no. He must

85

dream one who did not even exist, a fierce cat-woman all in white, whose beauty touched the edge of pain.

His own ache, unappeased, began to subside. He sat up, running his hands through his hair, worrying out the tangles. His mind stretched, struck walls. Reckless with sleep and the dream and the last rags of the darkness, he cast them down.

Silence. Utter stillness. No sound, no breath, no scent of alien presence. Thibaut lay in his blanket, unmoving. His mind—

Silence.

"Thibaut," said Aidan. Louder: "Thibaut!"

Nothing.

Aidan knew. He refused it. It could not be.

The dark head rolled as Aidan shook the boy's shoulder. The eyes were open, wide and black and empty even of surprise. Thibaut was gone. Emptied.

Dead.

In the smooth brown flesh above his heart, silver glimmered: the hilt of a Saracen dagger. And beside his body, still warm from the fire, the cake which was baked upon no hearth but one.

Aidan flung back his head and howled.

He had not, for all of that, gone mad. God had no such mercy. He had fretted over a woman. Fretting, he had brought down the wards. And the Assassin had come into his very chamber, while he dreamed and tossed and lusted after shadows, and taken Thibaut's life, and vanished away.

Utterly. No memory remained. The dagger was a lifeless thing, cold steel without scent or sense of its wielder. The cake was flour and water and honey, and no more in it of its maker than if it had made itself.

Thibaut's blood had stained it. So little blood, to mean so much. Aidan took a morsel in his mouth. He did not think why, only that he must. It was sweet.

He raised his eyes to a blur of faces. Mute, all of them; dazed; horrified. His mind, opened wide, reeled with grief, and grief, and grief resounding down every hall of memory. And fear. They were afraid of the hunter in the night. Of the white beast with its mad cat-eyes, crouched over Thibaut's body, his mouth full of honey and of blood.

Some of them knew then, and shrank from what they knew: the stranger in their house, the tale that was half open to the sun, half whispered in the dark. He had come singing on the wings of death. Now he held it in his hands. He had wrought it, he and no other.

"No," said Margaret. She held out her hand. It was frighteningly steady.

Mutely Aidan set the dagger in it. She barely flinched from the blood. "Damascus work," she said, soft and cool. "See, how the hilt is ornamented, and the blade. But the steel is too good for western forging—Indian, surely, and that of the best. It seems new."

"For each new murder," Aidan said, "a new blade." He rose with Thibaut in his arms. The boy's head lolled against his shoulder. He was as light as a leaf, as heavy as a world.

They stared. Joanna above all, mute with horror: she could not take her eyes from her brother's face.

"Maybe he's not dead," she said. "Maybe he's only stunned. Maybe he'll wake. Maybe—"

"He is dead." Aidan's voice was flat.

Her hand went to her mouth, stemming the tide of words. One of the serving women began to wail. Joanna whipped about. "Out, all of you. *Out!*"

They wavered. Margaret seemed oblivious. She turned the dagger in her fingers, staring at it, spellbound. Joanna lurched forward a step. The servants broke and fled.

She turned ungracefully back. Margaret had not moved. Aidan could not muster the will. The servants would let it out in keening and in rousing this whole quarter of the city. They three had only silence. Gereint was grief. This was grief on grief. It went beyond words and almost beyond pain. It numbed the soul.

"God is great," said Margaret in a low and dreaming voice, in Arabic.

The others stared, speechless.

She had not broken. Not quite yet. "It says so," she said, "here, on the blade. Most devout, our Assassin, and most like to his God. He fattens on the blood of innocents."

Her hate was diamond-pure, diamond-hard. "Joanna," she said. "Fetch Godefroi, if he has had his fill of wailing and gnashing his teeth. Bid him bring my writing-case."

Joanna did not even begin to argue. She went.

Leaving Aidan and Margaret alone. With all the gentleness in the world, Aidan laid Thibaut in the high curtained bed, closed the wide and staring eyes, covered the lifeless body. He straightened slowly, turned. Margaret regarded him with interest, and with a certain amount of pleasure.

This was her defense, this bitter calm. He spoke in it. "The blame is mine. My vigilance failed. His blood is on my head."

Her head shook infinitesimally. "I knew that he would be the next to fall, and I held fast to my resistance. We share this, you and I. But I the more. He was blood of my blood."

Aidan's heart spasmed. Thibaut, gentle Thibaut who had never spoken ill of any man. "Leave me my guilt," he said, low and raw.

"There is enough for us all."

Briefly he wanted to scream aloud, seize her, shake her, beat her into acting as a mother should act who has lost her only son. She stood where she had stood since she came, a small round woman in a loose dark robe. Her face was grey and old. She let the dagger fall. It pierced the Assassin's cake, breaking it. "I bore five sons," she said. "One only lived past his birth. Daughters I had none, except Joanna. If she dies," said Margaret, "I shall not want to live."

"Will you surrender, then?"

Her eyes lifted, black and wide. She smiled. He had never seen any face so terrible. "Surrender? Only," she said, "if I might be certain that, the night he bedded with me, he would die of yon dagger in his back."

So she wrote when Godefroi came, in Arabic but in the bare unvarnished phrases of the Frank. "Let him see for himself," she said, "that in taking from me my husband and my son, he has taken all that might persuade me to yield." She folded and sealed the letter, and gave it to her seneschal. "There will no doubt be a bird on the roof, with the mark of Masyaf on its leg. Give it what it waits for."

Godefroi's eyes were red with weeping, but he held himself stiffly erect. He bowed and went to do her bidding.

For her now there would be no tears, and no sleep. She set herself beside the bed. "Look after my daughter," she said to Aidan. Simply that. Even as she spoke, she turned her eyes and mind from him, toward her son.

Aidan moved without thinking, gathering up what garment came to hand: his cloak. He flung it over himself. Joanna had turned already. He followed her.

Just within the door of her chamber, she spun on her heel. Aidan stood just without. She spoke abruptly. "I can look after myself."

"I don't doubt it," he said.

Joanna's lip curled. "You haven't been much good so far, have you?"

It was pain, that was all. She needed to lash out. He was there, the best of targets, and the closest. He set himself to endure it. It was no more than he deserved.

She shook her head once, hard, tossing away tears. "What could you have done? That man is the devil himself. You're scarcely even a lesser angel."

His head snapped up. That was not what he was braced for.

His expression made her laugh, even as she wept. "Oh, yes: how dare I imply that you're not invincible? Grubby mortal I, who should be bowing at your feet."

"Not . . . grubby," he said thickly. His grief rose, choking him. "Oh, God! It was I who let him die."

"Hush," she said. "Hush."

This was not proper. That he should be on his knees in her chamber, weeping. That she should hold him, and rock him, and murmur words of comfort. She was the child, the slave of her temper, headstrong and sullen.

Her breasts were heavy still, aching with milk, that but for her stubborn will would have dried long since. She was a mother. She was not altogether a child or a lackwit or a fool. Whereas he . . .

"Stop it," she said, sharp as cold water in the face. But her hand was gentle, stroking his hair, moving down his back.

She knew what she was doing. She saw that he knew. She barely blushed. She drew back, not easily, but firmly enough. "I think," she said, "that we should try to get what sleep we can. When morning comes, Mother is going to need us both."

He raised his brows. His bed was occupied. Hers . . .

She could follow his thoughts with alarming ease, for a woman without magic. Her cheeks burned scarlet. "Not here!" It was too loud. "The roof—if any of the servants will —Dura!"

He rose, retreated past the door. The servant came from God knew where, red-eyed and stiff-backed as they all seemed to be. "Lay a pallet for my lord," said Joanna, "on the roof, where we used to sleep when we were children." The woman ducked her head and scuttled past Aidan: a scent of musk, a tang of fear, a heavy mist of grief.

Aidan lingered, unable to make himself go. "You, too," he said. "Sleep. We're safe enough tonight. They won't strike again until they have your mother's message."

She understood. The blood drained from her face, but she did not tremble. She kissed him quickly, and chastely enough, on the forehead. Almost he reached, clutched; knowing that if he did, she would not let him go.

His hand fisted at his side. Without a word, he left her.

8

Masyaf was a fortress, a stronghold. The village that served it, huddling round the knees of its mountain, hoarded every precious scrap of green, cherished every drop of water. But in the castle's heart, as in Alamut its master and its begetter, lay a garden like a many-colored jewel. It was smaller by far than the Garden of Allah in the Nest of Eagles, but perfect of its kind, and more than sufficient for its purpose. From the center of it, so cunningly was it made, one could not see its boundaries.

There, in summer's warmth, the Master of the Assassins of Syria raised his tent. No silken pavilion, that, but a simple dwelling of the desert, woven of goat's hair, black and unadorned. Naught lay within but his worn prayer rug and a single carpet, and the slave who attended his needs.

He had slept briefly after the prayer of the night, and risen again to pray, bowing southward to thrice-holy Mecca. His prayer as always was only that what Allah had willed to be, might be. If Rashid al-Din Sinan willed it also, then praise be to God.

He straightened, raising his face to the stars. Sweetness wafted over him: roses, jasmine, the blossom of orange and citron. The nightingale sang in her secret place.

His heart sang with it, ineffably sweet. "Thanks be to God," he said, "that He has set me in such a world as this."

"Thanks be to God," said a voice out of the night, "that you may take such joy in it."

That joy withered and died. Such had been her intent, he was certain. He would not admit to fear of the strangest of the slaves of Alamut, the oldest and the strongest and the most inextricably bound to the cause, but it was granted to any man to be wary of such a creature as entered the circle of his lamp's light. The form she wore now was that which she had worn before the first of the Masters of the Assassins, Hasan-i-Sabbah himself, on whose name be peace; and that was nigh a hundred years agone. A woman, it seemed to be, a maiden of some seventeen summers, too slender and cat-faced for beauty as it was reckoned in Persia, but beautiful for all of that, a beauty as fierce as it was strange. A man would want her, inevitably, but he might not be so swift to take her. The houris of Sinan's garden, like those of Alamut, were cast in a gentler mold.

She was more beautiful than ever, more wild and more strange. Sometimes she wore the turban; less often, as now, she let her hair fall as it would, staining her white garments like dark blood.

She bowed as was proper, kissing the earth between her hands. "It is done," she said.

His breath left him in a long sigh. "So. Is it well done?"

She raised her eyes. He met them, knowing that he was strong, that she could not match his will. Such eyes, green as emeralds, clear as glass, drawing him in, down and down and down. And at the bottom of them, a light: a face, a body, a boy of rather exceptional beauty. But to those eyes, nothing at all, save only prey. A heart, beating. A life for the taking. He took it, he who for this eternal instant was she; and he tasted its sweetness, and its gagging bitterness.

"He was," said Morgiana, voice without substance, clear as water, and as cold, and as still, "thirteen years old. Yesterday he confessed to his priest a terrible sin: he had exchanged sharp words with his sister. Such a tender lamb; it was almost a pity to rid the world of him."

Sinan reeled. He was free, in his own self, in his own garden where he and no other was lord. His slave knelt at his feet, and again her eyes were lowered, their power bound and hidden, as if it had never been.

Perhaps, after all, he had dreamed it. She was ifritah and

undying, spirit of air and fire, but above all, she was his. His slave, utterly, without will save what was his, without self save what he granted her.

Or so she had been. She had risen up not long ago, as shocking as if Masyaf itself had stirred and stood and begun to speak, and announced that she would shed no more Muslim blood. She had not spoken as if she expected to be refused. Sinan, taken aback, had set her on Christians instead, and she had seemed content.

Yet now he might almost have thought that she was bitter; that the glitter in her eyes was tears. Could an ifritah weep?

Her eyes lifted once more. He flinched; but there was no power in them. They were hard and flat, green-gleaming like a cat's. "That is the last of my murders," she said. "Now you will set me free."

For a moment Sinan could not comprehend plain Arabic. "Will? I? Set you free?"

"Release me from my oath. Let me go."

Yes. She had said it. "But," he said, "this is not the last of them. A daughter remains, and the mother herself."

"This is the last life I will take. I am done with killing. Set me free."

Sinan stood wordless in the face of such insolence. She did not even bow her head, still less address him as she always had, with deep and humble respect. She held herself as straight as a man, and spoke in a clear voice, not loud, simply telling him what she would have.

He had her name, and his own name written on the seal about her neck, the Seal of Suleiman which bound all races of the jinn. He had no fear of her. So he told himself, as he faced her and said, "No. You are not done."

She went whiter than he would have believed possible. He tensed. Seal or no Seal, she was deadly, always; and never more than now. But she did not move. She was utterly still.

"When this game is over," he said, "I will consider your plea. You have labored long on our behalf; I shall remember."

"Memory sets no slave free."

Sinan rose. He was growing angry. "Go, in the name of Suleiman, on whom be peace; by whom thy race was bound. Come not back until I summon thee."

In that much still he could command her obedience. She did not bow, but she obeyed.

Sinan shivered. Death was no stranger to his presence, and for his Faith he was ruthless; it was, after all, his Faith. But this was more than he had bargained for. The ifritah was gone. Not so the face with which she had branded his soul. The boy whom she had slain—whose death Sinan had willed.

Sinan faced him steadily, refusing fear, refusing regret; mastering him with strength of will. He was younger than Sinan had thought. He had been reported as a well-grown stripling, albeit small for a Frank; he had shown promise in the arts of war. The leper king had been crowned at his age, and ruled under the lightest of regencies, soon to be dissolved. Margaret de Hautecourt would have contrived the same for her son.

A strong woman, though her beauty was long and sadly gone. If she would but see the sense in what Sinan proposed . . . but no. She must resist. Her mother's apostasy from Islam had become, in her, crusading zeal.

What an Assassin she would make, who could sacrifice her only son for her faith. Pray Allah that now she would see sense, while she still had a daughter to be her comfort. And a grandson, it was said. A first grandson would be most precious to a widow without a son.

The dead face stared levelly back into Sinan's own, naming fidelity obsession, and just execution murder, and faith mere selfish greed. Sinan flung truth against it. The Faith demanded this, that any who opposed it be recompensed with death. The Mission was hindered while this child's mother held to her obstinacy.

What have I ever done but be, and be my mother's son?

His words, but the ifritah's voice, clear and hard.

You care nothing for our Mission. You wanted a woman; she

refused you. Therefore you take revenge as your power allows. There is no holiness in it. Only avarice.

Sinan flung up his hand, letting the wrath burn white and fierce. "Be silent, by the Seal that binds thee!"

She was, within and without. The boy's face faded. Sinan shivered in the cold of the mountains before dawn; but his heart was colder yet. Cold and implacable. He had done what he had done. No demon's spawn would trick him into regretting it.

Morgiana was all strange to herself. She had a chamber in the castle, high and apart, with the women's quarters between itself and the press of male humanity. But even that, now, was no refuge. Its walls closed in upon her. Its slit of window mocked her with the specter of freedom.

She stripped off her garments with their reek of death, not caring what tore, or what could not be mended. The blood on her soul was not so easily disposed of. She clawed at herself in a passion of revulsion.

A last glimmer of sanity set in her mind the image of a bath in Aleppo, where the service was both silent and impeccable, and where the attendants were all faithful to the cause. It was always they who cleansed her of the blood of execution; they knew her, and they knew what she was.

And they feared her, and hated her in silence, as they all did, all the mortal men to whom her oath had bound her. Only Hasan, Hasan-i-Sabbah the wise in the white light of his faith—only he had had no fear of her. Had, in his way, loved her. He had asked no oath or binding, only her fidelity to the Mission which his God had set so clearly in his soul. It was she, blind fool, who had insisted on an oath; who, in the flame of zeal, had begged him to make her his servant. The slave's bond had come later, when he was dead and she prostrate with grief. She had laid her freedom on his tomb, her last gift to him, and let herself be bound in body as in spirit. There was a fierce purity in it, a perfection of selflessness, a blessed certainty. She was nothing, no thing, no creature of her own, but utterly the Slave of Alamut.

She stood on the bare stone of the floor, in the cell that had always sufficed for her few hours of sleep, and saw it as a stranger would see it. Bare stone, plain box for what belongings she had, sleeping mat rolled and laid in a corner. It lacked even the beauty of simplicity. It was as empty as her soul.

She fled it as she alone knew how to do: that eerie, inward twist of mind and power, threading the world like a needle through silk, stepping from breath in Masyaf to breath otherwhere. Here, her own place, her secret.

Once, long ago, it had been a hermit's cell. His bones had been there when she found it, bare and clean and somehow welcoming. Though he had been a Christian and therefore an enemy, she had buried him with honor on the hill above the cave and its spring and its gnarled and ancient fig tree. From there his emptied eyes could gaze across the bleak and barren waste, the desert without life or water, save only here. Miracles must have fed him: apart from the fig tree and a blade or two of grass, there was nothing green or growing; and surely the lizards and the odd desert mouse could not have sustained him.

But the narrow mouth of his cave had hidden splendor. The way to it was dark and uninviting, a tunnel in the crag, but opening on a high vaulted space like the hall of a king. A smaller cavern abutted it; beyond it lay its secret: a chamber of flowering stone, and like a jewel in it, a pool of warm and everflowing water.

She, who needed but to step from the cave into the heart of any bazaar in the world, had made a refuge. Carpets covered the stone of the floor and hung from the rough walls. Chests, richly carved and inlaid with silver, held treasures from her wanderings. A divan stood against the wall, heaped with silken cushions; a table stood beside it, and on that a gleam of copper, all the proper instruments for the making and the serving of kaffé. The box beside them held within its ornamented protection her most precious possession, her copy of the Koran.

She entered warily, like a beast, as strange to it as it was to her. Years had passed since last she came here. A lizard scuttled under her foot. A mouse had nested in the cushions. But the rest had not changed, save to gather a veiling of dust, an air of emptiness.

It fit her soul. She scorned the hidden pool to scour herself in the biting cold of the spring, welcoming the pain, the outrage of skin accustomed to warm water and scented oils. She let the wind dry her, the cold wind of dawn. What matter how deep it cut? She was demon-born. She could not fall ill and die.

She prayed so, bowing before her God. Her prayers were empty. Somewhere she had lost her faith. She could not even remember where, to hunt it down and bring it back.

When the prayer was done, she remained, kneeling on the stones beside the spring. Her eyes, wandering, found her body. She had forgotten to cover it. Appalling; contrary to the Prophet's teachings.

He had been a man. Holy; possessed of God. But still, a man. Men found her beautiful. She could not make herself care. She was she, but not woman, not of kind to warm to a man's embrace.

She spanned the width of hips, weighed breasts in her hands. No, no male, she. Tall enough to pass if she must in the concealment of robes and turban, slender enough, quick enough on her feet; and strong enough most certainly, stronger than any man. But still, incontestably, female.

As that one had been male. She trembled in the wind of memory, seeing him as he had lain, all unguarded in sleep. He was young, she knew that surely. His power was growing still; strong, honed well for one so young, but soft with ease and arrogance. He would not think to use it, she suspected, where he thought his body's senses would suffice. As if, living among mortals, he tried to make himself one of them.

It was a strange kind of innocence. And he so beautiful, all moonlight and darkness, waking to the wonder of her face. Her hand rose to it. He had smiled at her. His body had warmed to her, most visibly, as men's bodies did. He had had no shame of it, no shrinking. Only clean desire.

"I will have him," she said to the wind and the stones and the eagle wheeling high against the morning. "He is mine. He was set on earth for me."

An enemy. A Christian.

"Ifrit to my ifritah. He will see. He will love me. And I—" Her voice caught. "I, him."

9

Gereint's death, beside this, had been a quiet thing, a lord laid to rest in the heart of his demesne. Thibaut had died in Jerusalem, the night before the opening of the High Court, when the king was to send out the *arrière-ban:* the calling of his vassals to arms against the infidel. The murder of one of their own, in their very midst, was no matter for quiet or for meek endurance.

But under the high voices and the cries for revenge ran a current of fear. Simple murder, a man could face. The Assassins were uncanny. They stank of sorcery.

He would lie in Aqua Bella, in the crypt under the chapel, beside Gereint who had been all the father he had ever known. It was nearer evening than noon when they set out, a great riding, all who could or would leave the court for a night and a day: a startling number, the flower of the kingdom, and about the bier a guard of the knights of God.

"He would have loved this," said Joanna.

They rode behind the bier, mother and daughter, and Aidan beside them. They were, somewhat unfortunately, downwind of the Templars. He could blame his tears on that, if he had any pride to salve.

Joanna's eyes were burned dry. He did not like the glitter in them. She had been too calm, too composed, too immovably strong.

Her hand took in the whole company, a force like an army, even to the baggage train: for Aqua Bella could not begin to feed or house them all. They were remarkably quiet in honor of the dead, the monks chanting soft and deep, the only other sounds the thud of hoofs, the chink of mail, the neigh of a war stallion and, now and then, a murmur of speech. "See," she said, "a royal escort; a riding out of a song. He would have been so proud, to know that it was for him."

"He knows," said Margaret.

Perhaps he did. Aidan could not know. Death and he were not on speaking terms.

He set heels to his stallion's sides. The beast was glad enough to break out of his strained and trammeled walk and plunge through the line. Templars' faces flashed past: sun-darkened, war-roughened, long-bearded. None moved to follow. He passed the vanguard of knights of the kingdom. One or two yearned after him, but duty bound them; and fear. And not only of Assassins, or of reivers on the roads. Of Aidan's white wild face.

Freed from the constraint of the march, Aidan gave his mount its head. The bay was a warhorse, built to be strong, to endure; he had no speed. But he could move well enough when he wished to, and he could run the day long without tiring. After the first mad gallop, he found his pace and settled into it. The road wound away before him. The cortege crawled behind.

Tomorrow they would bury Thibaut, a rite worn to custom, so soon after they had celebrated it for Gereint. The day after, they would return to Jerusalem, to duty that would not wait for mourning. And after that, Aidan must consider what he would do. The Assassin would come again, he knew that surely, to take Joanna. He could lay a trap there, and chance its failing as it had before. Or he could track the murder to its source, knowing that while he did it, Joanna would very probably die. He could not ward her from as far away as Masyaf.

He had not been able to ward Thibaut from across the width of a room.

He tossed his head and cursed both tears and self-pity. The bay stumbled. He eased it with legs and seat and hands. Green scent touched his nostrils through dust and sweating horse: outriders of Aqua Bella's groves. The castle was waiting, still and somber. Death had sunk into its stones and lodged there. No force but time would scour them clean again.

Aidan had a chamber to himself: the privilege of rank, and one which he did not try to refuse. It was a tiny cell at the top of a tower, barely larger than a closet. It happened, as he was too keenly aware, to stand directly above the one which Joanna shared with her maid and a pair of ladies from the court. He had to pass their door in going up, and again in seeking out the garderobe. Their scents were manifold, their voices soft and high as they settled to sleep. He did not hear Joanna's. Some remnant of sense restrained him from seeking her with his power. She was guarded. He need know, and do, no more than that.

There was just room in the chamber to pace, if he heaped his belongings on the bed. The window was high but wider than the usual slit, wide enough to lean out of, breathing the night air. He folded his arms on the ledge and laid his chin on them, and let his eyelids fall of their own weight.

He may have drowsed. He was aware, in his skin, that the stars had shifted. Thoughts of Thibaut, of Joanna, of grief and emptiness and sudden, inexplicable lightness, flickered through his mind. In a little while he would go down and keep vigil with the faithful few, watching over Thibaut's body.

He did not know what made him turn. There was no sound. No sense of mind or body, human or other than human, sparked with presence. Yet she was there. As he had dreamed her the night Thibaut died, so she was now, slender cat-eyed woman in glimmering white, her wine-dark hair pouring over her shoulders. She watched him with fierce intensity, a kind of hunger.

Hunger like his own. *My kind. Mine.*

A dream.

Her head shook, the barest flicker, more sensed than seen. Her beauty pierced his heart.

"Ah God," he whispered, "that you were real, and not the shape of my desire."

Her eyes burned. Half a step, and he could touch her. Half a step more, and she would be in his arms.

His foot shifted a fraction. His hand began to rise. She waited, chin lifted. She was small beside him, fine-boned, light and strong as an Indian blade. His nose began to catch a scent of her, vanishingly faint, like rare spices. He knew how her skin would be. Cream and silk, and warmth to burning.

Her breath caught, a gasp, soft and very distinct. Her hand half lifted. In protest. In longing. And she was gone.

Nothing remained, not even the suggestion of her scent. He had dreamed her, again, because she was not Joanna.

Swiftly, half angrily, he pulled on his cotte over shirt and hose, and descended to the chapel and the vigil. He did not, would not pause by Joanna's door.

There were mourners in plenty still about Thibaut's bier. Margaret was like a stone in the midst of them, dark, silent, motionless. Templars and Hospitallers, white robes and black, red cross and white, guarded both body and soul.

Aidan prayed for a little while, a prayer without words. He was stared at; his back felt it. At home they thought of the demon countess of Anjou, and Melusine of the Lusignans, and devils in monks' habits tempting saints to perdition. Here, they thought more often of the tales of the infidels: jinn and afarit, spirits of earth and air, and demons of the desert, and darker, older things, gods and demons long forgotten save in Scripture.

Someone had been talking. He had not been stared at yesterday; he had been a stranger knight like any other, if closer to royal than most. Now they all knew. That he was older than he looked. That he was brother to the King of Rhiyana, whom men had begun to call the Elvenking.

A gust of homesickness shook him; a dart of loneliness so piercing that he swayed. Gwydion was there at the bottom of his being, a core of quiet, a presence from which no force of hell or heaven could sunder him; but in body immeasurably far, who had slept twined with him in the womb. He ached with wanting that face which was the image of his own, that warm strong presence, that calm which no storm could shake.

Aidan stiffened his back. He would be his own man. He would stand on his own feet, and teach himself somewhat of Gwydion's calm. Truly; not the counterfeit which he had worn when each took the other's name and place, and Aidan served a time as king, and his brother cleansed his spirit with this or that bright errantry. The troubadour in Carcassonne had been Aidan, true enough. The trouvère in Poitou had been his royal brother.

This the greatest of Aidan's errantries had no time or place in it for Gwydion. It had not been easy for either of them. Aidan might have delayed a decade longer, but Gwydion made him go. Gwydion, of the pair of them, was the more foresighted, and the stronger in the face of his own pain.

He would not have let down the wards for fretting over a woman, if for no other reason than that he had his queen: Maura of the white wolves, who loved them both, whom both had loved, but who had chosen water over fire. Wisely, Aidan could acknowledge now that it was long past and done. She needed a place that was her own, and a mate who was not eternally yearning to fly free.

Aidan crossed himself and rose. The candles glimmered on Thibaut's pall. The illusion of sleep had faded from his face.

Death was in it now, stark as bone beneath the waxen skin. He had never looked more mortal, or more terrible. For all their beauty and their magic and their undying youth, none of Aidan's kind would ever hold the power of a single human soul.

He set a kiss on the cold brow, and turned blindly. The night beckoned. He took refuge in it.

In the shadow beyond the chapel's door, he stumbled against someone who lingered there, plainly too shy to join the gathering about the bier. A woman by the dress, one of the veiled ladies who had come with their husbands; remarkably tall and slender, this one, and strong in tensing against him as he steadied her.

His apology died. His senses opened. Veil and voluminous cloak of a Syrian lady, yes, and eyes dark enough within; but bright with defiance and a spark—an incontestable spark—of mischief.

Aidan got a grip on one thin strong arm, and led his captive forcibly to the nearest place of safety: as it happened, his own chamber. Of course Dame Fortune would choose that moment to send one of Joanna's bedmates to the garderobe. She saw the prince leading, as it appeared, a woman to his bed; she bolted with a little shriek.

Aidan shut the door with rather more force than necessary, and confronted his prisoner. "Just exactly what do you think you are doing," he demanded, "your majesty?"

Baldwin had been angry when he began, but his temper had cooled considerably. He sat on the bed in his preposterous disguise and let himself give way to laughter. "Did you see her face? Moral outrage, and jealousy—by our Lady, what she wouldn't give to be where I am now!"

Aidan stood over him, restraining with difficulty the urge to shake him. "My lord," he said with great care.

"Master William sounds exactly like that," Baldwin observed, "when he thinks I need cutting down to size." He tucked up his feet; under the veil, all too evidently, he grinned. His eyes were dancing. "Don't fret, sir. The right people know where I am. The wrong ones need not. You must admit, it saves fuss."

It did indeed. Aidan drew a deep breath. It steadied him, a little. "You're not here alone."

"Hardly. I've a lady's proper complement of guards. No maid, alas. There wasn't one I could trust on short notice; and Sybilla never did know how to play games properly."

"Except the game of man and woman."

"Well," said Baldwin. "That's what she was raised for."

"Do you envy her?"

The thin shoulders lifted under the cloak. "Would it do me any good if I did?"

"No," Aidan said.

"It hasn't gone that far," said Baldwin, "yet. But it will. Soon, I expect." His tone was cool. He did not pity himself. "I go to Saint Lazarus' hospital sometimes, to see what I'll have to face. That's how I slipped my leash this time: I went out as if I were going there, and doubled round, and fell in with your company as it passed David's Gate."

"In woman's dress?"

"This time. Sometimes I dress as what I am. The shroud and the clapper are wonderful for cleaving paths through crowds. Better than being king." Baldwin's head tilted as if in reflection; his eyes narrowed. "It's remarkable, Saint Lazarus. Some of the brothers there are knights, do you know? Templars or Hospitallers, once. Now they have an order of their own. When they ride in battle, they hardly need armor. They bare their faces, and the enemy runs away."

"Is it as bad as that?"

Baldwin's breath caught. Aidan trod a line as thin as a blade; he stood steady on it, meeting the king's dark stare. "You aren't merciful, are you?" Baldwin said. But then: "Judge for yourself."

It had barely begun, yet. The lines of his face were still

perceptible: the strong curved nose, the firm jaw, the mouth well modeled for both laughter and sternness. He would have been a handsome man.

His mouth twisted slightly. He swept the rest of the veil from hair still thick though the sickness had crept toward it, and held his gloved hands in front of him, considering them. After a moment he let them fall. "No; you don't want to see these." He lifted his chin. "Well?"

"You'll not put armies of infidels to flight quite yet."

"So," said Baldwin. "But I'm hardly a sight for a lady's bower. It's the idea of it, you see. Best they see a veil, and imagine a faceless horror. I'll be that soon enough."

"Never to me, my lord," Aidan said.

Baldwin regarded him for a long moment in silence. "No. It wouldn't matter to you, would it? It can't mar you. Body or spirit."

"Nor you, in spirit."

Baldwin shrugged. "I'm no saint. I've done my share of cursing heaven. I can feel uncommonly sorry for myself, when there's no one about to slap me down. But it doesn't do any good, you see. I have to get up and go on. The kingdom insists on wanting me. The wars won't stop for any silliness of mine." He touched his brow. "The crown is there, no matter what I do."

Aidan bowed his head, half nod, half obeisance. Baldwin yawned, childlike, as if he could not help it. He looked somewhat embarrassed, and somewhat angry, as any youth who is reminded that he is not quite yet a man.

"You," Aidan said to him, "will sleep. Here, lie down."

"I have a place in the camp," Baldwin began.

"You had one. Now, you have one here. I'll guard you better than I guarded the last of my charges."

Baldwin did not touch: that was trained in him from childhood and from bitter experience. But his eyes were like hands, warm and strong. "It's done, prince. Mourn him, swear vengeance for him, but let him go."

Aidan stopped, at gaze. "As you will?"

"As we all must."

"No," Aidan said. "No. This can't be your fight. You have the whole of Islam to face. Leave this one to me."

"Alone?"

"God will help me."

"Prince," Baldwin said. "I have knights, men-at-arms, servants of all descriptions. If you need them . . ."

"I need only your promise that when I am done, there will be a place in your army for me."

"Always. But, prince—"

Aidan shook his head. "No. In all gratitude, in all honor and respect and, God be my witness, love: no. You aid me best by remaining where you are, you and your armies, a bulwark against the infidel."

"You are going to do something rash," Baldwin said.

Aidan grinned, wide and wicked. "Not tonight. Not for a while yet, I think. Though if we're to speak of rashness, O my king . . ."

"I'm safe now, aren't I? And the lady didn't have to contend with a royal visitation on top of all the rest. I'll reveal myself tomorrow if you like. When it's too late for anyone to fret." He paused. "Thibaut wouldn't mind, I don't think. He was always a good one for mischief."

"I know who put him up to it," said Aidan with a hint of a growl.

Baldwin laughed, and yawned till his jaw cracked, and let himself be put to bed.

The king was present at Thibaut's burial, plainly and somberly dressed, with his veil drawn over his face. No one quite dared to ask how or when he had come. A short night's sleep and an early rising had quenched most of the firebrands; his presence silenced the rest, if it failed quite to quell them.

Aidan's presence at his back set their eyes to glittering. The tale was growing still, and not slowly. Fear, much of it, and false logic. Two men dead; a stranger in their house. Sorcery, and sorcerers, and Assassins.

Without the women to think of, he would not have cared. He would prove that he was no Assassin. The rest of it would come to nothing soon enough, once they had need of his sword.

The women had to face it now: a burden atop the burden of their sorrow. And there was nothing that he could do to make it lighter. He could not deny what was true. He could not alter what he was.

They were stoic in their endurance. But when the castle had emptied of mourners, courtiers riding away behind their silent and faceless young king, the walls themselves seemed to sigh with relief.

Margaret did not weep for her son as she had wept for her husband. She had no tears left. She sat in her solar, the night of his funeral, and stared blindly at the bit of needlework in her lap. Joanna had given up trying to make her go to bed, and dozed against her knee.

Aidan prowled, more restless even than he usually was. When he had picked up the same casket for the third time, and fidgeted it open, and found it exactly as full of sweets as it had been twice before, Margaret said, "There is a moon to-night, if you take a fancy to fly about the castle."

He stopped short, flushing. Her smile did not console him. He began to bow and dismiss himself.

"Don't go," she said. "Stay. I meant no rebuke."

He sat where he had been before the restlessness took him, and willed himself to be still. She perceived it; her eyes thanked him, a little wryly. He could, he admitted, see the humor in it. After a fashion.

When he thought that he would burst, or erupt into flight as Margaret had jested, she said, "Tomorrow we return to Jerusalem. The next day, or the day after, one of our caravans departs for Damascus, and then for Aleppo. Joanna goes with it."

Aidan sat bolt upright. "Aleppo! Why in God's name—"

Joanna had fallen asleep, frowning a little as she dreamed. Gently Margaret stroked her hair. The frown smoothed; Joanna sighed. "The House of Ibrahim," Margaret said, "has its center in Aleppo. As often as I can, I send a messenger there, with word of what passes in the kingdom, and such news as I can gather."

"That's treason."

She was unoffended. "How? I tell no secrets that will harm my king or his kingdom. Some, passed to the proper persons, can be of great aid to both."

"But first and foremost, to the House of Ibrahim."

"It is my House; its people are my kin."

Aidan raked his fingers through his beard. "But to send Joanna—to send her now—"

"Now more than ever. She needs escape from her sorrows. Our House needs to know what has happened here. And," said Margaret, "Assassins are men. In the harem of the House, under my grandmother's rule, even they might hesitate to trespass."

"They've done murder in front of the Qaaba itself, in their holy of holies in Mecca. They won't care whether your daughter is in a harem or in the Church of the Holy Sepulcher at high noon."

"So, then. If she is not safe wherever she is, what does it matter where she goes?"

"It should matter to you!" The echoes rang into silence. Joanna had not wakened. Margaret had not moved. Aidan made himself speak quietly, reasonably. "But, my lady. Aleppo, of all cities . . . it crawls with Assassins; it's their most loyal city. It's been under siege from the new sultan in Damascus, the one they call Saladin. It's rife with rebels and conspiracies. She'll have to pass through infidel lands to get there, and she'll be in infidel hands when she comes to it. Why not hand her over to Sinan and have done?"

Margaret left off stroking her daughter's hair and folded her hands in her lap. He could see Joanna in her then, in the careful precision with which she moved, and in the lowering of her eyes that was not meekness but altogether its opposite. "Do you think," she asked him softly, "that I intend to suffer this persecution in silence? That if I endure, he will go away, and I will have peace? No, my lord. He will know every moment of this suffering which he has caused me. He hoped for an empire; he will see how that hope is rewarded, now that he has killed in its name."

"And Joanna is your lure?"

"Joanna is my falcon." She paused. "I have no right or power to command it; but I will ask. Will you go with her? Will you guard her?"

He could not find words to speak. He was going to demand; to insist; to threaten if need be. And she asked. She trusted him so much. "And . . . if I fail?"

"Don't fail."

He blinked like a fool. She was always out of his reckoning; he did not know why he should be surprised.

"Guard her," said Margaret. "Watch over her. Keep her alive. Begin our revenge on Sinan, by proving that he is not invincible."

He pondered that. It was not enough; not enough by far. But for a beginning . . .

He nodded, sharp and swift and irrevocable. "I shall do it. I swear to you, my lady."

III

DAMASCUS

10

The caravan was a world of its own, a moving, swaying, many-legged city, a great slow dragon of a creature winding its way from oasis to oasis. Even in cities it kept its unity, growing or shrinking as it gathered new goods and sold the old, but centering itself on a single inn or caravanserai, arriving and departing together with its guards and its outriders and its master on his white camel at its head.

Joanna was a princess here, a scion of the House of Ibrahim and its hidden queen; as Aidan was no more than her guard. He took it well, she thought, for as proud a man as he was. Blank astonishment, at first, that these merchants should know his rank, comprehend his purpose among them, and conclude that he had not, yet, earned their respect. Anger, then, but a pause for which she could admire him, and in the end, albeit with clenched teeth, amusement.

He at least did not take issue with her refusal to ride in a litter like a proper princess. She rode astride as she always had, in Arab dress certainly, and veiled, but that was only sensible in the glare of the desert. It interested her how quickly Aidan shed Frankish garb for that of this country through which he rode. Two days out of Jerusalem, beyond holy Jordan on the marches of Islam, he appeared in the courtyard of the caravanserai in the light of dawn, in the swathings of Bedu robes. He seemed perfectly at ease in them; for all the whiteness of his skin, his narrow hawk-face with its new beard seemed more Arab than Frank.

But it was certainly a Frank who veered away from the camels and sought the horse which Margaret had given him: the tall grey gelding, half Frankish, half of the Arab breed, that had been Gereint's. Franks and camels did not understand one another.

She, on her own red mare, could hardly preach the virtues

of camelkind. As she took her place in the line, he fell in beside her. His greeting was civil but brief. She wondered if he had slept badly. It had been eating at him, his failure to guard Thibaut. She had not been supposed to notice, but in the night, each night, he had left his place among the men and spread his mat outside the room she shared with her maid. She had heard him come, light as his step was, and known when he lay down. His nearness was like a hand on her skin.

Daylight dissipated it. She was almost sorry. Yesterday and the day before, she had been too glad to be on the road away from Jerusalem, to feel the heat or the dust or the flies. And there had been Aidan to watch: for a little while again, a pilgrim, rapt as any mortal man in the wonder of the road to Jericho, and the thronging pilgrims, and the chanting and the jostling and the waving of palms as they went down to the river. The caravan had not paused, and he had not asked. He had simply separated himself from it, and she had followed him, hardly knowing why, perhaps with some dim sense of watching over him. Little as he needed it. He had his palm branch now, his badge of the greatest of pilgrimages; and when he took it, for once he was almost serene. A potent serenity. Within an hour, he was among the caravan again, no more or less quiet than he ever was, and the palm was laid carefully in his baggage.

And now even the cross was hidden, and he seemed all an infidel; and she was tired. She ached from two days in the saddle; her breasts, drying at last, throbbed dully in their bonds; sweat trickled down her back, itching abominably where she could not reach. But worse than any of it was memory.

They had been late leaving Jerusalem. Someone's brother had got himself lost among the taverns; the man being one of the richer merchants in the caravan, the master had suffered an hour's delay to hunt him down. He had come in a good hour after prime, still mildly drunk, and much bemused by the hue and cry.

Joanna owed him a month or two in purgatory. For if he had not got himself lost, they would have left at dawn, and Ranulf would not have found her.

He had bathed, for a miracle. His hair was cut; his chin was newly shaved, with a nick to prove it. He did not burst in as she might have expected, but asked admittance of the porter, and let himself be set in the receiving room to wait for her.

When Godefroi told her who had come, she said, "I won't see him. Tell him to go away." But, as the seneschal began to bow, his face as carefully neutral as any man's could be, she stopped him with a word. "No. Wait." She was shaking. Idiot. What was there to be afraid of? Ranulf was no Assassin. "Tell him I'll come."

Godefroi went. She lingered. Her room was empty, her baggage gone, taken to the caravan. She finished putting on her traveling clothes. Dura plaited her hair and wound it round her head. Her shaking came and went. Her stomach was a cold knot.

She swallowed hard. "Face it," she told herself. "Get it over with." She wiped sweating palms on her skirt and went down.

She was in the room before she saw who was there. Ranulf did not even look up. He was deep in colloquy with Aidan, the two of them looking as if they had sworn fast friendship. ". . . Cluny, yes," Aidan was saying. "Have you hunted the deep coverts of the Schwarzwald, in Allemania? I took a boar there once—God's bones, I'd never seen the like. I tell you plainly, he was—"

He broke off almost quickly enough to be convincing, rising and bowing and sweeping her into the orbit of her husband's eyes. Ranulf did not rise. He had no airs or graces; he was proud of it. A plain rough soldier from Normandy, he. Plainer and rougher than ever beside the Rhiyanan prince, glowering at her under his knotted brows. Some small part of her had begun to waver; to dream of surrender. That glower hardened her all anew.

He did not even greet her. He said, "I've come to take you home."

"This is home," she said.

He shook his head, ponderous as an ox, and as stubborn. "You belong with me."

Her eyes darted to Aidan. *Say something,* she willed him. *Do something.*

Did his brow lift the merest fraction? He bowed again. Hope bloomed.

Died. He was turning. Leaving. Abandoning her.

She hated him. She lashed him with it. He did not even pause.

Ranulf never saw. "You are my wife," he said. "You're coming with me."

She barely comprehended the words. They were noise; empty wind. She was all alone on the other side of hate. "Where," she asked him with perfect calm, "were you when my brother died?"

The sun had burned Ranulf's face the color of Roman brick. Perhaps, now, it reddened. His jaw jutted. "Away," he answered her, biting off the word.

"And you think I'll go back to you." Her lips drew back from her teeth. It was by no means a smile. "I will not."

His eyes were on his fists, clenched on his knees. Coarse fists, rough-haired, mottled with an ancient ailment of the skin. Her mind, ever wayward, recalled long white hands, a touch as light and soft as wind, warm as a hearthfire. She had to struggle to hear what Ranulf said. "I was away." He said it roughly, as if with anger. "Breaking compacts. If you come back, you can have the baby."

She froze in spite of herself. "The— Aimery?"

"Aimery." It half choked him.

Laughter burst out of her, high and wild. "Bribery! How long will I keep him this time? A day? A week? A fortnight? Then when I'm secured, off he goes, back to feed his father's lust for power." Ranulf said nothing. His shoulders had hunched; he looked more than ever like an ox: great, slow, tow-colored beast of burden, blind and deaf to human pain. "No," she said. "No, my lord. I will not go back."

He stood abruptly; so abruptly that his chair overset itself. She started like a hare. He made no move to touch her. His face showed nothing, not even anger. With deliberate care he righted the chair. When it was settled, he stood with his hands on its back, the broad scarred fingers flexing and loosing, flexing and loosing. The nails were bitten to the quick. Had they always been so? "You don't want the baby back?"

Her heart stopped. Part of her wanted to shriek aloud. Part, the cold part, the clear part, said, "Not at that price."

"What do you want, then?"

"Nothing you can give."

His jaw tightened. "I see. It's not fairy gold."

It was too subtle for her, at first, coming from Ranulf. "You think—you—"

"They seduce, that kind. They don't mean to, most times. They just are. But then they go their ways, and what's left?"

"More than you've left me."

He straightened, flexing his heavy shoulders. For an instant she thought that he would seize her. But there was not even that much passion in him. He merely stood, staring. His eyes were ox's eyes, sheer brute endurance. If there had been anger in them, or any emotion at all, it was gone before she could be sure of it. He opened his mouth. She curled her lip. His head shook, once, as if against the weight of a yoke. "And what do I do if you die?"

For a moment she had no words at all. "Do? What have you ever done?"

He stood unmoving. He seemed to ponder what she had said. Or maybe he was only waiting for her to burst into rage or tears, or to crumble into submission.

She would not give him the satisfaction. "Your pardon," she said with icy courtesy, "but I have duties waiting. Godefroi will show you out."

His eyes burned. Now he would do it; now he would act like a human man, and shout at her, and force her to yield. She almost—almost—wanted it. *Aimery,* her heart yearned. *Aimery.*

Ranulf shuddered. His teeth clacked together, sharp and sudden. "Come back alive," he said. That was all.

"He loves you, you know."

She started; her horse shied. Aidan watched her as she recovered reins and dignity. More Arab than Frank in those robes, yes, and more alien than either. "You were trespassing," she said with vicious softness.

"You were shouting for the deaf to hear."

She made a rude noise. "You only hear what you want to hear."

"Or what is meant for me."

Her cheeks burned with more than the sun's heat. He was maddening, but not as Ranulf was. He gave as good as he got. *He* would quarrel if she wanted it, with a high keen pleasure.

"He does love you," Aidan said. "It's great pain in him, that he can never show it."

"Love? Is that love, that rips a child from its mother's breast?"

"Love, and jealousy, and a deep need to matter in the world. He's twinborn, you know. Like me. But my elder-by-a-moment had the will and the wealth to give me a share in our inheritance. Ranulf comes of a house with little more to its name than honor, and he's Norman, and bound by Norman laws. His brother had it all. For him, always, there were only the leavings. He'd not even be a knight, now, if he hadn't won his spurs on the field."

She knew all that. She did not want to know what it meant. "He's kinder to his dog than he is to me."

"Of course. His dog doesn't demand that he love it. It simply knows. And," said Aidan, "it loves him back."

"He says I'm ugly."

"He told you once, under rich provocation, that you are not pretty. You aren't. On occasion, you are very beautiful."

"As when?"

"Not," he said, "when you're in a temper."

She spat at him, not accurately. And was quickly sorry. The hot air seared her mouth; and she would not, for temper's sake, soothe it with water while he watched with that infuriating expression. *"You,"* she said nastily, "are excruciatingly pretty."

"Alas for my virility."

"What does that have to do with it?"

"Nothing," he said.

Suddenly she was tired. Tired of remembering, and regretting, and knowing that she could have had her son, now, but for her own poisonous temper; tired of quarreling; tired of being herself. She wanted Thibaut alive, and Gereint, and Aimery warm and heavy in her arms, and Ranulf . . .

Not that memory. Astonishment, when he saw his newborn son; disappointment, a little, at the wizened red monkey-creature in its mother's arms; sudden, wondrous softening, big hands moving with utterly unexpected competence to cradle the small wriggling body, cold eyes warming into something almost like tenderness. And he had looked at her and smiled, and yes, that was tenderness; for her; for what she had given him.

The moment ended. He was Ranulf again, rough as old stone, and never a thought in him for her as Joanna and not as a mare in his stable.

"That is fear," said Aidan, shameless in his meddling. "Of baring the truth. Of being hurt."

She closed him out. It was bitterly hard, when he was there, under her skin, but she did it. In the end his own nature aided her: it sent him spurring away, whooping like a madman, hot on the track of a gazelle that had burst out of a hollow. She had not even known that he had a bow, until the arrow flew, a clean shot, unerring on the mark.

* * *

They dined on gazelle that night, in a caravanserai which they had to themselves, gathering in its court under the stars. Joanna's cookfire was a little apart from the others, in part for her rank, in part for her sex. She was glad enough of it. The choicest bits had found their way into Dura's pot; Joanna found that she could swallow a bite, then another, and another. Before she knew it she had emptied her half of the pot.

Aidan sat on his haunches beside her. His teeth gleamed white as he smiled. He was in a fine good humor: he had been among the guards, trading practice strokes with one of the swordsmen. She had watched as much as she could without seeming to watch. The guard had been teaching him Saracen strokes with a weapon lighter and more supple than his own.

He had it now, easy in his hand, turning the blade to catch the light. Wave-patterns upon it rippled and flowed.

"He sold it to you?" she asked.

"Lent it," he said. "Great honor that that is. I wish . . ."

"You want one like it."

It was alive in his hand. With loving regret he quenched it in its sheath. "I should give it back." But he did not move. His eyes were on the fire, full of it.

She shifted until she was close enough to touch, but not quite touching. She was aware of Dura in the shadows, a shadow herself, dark-eyed and silent. Voices washed over her; laughter; a soft, wailing song.

She blinked. "You," she said, "yonder. You spoke Arabic."

He glanced at her. "Did I?"

"You didn't even know?"

He shrugged. "It's my gift. It's not something I think of."

As simple as that. "Any language?" she asked him. "Any at all?"

"Any that a man speaks in my presence."

She whistled softly. "Gereint never told us about that."

"I doubt he knew. It was never obvious. Till I came here."

He hardly seemed to care that he had it, still less to be proud of it: a wonder and a marvel, to be free of Babel's curse.

"It's nothing," he said. "A trick."

Modesty. Truly. She laughed, astonished. He could not have been less human than he was now, or more.

She did it before she thought. Bent toward him. Set her palm against his cheek.

He tensed the merest fraction.

Her hand snapped back. She knotted it with the other, hating it, herself, everything but him. Him, she could not hate. Him, she—

Him, she . . . almost . . . loved.

This was what the priests thundered against. Lust. Unholy desire. This ache in her body. This fire when she looked at him, or thought of him, or was simply near him. She wanted to touch him again. And again.

She wrapped her arms about herself and rocked. Why did he sit there? How could he not know? And pity her, and despise her. *He* would know no such weakness. He was male, and royal; he could have any woman he wanted. Princess Sybilla had cast her eye on him, people said. He would never want such a poor creature as Joanna was, wedded as she was, to a man—who—

Who had no earthly use for her, except to breed sons. She scrambled herself up. He said something. She did not try to understand.

She cried herself to sleep. For all of it. Aimery, Gereint, Thibaut. Even Ranulf. But most of all, herself. She should have taken the baby, whatever the cost. Once she had him, she could have kept him. But anger had betrayed her. Had cast Ranulf out. Had brought her here.

Into, if the priests told truth, mortal sin. Simply to desire him who was not her wedded lord; and to have no power to stop, or even to wish to stop. Maybe she had gone a little mad.

She woke in the night, and knew that he was there, beyond her door, guarding her. The ache of weeping, the heaviness in her body, mattered nothing. She could rise, if she would. Go out. Touch him.

And be cast off. Rightly, properly; gently, even. It was in him to be gentle, when he wished to, though he would have died before he admitted it.

She lay on her face, though her breasts ached. She welcomed the pain. Dear God, what was this that she was wanting? Hot breath, hard hands, cruel weight atop her; the old pagan dance, great pleasure for a man, but for a woman only weary endurance. And yet she wanted it. Her body wanted it. Was going to drive her mad with wanting it.

She slid into a restless, shadow-haunted sleep. She dreamed, she knew that, but what her dreams were, she did not afterward remember. Morning was a blessing and a release.

And yet, for all the hideousness of the night, in some strange way it had cleansed her. She rose both calm and sane. Saner than she had been since before Aimery was born. She knew herself again. Grief was no less, guilt, shame, even anger, but she was Joanna; she could bear it.

Even Aidan in his Bedu robes that might have been made for his wild beauty: even him, she could bear. Flushing, she could not help it, but offering a smile. Which he accepted, and returned in good measure. "It gladdens me to see you glad," he said.

Such a pretty way with words, he had. She played the lady for him, all gracious condescension, which made him laugh. He laughed wonderfully, with all of him. It infected her; it filled her with a crazy delight. "What!" she cried. "Mock me, will you? Is that a knightly deed?"

"No," he admitted, "my lady."

"So, then. You shall pay for it. You call me your lady. Be my knight. Serve me in all humility."

His eyes glinted, catching a little on the humility. "Shall I sing for you, too, and be your troubadour?"

She clapped her hands, forgetting to be the lady. "Oh, will you?"

But he did not forget to be the knight. *"Ma dama,* your every wish is my command."

She checked for the merest breath of an instant. This was dangerous. He knew it, she could see it clearly. He thrived on it. And she?

It was morning; her spirit was scoured clean, and his eyes were dancing on her. She offered him her hand in her most queenly fashion, not even a giggle to betray her. He took it as a true knight must, and set a kiss in the palm, and folded her fingers over it. He seemed a little surprised at what he did. For a moment, as his eyes met hers, he seemed almost—frightened?

Not he. He had been a troubadour since the world was young. She held his kiss to her heart and lifted her chin. "Now then, my knight. Ride with me."

He knew where it was going, and he made no slightest move to stop it. She thought that she had mastered it. Brave child. There had been fairer ladies than she, but never one so valiant.

He could admit it, in the dark that was the center of himself. He had fallen in love with her.

No matter the catalogue of her many imperfections. She had no beauty as humans saw it. She was too young, too unschooled in graces, too damnably mortal. She had a husband, whom Aidan could not, even for his life's sake, dislike; who was cursed to be most inept where he loved most. She had a mother of whom even Aidan could stand in awe. She had been a daughter to Gereint, of whom even these mute thoughts were a betrayal.

No matter. He looked at her strong-boned, stubborn-chinned, inarguably Frankish face, and lost all will and wit.

"It's her spirit," he told his horse as he tended it in the evening. "Her high heart. Her adamant refusal to either bend or break. Grief only makes her stronger. And yet," he said, "that's not all of it. Her mother is the same; but the Lady Margaret is sufficient unto herself. One can admire her; respect her; serve her. But love her . . . no. Not I. Her circle is complete. There's no place in it for me."

The gelding was mercifully removed from such follies. He lipped up the last sweet grain of barley, and cocked an ear. Would there, perhaps, be more?

"Gluttony is a cardinal sin," said Aidan severely. He leaned against the accommodating shoulder, working a tangle out of the pale mane. "Yes, my friend, it's a fool I am, and too well I know it. She sees this damnable face and this damnable reputation of mine, and of course she thinks that she loves me. I who am thrice her age, I who have years and rank and power enough to grant me wisdom nine times over, I should know better. Dear God, I've oaths enough on my head, vengeance to take, a king to come back to or be forsworn; and I pine for a fair young body. Is it senility, do you think? Am I, after all, about to fall into my dotage?"

The gelding was hardly the one to answer that. He rubbed an itch out of his cheek and sighed. Aidan laid his own cheek against the warm satin neck, sighing his own deep sigh. They camped tonight on a stony level, having found the caravanserai full but no rumor of robbers near about. No one else hung about the horselines. They had all gone to feed themselves, as he should do soon, for his body's sake.

He felt the eyes upon him. He knew what they were. Clear green cat-eyes, his soul's shape cast in flesh. He bore it as long as he might, until he must turn or run wild. Running seemed, for a moment, the wiser course.

He turned.

She was beautiful in the dusk, more real than real itself, more solidly there than the horse at his side. Her head came just to his chin.

She saw that he had changed his manner of dress. He felt

her surprise as his own, and her pleasure. How not? She was his dream.

Her lips curved in the beginning of a smile. It could not be something she did often; she seemed to pause, searching out the way of it. It touched her eyes and sparked in them.

It smote him with such force that he staggered. "You are," he said. "You *are.*" He darted. She was solid in his hands, supple, inhumanly strong.

All at once, she ceased her struggle. She was rigid, her eyes wide and wild. He laid his hand on her cheek. She trembled deep within. Her scent flooded him. Sweet, impossibly sweet: scent of his own people, that was like nothing else under the moon.

Her arms locked about his neck. Oh, she was strong; wonderfully, splendidly strong. His head bent down and down. Her eyes were all his world. A moment more, and he would drown in them.

They closed against him. She let him go, thrusting him away. "God," she said. Her voice was hauntingly sweet, and heavy with despair. "God, God, God."

Allah, Allah, Allah.

Arabic.

He fitted mind and tongue to the way of it, aware of his gift as he almost never was. "Tell me, lady. Who are you?"

Step by step she backed away. He caught her hands. She tensed but did not resist.

"Lady." The words came faster now. "Lady, stay. Tell me your name. How did you come here? Where do you go? How did you find me?"

Her lips set. Her head shook, tossing.

"Please, my lady. Your name. Only that."

She twisted free, spun. The word escaped, flung over her shoulder. "Morgiana."

The air was empty. His heart cried its abandonment.

* * *

Morgiana.

She was a living creature. She was no dream, nor ever a midnight fancy. And yet, that power of hers, to be there, and then to be gone . . .

Aidan spoke her name in the night's silence. "Morgiana." Saracen name, Saracen face beneath the cast of his people. He yearned for her, and yet, deep in his soul, he feared her. There was a wildness in her, a power both old and strong. He was half a mortal man. She was nothing that had ever been human.

His mother had been mad, but even she had not been as mad as this. Was this the old true blood? Half mad, half demon: spirit of air and fire.

All the questing of his power found no trace of her. She was gone as if she had never been. Power, that, and stronger far than his own.

He shivered on his mat before Joanna's tent, and not alone with the cold of night in the desert. He had thought himself as fine a witch as ever raised the power. Beside this he was the merest child, a feeble halfling thing who only played at magery.

As she played with him, feigning shyness, letting him think her a dream. Surely she laughed at him now. They were cold, the afarit, and treacherous. Their honor was demons' honor.

But ah, she was beautiful.

He started. A shape stood over him. For an instant he hoped, feared—

No. Its scent was human, sharp and pungent. Always, beneath it, lay a hint of corruption, the promise of mortality; but seldom strong enough to be sure of. Tonight it caught at his throat.

Joanna squatted beside him, her face a blur without beauty, her hair straggling out of her hood. She was utterly human, utterly mortal. "I couldn't sleep," she said. Rough, barely musical, blessedly human voice. "Did I wake you?"

"No."

"Good." She rocked on her heels. Her bones creaked; she laughed, little more than a cough, and sat more sturdily on the edge of his mat. "Do I look appallingly clumsy to you?"

"No," he said. Truth. It was not appalling; it was endearing. Like a foal, or a wolfhound pup.

"I'm not a delicate lady. I'm a great Frankish cow."

He raised himself on his elbow. "Who says that?"

"I do." She pushed her hair out of her face. "It's true. Thibaut got all the pretty. I got the Norman reiver. I should have been a man."

"I for one am glad you're not."

"You don't have to be polite tonight. I can bear the truth."

"That is the truth." He paused. "My inclination is not toward men. Or even pretty boys."

"I should hope not."

She could not have read his face in the darkness, but hers was as clear to his eyes as in the first fading of dusk. What he saw there made him reach for her. There was no volition in it.

No more in her, who came as if to haven. She was warm and solid, an ample armful, nigh as tall as he and fully as broad. A fine figure of a woman, they would say in Rhiyana.

They lay together like children, content with simple presence, with the warmth of body and body. She stroked his beard, playing with it, taking pleasure in the feel of it against her palm. It shivered in him, that pleasure, even more than the touch of her hand upon his cheek.

She laughed into his shoulder. "You're purring!"

"I am." He was surprised. "I didn't know I could."

Nor could he, once he was aware of it. She settled again, the long lush curve of her fitted to his curvelessness. It was a wonder, how they were made, male and female wrought perfectly for one another.

But not he for she. He knew it very well. She was Ranulf's in the eyes of God and man.

It was hard to care, here in the mantling night. She would

have been astonished to know how close he was to innocent; how seldom he had wanted a woman enough to do what men and women did. They kindled slowly, his kind. But once they had begun . . .

"We should," he tried to say. "We should not—"

Her eyes, wide blue-grey mortal eyes, drank his words and left him dry. They were on their feet. He had no memory of rising.

She set a kiss on his cheek where her hand had been, chaste as a sister's. He watched, mute, as she turned and left him. Wise lady.

Wiser than he. He could not stand erect in her tent. She could, just barely.

Her maid was not there. Design? Accident?

He doubted that Joanna knew, either. "This is mad," he said.

She nodded. She let her cloak fall, stood in her shift.

A fine figure of a woman. Not a maid, not any longer. Her body had ripened; what it lost in firmness, it gained in sweetness. None of his kind could ever be as she was, full mortal summer, with spring in it still, and the shadow of a shadow of winter.

She shivered. He brought his warmth to her. Her heart was beating hard. She pulled away; she clung. "Here," she said, "damn it. We've got to—stop— Hold me!"

He was her knight. He could do no other than obey her.

"I don't care," she whispered fiercely. "I don't *care.*" She threw her head back, glaring into his face. "Do you despise me?"

"I—" He swallowed painfully. "I think I love you."

She froze. All but her tongue. "Don't mock me. At least spare me that."

"I don't lie. Ever. Or mock. Not where I love."

"But you can't—I'm not even pretty!"

"That should matter?"

"You," she said with trembling control, "are beautiful beyond any measure of mortal kind. Whereas I—"

"I am simply as I was made. You are yourself and no other, and I have loved you since first I saw you, ruffled and scowling like a wounded eagle. Your spirit is a white light, my lady, and mine beside it is a dim and faltering thing."

"You could charm the birds out of the trees." Her voice both mocked him and caressed him. Her hands had found the fastenings of his robes. She wanted to see. Just to see. Truly.

It was worth seeing. He knew that; he had never been able to be ashamed of it. Humility was a monk's vice. He was royal born, and no mortal man.

He was more alien when there was all of him to see, and more beautiful. His pallor glowed in the lamplight, whiteness less like living flesh than stone enchanted to life: moonstone, alabaster, marble. As white as that, and as smooth, no rough human pelt to mar it. Flesh like satin over steel, smoother than a man's, yet never like a child's. Oh, no. No child, this.

He was not a man, but he was male enough. Not appallingly so, for all the legends of the afarit. He was cut to human measure; he warmed in human wise. She watched in fascination. Ranulf had never given her time to see. To look, and wonder, and try to understand this mystery that was the other half of what she was.

Her eyes squeezed shut. Her cheeks were afire. Dear God, what was she doing? And he was letting her.

"Not letting," he said, soft and beautifully deep. "Wanting."

Bitterness flooded her. "Wanting. Anything female, yes? Anything at all."

"No."

Her eyes snapped open.

"No," he said again. "I haven't wanted a woman since before you were born."

Her lip curled.

He was not Ranulf. He did not wither before her contempt. "Believe me, or not. It changes nothing."

She tossed her head. Half of her was pain. Half of her was cold white anger. "Oh, come. I don't need to be lied to. Who was she, that night in Aqua Bella? Was she pretty under the veils? Did she give you pleasure?"

He laughed, shocking her into stillness. He was a long time about it. When he could speak, it came in gusts. "You—she— Joanna, ladylove, that was not she but he."

Her heart chilled and shrank. He saw. Damn him, he saw what her mind had leaped to. He seized her shoulders and shook them, not gently. "Joanna! Is that what you think love is?"

"How can I know what it isn't?"

"The heart knows." He set his finger under her chin, tilting it up. "My dear sweet lady, what your so-faithful friend saw was a bit of youthful mischief. That was no lover of mine or any mortal's. That was the king."

She gasped, and flushed. His hand was light, but she could no more have escaped it than if it had been iron.

He kissed her, light and swift. And, for all his protestations, with effortless skill.

She regarded him in something close to despair. She had no more grace in this than in anything else she ever did. She wanted him, all of him; but there was too much of him. She was like a child. Wanting every sweetmeat in the bowl, gorging on them, sickening with them; howling because they were so much and she so little.

Measure, she thought. Restraint. He was here. God knew why, God knew how, but he had chosen her; or been chosen for her. He did not look ancient or august or wise. He looked like a very young man who . . . sweet saints, who thought he loved her.

Her heart was a cold clenched thing, a knot of ice beneath her breastbone. All at once, as she stood staring at him, it melted. Flowed. Opened. Swelled and bloomed and sang. She could not breathe. She could hardly see.

Joy. This was joy. She laughed; it was like water bubbling, a spring bursting forth in the desert.

He knew. That was the beauty of him. He would always know.

They tumbled down into her blankets. He was laughing with her, quite as wild as she, and quite as deliciously mad. It was the greatest jest in all the world. He, and she, and sin and sanctity, and sanity, and how little, how very little, it mattered.

II

Joanna had not fallen into mortal sin. She had leaped into it with both eyes open, welcoming it with all her heart. And she could not make herself repent it. When she tried, a small demon-voice observed, *Men never do. Ranulf never has.* And: *How can it be evil? It's all joy.*

The world would destroy her if it knew. She was discreet; or he was. In daylight they were the lady and her knight, the princess and her guardsman. At dusk, in camp or in the caravanserai, she ate in her royal solitude and he among the guards. But in the deep hours between full dark and dawn, the masks fell. He had no more will than she, to end what they had begun.

Dura could not help but know. She was mute but not deaf, and she was far from blind. But she gave no sign. Her manner toward Joanna changed not at all; no more did her fear of Aidan. Sometimes Joanna wondered what she was thinking. There was a way to learn, but Joanna would not resort to it. It was too much like betrayal. Of Dura; of Aidan who could know her mind.

No one else suspected. Joanna was sure of that. She knew better than to court discovery with glances and smiles and brushings of hand on hand. There was no need. She could think love at him, and know that he knew. Though sometimes she would smile behind her veil, simply because she was happy; because she had been sick unto death, and he had healed her.

"I never believed it could be like this," she said to him the night before they came to Damascus.

It was late and they were short of sleep, but she was wide awake. He had been singing among the men; they had been slow to let him go. He was learning the eastern songs, high and wailing as they were, too subtle for western ears. It was their secret that he had sung for her.

He smiled now and stroked her hair where a curl of it circled her breast. Sometimes she could forget how imperfect her body was, how slack and heavy it had become; though, to be honest, it was thinning and hardening again with long riding. He made her feel beautiful. When he looked at her, she was all that she needed to be: herself, and beloved.

"Why?" she asked. "Why me?"

"Why anyone in the world? Maybe . . ." He pondered, or pretended to. "Maybe it's the way you sit a horse. Or the way you turn your head when you're startled, light and quick, like a well-bred mare. Or your temper. Yes, I think it must be your temper. It fascinates me. How you can be so gentle, then in a moment, like a storm in the desert, so fiercely angry. We can understand that, my temper and I. It makes us want to tame it. Or," he added, "to match it."

"I shouldn't think you'd find that hard."

He laughed in his throat. "See how the clouds gather!"

She thrust herself up, out of his embrace. "Is that all I am to you? A pet? A filly to be ridden until she submits?"

"You know you're not." He was perfectly calm, but his amusement had died.

A demon had found its way to her tongue. "I can't ever be

your equal, can I? I'm only human. I'm a diversion, a trick to while away the time until the Assassin comes. It's convenient, isn't it? You can pleasure me while you guard me."

"Convenient," he said, "yes." He sat up, shaking back his hair. He moved like a cat, always; a little more now, the only visible sign that she had pricked him. Like a cat, when he was up, he tended his vanity: combed his hair with his fingers, smoothed his beard.

Laughter welled up, putting the demon to flight. She fell on him, bore him back and down, held him prisoner beneath her. His eyes strayed from her face to the heavy sway of her breasts. "Damn you," she said. "I can never stay angry with you. Is it a spell?"

"If it is, it's none of mine."

She swooped down for a kiss. He was more than willing. She let it go on for a delightful while. He arched his back, warming below as above. But she paused. "Tell me the truth. What am I to you? Am I only human?"

It was hard for a man to talk sense when he held a woman so, but he was somewhat more than a man. He shook his head. "You are Joanna. No mortal woman has ever been what you are to me."

She was satisfied with that. When he had given her all that he knew how to give, she fell asleep, her long legs tangled with his own.

He should rise soon and find his own place, before dawn melted the image that seemed to sleep there. But he could not, yet, gather the will to move.

He had told her the truth. It was not supposed to be possible, what they had. Not with humankind. She had a gift; she could open herself as few mortals could, and give him fully of herself, without stinting. And the more she gave, the more there was to give. Her joy sang in him like the note of a harp.

And yet she could doubt. She could ask what she had asked.

She never forgot, no more than he, that they were not of the same kind.

What his mother had had with his father . . . it was different. They had not cared that he was mortal and she was not. Even at the end, he had kept his pride, his certainty that they were not lady and servant but mate and mate.

As for Aidan and Joanna—were they? He thought of her as a child, more often than not. And she knew it. She had seen how he indulged her temper.

Well then. She was a woman.

He grimaced. He knew perfectly well what his mother would have said to that. She had not been sane, but she had been strong, and firm in what she taught.

Human, then. Weaker than he. Under his guardianship, and sorely in need of it. But beloved—before God, she was that. It was not mere bodily lust which brought him to her in the night, and kept him there perilously close to the edge of prudence. He had tested himself. He had cast his eye on women at the well in a village through which they had passed, a day or two ago. Robes and veils were no obstacle to his eyes. He had tried to make himself desire the bodies beneath; and very fair one or two of them had been. He could as easily have raised his staff for one of the mares. They were not his kind. They were not, above all, Joanna.

She stirred in his arms and murmured. Her dream brushed past him. Aimery was in it, warm against her breast. And Ranulf. Ranulf saying, with as much courage as if he faced an army of infidels, "I love you. God be my witness, I do."

With utmost care Aidan slid away from her. She groped, bereft, but did not wake. He dressed swiftly but without haste. He paused, half bending over her, as if to kiss her, but straightened abruptly and shook his head. That was a human revenge, that claiming.

His fetch lay on the mat outside her door, dimming already though it was not yet cockcrow. It frayed and melted as he sat where it had been. He clasped his knees and rocked, and frowned into the dark. He needed to relieve himself, but something kept him there, some sense that touched the edge of his wards.

He greeted Morgiana with hardly more than a widening of the eyes. He was not aware until he had done it, that he had set his back firmly against the door. It was not guilt that moved in him. No, not guilt. Even though, looking at her, he knew that if he let it, his body would kindle for her. "Good morning," he said. "Is it light enough yet for your prayer?"

She shook her head. She was in white as always; he could see that it was a man's garb. Even, now, to the turban. Her hair hung below it in three long braids. It was hardly a disguise. She looked no less female, and no less feral. He could not help noticing that she wore a belt, and a dagger in a damascened sheath.

"Will you sit?" he asked her, being gracious. "I regret that I have neither food nor drink to offer you."

Her eyes were briefly wild, but she sat as he bade her, as far out of his reach as the width of the passage would allow.

"My name is Aidan," he said.

"Aidan." It rolled strangely off her tongue. "So easily you give it me?"

"You gave me yours."

Her shoulder lifted, an odd half-shrug. "It pleased my fancy."

"I come from Rhiyana, far in the west, between Francia and the sea. You?"

Her eyes had lowered under the long lids, but he felt them on him. "Desert," she said, "and empty places. It was Persepolis, once. Sikandar burned it."

"Sikandar? Alexander?"

"Sikandar."

His mouth had fallen open, he realized dimly. He willed it shut. "You remember Alexander?"

"I think . . ." She frowned at her knotted fingers: in that, so like, so damnably like Joanna. "I think . . . not. I am not so old. No. The land remembers. And the ruins, like ancient bones thrusting out of the earth."

"Persepolis," he said. "Persia." Was that the shape of her face, beneath the strangeness that was witchkind? Sharp, yes, narrow-chinned, eyes too large for human comfort under the slant of brows; but smoother than his own, a gentler oval, skin closer to ivory than to alabaster. Though perhaps a human eye would barely see it.

She raised her eyes to stare at him as frankly as he stared at her. Amusement sparked them; unwilling, he might have thought. "You could almost be an Arab," she said.

"So I'm told." He was rubbing his eagle's beak of a nose; he lowered his hand. She bit down on a smile. She was no dainty snubnosed lass herself; that was a fine high arch, and all Persia in it. "Why are you dressed like a Turk?" he asked her.

"I am not—" She fixed him with a hard bright stare. "How should I dress?"

"Any way you like."

That pleased her. "I like you in the *djellaba*. It's more fitting. Even if you are a Frank."

"Rhiyanan," he said.

"Frank." It was beyond argument. "Al-Khalid," she said, "outlander, what do you do in our country? Are you a spy?"

"What would you do if I were?"

"Kill you." There was no hesitation in that at all. He shivered lightly. Old and cold and wild: oh, yes. She was perilous.

He leaned back against the door and folded his arms and smiled his whitest smile. "I'm not a spy. I'm guarding a caravan. May I ask what you were doing in Jerusalem?"

"Admiring your fine white body."

Bolder words he had never heard, and she seemed to know it. The faintest of flushes stained her cheek. It was, in spite of everything, enchanting.

His blush was fiercer than hers. It took all the strength he had not to leap at her; to say coolly, "I trust you found it to your liking."

Her teeth flashed, white and sharp as his own. "It serves its purpose. How is it that you grow your beard? Franks of your . . . prettiness . . . most often do not."

His hand went to it. "You don't like it?"

"Allah!" She was laughing. "Franks! We of the civilized world maintain that a man's beauty is only fulfilled when he grants it its fullest expression."

He had not known that. He rubbed his chin. Somehow, at the moment, it did not feel quite so roughly unkempt.

"You are vain," said the Saracen, more amused than not, "for a hired soldier."

He stiffened. "Madam, in my own country I am the son of a king."

"I don't doubt it." Nor did she sound as if she cared. "Here, you are a foreigner who tries unskillfully to ape Muslim manners. Will you be advised, al-Khalid? Tell the truth where you can. Where you cannot, do as you see Muslims do. And never," she said, "never let them see what lies between your navel and your knees."

He stared, uncomprehending.

She hissed with impatience. She sounded like an angry cat. "Modesty," she snapped. And when he did not respond quickly enough: "You are not circumcised!"

That, he could understand. His cheeks were flaming. She had seen altogether too much. Unless she was guessing. She must be. She would know the tales. Saracens called Franks the Uncircumcised.

Her cat-eyes were bright with malice. "And, if I may advise you further, you might do well to consider your accent. You look like a prince of the desert. You speak Arabic like a camel driver from Aleppo."

He shifted it to that of a she-demon from Persepolis. "Would this better please my lady?"

She laughed, not at all dismayed. "Better, yes." Her head lifted. He heard it as clearly as she. The wailing cry of the muezzin, calling the faithful to prayer. But, much closer, the murmur of waking voices. Without so much as a glance of farewell, she vanished.

He had felt it. Perhaps. A flicker of power. But how, or why, or where it had taken her, he could not begin to tell.

It maddened him, like a name not quite remembered. For all his trying, he gained nothing but an aching head.

And a swelling certainty. The next time, he would follow her. He would learn who she was, and where she went, and why she came. Though perhaps the last was not so hard. She came for him. Because she knew what he was.

Once he had tracked her to her lair, what then? She was as dangerous as a lioness with cubs. What if she had cubs indeed? And with them, a mate?

He did not like that thought at all. No; not in the least.

The door opened at his back, nearly casting him into the room. Joanna frowned down at him, but with a smile somewhere under it, and warmth as strong as an embrace. "What is it? Were you talking to someone?"

"No," his tongue said for him. "No. No one at all."

He was beginning to see the virtue in the Muslims' philosophy of love; and the diamond edge of irony. A score of years without so much as a spark of desire, and suddenly his body yearned not for one woman, but for two.

No; not exactly. Joanna, he loved for all that she was. With Morgiana, it was simpler. It was the plain call of beast to beast. Not love, there. Mating.

And yet it was Joanna whose body he knew in its every detail; from whose bed he had come, and to whose bed, God willing, he would go. She would never understand why he seized her then and there, where anyone might see, and kissed her thoroughly, and left her gasping and tousled and beginning, astonished, to laugh.

12

Damascus grew like a mirage across the northern horizon. Mountains walled it, desert besieged it, yet in itself it was a vision of the Muslims' Paradise. The caravan had been lost for an age, it seemed, in the bleak bare desert, taking refuge in the rare patch of grudging green, prey to wind and sun and hordes of stinging flies. Here was peace. A city of orchards and gardens, alive with the song of water; walls and minarets, domes and towers mantled in greenery, pale gold stone seeming to grow out of the earth. No city in the world was older, no place more blessed. The roads of gold and silk and spices came together here; kings had made it their dwelling place, and princes taken their ease among its gardens. Here, blinded by the light on Kaukab that looked upon the city, Paul had begun his preaching; here Abel died at his brother's hand; here, if legend were true, had been the Garden of Eden.

It was human enough as one rode close to it, a babel of clamor and stenches. But beautiful still; and the green smell was all about it, the scent of living things. It was utterly foreign. Yet, for a moment, to Aidan it recalled nothing so much as the deep places of his own forest of Broceliande.

In Damascus the House of Ibrahim had its own caravanserai, a great space like a palace, half of it just beyond the walls, half just within, so that the wall itself was part of it. It had its own wells, its own gardens, even its own finger of the river. A king might have claimed less; in the west, certainly, many had.

Determined though he was to cling to his pride, Aidan was hard put not to gawp like a yokel at the splendor of the inner house. Not the King of Jerusalem himself had carpets half so fine, or furnishings so exquisite in their perfection.

Here at least, it seemed, he had his proper rank. He was damnably slow to understand what it meant. The silent, perfect servants, the long luxurious bath, the delicacies laid before him to assuage his hunger, all conspired to make him forget what he should never have permitted: that from the moment he passed the door, he had not seen Joanna.

This, truly, was Islam. He was a man; here was his place. She was a woman and a great lady. The harem had her. And there, quietly but most firmly, he was forbidden to go. He was not her close kin, or her master, or—as God and the world well knew—her husband, to be granted the honor of her face. No matter that he had seen it every day since he came to Jerusalem. The custom was different here, and even a prince might not easily stand against it.

The master of the caravanserai was no menial; he was a prince of merchants himself, brother to Margaret's mother. He apologized with eastern profuseness, and agreed that it was insufferable, but he would not revoke the prohibition. "Yes," he said over the dinner which Aidan could hardly touch for fretting. "Yes, O prince, truly I understand. But I pray you humbly to consider where we are, and what rumor will make of your insistence. You are young, and she, and her husband far from here, and honor is much more delicate a thing among our people than in the land of the Franks. Would you dishonor her for no good cause?"

"What use will honor be to her when she is dead?"

Hajji Mustafa raised his plump ringed hands in protest. "Allah forbid!" he said. "And we, as He will allow. Be at rest, O prince. She is safe here. Her guards are of the best; my wives and concubines will watch over her and make her welcome. We are all her kinsmen. We will defend her, if need be, with our lives."

And so they might. Aidan chose not to say it. This soft-seeming man had Margaret's core of steel; and this was not, as he had so courteously pointed out, Aidan's world. He had no place here except on the sufferance of the House, nor would he be wise to begin by testing it to its limits.

Joanna was not suffering. She was not even thinking of him; she was exchanging gossip with her uncle's senior wife.

Hajji Mustafa was excellent company, even for a sullen and snarling prince. It was little enough credit to Aidan that he muted his snarls and mustered a smile, albeit with clenched teeth. That was merely prudence, the instinct of the courtier waking almost too late. It would ill serve Joanna to have her uncle wondering why her guardsman was half mad at being parted from her.

Aidan escaped as soon as he might, with as much courtesy as he could muster. It seemed to be enough. Fatigue excused it, and the strangeness of a new place to senses trained in the west. He was aware that he was being studied. Some of the servants seemed disappointed that he looked so ordinary, except for his height. They had been hoping for red hair, or yellow at least, and a shaven jaw.

They would have been interested to see him in his chamber, pacing like a leopard in a cage, weighing his chances of slipping into the harem. Not so difficult for his powers, that. But if she was heavily attended, as she must be, his entry alone would do no good at all.

Someone scratched at his door. He opened his mouth to call out a dismissal, but snapped it shut. He sprang to loose the bar.

Dura stood outside in her veils and her fear and her tongueless silence, her eyes like a rabbit's when the hawk flies over it. Her reluctance was as clear as a cry, but with it an odd, twisted approbation. She loved her mistress; she took a perverse pride in her mistress' choice of lover. A demon prince, it seemed, was preferable to a Norman baron.

She pointed to Aidan's cloak that hung by the door, and beckoned. Her mind bore an image of water and of greenery; of a place well hidden from unwelcome eyes: a grotto in the garden, patently designed for such trysts as these.

Joanna was there, sitting on the grass in a glimmer of lamp-light. She was no Joanna that he knew. Not the Frankish lady in the black that so ill became her; not the trousered rider of the caravan, sitting her horse with the light free carriage of a boy. This was a princess of the House of Ibrahim, her hair washed with henna and combed into curls and scented with rosewater, her eyes painted with kohl, her body clothed in silks that did its richness justice.

Her swift blinding smile was Joanna's, her arms about him, her quick darting kisses. So too the way she pushed him back, searching him with her eyes. She laughed her light clear laugh, which always startled him, husky as her voice was when she spoke. "They've made an Arab prince of you!"

He had not even noticed what they dressed him in, except that there was a great deal of it. Her embrace had dislodged the jeweled cap. He made no move to regain it. "And you," he said. "You've become an odalisque."

She paused and sobered wholly. "You don't—"

He pulled her to him. "You look splendid. You smell like heaven. You feel . . ." His hands lost themselves in silk. "You feel like a queen in Araby."

"I *am* a queen in Araby."

They had done something to her skin. Scented oils; powders of improbable richness. Something in him wanted to hate it. His hands reveled in it.

She had to show him how it all came off, his own as much as hers. Naked in the nest of it, her hair tumbled out of its bindings, she was as splendid as this land they lay in.

"You're smooth," he said, startled. "All of you."

He had not known all of the places a woman could blush. "It's the custom here. For cleanliness. When they started, I—I didn't think to argue." She looked angry. "You hate it. I can tell."

"It's different. I've never imagined . . ." He knew where a man could blush. He was doing it. So: that was what they had been offering, in the bath. He had been indignant in refusal. Shaggy barbarian, they would have been thinking him.

He must have said it aloud. She was shaking her head. "Not you. You're as clean-skinned as a boy. Except . . ." Her hand was in the thicket, teasing him into pleasure. "Don't let them shave your head, my love. You have beautiful hair."

That was not where her hand was. "How strange. Every-thing but the beard. Whereas the Franks—"

"Nothing but the beard." Her free hand tugged at his. "This, too. I think I like it. It gives your face a certain air."

"Age."

"That, yes. You look all of twenty-three."

"I was hoping for twenty-five."

"Maybe in an inch or four," she said. She was doing wanton and wicked things. Some of them were as new to him as the kohl on her eyelids; and much more distracting.

"Did you learn all that in an afternoon?"

She was drowsily sated, but she had strength left for a grin. "Wouldn't you like to know?"

Somewhat belatedly his mood impressed itself on her. She peered at him, near blind as always in the dimness. Her fingers found his knotted brows. He would not smooth them for that. "Is something wrong?" she asked him. "Is it something I've done?"

"You," he said, "no."

It took her alarmingly little time to understand. Which, he reminded himself, was why he loved her. "Aidan," she said, half laughing, half tender. "Aidan, love, I should have warned you. I thought you'd know. It was evident enough in the caravan."

"Not to me." His body was knotting dangerously. Grimly he quelled it. No; no rage here. Not with her honor as its price. Though she dared—she dared—to speak to him in that tone. Warm. Indulgent. As if he had been a child.

She tried to soothe him with kisses. His lips were set against her. "Do you think I like it, either?" she demanded. "It's a nuisance. But you see how easy it is to evade. Easier than the caravan. Here, no one will trouble us, and no one will suspect that either of us is in any bed but the proper one."

"How can you be sure?"

"I can. I have a room with a bolt on its door, and Dura is guarding it. And this isn't a harem with intrigues. Not of that kind."

"So," he said, "here. And what, when we come to Aleppo? Will it be as easy there? Or will I ride out with my ballocks for a necklace?"

She gasped. It was trying not to be laughter. "Believe me, my dear lord, whatever comes of this, that will not be how you pay for it."

"You haven't answered the rest."

Nor did she, for a long moment. "I . . . don't know. Can't we leave it for when we face it? We have a fortnight here, or more, if the caravan's business warrants. Then the road again. Maybe by then we'll be at each other's throats."

"Not I."

She stroked his cheek. "Nor I," she confessed softly. "Please, love. I was so miserable, and suddenly I'm so happy. It can't last, I know that. But while it does, I want to savor it. Will you give me that? I've never asked for a gift from you. I'll never ask another."

She was too wise. Too wonderfully, damnably wise. He laid his hand over her heart. It beat like a bird's beside his own, mortal-hard, mortal-swift. "Have I told you that I love you?"

He never had. She had always known without telling. But words were strong; they had power. With a cry almost of pain, she flung herself upon him. Hot tears scalded his shoulder. They were not tears of grief. Not entirely.

"For this little while," he promised her, holding her, "I shall be joyful. For you."

She raised a tear-stained face. "With me?"

"With you," he said.

She smiled, damp and luminous and immeasurably happy.

Poor prince, Joanna reflected. He was not only wild with fear for her safety. He was jealous; and, however briefly, out of his element. He would settle to it. This was a fine wide world for a man of rank, and a high adventure.

For a woman it was different. Stranger, more secret. Yet not, as the ignorant might think, altogether like a cage. The bars were gilded, and the key was in her hand, if she took care to wield it wisely.

Men had their world under the sun, their bright swords, their wars and their conquests. Most of them never knew, or chose to forget, that there was another world, an inner world, a world of veils and lattices and curtained litters. No swords glittered there; the sun was shaded, or trapped in walls. Yet a kingdom could rise and fall on words spoken within those hidden places.

Joanna was no mistress of the inner realm. For that, one needed to be born and raised to it; and she was distressingly prone to fits of rebellion. Still, her mother had taught her all that she could learn, and she had spent two years in the harem in Aleppo. She knew how the game was played, if not the fullness of its complexities.

Frankish blood and breeding would earn pardon for some of what she lacked. Her standing in the House of Ibrahim would serve for the rest. Trade, at least, she knew, and some of the ways of courts.

She had always got on well with Uncle Mustafa's wives; Umm Jafar in particular, who was older than he and eminently sensible. It was she as much as he who managed the House of Ibrahim's affairs in Damascus.

It was she who took Joanna to call on the ladies of her acquaintance. Not all were merchants' wives. Nor were all Arab or Syrian. Seljuk ladies were not, like Franks, overproud of the division between war and commerce. To these, of late, had been added a Kurdish *khatun* or two, the new sultan being of that nation, and as given as any other man to filling high offices with his kin.

As was only logical. Whom else could one trust, if not one's family?

They were all intrigued by the Frank who spoke Arabic like an Aleppan noblewoman. Damascenes, however, had grace. They did their best not to make her feel like a hulking foreigner. They did not, out of delicacy, ask her why she traveled without her husband. They were quite willing, even eager, to hear of her escort, the Frankish knight of whom their husbands were speaking with no little interest.

She should have been better prepared. She kept wanting to blush and stammer: and these eyes, trained to intrigue, would reckon up every slip and stumble, and know exactly what it signified.

And what if they did? What could they prove? Why should they want to? She would have wagered that she was not the only woman in Damascus who found contentment elsewhere than in the marriage bed.

She did not stop blushing for that, but her voice steadied admirably. "Handsome?" she would repeat when they asked. "If you like the Persian beauty, plump and toothsome, no, not at all. But if you like them long and lean like hunting cats, oh, yes, he is a handsome man. Like the young moon in Ramadan. Like a hawk in the desert." Then she would smile, white and wicked. "No, not like a Frank at all. He actually looks civilized."

Then they would all laugh, and the sweets would go round again, and sometimes she would have to go on and tell one or two of Gereint's less perilous tales, but more often they would tell their own tales of beautiful men whom they had seen or heard or dreamed of. Some of the tales would have burned a man's ears, could he have heard them. Women in the harem saved their prudery for their menfolk.

* * *

This morning Umm Jafar was particularly insistent that Joanna pay proper attention to her toilet. Joanna was never at her best in the morning, even when she was allowed to lie abed until the sun was high; and last night had been rather more strenuous than usual. She wanted to lie about the garden and dream, not play politics in the guise of harem gossip.

She submitted with poor grace to prinking and preening and painting. There was a new wardrobe for her, from drawers to cloak, even finer than the one she had been wearing. This had gold thread all about its edges; the overgown and the cloak were the same cloudy blue as her eyes. Alia insisted that Joanna—Jahana, they said here—borrow her lapis necklace, and of course the eardrops must go with them, and the fillet to hold the veil. When all of them were done, she was hung with jewels like a sultana, and her mood was, in spite of itself, beginning to lighten.

If he could see her now . . .

Tonight.

Umm Jafar was waiting. There was the ordeal of the litter to face, the rocking and swaying in stifling confinement, each of them doing her best not to fall into the other's lap. Umm Jafar, even at her age, had a dancer's balance. She never lost it, not once.

Joanna was learning to treat it like a horse or a camel. Ride with it, yes. Distract herself with chatter. Resist strenuously the urge to rip the curtains aside and leap out into the street.

"Where are we going today?" she asked when they were well on their way, the porters settled into their jouncing stride, the eunuch clearing a path with a voice like a war trumpet.

Umm Jafar was a stout comfortable woman, her figure long since gone in bearing her brood of sons, but there was spirit in her yet. It made her black eyes sparkle. "To the palace," she answered.

Joanna gave that the pause it deserved. "You have friends there?"

"Kin," said Umm Jafar without excessive smugness. "You

wouldn't know my cousin Rashida who married an emir from Baalbek. Her daughter married an emir from Damascus, who happened to be related to Muin al-Din, who was ruler of the city before the old sultan seized it. Muin al-Din, of course, is father to the Emir Masud, and to Ismat al-Din Khatun."

Joanna had been keeping track of the spate of names. It was easier than it might have been a week ago: she was learning rapidly. "Ismat al-Din? The old sultan's widow?"

"And the new sultan's wife. They were married just before you came."

Joanna sat back among the cushions. Here, indeed, was a coup.

Umm Jafar smiled at her expression. "The men might wait a year for a private audience with the sultan. We—why, we make a social call on connections of the family, share our gossip, tell a tale or two, while away an afternoon. What could be simpler?"

Joanna laughed and applauded her. "As simple as sunrise. You should have been an empress."

"What, and leave Mustafa to manage by himself? He'd be selling gold at barley prices, and then where would the House be?"

It was possible, with practice, to see the city with one's ears, and with one's rump on the litter's cushions. Joanna knew enough not to peer out. She would likely see nothing but the sweating shoulders of the porter in front. She was aware that the crush of the city had changed, muted, cleared somewhat. That would be the gate of the citadel after the knot of the market about it. Somewhere a camel roared. Hoofs clattered: a horse; a donkey would never make that swift arrogant sound. They did not pass any of the inner gates open to the men. There was another for them, smaller and more secret, and its guards called the challenge in eunuchs' voices.

Here, abruptly, was quiet. The litter lowered to the ground. Joanna blinked in the dazzle of a courtyard, sneezing in surprise at the scent of sun and dancing water and, heavy and sweet, roses. A servant was waiting, a black eunuch of impeccable dignity, who greeted them and offered them the ritual basin to wash their hands and faces. Umm Jafar, Joanna could see, was pleased. He was a servant of some standing; that implied that the guests were reckoned worthy of him.

Joanna moved carefully, with an eye on Umm Jafar. A sultan's harem was different even from that of a great emir. Richer, immeasurably, and larger, though this one seemed to boast more space than occupants. Saladin was new still to his place; he had been sultan of Egypt before he took Syria. The bulk of his family would be in Cairo; here was only what was necessary for the dignity of his Syrian wife.

From that lady's perspective, such might not be an ill bargain. She was spoils of war, but she had been a queen. She had value; she had her husband to herself, without the interference of her fellow wives.

Joanna shivered lightly in the cool of the passage. When she was feeling sorry for herself, she needed but reflect that she could have been born in Islam.

The austerity for which the Sultan Nur al-Din had been famous, and which Saladin was said to imitate, was hardly apparent here. Muslim places always seemed bare to Frankish eyes, because they were so sparsely furnished—a cushion or two, a table, sometimes a divan—but that bareness was made luminous by the adornment of walls and floor. Carpets that widened her trade-wise eyes; tiles of gold and green and white and the pure, piercing blue of Isfahan; and everywhere, the words of the Koran transmuted into flowing art.

The queen entertained guests in a chamber like a pavilion, open on the garden and another of the dancing fountains that were peculiar to Damascus. Today there were but one or two other callers, and those known to Umm Jafar, who was met with every expression of delight. She made obeisance, with Joanna a breath behind; Ismat al-Din accepted it as her due, but dismissed further servility with the flick of a tiny hennaed hand.

She was small, even for a Syrian: hardly larger than a child. Joanna could not decide if she was beautiful. Supremely artful, yes, in her dress and in her enhancement of what Allah had given her, and she had the shape so beloved of the poets: full breasts, tiny waist, extravagant swell of hips and haunches, full round thighs tapering to dainty feet. A Frank might have found her grotesque. A Muslim would have lusted after her body, but wondered if her chin were perhaps a little too pointed, her mouth too wide, her eyes large and dark enough but never the great languid calf-eyes of perfect beauty. Her gaze was bold and direct and most disconcertingly intelligent, with a light in it that bespoke anything but meek docility.

She seemed not too taken aback by her hulking Frankish guest. "Here," she commanded. Her voice was clear and rather sharp. "Sit by me. It's ages since I saw a new face."

"Not even your husband's?"

Joanna would happily have bitten her tongue in half. Ismat laughed, full and free. "Except his! Not that he was new. His sister married my brother years ago. He used to come and visit when his wars would allow."

There were sighs around the circle. Ah yes, the glances said. A long romance, a love tragically sundered by her marriage of state to the old sultan.

"He was," said Ismat, "a remarkably callow boy."

"I hope he grew up," Joanna said.

The queen smiled. She had excellent teeth: not an easy accomplishment in the sugared idleness of the harem. "He grew," she said, "indeed." For an instant her eyes softened. "A maiden has no choice. A widow does. Even a widow who is spoils of war. I accepted him for my family's sake. I remain for my own."

That was remarkable candor before a stranger, but it seemed to be her way: no one was unduly shocked. Joanna had to remind herself that she was not talking to a Frank. "My mother's second marriage was like that. The first husband for the family, she says. The second for herself."

"And she is content."

Joanna's throat tightened. "She was."

Umm Jafar was making troubled noises. One of the others bent toward Ismat al-Din. Joanna forestalled them both. "He's dead. He was killed. By an Assassin."

Suddenly the pavilion was very still. Even here, that name was not uttered lightly. Muslims did not cross themselves. They murmured words of prayer and guard.

"Tell me," said Ismat al-Din.

If she had been a man, she would been a formidable warrior. Joanna, in answering, could be surprised at how swiftly they had come to the point. It was far more like the easterners to talk in circles round it for days on end, then to edge toward it by excruciating degrees.

Ismat al-Din had decided to be direct. Like a Frank. Perhaps it amused her, so to indulge the barbarian.

No, Joanna thought, watching her face as the tale unfolded. It was nothing so petty. It was courtesy; courtliness as a westerner would perceive it. And—yes—some small degree of pleasure in playing at foreign ways. To a Syrian, it would be like galloping headlong down a mountainside, and Allah alone knew what was at the bottom.

The others, even Umm Jafar, seemed giddy with the speed of it. Ismat was intent. When she asked questions, they were to the point.

It was not as hard to tell as Joanna had expected. She could set herself apart from it; tell it like a story, like something long ago and far away. She had to put in Aidan, and Ranulf, and because of Ranulf, Aimery.

"That is barbaric," said one of the women. Later, Joanna promised herself, she would trouble to remember her name. "They take our darlings away, yes, it is written that they must. But not from the breast. Ya Allah! The man is mad."

Ismat silenced her with a long level look. To Joanna she

said, "It was bold of you to leave him. Is it true, Christians have no divorce?"

"None for a woman. A man can put his wife aside, if she gives him no sons, if he can afford to buy a dispensation. If she's borne him sons, there's no recourse in law. Though maybe, if he's strong enough to get a bishop in his pocket, and to cozen Rome . . ."

Ismat shook her head. The jewels on her fillet glinted, bright as the fountain's fall in the sunlight. "It would be enough to make a woman profess Islam."

"Or a man," Joanna said. "One wife at a time is a grievous burden."

"Even for the wife?"

"At least your husband won't lie and hide when he takes a fancy for someone else. He goes, satisfies himself, and if you've done your work well, comes back to you."

"And if he does not, why then, God has willed it, and God will judge." As would Ismat, from the glitter of her eyes. "I grieve for you, Jahana. I marvel at your courage. My husband is no stranger to the death that comes from Masyaf. Twice he has been assaulted in the midst of his armies; this past month and more, he laid siege to the fortress itself. Alas, God willed that he fail. The Old Man of the Mountain is no easy opponent."

"Nor am I," said Joanna. "Nor is the prince who rides with me. We have sworn vengeance on Sinan. God will see that we win it."

She must have looked more deadly than she knew. The women seemed shocked and rather frightened. Ismat regarded her with a degree of respect. "I wish you good fortune," she said.

"You honor me," said Joanna.

Again Ismat dismissed the courtesy with a gesture. "We are friends. I give you your due. Come; would you see my garden?"

13

While Joanna made her way through the harems of Damascus, Aidan had been establishing his presence in the outer chambers. He, like her, was a curiosity; unlike her, on Mustafa's advice he went about without disguise, as Frank and knight and, when it mattered, prince.

He went more than once to the palace. He was not granted audience, but he did not seek it. He wanted to see what this man was who was Sultan of Syria, what kind of men he kept about him, how he went about ruling his domains.

To the eyes of a prince from Rhiyana, Salah al-Din Yusuf ibn Ayyub was an upstart, an adventurer, a hired soldier who had risen out of nothing to seize a throne. He was neither Arab nor royal Seljuk but a Kurd, a mercenary's son, pupil of the irascible old warrior who was his uncle. The old man had gone into Egypt with his nephew unwilling behind him, to win it for the Seljuk sultan; and win it he had, and well. Too well. Nur al-Din did ill to entrust that venture to a hireling while he tarried in Damascus. He who had looked to become lord of Egypt as of Syria, saw the hireling's young kinsman made sultan in Cairo: the servant become, all unlooked for, a master and an equal. Then when the sultan died, Saladin came out of Egypt, to secure Syria, he attested with limpid sincerity, for the old sultan's heir. Now the young heir was mewed up in the walls of Aleppo, and Saladin was sultan in Damascus, lord by force of arms of both Syria and Egypt.

He was still young for such an eminence: two years short of forty. He followed Nur al-Din's example of austerity, in that he affected no richness of dress, nor any ostentation but what his office could not escape. He favored black, knowing perhaps that he looked well in it: a slender man of middle height, with a fair olive skin beneath the weathering of war, his dark beard cut close about his narrow jaw, and a healing scar running into it: swordcut, perhaps, or dagger-slash. When Aidan first saw him sitting on the dais in his diwan, the time of public audience, he had little enough presence, except what people gave him by making him their center. When the discussion wandered, he shrank into obscurity.

Then, it seemed, he had had enough. He did not move, nor for a moment did he speak, but suddenly he loomed in his place. When he spoke, although he hardly raised his voice, he spoke in silence. It mattered little what he said. He had mastered his diwan.

That was kingship. Not inborn, perhaps, and certainly not in the blood, but long studied and most well mastered.

Aidan was discovering that he liked these Saracens. Their art of graceful indirection was not one for which he would ever have much patience, but as a game it was entertaining, and it was conducted in an atmosphere of unfailing civility. That was not to say that they were gentle people. They were as cruel as cats, predators to a man, but graceful predators. Fire of spirit was much admired among them, particularly if it went hand in hand with sweetness of speech; their tongues, like their daggers, were subtle and wickedly sharp.

He, enemy and infidel though he was, was made most welcome. Hospitality was as holy as war, and as long as he did not wage the latter, the former was his for the asking. Among the emirs it was the fashion to vie in generosity; there was always a tale of a man who had beggared himself between the giving of alms and the entertainment of guests. Often he won it all back again, by the simple expedient of accepting alms and being a guest where before he had been the bestower of largesse.

"I think you could teach the Christians a thing or two," Aidan said.

He was in the palace yet again, accompanying Mustafa on an errand to one of the ministers in the House of Justice: a matter of trade, in which he would admit no interest. As often happened, there was a company drilling in one of the courts, and a gathering of hangers-on to watch and lay wagers. Some of these had found a stranger more engrossing than exercises with spear and sword, and wandered over to make his acquaintance.

In his own country he was no more than respectably tall. Here he towered over all but the tallest. That and his Frankish cotte, and the cross on his breast, made him remarkable.

It was something, to be stared at as a Frank and not as a witch's get. There was no one here to spread rumors of his lineage. He settled in to be what they took him for, a young infidel knight with a taste for travel and a kin-tie with the House of Ibrahim.

They happened to be talking as young men will, not of hospitality but of war. Before he came to Outremer, Aidan had been proud of his handsome longsword; it was a good blade, as good as the west could offer, but here it was only middling.

"Your armor, now," said one of his new acquaintances, "that's as good as any there is. Your horses are slow, but their weight overwhelms our slender-legged beauties. But when it comes to blades, you could, indeed, learn from us in Islam."

The others nodded, agreeing. He was the youngest, a bright-eyed youngling just beginning his first beard, and he was somewhat given to the pomposity of youth; but the rest seemed to think that he was entitled to it. He raised a finger like a master in a *madrasa,* and went on with his instruction. "The best blades come from India, or from Ch'in. They have arts there, secrets passed down through long ages from master to apprentice. Some say there's magic in it. Certainly there is a power in the forging of fine steel, that comes to reside in the steel itself, and gives the blade a life of its own."

"Is there truly magic in the working?" Aidan asked.

The boy's mask of solemnity slipped; he grinned. "Didn't I say it was a secret?"

"I've heard tell," said a slightly older man, "that part of the mystery is the quenching of the blade in blood. Fresh blood, for choice. So every blade, as its first act in the world, pierces the heart of a captive."

"Maybe," said the boy. "Maybe not. Maybe only for the very best of all."

"Therefore," said Aidan, "magic. A great blade is like a living creature. It has its pride and its temper; it becomes a part of the arm that wields it."

The boy regarded him with dawning respect. "You know steel."

"We have a nodding acquaintance. I've worked a blade or two myself: enough to know how exacting a mystery it is."

The boy's respect deepened, but leavened with a healthy skepticism. "I've never heard that a Frankish baron would set his hand to a trade."

"To an art," said Aidan, "even a prince might condescend."

"Did you make that?" the boy asked, indicating Aidan's sword.

Aidan laughed and shook his head. "You flatter me beyond my deserts. A sword is more than I shall ever aspire to; even a dagger taxes my poor skill." He drew the one he carried and held it up. "You see," he said.

The boy examined it with every evidence of an expert's eye, from fine-honed point to plain and rather worn silver hilt. "It's not bad. Well balanced; a decent edge. No nonsense about it."

Aidan welcomed it back, sheathing it. It was not displeased to be judged as it was. "You know steel," he said, returning the boy's own words.

The boy shrugged. "I know what I was taught."

"Ishak," someone explained, "was taught in the best school of all. He's a swordsmith's son."

Ishak shrugged again. "That's nothing wonderful. I'll never make a smith myself. Allah's jest on our family. I've no gift at all for the making of steel, but I seem to have the glimmer of a talent for wielding it. I can judge it, a little, but as a swords-man does, not as a smith."

His friends snorted. "Don't listen to him. He's the best swordsman in the company, and the best judge of a blade. His father is the best smith in Damascus."

That last, at least, Ishak could agree to. "He has the art from his father and his father's father, back to the first of us, who came from India. His blades are as good as any in the world."

Aidan tensed like a hound on a hot scent. He kept his voice cool, his expression mildly interested. "He must offer his wares only to kings."

Elegant young lordling though he seemed to be, Ishak had an artisan's scorn for pretty fancies. "Where's the sense in that? Kings aren't thick on the ground here. He's not cheap, it's true, but if a man can pay, my father will give him what he's paid for."

"Surely he's much in demand."

"He has as much work as he wants to do."

Aidan nodded, smiling. "Someday I'd like to see a blade from his forge."

"That's easy," said Ishak. "Come and visit it."

"Ah," Aidan said. "Surely—his valuable time—his se-crets—"

"He's always glad to talk to a man who knows steel. Even—" He caught himself.

Even a Frank. Aidan's smile did not waver. "Maybe I will come," he said, "one day. To talk about steel."

Ishak was delighted. "Then let it be soon! Come—" He paused, struck with a thought. "Come tomorrow. I've a day's leave then. I'm with the Emir Masud; everyone knows where his house is. Meet me there after the morning prayer."

As easily as that. Aidan presented himself when and where he was bidden, and found that he was expected. He had cho-sen not to be a Frank today; Ishak grinned at the Arab nobleman who seemed to be calling on him, and embraced him as if they had been brothers. "Sir Frank! You make a fine soldier of the Faith."

Ishak, it seemed, reserved his solemnity for strangers. He linked arms with Aidan and bore him out of the emir's house, calling farewells to his poor imprisoned comrades.

He was older than Thibaut had been, and there was not a grain of shyness in him. Yet, slight and dark and slender as he was, delighting in his possession of such a prize as Aidan, he was painfully like the boy who was gone. Even his standing in the world. He was like a squire, a youth in training for war under a knight, the Emir Masud who was the sultan's friend and champion. It had been a gift, he said, a favor to a kins-man; the emir did not seem to be regretting the bargain. "My lord got a sword out of it, and my father got rid of an embar-rassment. Nine generations of smiths like no others in the world, and I had to be worthless even for shoeing horses."

"You're the only son?"

"As Allah willed," said Ishak, not too mournfully. "By God's good fortune, blessed be He, my father found an ap-prentice with every bit of the talent I lack, and he was of an age and an inclination to marry my youngest sister and get her a son. The house and the art are safe, and I'm free to be what God ordained me to be. God," he said as one who knew, "is very great."

"Amen," said Aidan, catching himself before he signed the cross.

Ishak skipped round a beggar, and flashed his teeth at a whore who was either excessively late to bed or unwontedly early to rise. "I'm not expected home till after the noonday sermon. There are places where a man can go, if a man be a Muslim . . ." His eyes danced sidelong. "Are you a hellion, sir Frank?"

Aidan laughed aloud. "From the cradle."

Ishak clapped his hands. "Wonderful!" He tilted his head. "You need a name. In case, you know . . . I can't be calling you Sir Frank, or Aidan." He said it as oddly as Morgiana had. "So, then. What shall we call you?"

"Khalid," said Aidan promptly, barely checking even after he had said it.

"Khalid," said Ishak, approving. "Friend Khalid, I do believe I like you."

It was impossible to dislike this young imp with no talent for smithing. Aidan had come for the father's sake. He was amply pleased, now, for the son's. Even if he gained no blade from this, he had gained a friend.

It was Friday, the Muslim sabbath. Therefore every true believer was enjoined to purify himself in the bath, the *hammam* that was one of the wonders of the eastern world.

Under the name Morgiana had given him, Aidan was reminded of her as he stripped to bathe. Muslims were modest: they covered their bodies, always, from navel to knee. It served well for the concealment of an uncircumcised Frank.

They took Ishak away for the more arcane rites of the bath. Aidan lacked the courage for them. He lingered in the outer room, watching the men who came and went, listening to their talk. He attracted hardly a glance. They were plain folk here, no princes, no beggars; solid, respectable citizens, their sons, occasionally their servants. Here he heard pure the grace of speech that was Damascus—mincing, an Aleppan would say, with resort to the proverb: *Aleppans have the tongues of men; Damascenes, of women.* To which a Damascene would reply with reference to the boorishness of Aleppo.

There was a lute-player in a corner, and a player on a drum, and a blind singer with a voice of that mingling of strength and purity which only eunuchs can attain. There seemed to be no words to his song, only the stream of pure notes.

"You are civilized," said Ishak, appearing beside Aidan, smooth as an egg but for his brows and his long lashes and the tentative foray of his beard. Aidan had to labor not to stare. He was not, mercifully, the only long-haired man in the *ham-*

mam. Here and there was a Turk with his braids hanging down his back, or a curly-headed boy, or, once, an Arab with the look of the desert, tense as a wolf in a cage.

A tension which Aidan could well comprehend. He followed Ishak through the stages of the bath, strange as they were, but a wonder to his skin. He could learn very quickly to find this luxury a necessity.

"You have none at home?" Ishak was appalled. "What do you do?"

"Little enough," Aidan admitted. "Rivers in summer, or the sea. Water in tubs in the winter, if we insist on it; though it's said to court one's death of cold. In my city there's still a Roman bath, but we've long since lost the full rite of it. We swim in the pools. Sometimes we fire the furnace and have a festival."

Ishak shook his head, incredulous. "No *hammam.* I can't conceive of it."

He was still shaking his head when they came out, purified to their fingers' ends. Aidan had decided what he would do when he came home again: revive the Roman rite, or as close to it as he could manage. The priests would howl. He could hardly wait to hear them.

They would howl louder yet if they could see him now. Full of Saracen meat and bread, beside a Saracen whelp, in a Saracen mosque. Not the Mosque of the Umayyads that was the greatest in the world, in which the sultan would pronounce the sermon; Ishak was a man of lesser pretensions. There were half a thousand smaller mosques in Damascus: many, like this one, the gift of a rich man's piety. A court, a fountain in which the faithful cleansed themselves for prayer, a minaret from which the muezzin called them to it, and within, the wide, empty, carpeted expanse with its many hanging lamps, its carven pulpit, and its *mihrab,* the niche of prayer facing south toward Mecca. No image, no icon, no shape of living thing in paint or glass or stone; not even an altar. An elder led the prayer, but he was no priest as a Christian would under-stand it; he merely guided where any could follow.

Aidan's back stiffened in revolt. What was he doing here? What madness was this, this dance of standing, kneeling, grov-eling before an alien god?

And he had been shocked that the Knights Hospitaller could enter a pact with the Saracen sultan. They at least kept their faith unsullied. They did not bow before Allah, even in show.

"All one has to do," Ishak had told him, "to profess Islam, is to utter with a pure heart the words of faith."

There is no god but God, and Muhammad is the Prophet of God.

No. Aidan did as Muslims did, here in their place of wor-ship where no infidel should come, but the prayers he mur-mured were not the prayers of Islam. His Church had no love for such a creature as he was, but it was his Church. He would not forsake it for the preachings of a madman out of Arabia.

To be sure, it was a splendid game. Ishak's youth was infec-tious. He was, Aidan realized, a season or two older than Joanna; yet, for all of that, years younger. He was a child still, with a child's lively sense of mischief.

And he did not know what Aidan was. A Frank was alien enough; he was amply content, and quite wickedly eager to present his father with it. His father, Aidan could hope, would survive the shock.

14

"Are you ripe for mischief?"

Sayyida almost dropped the jar of oil which she was fetching from the storeroom. Hasan, who had followed her ably on all fours, rolled to his fat rump and crowed. Morgiana swept him up, to his high delight, but her eyes were on Sayyida. "Well?"

That was utterly like her. Gone without a word for however long she pleased, then back without a word of greeting, proposing some new deviltry. Sayyida, for whom the month between had not been of the best, was sorely tempted. But . . .

"I can't," she said. "What will I do with Hasan?"

"Bring him with us."

"Where?"

It had slipped out, past a stronger refusal. Morgiana's eyes sparkled. "Out. To the bazaar. To the mosque. When did you last hear a Friday sermon?"

"I can't," said Sayyida, taking a firmer grip on the jar and setting off for the kitchen.

Morgiana let her deliver the oil to Fahimah and discover that she would not be needed again for yet a while. "Go," said her father's wife, who always spoiled Sayyida when Mother and Laila were not there to restrain her. "Take the baby and have a little rest in the garden."

Sayyida strode out of the kitchen with fire in her eye, to meet Morgiana's wide and wicked smile. "You put a spell on her!"

"I did not," said Morgiana. "Fetch your wrap, and a shawl for the baby."

There was no doubt of what Hasan would choose, if anyone happened to ask. Sayyida paid one last desperate tribute to duty and respectability. "I'll miss Ishak when he comes."

"Ishak is not expected until after the sermon. We'll be back well before him."

"You," said Sayyida, "are a limb of Shaitan." Morgiana only laughed. Sayyida went to find her mantle.

Well and modestly swathed and veiled, a pair of women made their way to the bazaar. One carried a basket, the other a bright-eyed baby in a shawl.

Mother and Laila were very thoroughly occupied, Mother in resting for her son's arrival, Laila in calling on a friend or two. Father, unlike Maimoun, did not object to his wives' passing the front gate, if only they were circumspect about it, and did nothing scandalous.

Sayyida put them firmly out of mind. She had not passed the gate of the house since before she married Maimoun. Then, with the servants, she had seen to the marketing. But a married woman of good family, mother of a son, with servants at her call, did not need to set foot outside her own door. Her honor and her duty were to remain in seclusion. Maimoun had been most eloquent on the subject, when once she had asked if she could go out. "Just to take the air," she had said.

"You have the air of our garden," he replied, "which is surely sweeter than the effluvium of the streets."

Maimoun, for all his lack of family, was an educated man, and he was most conscious of the honor of this house which he had made his own. He had overridden Laila, who would happily have seen Sayyida continue to be little more than a maidservant. Mother had taken his side, which had settled the matter. Sayyida was not to go out. Shahin and Rafiq could do all that was needed of tramping about the city.

Safe in her voluminous wrapper, Sayyida did a little dance in the street. Hasan grinned at her over Morgiana's shoulder. She grinned back and ruffled his curls.

It hardly mattered to Sayyida where they went. The walls were not the walls of her house. The sun was hidden more often than not, slanting through louvers in the roofs of the streets or making its tentative way between high walls, but it was sun that came at a different angle than that in the house. The dark, twisting, tortuous streets were a wonder and a delight, the bazaar a dizzying marvel. She was like Hasan, discovering it all over again, as if it were wholly new.

They bought a sugar tit for the baby, and bathed in a *hammam* that was open for that hour to women—by great good fortune, seeing no one Sayyida knew—and dawdled along the street of the cloth merchants. One could dream long and joyously among the silk and sendal, damask, brocade, cotton fine as spidersilk, sheer fabric of Mosul, cloth of gold and silver, turquoise, sea green, scarlet and vermilion and rose, saffron, blue, violet and royal crimson. There was silk exactly the color of Morgiana's eyes, and Damietta brocade as pure as the snow on Mount Hermon, embroidered with gold, and wool as soft and deep as sleep. Morgiana had a long and lively chaffer over a length of silk which the merchant swore had come from Ch'in, the color of flame, embroidered with dragons. When at last she consented to a price, she paid it in gold. Sayyida laughed to see the seller so visibly torn between wailing that he had been beggared by her bargaining, and singing praises to the quality of the coin.

Sayyida folded the silk in her basket and covered it with a bit of rag. Hasan, having nursed in the *hammam,* was asleep on Morgiana's back. "He's never this placid for anyone else," Sayyida said.

"Sorcery," said Morgiana, taking the basket over Sayyida's objections and herding her past a laden donkey.

One of the greater pleasures of facing Damascus from behind a veil was that of observing the men who passed, and not being observed in turn. The slave with bent and often shaven head, but sometimes a handsome face; the laborer under his burden; the man of substance strutting importantly about his business. Often he would meet another who could have been his brother, stout with good feeding and well content with himself and his world.

"Peace be with you," one of them would say.

"And with you, also," the other would reply.

"And on your day prosperity," the first would continue.

"And on yours, blessing and prosperity."

Then, the ritual fulfilled, they would go their stately ways.

They were amusing, but the young men were fascinating. Tradesmen's sons with the sweat of their labors on their fine smooth brows. Soldiers strutting as if they owned the city. Merchant princes in the best of their fathers' wares. Noblemen mounted or afoot, with swords at their sides and bright mail on their breasts, turbans wound about the sharp points of their helmets, fierce and haughty as eagles. Dark slender Syrians, hawk-nosed Arabs, sleek full-cheeked Persians, almond-eyed Turks with their hair braided down their backs; even curly-bearded Jews, and fair Circassians, and a golden giant who was, Morgiana said, from somewhere called the Rus. No Franks, today. Sayyida had seen a Frank once. He had been as big as the Rus, but smooth-shaven, and his hair had been the color of a new copper pot. Urchins and beggars had followed him, marveling loudly at his strangeness.

The women paused to slake their thirst at a fountain which danced where two streets met. Sayyida sat on its rim to rub an aching foot. She was grievously out of training, but her wind seemed likely to hold. She slanted a glance at Morgiana, who played beast of burden without the least evidence of strain.

The ifritah had gone very still. Sayyida followed the direction of her stare. At first there was nothing worth staring at, unless it were the *qadi* in his robes and his dignity, making his way on an errand of significance, most likely the partaking of his dinner. Then, behind him, a pair of young men arm in arm, fresh and shining as if from the bath. One was extraordinarily tall. The other was Ishak.

Sayyida's instinct gibbered at her to flee. Sense, as well as shock, held her where she was. She was a faceless shape in black, a pair of shadowed eyes, invisible.

Once the terror was in hand, it was wickedly pleasant to sit there in full sight and not be seen at all. They paused to drink as she had, keeping to the other side of the fountain, which was their only concession to the women's existence. Ishak was in high good humor. His friend was . . .

Striking. That, first. His height; his carriage, light and proud; his moon-pale skin. His eyes were grey. She had not known that eyes could be that color, like fine steel.

Morgiana might have been carved in stone.

The stranger bent to drink, cupping water in a long narrow hand. Ishak flicked a handful at him; he laughed and gave it back fourfold. Still laughing, skirmishing like young lions, they went on their way.

"I think," said Sayyida after a very long silence, "that we are going to have a guest."

Morgiana seemed not to hear. Sayyida had never seen her like this. All at once she stirred, eased, shook herself. "Yes? Did you say something?"

Sayyida swallowed a sigh. "Nothing." Her eyes sharpened. "Morgiana. Are you in love?"

The ifritah whirled on her in such passion that she recoiled. *"No!"*

Sayyida let the echoes die. Carefully, she said, "I think we should go home."

Morgiana did not even argue.

He was, Sayyida conceded, a very handsome man.

As far as anyone in the house knew, Morgiana had come in shortly before noon in her guise of the lady of Damascus, and gone to keep Sayyida company in the garden. They prayed together there, the only words Morgiana spoke until the other women came and required greetings and some semblance of conversation. The announcement of guests was a welcome release.

When it was only Ishak, Father and Maimoun had their greetings, but then he went straight within to pay court to Mother and be fussed over by Fahimah and be polite to Laila, and thereafter, if there was time, Sayyida would get him to herself. When there were guests, the women had to wait, except for Sayyida who put on her veil and served the men their dinner. Or so it had been until Maimoun put a stop to it. Now Shahin and Rafiq did it as they did everything else.

Mother and the aunts had to suffer in patience. Sayyida was less high-minded. Behind the room where the men dined was a passage for the servants, with a door that had an inclination to hang ajar. Rafiq stayed in the room, serving as he was needed, or pretending to; mostly, he napped against the wall.

Shahin, having brought the bowls and platters from the kitchen, never came back until they were ready to be cleared away. Neither of them need know that the passage was in use while they were out of it. With the ease of long practice, Sayyida set her eye to the crack of the door. She felt rather than saw Morgiana crouch in front of her and do the same.

Farouk the swordsmith was an older, stouter, sterner version of his son. The solemnity which Ishak only played at seemed to be his natural condition. If there was any lightness in him at all, he did not display it to strangers.

Maimoun his apprentice seemed intent on being the master's image: a solid young man with a faint and perpetual frown, very full of his own dignity. But again, perhaps that was the face he put on for strangers. It slipped alarmingly when Ishak brought Aidan in with all the proper formalities, saw him served with the best of the table's offerings, and then, and only then, said with utmost casualness, "Khalid is a Frank. He's come up from Jerusalem in search of good Indian steel."

Maimoun looked as if he had opened a bottle of rosewater and breathed in a noseful of asafoetida. Farouk merely frowned. "I don't suppose you call yourself Khalid at home."

Aidan bowed. "Aidan of Caer Gwent."

"Khalid, then," said Farouk, "if you don't mind. Your Arabic is excellent."

Aidan smiled, shrugged. "I do my poor best. I have kin in the House of Ibrahim."

Which might have been meant to follow logically, or which might not. Maimoun's expression had not altered, unless it had grown more sour still. He had stopped eating. Clearly it appalled him to have broken bread with a dog of a Frank. Even a dog with pretensions to respectability. "That's your accent, then," he said. "Aleppan."

"No doubt," said Aidan. "I've been told I sound like a camel driver."

Ishak choked on a bit of spiced mutton. Farouk pounded

his back with no slightest sign of emotion. Aidan's eyes sharpened. He knew a word for that. Deadpan.

Farouk, he was beginning to suspect, was no one's fool.

He let himself settle slowly. The food was plainer than he was used to in Mustafa's house, but plentiful, and well prepared. So too was the house less rich than the merchant's, yet still prosperous, more so than many a western lord's: clean and well looked after, with a good carpet, and dishes of silver, some rather fine. The manservant—slave, no doubt—did not exert himself a whit more than he must, but he was attentive enough. He and the woman seemed to be the only servants, unless there was a gardener, or someone hidden in the harem.

That, Aidan could not accustom himself to: the utter absence of women. One saw them in the street, veiled to the eyes or, if they were slaves, unveiled but returning no glances. He had not known how much he valued the presence and the voices of women in court or at table, until he was deprived of them.

They were not spoken of. A gentleman might, after sufficient preparation, speak in general and poetic terms of feminine beauty, but to his wives he never referred, save indirectly. A woman who was talked of was a woman without honor. A lady was a secret kept among kinsmen.

Aidan's secret was sweeter and deeper than most. He drank water flavored with lemon and that essence of sweetness called sugar, and tried not to yearn for wine as for women. Good Muslims did not drink wine: as good a reason as any, to cling to his own faith.

When Ishak let drop that his friend was a Frank, Sayyida had all she could do not to gasp. A Frank. Here. In their house. Eating their food, at their table, in her father's company. Looking and sounding and acting like a human being.

She choked down a giggle. Why should she be startled? Her family had inherited an ifritah. They should know all there was to know of entertaining devils.

Morgiana did not move, and barely breathed, until he spoke of camel drivers. Then her shoulders shook against Sayyida's side. Laughing, surely. It was not a camel driver he sounded like. Not in the least.

Maimoun would not eat, would barely sit still, now that he knew what he ate with. Her father seemed to have accepted the inevitable; she wondered if he would tan Ishak's hide later, for tricking him with such utter disregard for law and custom and sacred purity.

The Frank had pleasing manners, although he did occasionally forget and take his cup in his left hand. That seemed to be the hand he favored: his dagger was on the left side. Sayyida noticed such things. It went with being a swordsmith's daughter.

Her father had taken to this man, Frank or no. When the talk turned to steel, the dull air began to glitter. Even Maimoun came out of his sulk to answer a question, and in answering it forgot to be rude.

Ishak was looking most pleased with himself.

When the discussion adjourned to the forge, Ishak excused himself to pay his respects to the harem. The others did not look as if they expected to miss him.

Sayyida looked about, startled. Morgiana was gone. She had not even felt her go.

"Well, little sister? What do you think of him?"

Ever since he grew taller than she, Ishak had called her that. She stuck out her tongue at him. "What do I think of whom? Maimoun?"

Ishak rolled his eyes. "Don't be stupid. I know you were spying. You always are." He poked a finger in Hasan's belly to make him laugh, glancing up bright-eyed. "Well?"

He was unconscionably proud of this one. Sayyida almost lied and pretended to be unimpressed, simply to see him lose his temper. But there was something about this Khalid which did not welcome deception. "He's . . . different. Where did you find him?"

"In the House of Justice, watching the mamluks at their exercises. He's with the House of Ibrahim. He knows steel."

"I gathered that," she said dryly.

"I thought Father would like him."

"Or be appalled by him."

"That was Maimoun." Ishak made a face. "Sometimes that boy can be a perfect ass."

That boy was a good four years older than Ishak. Sayyida raised her brows and let it dawn on him.

Ishak flushed under his few proud wisps of beard. He still had a girl's soft skin, which showed a blush to splendid effect. "Well, he is. He's brilliant with steel, but with people he's hopeless."

"Not completely," said Sayyida. "Once your friend seemed to know steel, he came round marvelously."

"He did, at that." Ishak wiggled Hasan's toes for him, meeting grin with grin. "I suppose it was a bit of a shock. Sitting down to dinner with a perfectly presentable person, and finding out that he's not only a Christian, he's a Frank. Franks don't eat babies, you know."

"Did your Frank tell you that?"

"He didn't need to. He's remarkable, isn't he? I've never met anyone like him."

"How many Franks have you met?"

"One," said Ishak. "He didn't speak a word of Arabic, and from the look on his face he didn't want to. He shoveled in his dinner with both hands. He stank like a goat." He spread his hands. "I think this one is as unusual for a Frank as he is for one of us."

"I think you're babbling." Sayyida bundled Hasan into her lap. "Morgiana was here this morning."

She did not know why she said that. Ishak did not like Morgiana. He knew what she was: as the heir of the house, he had received that secret as his due. He spat. "That one. What did she want?"

"Company. We went out." Ishak's brows went up. He knew about Maimoun's prohibition. He also thought it ridiculous. "We saw you in the bazaar. I think . . ." Sayyida let it dangle for a while. "I think she liked the look of your Frank."

"Ya Allah!" Ishak had gone white. "Where is she now?"

"Gone. You know how she is."

"I know . . ." Ishak gulped air. "Liked the look of him, you said? Liked the scent of his blood. She'll eat him alive."

Sayyida refused to let him shake her. "She doesn't kill for pleasure. You know that. I think she's in love."

"That's all you women ever think."

"You didn't see her," said Sayyida. "Why shouldn't she be in love with him? You are."

"I don't eat men's livers for breakfast."

"She's always been good to me."

"Well," said Ishak. "You're you."

Sayyida thanked him for the compliment, which made him scowl. "Hasan likes her better than anyone else in the world. Even me. Who's to say she wouldn't be as gentle with a lover?"

"It's not that, that frightens me. What if she tires of him?"

In spite of herself, Sayyida shivered. "If he's what you say he is, he can take care of himself. Maybe she'll never go near him at all. She's shy."

"Oh, yes," muttered Ishak. "Like a tigress, she's shy."

"If you say anything, you'll break your word."

"Damn my word." But Ishak was very quiet after that. In a little while, he kissed Sayyida, favored Hasan with one last, halfhearted smile, and left them.

Aidan was in a state of bliss. He had seen the forge. He had looked on blades of excellence beyond the dreams of western smiths. Even the toys were as deadly as they were beautiful: the little jeweled poniards which had been Maimoun's inspiration, to catch the eye of the buyer with gold to spare. Pretty though they were, they were living blades, keen enough to draw blood from air.

But the swords were the smiths' pride and the proof of their mastery. Farouk had but three which he would let Aidan touch, and all three bespoken: one for the caliph in Baghdad, one for the lord of Mosul, and one for an emir of Damascus. Each had its hilt and its fittings in accordance with the man who would own it; on each, with consummate skill, was graven a verse from the Koran. "To hallow it," he said, "and to aid in the growth of its soul."

"What," Aidan asked, "if it were for an infidel?"

Farouk's eyes glinted, as if he had been expecting the question. "Then the infidel would have to endure a blade with a Muslim soul. I have no power to impart any other."

"May a Muslim soul shed Muslim blood?"

"It's been done often enough."

"Ah," said Aidan, trying the balance of the emir's blade. "This would be a tall man, as men go here, but narrow, no? Like me. And not overfond of opulence; though he likes a bit of gold in the inlay of his scabbard."

"Yes." Farouk looked him up and down. "You'd take a longer blade. Heavier, to go with your armor and your way of fighting, but feather-light in the balance. Silver, I think, on the hilt, and a ruby in the pommel, for you to carve a cross in if you're minded to profane a good Muslim blade. And in the blade, flame-patterns; a soul of fire."

Aidan's neck prickled. This was power, this soft, measured voice, naming him true. "What would you take, master smith, in return for such a blade?"

"Did I say that I would do it?"

"I say that you can."

"Would you want a sword with a Muslim soul?"

"If the sword could endure a Christian hand on its hilt."

"Does that hand belong to a swordsman?"

"Would you test it?"

Farouk nodded once. Aidan could taste his pleasure in the game. His own was rising, heady as wine.

There was a post in the yard, a lopped tree-trunk as tall as a man—a short man, as Aidan saw it. The sword which Farouk gave him was a practice blade, blunted, as heavy as a cudgel, but strangely alive in his hands. His nose twitched at the tang of iron. There was no truth in the tale that his kind could not abide cold iron, but he was aware of it as he would not be of any other metal, even steel: dark and strong, its fire buried deep but burning the hotter for that.

He raised the sword, trying its balance. It was a sullen beast. He gentled it slowly through the movements of the swordsman's drill in Rhiyana, that done properly was like a dance. He did it properly. Faster, then, in the cadence that was indeed a dance, though it needed the skirling of the pipes to make it whole. The blade had found its balance. It would never wake to joy, but willingness, it could know. It bit stoutly into the hacked and motionless wood, caring not at all that it was not flesh and bone.

"A longer blade," said Farouk in his cool dry voice, "yes. But not, after all, as heavy as I'd thought. Would you have a use for a sword that can thrust as well as cut?"

"Would it stand against a Frankish broadsword?"

"Stand, and thrust home."

Aidan bowed over the hilt of the iron sword. "I defer to the master's judgment." He paused for a breath, two. "Will you make me a sword?"

"I will make you a sword," said Farouk.

15

The message was brief and to the point. The prince from Rhiyana, if it pleased his highness, would accompany the Lord of Syria on a hunt.

"I like the way he puts it," said Aidan. *"From* Rhiyana. Is there no way in Arabic to say 'the Prince of Caer Gwent'?"

"Not easily." Joanna ran her fingers through his hair. She could never get enough of its thickness or its fineness or its ravenwing sheen. "His messengers know something of your proper title, at least. They do try to be courteous."

He turned his head in her lap, to meet her smile with a hard stare. "You had a hand in this."

"Do you object?"

His brows knit. "No." He did not say it quite as if he believed it. "Mustafa is beside himself. An invitation from the sultan, all at once, and never a bribe sent or a chamberlain bought. What is the world coming to?"

"Women's rule." She traced the line of his cheek from brow to rigid jaw. "All I did was make friends with the Lady Ismat."

"And tell her about me."

"I hardly needed to. All the women know about you. If you were a woman and we men, you'd be a celebrated beauty."

His blush in the lamplight was as vivid as a banner. She let her finger continue its wandering way. He caught it. "Why do you let us even pretend to rule you?"

"Something has to occupy you while we contend with matters of consequence."

He laughed unwillingly. "I wish I could scoff at you as any proper man would. That's a curse, you know: to perceive the truth."

"Poor love." She slid down into his embrace. There was no

urgency in it, though he would be ready if she wanted him to be. As, now, she did not. His warmth was enough. "I wish I could go on the hunt," she said wistfully.

"You could wear boy's clothes."

"Who'd be deceived?" she said. "No; now's no time to shock the proprieties of Islam. I'll be good and wear my veil and keep the Lady Ismat company. She listens in on councils, you know. There are rooms made for that, with rooms behind them, and hangings over the lattices between."

"And the sultan knows?"

"Of course. He asks his wife's advice. She's Syrian born, and she's been in the palace since she was a child. There's little she doesn't know of how this kingdom is ruled."

He nodded slowly. "Logical. But strange. So strange . . ."

It took him a long while to understand why she laughed at him.

It *was* strange, Aidan insisted to himself as he joined the gathering at the westward gate of Damascus. No matter that he was not even a human man. He was half a Frank and all a foreigner, and dressed for it in this clear dawn, in the hunting gear of a knight in Outremer. The falcon that had come with the sultan's invitation rode hooded on his fist, calm in the tumult. Its falconer was an easygoing man, God and the sultan be thanked: he indulged a foreigner's eccentricity, and troubled neither bird nor prince with the intrusion of his presence.

"Sir Frank!"

Ishak's voice was unmistakable. After a jostling moment, its owner followed it, halting his desert pony beside Aidan's tall grey. He grinned up at the prince.

Aidan could not help but grin back. Since Farouk promised him a sword, Farouk's son had managed to spend as much time in Aidan's company as duty would allow. If not more, Aidan thought, replacing the grin with a frown. "Aren't you supposed to be waiting on your lord?"

"I am," said Ishak. "He sent me to look after you. It's not proper you should ride unattended."

Aidan's throat closed. The grey gelding jibbed; the falcon bated wildly, struggling against jesses and hood. Grimly Aidan set himself to calm them both. For long hours he could almost forget; then it would smite him to the heart. Gereint; Thibaut. His own cruel folly.

The boy was beginning to be alarmed. Aidan made himself ease, though he could not smile. "I don't suppose you had anything to do with it," he said with creditable lightness.

"Well," Ishak admitted, "it was supposed to be Ali. I bought him off." He paused. "You never told me you were a prince."

"You never asked."

"I suppose I should be more respectful."

"Why?"

"Your father was a king. Mine—"

"Yours is a king of smiths."

"I do," said Ishak carefully, "know the proper courtesies. For one of us. I want to be sure you know that. If I had known before . . ."

"I'm glad you didn't." Aidan could smile again, rap Ishak lightly on the shoulder, startle a grin out of him. "There, now. Shall we be equals?"

It was interesting to watch the boy's thoughts play across his face. Artisan's son and the son of a king. True believer and infidel Frank. "Equals," Ishak agreed without excessive reluctance.

There was more than a single boy in that company, and rather more than one greeting to acknowledge: a remarkable number, in truth, once Aidan was disposed to notice. No one seemed unduly angered by his presence or his very visible Frankishness. He was a guest; what he had been or what he would be, they did not for this moment choose to consider.

Saracens did not know how to ride in ordered ranks. There were circles of precedence, centered on the emirs, that shifted and mingled apparently at will. A flurry marked the coming of the sultan. He rode with less attendance than any of his captains: a kinsman or three, his huntsmen and his falconers with their charges, a handful of his guard in their sun-colored coats. He himself was in black without mark of rank, his only distinction the golden inlay of his bridle, and the mare that wore it, a queen of queens of the line of Arabia.

His coming roused a cheer; the flash of his smile and the wave of his hand sent them all thundering through the gate.

The life's blood of Damascus was its river, the cool stream of the Barada that flowed down out of the mountains, and parting manifold fed the myriad wells and cisterns of the city. The hunt rode up its course, through the orchards heavy with fruit, past the pleasure houses of princes, round gardens awash in the fragrance of roses. The horses danced, fresh and eager in the rising morning; one of the riders burst into song, and others took it up. Even Aidan, once he was sure of it. He had been proud of his endurance in the city, that he could dwell there so long and never once break and run for the open sky; but now that he was set free, he was half mad with it. It was all he could do not to set heels to the gelding's sides and outrun them all.

Ishak anchored him. Ishak, whose every movement sparked memory of Thibaut. Ishak, who was no prey for an Assassin's dagger, nor ever—before God—would be.

So anchored, Aidan rode well back in the company, singing when he was moved to sing, being princely pleasant to any who would speak to him. Most of the emirs, he knew. A Kurd of the sultan's nation; a Turk keeping well away from him; a Syrian or three. Two of them were almost princes: Masud, the Lady Ismat's brother, who looked little like his sister as Joanna had described her, a heavyset, ungraceful man afoot, but pure beauty ahorse; and Murhaf of Shaizar, the sultan's table companion, nigh as tall and nigh as narrow as Aidan, riding with a very old man to whom he offered a degree of respect astonishing in one so haughty. The old man rode well and easily, with the air of one who has spent his life in the saddle; his back was erect, his hand steady on the rein of his mare. Not only Murhaf treated him with deference: even the sultan, falling back once, greeted him as *sheikh* and *father,* and he seemed to accept both as his due.

They hunted rather differently here than in the west: with hawk and hound, yes, but also with cats, lean spotted cheetahs that rode to the hunt on the backs of iron-nerved horses. Drummers rode before the hunters to flush the prey, whatever it might be—birds, rabbits and smaller beasts, a herd of gazelle that burst like winged things out of a thicket. Aidan barely remembered to fly his own falcon at first, for watching the cheetahs. Delicate as they were, somnolent almost to insensibility, when they were let off their mounts they transformed into the swiftest and most deadly of hunters. Whatever they were loosed at, they brought down. Sometimes they had aid: the saker hawks that would fly at anything that drew breath. The saker would strike the prey in the thickets; the prey would flee into the open; the cheetah would bring it down. Or the cheetah would spring upon it in the open spaces, and it would escape, and the saker would pursue it into the reeds. Then the hawk would come back to the lure, the cheetah to its pillion; the hawk would wait in blood-red patience to be loosed again, the cheetah would return to the sleep which seemed to be its natural state.

Aidan's falcon, unhooded, screamed and struck at his gauntlet. *Hunt!* it raged at him. *Hunt!*

He laughed and flung it into the air.

Chance and the pattern of the hunt divided the company, some cleaving to the river and its coverts, others venturing into the hills. Aidan found himself with Murhaf and the old man who must be his father, and Ishak, and their attendants and their falconers, and a hound or two. The drummers were all down by the river, likewise the cheetahs. It was quieter without them. The hounds led them away from the Barada, up the path of a streamlet that fed it: hardly more than a trickle in a stony bed, but the thickets about it were full of birds.

Aidan's bag filled quickly. His falcon was hardly tired; appeased but not sated by a mouthful of its last kill, it circled lazily, not hunting, simply riding the air. It was aware of Aidan, but not as it would be of a human man: as a power like wind and sun and the joy of the kill, riding with it, part of it.

Human speech came dim and strange. Words of stopping, resting, sharing water, apples from the orchards, a mouthful of bread.

Aidan wandered a little away from them, following his horse as it grazed. He drank from the stream, slaking the thirst that was his own, but the blunted edge of hunger was the falcon's. He filled his eyes with sun and sky, his mind with the freedom of the air.

The falcon was tiring. Its temper, never sweet, had grown uncertain. It bethought itself of the wideness of the world and the narrowness of its captivity, and remembered that no bond or creance bound it, only the will of the one who flew it.

A dove burst out of cover below it, flaring fear. The falcon stooped upon it, drank its terror with wicked delight, veered aside in the last hurtling instant. The idiot bird darted back into its tree, startling the whole flock into flight. The falcon chose at its royal leisure, sighted, plunged to the kill.

Aidan let it feed, bound lightly with it still, demanding nothing. The falcon quieted as it gorged; it yielded before it knew what it had done, raised its head to his approach, sprang to his fist. He gave it the gift of his pleasure, swift and falcon-fierce.

The others had eaten and drunk and settled to rest. That it was for the old man's sake, they very well knew, and the old man as well as any. He did not, Aidan noticed, betray that he understood. That was wisdom. It was also kindness: Murhaf, no youth himself and contending with a wound gone bad and still barely healed, was in hardly better case than his father.

They greeted Aidan in their various ways, Ishak with guilt and a word about bread. Aidan shrugged it off. He sat in the space they left for him, between Ishak and the old man. His falcon regarded them with a baleful eye. Their own birds waited in bound and hooded silence near the horses, with the falconers watching over them. Aidan stroked his falcon's back with a feather, gentling it. It settled; its eyes blinked shut. Softly he shifted it to the perch that its falconer had set beside him. Unhooded, lightly jessed, content with its hunt and its full belly and his presence, it slid into a drowse.

"You are a falconer," the old man said.

Aidan bowed his head. Murhaf, belated, a little irascible with his wound and his oversight, named them to one another. The old man was, indeed, his father: Usamah of the house of Munqidh in Shaizar. Usamah was hardly awed to greet a king's son of a country he had never heard of, although his courtesy allowed a modicum of respect. It mattered rather more to him that Aidan knew how to hunt with falcons. "They know the art, then, in your country."

Which, his tone said, was as far away as the moon. Aidan swallowed a smile. "We have some small pretense to knowledge."

"Do you fly eagles?"

That was a test. Aidan's smile escaped its bonds. "Once. When I was young and mad. I'd rather fly a good goshawk, or a gyrfalcon. The hunting's better, and the weight's less burdensome on the fist."

"I used to hunt lions," said Usamah.

The others exchanged glances. The old man's mind was wandering, surely. Aidan, who knew better, said, "I went against a boar barehanded once."

"How long were you recovering?"

"A whole winter. The boar," said Aidan, "lived to a ripe age."

Usamah laughed. Age had thinned his voice, but it was still rich and deep. "No doubt you took revenge on the tribe of his sons."

"I tried," Aidan said. "Sometimes I succeeded."

"Ah," said Usamah: "we're all reckless in youth. I went after a serpent once, when it chose to make its nest in our house. In the inner court, mind you, amid the carvings of the portico: hardly a pleasure for anyone who walked beneath. It would sleep with its head hanging over the arch, looking like part of the carvings. When I had had enough of it, I went for a ladder and set it under the nest, with the snake watching every move I made, for though it was asleep its eyes were open, as serpents' always are. Then, while my father watched and did his best not to upbraid me for a fool and so startle the beast, I went at its head with a little dagger. No room up there for a sword, you see, and I never thought of trying my archery. Its face was a bare elbow's length from my own, and as hideous as you may imagine. I sawed at the neck. The body whipped out and wrapped about my arm. And there we were, swaying on the ladder, I sawing for my life, it coiling for its life, and just when I was sure that I would topple, head and body parted, and it was the snake who went down, and not I. It would have been fair justice had the ladder gone down with it and left me clinging to the carving, till the stone let go or my fingers did, and I fell. But Allah was merciful. My father," said Usamah, "flayed me handsomely thereafter, for risking my neck in front of him."

"Would he have preferred that you do it out of his sight?" Aidan inquired.

Usamah's eyes glinted. "I think he regretted that he had not thought of it first. I was a wild youth, but my father, given cause, could be wilder than I."

"Mine had trained himself out of it before I knew him, since he had to be king; but there were many who remembered what he had been before he was crowned. When I drove my tutors to distraction, they would console themselves with remembering. 'Lathan was worse,' they would say. Until they learned not to do it in my hearing. I could never abide a rival in deviltry, even if it were my father."

"I should be stern," the old man said, "and speak of honoring one's elders."

"So you should, sir," said Aidan; "and I shall consider myself chastised."

"You are well-spoken," said Usamah.

"For a Frank," said Aidan.

"For a Frank," the old man conceded, "and for many a Muslim. I have had friends among your people. The best are as good as any man living. The worst are no worse than we, and sometimes less misguided. When I was in Jerusalem on an errand for my lords, I was suffered to do my devotions in the little mosque, the Father Mosque that lies in the shadow of the Dome of the Rock. A Frank who was new come from the west saw me praying south toward Mecca, and could not abide it; he lifted me bodily and flung me down with my face to the east. '*This* is how to pray,' he said to me, not at all with hostility but as if he wished to teach me the error of my ways. Nor would he hear aught in opposition, until my friends of the Temple came to escort him out. They were most apologetic, and most courteous."

"Templars?" Aidan was startled.

"Templars," said Usamah, much amused.

Aidan shook his head. "No one in my country would ever believe it. It's so very simple there. Enmity pure, without taint of expedience. Or of plain courtesy."

"So is it often here. I had occasion to learn otherwise. Men are men, in the end, whatever their faith."

"Do you regret your battles, then?"

Usamah's eyes were clouded with age, but the fire behind them was as fierce as a boy's. "I do not. War is the one great test of a man. Without it he is but a woman, or a woman's toy. And you, king's son? Are you a child of peace?"

Aidan laughed, full and free. He had to pause to breathe, to muster words. "Your pardon, sir. It is only . . . my people say that I am too well named. I'm the fire in the dry wood, the hawk of battle. For that there was no war at home, I came here seeking one."

"Have you found it?"

Aidan lowered his lids over his eyes, lest the glamour fail and bare the wild green light. "I have found it."

"May God give you good fortune," said Usamah.

While they spoke, Aidan had been aware of hoofs on the stones of the watercourse, the ring of bit and bridle bell, the approach of a small party riding without haste. He looked up unsurprised as two men in golden coats came up side by side, and behind them one in black, with one lone falconer. The hounds leaped up baying; the huntsman whipped them down.

The sultan swung lightly from the saddle, returning Usamah's calm greeting, Murhaf's sketched bow. Ishak was all eyes and awe. Aidan sat unmoving, and let this lord of the Saracens choose how he would greet a Frankish prince. That this had been intended, he could well see. It was like these people's subtlety.

Saladin regarded him with eyes as clear as a child's, taking in the whole exotic length of him; fascinated, and delighted with that fascination.

"There was once a king in the west," Aidan said, "who would not dine of a festival, until he had seen a marvel. Has my lord dined yet today?"

The sultan laughed. "Now I think I may. We are well met, sir prince. How fares your hunt?"

"Well, my lord, and well companioned."

"I had thought you might take pleasure in their company." Saladin sat by Aidan with the ease of all these easterners, to whom a chair was a useless inconvenience. He was smaller than Aidan had expected, and slighter even in mail, and although sun and war and the livid new scar had aged his face, he still seemed younger than his years. It was his manner. He had no hauteur; he saw no need of it.

With a small cold shock, Aidan realized that this was a rarity indeed: a man whom the glamour could not touch. He saw Aidan as he was. All the strangeness, but for the eyes, which Aidan would not give him. And more than that. He did not see youth in the white smooth face. He saw no age at all.

It was most strange, not to be looked on as a raw boy; to be granted from the first the respect due a man's years. Aidan knew a moment's emptiness; even a flicker of resentment. Where was the pleasure here, in indulging mortals' folly?

Joanna would have had a word or two to say to that. Aidan settled against a tree-bole, because he must move, however little, and it was no courtesy to leap up and stride away from a king. Even Ishak had more native quiet; the sultan's presence had frozen him where he sat.

Saladin beckoned to the nearer of his guards. The man—youth, more nearly, blue-eyed and ruddy-fair, which was startling under the turban of a Muslim—brought forth a flask and a pair of silver cups, which he filled. The sultan took one with simplicity that was almost ceremony, and held it out to Aidan. "Drink," he said.

That was more, far more, than courtesy. A Muslim should not share nourishment with an unbeliever, lest his purity be polluted. Ishak had sinned in setting Aidan at his father's table; youth and recklessness and the witchery of Aidan's presence barely excused him. But the sultan, the king and defender, the rectifier of the Faith, could never do so lightly what a swordsmith's son had done.

A certain form was observed. Saladin waited until Aidan had drained his cup of water freshened with lemon, before he set lips to his own. The cup, he bade Aidan keep. It was ruined, certainly, for further use by a Muslim, but it was a beautiful cup, and a generous gift.

It always took these people an age to come to any point, and Saladin, though Kurdish born, was raised a Damascene.

He could discourse, it seemed, for hours on the weather, the virtues and vices of falcons, the quality of the hunting; anything but what a Frankish prince was doing in Damascus. He honestly did not seem to care. It would be a release for him, this long drowsing noon away from the cares of his kingdom. Usamah had actually gone to sleep; Murhaf's beard was on his breast, his awareness half in a dream. Guards and servants had sunk into quiet watchfulness. Even Ishak was nodding.

The sultan paused. Aidan had already forgotten what they were speaking of. He was on his feet, prowling among the sleepers, hardly aware that he had moved at all. Saladin watched him as people always did, as they would watch a leopard pace its cage. As a leopard would, he met the sultan's stare.

Too late he remembered what this man of all men could see. Saladin's eyes widened as if of their own accord, the mind hardly aware yet that it had perceived anything amiss. He peered closer, but Aidan had lowered his lids, half turning to sit where he had been before, and would not look up. After a moment Saladin sighed, shook his head, decided that he had seen but a trick of the light.

"What do you think of our city?" he asked.

"It's very beautiful," Aidan answered. "Like a city from a legend: old beyond measure, richer than kings. There's strong magic in it."

"Do you think so?" The sultan was pleased, but his eyes were intent. "Was it for the magic that you came?"

Aidan smiled a sword's-edge smile. Still he would not raise his eyes. "I came because the road led me here. I stay while my caravan stays. The beauty of it, the excellence of its welcome, come as a surprise and a delight. I could wish that I had come in a happier time, to do the city justice."

"If any of my people has done aught to offend you, I would know, that we may offer recompense."

"Your people," said Aidan, "have been the unfailing soul of courtesy."

"Yet we have not eased your heart."

"Only one man may do that, my lord, and that with his blood."

The sultan sat for a while in silence, smoothing his beard along his jaw.

No; not his beard. The scar that ran into it, a thin livid line. "I have heard," he said, "that that man is one whom I know." And when Aidan said nothing: "You must forgive me that I do not name him. His terror is not easily forgotten."

"Yet you laid siege to his castle," Aidan said.

The sultan smiled, tight and small. "You know how panic is. Some, it causes to flee. Others, it drives full upon what they fear."

"And the first are called cowards, but the rest are reckoned valiant."

"Or mad." The sultan was a little pale beneath the sun-stain of his skin. He touched the glint of mail at his throat. "This never left me, even when I bathed, from Ramadan to Ramadan, and half a year about it. For I had taken arms against Aleppo that is a Shi'a stronghold, and they are Shi'a, those of the Mountain and the dagger; and their master paid well to remove my upstart presence. First before all my army, at the meal we shared in the camp, the servers turned on me and would have killed me, but that one of my emirs knew them and cried the warning. He died for it. They died, twelve and one of them, but I lived, and lived in terror. Every shadow must surely be my murderer; every man about me must owe fealty to the Master of the Knives. Asleep and awake I was on my guard. I trusted no one. I nearly died for nothing more than fear.

"And so I lived for a year and half a year, easing a little with time, until I had almost remembered the taste of peace; and he struck again." His fingers trembled on the scar. "One of his slaves gave me this. Another pierced my mail but drew no blood. They died, all four, but one of my own men was dead, and they tell me that I had gone mad. I built a wall about my tent. I suffered none in my presence whom I did not know, nor spoke to any save those who had been with me from my youth. Then when I could bear it no longer, when I must act or break, I laid siege to Masyaf."

Aidan leaned forward, rapt. The sultan sat with fists clenched on his knees, a sheen of sweat on his brow, eyes wide with memory. "I laid my siege. My men were starting at shadows, but they followed me. Maybe they loved me. Maybe they feared me a fraction more than they feared my enemy.

"But when I had established my camp, set up my engines and settled for the long game of waiting and testing, a man came to me. He passed all my guards and sentries but those about my tent, and of those he asked leave to approach me. They gave it to him. He was one man, alone, not young, and they ascertained that he carried no weapon; and I was within the company of my captains and my servants and my most trusted slaves.

"He came before us, and named himself with calm that was not even insolence, as the very enemy we had come to destroy. My guards closed in on him, but I did not bid them seize him. He smiled at me and said, 'We have somewhat to say to one another, I think. Will it please you to speak with me alone?'

" 'There is nothing you can say which my captains cannot hear,' I answered him.

"His smile never faltered. 'Are you, perhaps, afraid?'

"If he had sneered, I could have defied him. But he was gentle; he was compassionate. He maddened me. I dismissed my emirs, ill though it pleased them. But my servants, I kept.

" 'Alone,' said the Old Man of the Mountain, gentle and inexorable.

"I sent away my servants, all but two mamluks. 'These are as my right hand and my left,' I said. 'They have been at my side since they were children. They are part of me; they do not leave me.'

"My enemy inclined his head. He addressed my mamluks,

gentle as ever, without heat, without mockery. 'Isa; Buri. If I said the word, would you slay him?'

"And their daggers were in their hands, one at my throat, one at my heart, and they wore no expression at all. They were his. My very hands were not my own; I was all betrayed.

" 'Let be,' bade my enemy, gently, gently. And they obeyed him; but he took no notice of them. 'Your power is great, O sultan, and shall grow greater still. I confess that I erred in seeking to put an end to it. I shall not serve you who would raise the banner of the Sunni heresy over the House of Islam, but while you make our world one, while you pursue the Holy War as it is written that you should pursue it, let there be truce between us. I shall not again send my faithful against you, if you will undertake to withdraw from my lands, and to restore what your armies have pillaged and burned.'

"I gaped like a fool. One word only came to my mind. 'Why?'

" 'I read what Allah has written. I see what you will do in our country. You are better for it than any who might take your place.'

"Blunt words enough, but I sensed the truth in them; or the truth as he chose to see it. I was not swift to yield, but in the end I accepted what he offered. He went away, and took my mamluks with him. In the morning I broke camp. Since then I have let him be, and he has made no move against me. I begin to believe that he will keep his word."

"Sinan is a man of his word," Aidan said. "As am I. I have sworn to exact payment for a pair of murders; with his own hand he shall pay it."

Saladin shook his head slowly. "You are as mad as I was."

"He killed my sister's son. He cut down a child whose only crime was that he was born of a woman whom Sinan desired. He threatens her daughter, whose guard I am, insofar as I may be where men and women live so endlessly apart."

"Has he threatened you?"

"Why would he? His feud is only against one certain woman

and her blood. But one of that blood was kin to me in the degree which is sacred among my people; the other had made himself my own. Therefore he is my enemy."

"I think," said Saladin, "that you are an ill man to cross." He did not smile as he said it. "Has your lady considered yielding, for her family's sake?"

"It is for her House's sake that she refuses. Would you have Sinan at the head of the House of Ibrahim?"

Saladin shivered in the heavy heat. "Allah have mercy on us all! Small wonder then that he withdrew his hand from the lord of Egypt and Syria. He had his eye on larger prey."

"A Frank would never do that," said Aidan: "pass by a king-dom for an empire of trade."

"Assassination is hardly a Frankish weapon, either. When you kill your kings, you prefer to do so openly, in battle if you can. Sometimes I could envy you."

"You wouldn't want to," Aidan said. "You haven't lived in a Frankish castle."

"I've . . . heard of them," said Saladin. He grimaced. "No baths?"

"None. And only one wife at a time. Even the wine," said Aidan, "is mostly horrible. As for the climate . . ."

"Ah," said the sultan: "cold, endlessly. And wet. But green. Do you yearn for green, here where it is as rare as emeralds?"

"Not exactly here," Aidan said in the whisper of leaves and the ripple of water; but over it the hammer of the sun. He rose again, stretching till it seemed that he could pluck the sun out of the sky. He faced the sultan. "I understand what you've been telling me. I never asked or expected that you help me against my enemy. I didn't ask it of my king in Jerusalem, either. He set me free to do as I must. Will it please your majesty to do the same?"

"What will you do?" asked Saladin, peering up at him, blinking, for he stood against the light.

"Whatever I must. Nothing that will harm you or your kingdom, unless need drives me."

"Let me see your face," said Saladin.

Aidan was slow to move. At last he sank to one knee, bringing them eye to eye as the ground bent. The sultan's breath caught. "You are—not—"

Aidan smiled with terrible gentleness. "My father was a king in the west of the world. My mother was—is—a daughter of sea and stone. My brother is the sea. I am flint that, struck with steel, breeds fire. Are you afraid of me?"

The sultan stiffened, stung to pride. "I am neither child nor fool, to be utterly without fear. You—I had not expected you. What are you?"

Aidan was suddenly very tired. "Half a man," he said. "All a fool. But what I have sworn, I intend to fulfill. However I may. However I must."

Now it was the sultan who stood, and Aidan who looked up at him, emptied of either pride or defiance. He could not even care that he was unmasked. "I must ponder this," said Saladin. "And you." He stretched out his hand. Aidan did not flinch from it, even when it gripped, sparking pain. "I shall summon you," the sultan said.

16

Aidan, who knew kings, did not wear himself out in waiting to be summoned either soon or urgently. Which was as well: it seemed that Saladin had forgotten, or elected to forget, his promise. If the caravan left before he remembered, Aidan intended to go with it.

It was close to leaving. Three days at most, Mustafa said. He seemed honestly regretful.

Aidan did not know what he felt. Relief, that he could advance at last out of this stalemate. Regret that he must leave a city so beautiful, and people in it who had become friends.

And fear, certainly, leavened with eagerness. Sinan had not moved against Joanna in Saladin's city. The road would be a different matter. And Aleppo, that was in large part Sinan's.

Word came to him as he waited, with Ishak to bear it, both eager and proud. "Your sword is ready," he said.

So soon; so miraculous. Aidan was halfway to the gate before Ishak caught him.

This time he was not offered the hospitality of Farouk's table. He did not care. Food and drink were common things, distractions. He had come to claim his sword.

Even the rite of washing feet and hands and face, of greeting and being greeted, of being courteous and receiving courtesy, tried his patience sorely. It was a measure of his acceptance into this world, that he could bear it at all.

He felt Ishak's amused understanding, Maimoun's sour dislike, Farouk's eagerness that was hardly less than his own though infinitely better hidden. They were like libertine monks gabbling the mass, all their minds fixed on the ale that waited in the refectory.

At last civilization was satisfied. Aidan was allowed past the outer courtyard; he was led to a room he had barely noticed before, except as an adjunct to the forge. There he was bidden to wait. Ishak stayed with him, silent for once, looking damnably pleased with himself. Aidan would have liked to hit him. Would have done it, if he had trusted himself not to break the boy's neck.

The silence lengthened. Aidan's back was taut. Soon now, God and the smith willing. His fingers itched for the feel of the hilt.

After an eternal while, Farouk came back, with his apprentice dour and silent behind. The master smith carried something wrapped in a cloth. Maimoun spread a carpet hardly wider than his body, hardly longer than a sword, woven of plain dark colors in a pattern as subtle as a hillside in winter.

Farouk, kneeling, laid his burden down upon it. With loving care he folded back the cloth.

Aidan did not move, still less reach to touch. The sheath was a beautiful thing, black damascened with gold in the endless curving patterns which the Saracens loved. The hilt was plainer, a hilt made for use, of silver unadorned, but the guard was inlaid with gold, and the pommel was a ruby as Farouk had promised, a great glowing eye in the nest of cloth and carpet.

Aidan glanced at Farouk. The smith inclined his head. Quietly, without haste, Aidan took up the sheathed sword. Its weight was sword-weight, lighter than some, longer than the blade he had brought from Rhiyana. He closed his right hand about the sheath, his left about the hilt. The silver was cool and quiet in his fingers. Slowly he drew the sword.

It shimmered as it drank the light. Its patterns were subtle, wave-patterns, flame-patterns, flowing from the hilt to the diamond-glitter of the point. Almost, as he turned it, they vanished; then they glimmered into clarity. Words flowed together with them.

> *Verily We created man of potter's clay of black mud altered,*
> *And the Jinn did We create aforetime of essential fire.*

Aidan's fingers convulsed upon the hilt. The sword leaped in his hand like a living thing. It knew him. It tasted his essence. It was his.

He gave it tribute of his own blood, a drop to sate its thirst when it had danced for him. Maimoun, unnoticed, had brought two things to test it: a billet of wood and a silken cushion. Aidan curled his lip at the wood. With the gentlest of strokes, he clove the cushion in two. The down within barely scattered. One feather rose, met the blade, parted.

The air would weep when he wielded that blade. A man might ride against him, be cloven, and never know it until his head slipped free of his body.

Aidan sheathed it reluctantly. *Later,* he said to it. *Wait for me.*

The others watched it all in the silence of perfect understanding. Aidan bowed low to the smith. "You have outdone yourself," he said.

Farouk nodded to plain truth. "I've never wrought a better blade. I may never do as well again. God was with me; He guided my hand."

"And . . . your choice of verses for the blade?"

"The steel chose," said Farouk. "That is its soul."

He spoke the truth as he saw it. Aidan was mute. This was power, a magic deeper and stronger than his own. The forging of steel; the waking of its soul; the binding of them both, each to each. Earth and fire. Mortal and immortal. As the bearer, so the blade.

Aidan bowed over it, lower even than before. "Master," he said.

With the sword in its proper place at his side and both gold and tribute well paid to its maker, Aidan eased in body and mind. The city through which he passed seemed all made new. He rode it like a river in flood; he could blunt his senses to it, but not quell them wholly, so that he was not left blind and deaf. So balanced, so poised, he found strength not only to endure the press of humanity but to move as part of it.

It was a kind of freedom. Not as simple nor as sweet as the silence of the greenwood, but keen-edged like the hunt's end, when the boar waits, and the hounds have drawn back, and the hunter knows that now he will be master, or he will fall.

He found that he was striding lightly, hardly hindered by the narrowness of the streets or the jostle of people. Now and again he touched the cool smoothness of the swordhilt, for the simple joy of its presence.

He paused once for a napkinful of something deliriously sweet, and once again for a dipper of cool water of Barada. He heard a street singer with a voice like a mating cat; he nearly fell into a brawl of uncertain beginnings and impressive extent, the center of which appeared to be a Turk and a Kurd.

He was mildly startled to come out of the clamoring dimness of the bazaar and find the sun still high in the sky. He had come out face to face with the eastern gate of the Great Mosque, just as the brazen falcon bent down under its twelve narrow arches to drop the ball of the hour into its basin, and the arch of the second hour past noon vanished behind its shutter. Aidan stood staring at it, though he was cursed for barring the way, and although he had seen it before. Even at night it was a marvel: the falcons continued their sleepless round, and lanterns marked the passing of each hour through a circle of blood-red glass. It made time seem real, a graspable thing, a matter for man's mastery. But he could only measure it; he could not stop it, nor make it run backward.

"Your stars, my lord—shall I read your stars for you?"

Aidan glanced down. A man peered up, crouching on the step, clutching charts and pens and abacus: the tools of the astrologer's trade. He was marginally preferable, Aidan supposed, to the sellers of relics who infested Christian churches. Though there would be a few of those within, keeping their heads low for fear of Sunni wrath, but offering the odd, bold Shi'a pilgrim a glimpse of the casket in which reposed a strand of the Prophet's hair, and beside it one which held the head of the great Shiite martyr Husain. The Sunni did not bow to relics, which they reckoned—like nearly everything else—a kind of idolatry.

They were not fond of astrologers, either; which did not keep the creatures from flocking to the steps of the Gate of the Clock.

This one sighed in Aidan's silence. "Business," he said, "is bad, though I ask barely enough recompense to keep flesh on these worthless bones. Would not my lord be pleased to know what days are propitious for his undertakings?"

"Is that all you can tell me?" Aidan asked him.

"I hardly pretend to foretell the future," the astrologer said. "Simply to surmise by my science what it is likeliest to hold."

Aidan dropped to the step beside him, caught in spite of himself. "An honest soothsayer! No wonder your business is bad. You should be promising miracles of prophecy."

The man drew his skinny body erect, all offended dignity. "I am not, great lord, a charlatan. I am a student of the stars."

And young under the straggling beard, and painfully earnest. He clutched his charts to his chest and glared at Aidan's smile. "You may mock me, O sultan, but my science is my science."

"Certainly," said Aidan. "I was merely surprised. What is a true philosopher doing, selling horoscopes on the steps of the Great Mosque?"

"Allah's will," the astrologer replied with humility as striking as all the rest of him, "and necessity. My family is impoverished; my father is newly dead, God grant him peace; there is no money to spare for the completion of my studies. Therefore I make what use of them I can, for what little it will bring. Very little," he said, "but anything is better than nothing. And I will not—I will not—beg."

"A man has his pride," Aidan agreed. He paused. "I don't know when I was born according to your calendar."

"Ah," said the astrologer, coming to attention, like a hound on a scent. He peered. "Greek?"

"Frank," Aidan said.

"Ah," the astrologer said again, not a whit dismayed. He riffled through his charts. "I think . . . yes . . . close enough, if I add here, and subtract . . ." He trailed off. "The day?"

"May Eve," Aidan said, "nigh midnight."

It meant nothing to a Muslim, except as a number on a chart, that Aidan's first sight had been the Beltane fires. "The year?"

Aidan told him.

He scribbled. Stopped. Looked up. "My lord will pardon me, but I think my lord has erred by a decade or four."

"I think not," Aidan said, smiling.

The astrologer blinked. "My lord, you cannot be—"

"I can."

He shivered. He considered, visibly, a number of responses.

With feline delicacy, Aidan set a coin on the step between the astrologer's feet. It glittered gold.

"Numbers," the astrologer said in a dying fall, "are numbers. Even . . . for a . . ."

Another bright bezant appeared beside the first. Aidan had not moved, in body, to put it there.

The astrologer stared at it. He was remarkably calm. An error in mathematics was a shudder in the heart of him. Magic . . . that was different. He inclined his head, not at all ridiculous in his dignity. "My lord," he said. He bent again and peacefully to his calculations.

Aidan waited in rather more patience than some would have believed him capable of. People came and went. The other astrologers were well occupied; their colleagues in the gate, the notaries, plied a lively trade. Some went from one to the other. First the stars, then the contracts; and if the stars were bad, they passed the notaries by and went within, probably to pray for a more auspicious day.

The second falcon dropped its ball with a clinking of metal on metal, like the ringing of a bell. The astrologer muttered over his charts, and gnawed his beard, and scored through a whole line of calculations. He looked up, rumpled and almost fierce. "I have never," he said by way of explanation, "cast a horoscope for a prince of the jinn. You are a prince. I read that properly. No?"

"Yes," Aidan said.

The astrologer was too preoccupied to bow. "It's all most interesting. Incredible, I would say, but you are what you are. Between Venus and Mars; but Mercury has power in your house. You are as much loved as hated; one who would possess you, would possess you utterly. Death rides close to you, but has no dominion over you." His finger, ink-stained, traced the line of the chart. "See, there is danger, and there. And great joy, but a great loss. A journey—journeys. Look to your wives. One is jealous, and will harm the other, unless you take care."

"But I don't have—" Aidan began.

The astrologer did not hear him. "You were born under a singularly brilliant star. You fly with kings; kings look to you —not for guidance. For strength, yes. And the fire of your presence. Where you are, stability seldom is. You move in power, you are power, but you rein it in; you clip its wings. That's not wise, in what you have to face. Learn to wield what you bear, prince, or you will fall. How low, my science is insufficient to foretell. Whether you will rise again . . ." He underscored a figure, glared at it. "Venus in the Virgin. Fire in a cold heart. Death. Even a jinni may die, prince. Remember that."

"I never forget," Aidan said.

The astrologer fretted with his beard. "It's bad. I don't pretend to deny it. But there's hope. There's always hope. What can kill you, can save you. It's a matter of proportion."

"It's all dark before me, then?"

"I didn't say that." The astrologer held to his patience with difficulty. "You've been blessed with a royal share of good fortune. Now you're asked to pay for it. If you are wise, and move carefully, and forbear to tempt heaven, you will end more blessed than before. Look, here, you can see it. All the paths come together; they seem dark, because of their density. Either they end here, in an inextricable knot, or they unravel again under fortunate stars. The choice is yours to make, in the sum of your choices."

"Thereby," said Aidan, "encompassing both destiny and free will."

"Exactly," the astrologer said, oblivious to irony. He looked like a very young bird, hunched bright-eyed in his nest of charts. "I've never done a more interesting horoscope. So many choices—take mortality out of it, and you touch infinity. It's a fascinating way to go mad."

"God be thanked, then, that you did not."

The astrologer flushed slightly. "I confess, I kept myself within very limited bounds. I used the quickest calculations wherever I could. It's not a wonderful horoscope, my lord. It's barely even adequate. There are a few paths . . . if I'd followed them, instead of . . ."

"Enough!" cried Aidan, "or you really will go mad, and it will all be on my head."

"You should have thought of that," the astrologer said severely, "before you let me cast the horoscope."

His illogic was sublime; it touched the edge of perfect logic. Dark as his foreseeings had been, Aidan could not, for the moment, be cast down. He had a lover and not the warring wives of his stars, and in a little while he would see her; and in a day or two they would leave the city. He had grief enough, as the astrologer had seen, but there was joy in it. He filled the man's hands with gold, all he had in his purse—all, maybe, that he had in the world, but he did not care. There was too much joy in it, in seeing the eyes go round in the thin face, and the narrow brilliant mind open wide in astonishment, protest, guilty delight. "But," the astrologer said, "but this is an unlucky day for me."

"Certainly it is," Aidan said: "for your career as a street-corner astrologer. You, my fine philosopher, are going to go back to your schooling, and prosper at it, and end the master of your own school. Promise me you'll do that."

"But," the astrologer said. "But—"

"Promise!"

"I promise. I—" He swallowed audibly. "My lord, I foretold disaster!"

"You gave me fair warning. Which I shall remember." Aidan rose, smiling. "May God prosper you."

* * *

As Aidan turned away, the astrologer still babbling but beginning, incredulously, to praise his God and his benefactor, he nearly collided with a figure in a scarlet coat. A youth, a Turk with his long braids and his necklaces and the heavy rings in his ears, wearing an expression half of triumph and half of patience taxed to its limit. When Aidan stopped, beginning an apology, the Turk's face smoothed itself flat, though his narrow black eyes were glittering still. "Sir Frank," he said, "the sultan asks you to attend him."

And the hunt, it was readily apparent, had taken most of the day. Aidan forbore to blush, but he moved quickly where the messenger led. There was a horse waiting, with a very small page holding her bridle, and a pony which, on sight of the Turk, lifted its blocky head and neighed. The mare, tall for an Arab and most well aware of her beauty, regarded Aidan with wary respect. Beasts always knew him; beasts of mettle were sometimes slow to trust him, because they saw his power, and knew what it could do to them.

This one had courage. She barely flinched from his hand on her neck. Her great nostrils flared; her lean ears quivered. "By your leave," he said to her, setting foot to stirrup. She jibbed, stilled. He stroked her sleek bay neck. It arched; she pawed the ground. The page clambered nimbly up behind, quick as a monkey and no more inclined to ask whether he was welcome. Once the child was settled, the sultan's messenger kicked his pony into a trot. The mare, insulted, sprang into a dancing canter.

Aidan was sorry to part with the mare whose gaits were fire and silk. But the sultan was waiting, and the messenger was not minded to linger. They left horses and page in the outer court of the citadel and passed within, going deeper than Aidan had ever gone before: past the public portions into regions less meticulously splendid. Opulent still, certainly, but time had been allowed to tread here. Paint and gilding grew worn and faded, tiles cracked, staircases hollow with use. But the garden into which they emerged was most well tended, heavy like all of Damascus with the scent of roses, sweet with the sound of falling water.

Beyond the fountain was a pavilion nigh as large as a king's hall, its columns twined with roses, its doors all open to the garden, so that one could scarcely tell where inside began and outside ended. Cool airs played through it; a fingerling of Barada filled the pool in its center and bubbled away beneath the tiles of the floor.

By the pool in a circle of attendants sat the sultan. He had been at work: a pair of secretaries scribbled amid a tottering heap of charters and registers and dispatches. The man nearest him, young to bear as great a weight of dignity as he patently did, wore the robes of a *qadi,* a judge, and scribbled as assiduously as either of the secretaries. The emirs beyond him, by contrast, looked as fiercely out of place as falcons in a dovecote. Aidan knew Murhaf ibn Usamah, and Ishak's lord Masud; the third was a stranger, a haughty personage who, beneath robes of dazzling extravagance, bore a marked resemblance to the sultan. It was he who seemed most ill at ease in the scratching of pens and the riffling of pages; even the peace of the garden seemed to give him no pleasure. Left to himself, he would have disposed of the busy scribblers and called for dancing girls.

Saladin, thin and dark and clerkly in spite of the sword at his side, seemed in his element. He caught Aidan in the midst of a low and careful obeisance, embraced him, kissed him on both cheeks. "My lord prince! Well met, and welcome. I'd begun to fear that you had left the city."

"Not quite yet, sire," Aidan said, recovering himself quickly enough once he had recalled the eastern propensity for effusion. "I fear I gave your man a hard chase. I was dallying about the city, and taking little enough notice of where I went. It's a miracle he found me."

"Arslan is a better hunter than most," said Saladin, smiling.

The young Turk, catching his eye, bowed low and took himself elsewhere.

The sultan's smile broadened to take in Aidan. "Come, sit, be at ease. You came in a good hour; I'd all but finished here. A moment longer, of your charity . . ."

Aidan inclined his head. A servant appeared with sherbet, fruit, a plateful of bread sprinkled with salt. Aidan understood the significance of that; and if he was not hungry, he had a respectable thirst. He nibbled a bit of the flat unleavened bread, finding it good; drank deep of the sherbet that was cooled with snow from Mount Hermon. The sultan bent toward his *qadi,* intent on the wording of a letter. His emirs waited in varying degrees of patience. Murhaf's head was bowed; his lips moved: reciting the Koran as a Christian would tell his beads. Masud observed the pattern of rose-leaves against the twining arabesques of the tiles. The third emir, who was Saladin's brother Turan-Shah, watched Aidan.

Not with hostility, Aidan took note. Not quite. Measuring. Pondering his usefulness.

This man had not his brother's simplicity. Saladin was no more and no less than what he was. Turan-Shah was the elder, born to rule among the sons of Ayyub, condemned by the fortune that had left him behind while his brother forayed into Egypt, to see one younger and, in his mind, lesser, made king twice over, while he remained but the servant of a king. He who coveted splendor saw his brother spurn it as if it were dust; he who would have ruled like a proper emperor, must bow to a man who could not even keep order in his council. Who—his eyes began to glitter—entertained Franks as if they had been decent Muslims, and never gave a thought to the propriety of his station.

Aidan struggled free of that small cold mind, clinging to his cup as to an anchor, fighting a fit of trembling. Dear God, who had this Ayyub been, that his sons should come so close to power? Saladin, who could see through any veil of glamour. Turan-Shah, whose mind was more than open; who drew the power in and all but drowned it.

They were mortal enough. There was grey in Turan-Shah's beard; his face bore the marks of time and war and self-indulgence. His scent was man-scent, heavy with eastern musk. Aidan breathed deep of it, little comforted by it. He traced the cross on the hilt of his dagger, for strength, and for remembrance. Of what he was; of what he was sworn to.

The *qadi* withdrew at last, taking the secretaries with him. Saladin sighed and stretched and rubbed his eyes. "Allah be my witness, I could never be a scholar." He captured an apple from the bowl which Aidan had not touched, and bit into it with every expression of pleasure. His eyes on Aidan were bright and appallingly clear, but his mind laid no traps for unwary power. "You leave the city soon, then, prince?"

Aidan nodded. "The day after tomorrow, sire."

"So soon." Saladin sounded as if he regretted it. "Will you still do as you swore to do?"

"I must," Aidan said.

The sultan nodded. His fingers sought the scar of the Assassin's dagger, rubbing it as if it pained him. "You cannot in honor do otherwise. As I cannot, by my given word, grant you aid."

"You know I ask for none."

"I know," said Saladin. "But what I know and what I could wish . . ." He sighed, gestured as if to thrust the thought away. "You who are royal know what choices royalty can force upon us. You who are . . . more than that . . . know why I do what I do. I've pondered you, prince, and all that we spoke of. This is what I shall do." He smote his hands together.

A pair of servants came, burdened with what looked like a bolt of silk. They shook it out. It was a coat, a robe of honor, black but for the bands embroidered high on the sleeves: the *tiraz,* the graceful flow of Arabic in letters the color of blood.

Aidan's name, and the sultan's, and the greatness of God woven through the word for honor.

And it was more than a coat. Its weight was steel weight, mail weight—the Syrian fashion, to conceal mere naked armor in the beauty and subtlety of silk. It was like the scabbard of Aidan's sword, damascened. Gold shimmered through its blackness.

The others looked away for their modesty's sake while the servants clothed him in it. It was lighter than his Frankish mail, and more supple, yet he suspected that it might be stronger. They bound it with a silken belt, and hung his sword from a baldric worked with gold. He looked barbarically splendid: quite properly civilized, to the eyes which saw him now.

The sultan smiled, and clapped again. Swift feet sounded. A company of mamluks entered at speed, in cadence. They all wore scarlet coats which, Aidan was certain, concealed the weight of armor. One of them was the Turk who had brought him here. They dropped down in the grovel of Muslim obeisance, but not to Saladin. They kissed the floor at Aidan's feet.

"These," the sultan said, and his expression was frankly wicked, "are yours. What you choose to do with them is your affair. They are," he added, "most well trained. And they have reason not to love our common enemy."

Aidan could not say that he had ever in his life been truly dumbfounded. He had always been able to find something to say.

He contemplated the row of scarlet rumps and abject turbans. Each coat bore the *tiraz* which marked his own. The bodies within suffered none of the prized oriental plumpness. They were all youths—the eldest could not have been past twenty—lean and awkward-graceful as young wolfhounds. One or two might be as tall as he. Several were certainly broader. One long braid beneath its turban was the color of wheat in the sun.

"But," Aidan said at last, "what in the world would I do with a company of mamluks?"

"Whatever you please," said Saladin.

"Then I give them back to you." Aidan raised his hands, pressing on before anyone could stop him. "Sire, this is a gift worthy of a king, and I cherish it for the splendor that it is. But these are soldiers of Allah. How can you so endanger their souls as to give them to me?"

"I trust you," said Saladin, "not to forbid them their salvation."

Aidan flung up his head. His eyes were wild. "You know what I am!"

The sultan nodded once.

Even half-mad, Aidan could not seize a king and shake him till he came to his senses. Nor would it do any good at all to blast the pavilion to its foundations. He clutched the rags of his temper and made himself speak quietly. "My lord. If I speak to them—if I give them the truth—will you allow them to choose?"

"It is not my part to allow or disallow. They are yours."

Aidan bit his tongue. He clapped his hands. Sparks flew. He started; cursed. Only the sultan seemed to see, and he was more amused than not. "Up!" Aidan commanded this army which had been thrust upon him.

They obeyed with laudable alacrity. Boys, yes. Some were still beardless, or too fair for the down to show. He scanned their faces. Tallest to smallest. Clear blue eyes in a face that was pure northern snow. Grey eyes; green, below ruddy brows. Blue again, like ice, but startling in a face as olive-smooth as any Syrian's. Brown, thereafter, and eastern certainly, Turkish braids, Turkish ornaments, round Turkish faces. And on the end, as like as two reins on a bridle, a pair of broad-cheeked, yellow-skinned, slant-eyed imps of hell who dared him outright to remark on their manifold oddities.

In spite of himself, he smiled. "I, too," he said, "am twin-born. And I'll wager I'm odder than you."

"How much?" one demanded promptly. He would be the fire-twin. He was, perhaps, a shade the stockier, a whisper the shorter.

"Your freedom," Aidan answered him. "You lose, you choose. Whether to follow me or go your ways."

"That *is* odd," said the other, the water-twin, with interest.

"Where's your brother?" the first asked: always one for the essentials, he.

"Home in the west, being a king, poor victim."

"Odder and odder," said the water-twin.

The others did not move, but the air about them rippled with impatience. Aidan addressed them all. "Your sultan has told you that you are a gift. Now you know that you are given to a Christian and a Frank. What you are given to do, you may well guess. Do you fear the Assassins?"

They paled. None of them, to do them credit, either moved or spoke.

Aidan smiled a cold white smile. "Good. I see that you are sane. I see also that you are brave. Are you brave enough to serve me?"

He gave it to them whole, without mercy. The truth of his face. The truth of his power, piercing their minds, reading their souls. None of them was secret slave to the master of Masyaf. None of them was such a fool as to be unafraid of the creature who faced them. *Ifrit,* they agreed, implicitly. The twins had another name, but it meant much the same.

None of them had the wits to turn and bolt. The young Northman wore a berserker's smile. "This is better than a song," he said in a voice both light and startlingly sweet; a singer's voice.

The imps—Kipchaks, they called themselves—were grinning like mad things. "I like this," said the fire-twin with wicked relish.

Aidan had all their names. His finger stabbed at each.

"Conrad." The fair singer, who for all his size was one of the youngest.

"Andronikos." The grey-eyed Macedonian with the Byzantine smile.

"Janek." The Circassian, ruddy as a Frank.

"Raihan." Half Frank, half Syrian.

The Turks: "Shadhi; Tuman; Zangi; Bahram; Dildirim; Arslan."

And the imps last of all, water-twin, fire-twin, elder and younger: "Ilkhan. Timur."

They went down one by one as he named them, abject at his feet. But not in their minds; ah, no. In their minds they were giddy with the joy that is the heart of terror.

The more he strove to drive them away, the tighter they clung.

He spun away from them, upon the sultan. "They are all mad!"

"But most well trained," said Saladin, "and utterly loyal. They'll serve you well."

Damn him. He had known what he was doing. He had chosen the best fighters and the worst hellions, and the ones least likely to balk at serving a demon. They were all pagans; even the ones who were born Christian. Even under the yoke of Islam.

They were, Aidan had perforce to admit, perfectly matched to their master. Their entirely unwilling, utterly nonplussed master.

As he would be whether he kept them slaves or set them free. Once his own, always his own. He was obligated to them as they to him, while their lives should last.

It was damnably like being a king. "What am I to do with them?"

"Use us," Arslan ventured to say. He was the eldest but one, and stood as their captain. "We all hate the one you hate. Our master before you—it was he who died when our sultan took his wound. He had no son; we passed into the hands of our sultan. We asked him for the right to vengeance. He promised it. Will you break his promise for him?"

"You could die for it."

"Then we will go to Paradise, and Allah will reward us."

Aidan threw up his hands in despair. "Do you know who would be glad to see this? Half the High Court of the Kingdom of Jerusalem. They wanted me with an army at my back. And now, by God, I have one. But I'll not command an army of slaves, even if your law would allow a Christian to master Muslim souls. You'll be free, or you'll not follow me."

"It has been witnessed," the sultan said.

He was inordinately pleased with himself. His emirs were more than slightly puzzled. His brother did not know what there was to fail to comprehend, except that a Frank had been given a gift as far beyond his deserts as if a dog had been granted entry into Paradise.

Saladin rose; he managed, by sheer force of will, to stand eye to eye with the tall Rhiyanan. He said, "Now you go as well attended as any man may. I pray God that He may grant you His good fortune, and somewhat of His providence. Walk warily, my friend. Look always to your back. You may know better than I what weapons of magic your enemy may wield, but that he has them, you may be certain. There may even—it is whispered—there may be some among his servants who are not merely human."

Cold walked down Aidan's spine. But he held up his head; he smiled. "Whatever his servants may be, he himself is beyond all doubt a mortal man. I go well forewarned, and most well armed."

Saladin's smile was as brittle as Aidan's own. He embraced the prince, as if with his strength alone he could will it all to end as he would have it. "Allah defend you," he said.

Aidan bowed to the floor. The mamluks—his mamluks—followed him in a body. That made him laugh. Still laughing, with the sultan's wide and sudden grin to bear him company, he led them away.

17

Joanna did not, as Aidan had half feared, react with horror to his new army. She was not even surprised. "Ismat told me," she said. "It was partly her idea. She thought you ought to have followers you can trust."

Aidan barely raised a brow. He was beginning to understand how these women ruled while letting their men believe that the world was in their own hands. No doubt Joanna was a traitor to her sex, for letting him know what she knew; or she would have been, if he had been a human man. Sometimes he wondered, a little bitterly, if that was why she accepted so easily what was between them. He was like a dream lover, not human and therefore not quite so mortal a sin.

Then he would look at her and upbraid himself for a fool. She had begun in fascination with a creature out of Gereint's stories. She was seeing him entirely and simply, now, as himself; as no one not of his own kind had ever seen him, even his father.

On this last day in Damascus, she had damned the proprieties and come out of the women's quarters. She wanted to see the city plain, for once, before she left it. She saw it from horseback, wearing a veil to keep from being spat on, but she was a Frank and that was obvious. Aidan had his doubts of her wisdom, but in the circle of his mamluks—his; God's bones; he was still not used to it—and with him at her side, she was as safe as she could ever be. His hellions were unsure of her, as yet. Raised in Islam as they had been, and drunk with their young blood, they did not like the thought of a woman riding like a man. Even if she was as tall as one, and a Frank.

She had enough Saracen in her, and enough Norman noblewoman, not to care in the least what a pack of freed slaves thought of her. She was more interested in seeing this jewel of earthly cities. Sometimes she was even more interested in seeing how close she could ride to Aidan without either being seen or rousing her mare's dislike of being too close to a male, even a male who was a gelding.

Aidan, who was hardly that, encouraged his horse to snake his head and sidle. Otherwise he would seize her then and there and overwhelm her with kisses, and that would not be wise at all.

The astrologer was gone from the Gate of the Clock. Aidan smiled to himself.

Joanna wanted to go inside. It was not forbidden to a woman, but a Frankish woman was hardly welcome. But she was stubborn. She caught his eyes and held them. "Why does anyone have to know? Do they all know what you are?"

His breath hissed between his teeth. That was boldness beyond belief. No mortal had ever asked—ever dared—

She said none of the things she could have said, that would have presumed on what was between them. "I'd like to see," she said.

After a long moment he spoke. "We are," he said, "emirs come to pray for success in our enterprise. It would help if you tried to walk accordingly."

Her grin was too wicked to stay angry at, her swagger too perfectly like that of a Seljuk princeling with a fine sense of his own importance. One of Aidan's mamluks—not a Turk—snickered. He left that one, and five more, on guard over the horses. The others fell in about the two tall figures who might have been good Muslim captains come to pray in the holy place. Aidan at least had no need to pretend to more than his usual semblance of humanity. He was still full of Joanna's reaction to him in his splendid new coat.

The mosque was as much a city as a place of worship. Its galleries were full of merchants: perfumers and sellers of bread waging a war of scents, and bookbinders and jewelers and crafters of glass like jewels sending forth a manifold dazzle of light, and all of them raising their chants to beckon the pilgrim in. The western minaret was full of holy men, and the higher they were, the holier they grew, until the highest seemed to sit directly under heaven. In the regions below, circles of boys chanted the Koran round their teachers, and men stood guard over the first Koran that ever was made, and a veil concealed the cell from which Aisha, beloved of the Prophet, had kept his word alive when he was dead. About them all, the mosque was like a garden of stone: many-colored marble to twice man-high, then the jeweled glitter of the greatest mosaicwork that was ever made or conceived of, every city of the dawn of Islam set living on those walls to endure, it was said, beyond the end of the world.

The center was peace, and the ornate simplicity that was Islam. It was vast, the hall of prayer, and empty, its lamps of gold unlit but glimmering in the gloom, its massed carpets glowing between the pillars, and the golden vine winding round its *mihrab*. There were people here in numbers enough, but the space was wider than they, and quiet. Somewhere, someone chanted the Koran.

It seemed most logical, and most natural, to sit on the carpet by a pillar, face toward the niche of prayer, and simply be. Joanna sat close. With no one to see but the mamluks, whom he trusted, Aidan wound his fingers with hers. She smiled at him, a quick smile, with promises in it for later. "This is holy," she said softly, "even if it is not our holiness."

He nodded. It was like her, to understand without needing to be told. They needed it, this peace. He had no great gift of prescience, but because he was what he was, he could know that they would not have such quiet again.

Almost he clutched at her, to hold her, and this hour, and all that they must lose. She had turned from him; she was taking in the purity of the space. It was Roman once; then it was Christian, full of the chants and incense of the Greek rite. Now it was Allah's.

He kissed her fingers one by one. She smiled, although she did not look at him. Her hand curved to fit his cheek.

Ishak saw them down the length of the mosque. At first he thought that his eyes were failing him. The mamluks were clear enough in their scarlet livery, but the two in the middle blurred and wavered like heat-shimmer in the desert.

It was only that they were in black and the hall was dim, and he was winded with tracking them down. Aidan, he could see well enough once he set his mind to it. He wondered vaguely who the other was. Another Frank, maybe; or someone from the House of Ibrahim.

He could not spare breath to care. He had tried hard, so hideously hard, to forget what he knew; and he had succeeded. He had never even been tempted to tell the Frank his family's secret.

Tomorrow the Frank was going. Probably he would never come back. Ishak was not moved, except as a child is, wanting what it knows it cannot have, to beg the Frank to take him on the caravan. There was the family to think of, and Masud, and the sultan.

But the Frank had been Ishak's guest, and Ishak thought that they might be friends. The Frank was exotic and splendid and more apt for mischief than anyone else Ishak had ever known. Ishak was going to miss him sorely.

If he died because Ishak had not warned him . . .

That was not a man with him, though she was as big as a man, and ugly in an inescapably Frankish fashion. And shameless. Stroking him, here, in the very house of God.

Franks had no decency at all.

He shivered. His stomach clenched tighter even than his fists. People said that Franks were too pallid to have any passion, all their fiery humours chilled and quenched by their cold northern climate and their taste for unclean meats. Not these two, he could well see. They were unseemly.

But, like animals, oddly beautiful. They knew no better.

Aidan knew steel. Ishak's father would say that that was enough.

He was avoiding thinking of what he ought to be thinking of. He should escape, now, while they were occupied; before they saw him.

He swallowed hard. He had not come so far, to turn coward and slink away.

He drew himself up, tugged his coat into order, smoothed what beard he had. With his best face forward, he went to break his given word.

The woman was not so ugly, close up. Merely plain. She was modest enough to snatch for her veil when she saw him coming, Frank enough to shrug and give it up since he had already seen what there was to see. She had bold eyes. He blushed under them, and could not even begin to pretend that he had come here by chance.

He could at least pretend to ignore her. He greeted Aidan with none of his usual lightness, squatting within the circle of mamluks, who knew him and did not try to stop him. But once he was there, he could not say what he had come to say. He could not even circle round to it. He scowled at his boots instead, and let them think him impossibly rude.

Aidan touched his shoulder, lightly, as if to bolster him. "Come, sir. You knew I'd be leaving as soon as I could."

Ishak nodded, swallowing. "It's not—I—" He gathered himself under those eyes like his father's steel, rippling like it, dazzling him, and said as levelly as his body's trembling would let him, "Sir Frank, it's not that you must go. I understand; it's no pleasure, but I accept it. It's what you go to. I don't think you understand what the sons of knives are."

"I think I may," said Aidan, but not as if he had taken offense. "They're very subtle, and very deadly. They almost never fail to kill where they are commanded. Except with your sultan."

"Allah's hand was on him," Ishak said.

"And it can't be on me, because I am a Christian?"

Ishak shook his head until his turban rocked on its moorings. "No, no, no! Allah defended him: kept the Old Man from using his strongest weapons. Nothing but human force went against the sultan."

Aidan, for a wonder, seemed to be listening to Ishak, and heeding what he heard. "He said something to me of that. That not all the *Hashishayun* are human men."

"Ya Allah! Don't name them!" Ishak caught his voice before it spiraled into hysteria. "What . . . what do you know of their magic?"

"Little," said Aidan. "They're masters of stealth. They're mad—bewitched, some say; or drugged. They live to die and pass to Paradise."

"Nothing more?"

"Is there more?"

Those eyes were too damnably keen. Ishak fixed his own on his feet. "They have magic, prince. Devil-magic. And they are mad. What law or reason or sanity can any man compel, on folk who care only to kill and then to die?"

"Then," said Aidan with such lightness that Ishak groaned in despair, "I'll have to be madder than they."

"Can you be stronger, too? And deadlier?"

"I can try."

"You'll still die," Ishak said. "Unless you have magic, too."

Aidan smiled. "I have magic."

Ishak's chin snapped up. "Are you first cousin to Iblis?"

"I've been accused of it," said the Frank.

Ishak ground his teeth in frustration. He wanted to burst out with it, all together, all bare. And he could not. His throat clenched when he tried to speak; to name her. To warn this innocent of the Old Man's devil-bitch.

Magic. What could Franks know of true and high and deadly magic? They were hardly more than savages.

Even this one, who looked like an eastern lord. He smiled at Ishak, thinking no doubt to calm a child's fears. Child that he was himself. What power did he have, to face what laired in the Mountain?

Ishak could not—could not—speak of her. The spell's shape was as distinct as bit and bridle, as a shackle on his tongue. He cursed her to blackest hell, but he was silenced.

He rose without grace, choking on tears as much of rage as of grief for a friend. "Prince," he said. "Prince, if you will not be wise, at least be warned. Trust no one. No one, do you understand?"

"Not even myself?"

Ishak tossed his head. "Allah! You would drive a saint to murder." He thrust the words out one by one, with all his strength of will and wit. "You are hunted. Your life is worth no more than a pebble in the desert. Pray your God to watch over you. No lesser power can defend you."

"I understand," said Aidan. The light mad mockery, at least, had left him. "I do, Ishak. How much have you risked, to tell me this?"

Ishak's blood ran hot, and then cold. His shoulders hunched. "It doesn't matter. My father—makes knives—for—" His voice died. His throat throbbed and burned. He was dizzy, sick.

The Frank caught him before he toppled. He leaned against that slender strength; but only briefly. He willed himself erect. "I have to go," he said. "Go—go with God. May God defend you."

The boy all but fled, head down, stumbling as if he had gone blind. Aidan started after him, stopped. There was power on him. To break it, or to pierce it, might break his mind.

The cold that had struck when the sultan spoke of magic, had sunk to the bone. It was real; it was true. And Aidan had never seen. He had held in his hand a blade of Farouk's forging, stained with Thibaut's blood, and he had never understood, nor remembered.

There was a power in Masyaf. Stronger than he, perhaps; older; less human than he could ever be.

He had never had to contemplate such a thing. They had always been human, all his enemies. His own kind were his own kind. They did not turn on one another. That was a mortal madness.

Memory quivered. The Saracen, the cat-eyed beauty, Morgiana. If he could find her—if she knew what was in Masyaf—perhaps—

Would she aid a Frank? Others had, Ishak not least of all; but Aidan would never presume on Saracen charity. Perhaps she would not even know what demon answered the call of the Master of the Assassins.

If he ever saw her again, he could but ask.

He turned back to Joanna. She reined in her fear, but it was rising, draining the blood from her face, the light from her eyes. He drew her up and kissed her. "I'll defend you," he said.

She clung as briefly as Ishak had. But she knew more of him than the boy had been allowed to see. She let herself believe him.

IV

ALEPPO

18

Aleppo was white. White as chalk, white as bone, white as the blindness of sun on snow. The rock of its citadel loomed up to heaven, dazzling in the glare of noon; the green of poplar and cypress blurred to a shadow beneath it.

This was a starker beauty than Damascus. Its people were less languidly graceful, its orchards less inviting. The flow of its speech was deeper, harsher, closer to the stone on which it stood.

Even its lordship was different. Saladin was not sultan here. The child al-Salih Ismail, whose father had been sultan in Damascus before his death brought the upstart out of Egypt, ruled with his regent, Gumushtekin. That he ruled by Saladin's sufferance, mattered little to a city which had weathered years of siege against the interloper. Which had, above all, set the Assassins on him, until he made his own peace with them.

The House of Ibrahim was a city within the city. Here at last even a western nobleman could see what power was in a kingdom of trade: in its hand upon the caravanserais, and its holdings in the city, and its strength to rule as it chose without regard to the one who held the citadel. Where the caravan passed, no one presumed to hinder.

Yet the house itself, though large enough, did not ape a palace. It had begun as a simple dwelling, a house of a single court with a garden at its back. Years and need and the swelling of its dependents had stretched its boundaries, until its wall enclosed a fair half-dozen lesser houses and their gardens. But its heart was still the house of Ibrahim the seller of spices, Abraham the Jew as he had been then, before the dawn of Islam.

For Joanna it was another face of home. Hakim the porter was at his post as he had always been, a shade greyer, perhaps, a shade more dry and sinewy, but still the guardian of the gate. The gap in the arch where one of the cousins had proven his prowess with a sling had never managed to get itself mended. The broken-backed pomegranate tree still shaded the first court, laden now with fruit, with a boy to drive away the birds. There was, as always, a cat on the fountain's rim and a servant or three trotting from sun to shade, and a gathering of cousins escaped from duties to see who had come.

They had an eyeful: twelve mamluks in scarlet with hands to weapons, and a Frankish prince in the robe of a Damascene emir, and Joanna with her maid as drab as peahens in the midst of them.

This time, she knew without asking, Aidan was going to be difficult. On the road he had been no more restive than he ever was; he had seemed as glad as she, to be free to ride together by day and to lie in one another's arms at night. But since Aleppo came in sight, he had been as twitchy as a cat.

Even in the few moments between surrendering his horse to a groom and facing the uncle who had come to give them formal greeting, he could not stand still. He prowled to the pomegranate tree and back, pausing to exchange stares with one of the youngest cousins, gathering up the cat that had come to weave about his ankles. He was a lodestone for cats, always. He came to stand at Joanna's back, as the cousins scattered and their elder advanced like a ship in full sail: Uncle Karim, no less. They were being honored.

Though Aidan might not think so. She willed him to keep quiet, to stand still, to let her do the talking. Uncle Karim was not an easy sight for Frankish eyes, nobly rotund as he was, attired as always in the extremest height of fashion, with a beard dyed blacker than any natural beard could be and curled extravagantly, and a turban of truly astonishing dimensions. One's first impulse was always to goggle, and then to laugh aloud.

People who laughed at Uncle Karim usually lived to regret

it. He had a mind like a Damascus blade, and a propensity for repaying slights in the purest unadulterated gold coin.

Aidan was not laughing, that she could hear. She could not in courtesy twist about to see if he was grinning. Those of his mamluks whom she could see, seemed to have frozen in mid-goggle. She could not, unfortunately, see the two she was most afraid of. The Kipchak imps were behind their master, doing God alone knew what.

She was free at least to accept her uncle's greeting, all of it, in all its intricacy. But it was heartfelt; his embrace had a quiver in it, and while his tongue ran on, his eyes took in every travel-weary inch of her. And her escort. And, narrowly, her prince.

Then at last she could turn. Aidan was not grinning. His face was marble-still, his voice soft and careful in acknowledging his host. The cat was on his shoulder, purring thunderously. It made him no less alarming to look at.

She hardly heard what they said to one another. Will had met strong will, and found its match. Grey eyes and dark crossed, clashed, disengaged.

Uncle Karim smiled. The slight inclination of his head had more respect in it than all the bowings and effusions before it. "Come," he said, "if you will, and rest, and take refreshment. All that is here, is yours. May your sojourn with us be long and blessed."

Aidan did not want to go where the plump hand beckoned. She could not touch him, not under all these eyes, but she said, "Go. It's safe. I promise you."

He shook his head tightly, lips set. Her heart constricted. Not a battle; dear God, not here.

He seemed to catch her thought. He went stiffly where he was led, but he went without argument.

Her breath left her in a long sigh. She loved him; she ached with wanting him. But he was not a comfortable companion. If he ever took it into his head to run wild, nothing in the world would stop him.

He was close to it now. She almost broke away from the women who were leading her to the harem and its bath, and ran back to him. But she mastered herself. She would only make it worse.

Even with all her troubles, the bath was heaven. The aunts and the cousins were all there to spoil her, to hover about her, to make her feel loved and pampered and protected. They had all the gossip ready for her: who was married and who was pregnant and who was at odds with whom, both within the harem and out of it. It was all a warm and steady stream, like the water, the soap scented with roses, the oil rubbed into her skin.

Languid, at peace, with fear driven deep into the shadows of her consciousness, Joanna could look at herself and see what she had been blind to for so long. She was surprised. She had a shape again. Her waist would never win back its maiden smallness, but it was less thick than it had been. Her breasts were tender still, but their milk had dried; though their high round firmness was gone, this new fullness was not unpleasant to see. Her hair had darkened, gone from oak-gold to bronze, but it had won back its luster; it tumbled about her face, softening the long strong lines of cheek and jaw, widening her eyes and deepening their cloudy blue to misted violet. She stared at herself in the silver mirror, astonished. She looked like a woman with a lover.

She hid her flush behind the curtain of hair, attacking it with a brush until someone interfered. She looked into the withered face of the oldest aunt, and eyes that saw all there had ever been to see. A gnarled finger prodded her breast. When she flinched, Aunt Adah grinned, baring her toothless gums. "So, little one. Is it another baby we'll be raising for the House?"

Joanna's teeth clicked together. No. Oh, no. "No! I had one. He was taken away from me. I'm still—not—entirely—"

Aunt Adah nodded altogether too willingly. "Yes. Yes, of

course. Poor little one. Franks are barbarians, to take babies away from new mothers and leave them all alone."

Slowly Joanna's heart stopped trying to leap out of her breast. She was not deluding herself. She was being sensible. Her courses had not begun yet: her body was still off its balance after Aimery. She was not carrying another child. Which could not possibly be Ranulf's. Which would not likely be human at all.

And if she were . . . if she were . . .

No. She turned her back on the thought and slammed the door. She set herself to be welcome and welcomed, bathed, fed, laid to rest in a high cool room full of the song of wind and falling water.

Aidan did not want to be quiet. He did not want to eat. He did not want to rest. His mamluks were taken away from him, led away to some inner fastness of servants and of lesser guests. His lover was locked in the harem. He had walked open-eyed into a city of Assassins, and he knew that he had been mad to dare it.

He lay on the mat in the room which he had been given, not because he wanted to lie there, but because the patchwork cat, coiled on his middle, was content. Its purring rumbled through him; its peace stilled the worst of his compulsion to leap up and bolt.

And why, except for the cat, did he not do just that? Why did he not fly, if he was minded to? He could. It was there in him, the power.

The cat butted his hand. He rubbed its ears, aware of its bliss, as a murmur on the edges of his rebellion.

He had done nothing that a mortal man could not do, except blur the truth of his face, and walk in a mind or two, and sustain the wards against the Assassin—ill as that had served Thibaut—since he left Rhiyana. In all else, he had wielded no power. He had made himself human.

It had seemed prudent enough when he began. This was a

mortal world, and mortal fear could kill. He had seen the threat of it in Jerusalem, in the whispers that he was the Assassin, that he was worse, that he was the devil's own.

But he was not mortal. He was not human. Here in Islam, which not only accepted the possibility of his kind but granted it the hope of salvation, he was perhaps not safe from fear, but he was less likely to be burned at the stake for it. And his power chafed in its confinement.

He uncurled a tendril of it, delicately. Nothing so common to his kind as wards or mindsight; those had had use enough. But the deeper power, the fire that was his name and his essence, woke with joy. A flicker, only, for a beginning. A wash of flame over his body.

The cat regarded him wide-eyed. He was clothed in fire. He raised his hand, each finger like a candle, crowned with a flame. He laughed for the freedom of it.

The edge of his awareness rippled. Presence, and human. He damped the fire. The cat sneezed. He sat up to face the man with the ridiculous turban and the blade-keen wits.

If Karim had seen or sensed the wildfire, he had chosen to reckon it a delusion. He bowed with grace astonishing in a man of his girth, in the exact degree due the second son of a king. Aidan acknowledged it with a raise of the brow and an inclination of the head. It was more than he would have given a merchant at home.

But, having acceded to the proprieties, this merchant recalled that he was Aidan's equal in the kingdom of trade, second heir after his sister. And that was strangest of all, that a woman could inherit, and rule, in her own right, when there was a man of years and strength to do it for her.

Karim established himself in comfort where the breeze was coolest, near the door that looked on the garden. His robe was of sky-blue silk. His slippers were scarlet, embroidered with crystal and gold; their toes turned up with elegant extravagance.

Aidan, barefoot in cotton drawers, sighed for his dignity and kept to his mat. The cat drowsed in his lap.

Karim spared it a glance. "You have a friend in the house, I see," he said.

"But not, God willing, the only one."

The merchant smiled in his curled beard. "You are welcome here," he said, "as the kinsman of our kinswoman, and as a lord of Rhiyana. That is pearls, no? And a little tin. And a beautiful fine woolen cloth that sells for a princely price in the proper places."

"And a very little metalwork, though maybe that is not well thought of here, where the smiths are the best in the world."

Karim was not in the least discomfited. "And, as you say, a craft in gold and silver and somewhat in iron, and a rare art in the cutting and setting of gems. The King of Jerusalem's emerald is known even here."

"Is it?" Aidan smiled. "And so it might be. The stone came from your caravans, though it was cut and carved in Caer Gwent."

"Such is the kingdom of commerce," said Karim.

"I begin to see the extent of it," Aidan said. "That you should know our little country . . . have you kin who trade there?"

"A distant cousin, and an ally or two. They speak of a country well ruled, prosperous and at peace: a haven for the gentler arts."

"But not fair prey for any barbarian with an axe and the will to use it."

"Certainly not," said Karim. "Even, I trust, without the marshal of its armies."

"My royal brother is at least the soldier I am, and twice the general."

"Then he must be remarkable indeed."

"His failing," Aidan said, "is that he let the monks corrupt him. He lets everyone else claim the praise, and takes the blame on himself. There is such a thing as an excess of Christian charity."

Karim could not in courtesy answer that.

Aidan nudged the cat from his lap and drew up his knees, clasping them. The cat contemplated sinking claws into his ankle, but reconsidered. It turned haughtily and stalked out.

"I am not," he said to the final fillip of its tail, "the Christian that my brother is. Nor have I his patience. Tell the lady of this house that I shall do my utmost to wait upon her pleasure, but my temper is uncertain at its best. Which, now, it most certainly is not."

Karim regarded him in grave astonishment. "Sir! Have we failed of our hospitality?"

"I have been at the mercy of the caravan since it left Jerusalem. Now the caravan is ended. The one whom the Lady Margaret charged me to guard is locked away from me in the harem. I have nothing to do but wait, and look for death that comes out of the air. As it will, Master Karim. As it most assuredly will."

Karim looked long at him, with no fear that he could discern. After an endless moment the merchant rose. "Rest," he said, "if you can. I shall see what I may do."

It was better than nothing, Aidan supposed. He had trampled on every rule of eastern courtesy; but he was, truly, out of patience. He did not intend to cool his heels in this city of Assassins, until Joanna died for Muslim propriety.

If they did not let him in to guard her, he would find his own way there. Soon. Tonight. The air was limpidly clear, the air of Aleppo on the threshold of autumn, but beneath it was a tension like the gathering of thunder. It was going to break. And when it broke, it would break in blood.

He put on the garment that had been laid out for him, a light silken robe, and went out to the gallery. The garden lay below, green and empty. The rooms beside his own were likewise untenanted, their inhabitants gone now about the business of the House of Ibrahim.

He swung over the rail, dropped lightly down. Beyond the wall he heard children's voices, and a woman's raised in remonstrance. He walked along it, hand resting lightly on it, as if to promise that he would conquer it.

In the corner of the wall, an almond tree shaded a space like a bower. He bent beneath the branches, and started, recoiling.

Morgiana tossed him an almond. He caught it, by instinct, as he dropped down under the arching green. She cracked a pale-brown shell and freed the meat, but did not eat it. Her expression was almost frightening in its stillness.

She wore woman's dress, drab and voluminous black, with a veil over her hair. She would have been beautiful in sackcloth, which this very nearly was; its perfect propriety was more alluring than the man's garb in which he had seen her before.

The almond broke in the clenching of his fist. A jagged edge sank deep, drawing blood. He stared at it in surprise.

She took his hand in warm steady fingers and drew out the shard. The blood welled, dark and thick. She set her lips to it.

He could not move. She was only cleansing the wound by what means she could. Only that. She raised her head; she was as calm as ever. "You should take care," she said. "You have more strength than a man."

Temper burned away his astonishment. "Am I so much a child beside you?"

"Allah knows, you are not." She was still holding his hand. "I've been waiting for you."

He glanced about. "Here? Do you live here?"

She shook her head. "I saw you riding in. You were beautiful in your robe of honor. Almost civilized."

"Almost?"

She laughed and kissed his palm, swiftly, as if there were nothing else one ought to do with a man's hand in one's own.

"I should not like you to lose your wildness. It makes you fascinating."

"You . . ." he said. "You could quickly drive me mad."

He was half jesting. But even the half that was in earnest had not looked to drive her back against the tree-bole, green eyes wide, white face stricken.

His hand, that had known no pain of its wound, began to throb. He flexed it, staring at her. She looked ready, impossibly, to weep.

He gathered her to him. "Hush," he said, though she had made no sound. "Hush. I meant no hurt."

Her head shook, hard, against his shoulder. She was smaller than Joanna, lighter, slender-boned as a bird, but wonderfully, uncannily strong. Her fists knotted in his robe. Her voice came muffled but distinct. "I have no art; no skill. I know nothing of gentle things. I can only say what is in me to say. And that—and that—is all amiss."

He drew a breath, two. "Are you telling me . . . that you . . ."

She thrust herself back. "Oh, you beautiful, innocent fool! I love you. I have loved you since I saw you in Jerusalem. I have followed you, watched you, waited for you, wanted you. If I shall drive you mad, what is it that you have done to me?"

He opened his mouth, closed it again. He could think of nothing to do, except to touch her. She was burning cold. "I don't," he said, "I don't yet—" He swallowed. "Yet. But when I see you, touch you . . ." He had her hands in his. He held them to his heart. He could not help the sudden smile. "If you would seduce a man, my lady, you had best begin by letting him see you as often as you see him."

She stiffened, offended; but listening with fierce intensity.

He raised her hands and kissed them. "When I first saw you, I thought that I had dreamed you. You were all that I had ever yearned for in a woman."

"And now?"

He met her eyes. "And now, you make my heart sing."

Her arms locked about his neck. "Will you love me? Will you love me now?"

He checked, startled. She was shaking, and not with passion. As if she were going to die before the sun set, and once again, just once, she craved the body's pleasure. "Lady, why in the world—"

She spun away from him. "No. Of course not." Her voice was bitter. "You are Christian. I forget. You make a virtue of denial."

Aidan laughed with his own fair share of bitterness. "That may be, but I was not born a Christian. No, lady. It's only . . . are you sure you want it? I hardly know you."

"That is why," she said. "That is why I want you now."

He reached for her, but she had gone too far, almost out of the tree's shade. "Lady," he said, "have mercy. I've seen you thrice before this; I know no more of you than your name. If you have a husband, children, kin—"

Her laughter was like a cry of pain. "None! I have none. There is only I. Only—only—"

He leaped. He was surprised that she was there, that she had not vanished. But no more, it seemed, than she. She had to tilt her head back to see his face; to reach high, to smooth the hair back from his brow. Her hand trembled. "I love you," she said.

She was gone.

He dropped down, boneless. "God," he said. As she had once. "God, God, God."

Two wives, the astrologer had said. Had he meant this impossible tangle? Fretting into madness over one; driven truly mad by the other. And if one was jealous . . .

That would be Joanna. Muslim women knew how to share their men.

He tossed his aching head. What was he thinking? Joanna had no cause for jealousy. This was a madwoman, a demon-creature gone wild with age and loneliness. That he found her beautiful was proof only that he had eyes. The rest was pity and fascination and a little—more than a little—desire. Their bodies fit well together. Almost too well. The memory of her was strong on his skin, her absence an ache that mounted to pain.

He dragged himself to his feet. He had come to the garden for healing; it had dealt him a wound worse still.

God had not done with mocking him. He could rest now. He could fall without effort into a sleep like death. Therefore he was not allowed it. A servant was waiting in his chamber with fresh clothing, a cup of sherbet, a cloying obsequiousness. Now that he had rested, he was informed, he would dine, then the masters of the house would rejoice in his company.

He contemplated a feast for a prince and a long evening's discourse on nothing in particular, and came deathly close to defying it all. But training held, and bone-weariness. He bowed to the inevitable.

19

Joanna was well guarded. Too well by half. She and Dura shared a chamber with two of the cousins, light sleepers both, and one heavy with pregnancy and given to rising every hour at least to go to the privy. Samin the eunuch, who was well-nigh as vast as the Dome of the Rock and armed with a sword, slept across the door. An Assassin would have been hard put to enter the room, which had only one latticed window; and if he had found a way to walk through walls or the mountain of Samin, he would have had to unravel Joanna from the knot of her maid and her cousins.

A lover, even a lover who was Aidan, could not begin to approach her.

It was not as if she had been taken unawares. The House

knew the danger she was in, for its sake; and the harem was crowded. The unmarried women, the women with child, the women whose husbands were elsewhere on the business of the House, had perforce to sleep in twos and threes.

She had not spent a night without Aidan since he first came to her tent. In that warm and airless room, filled to bursting with humanity, still she was cold. Alia's back against her side, Nahar's exuberant flesh crowding her, Samin's thunderous snores, all made her ache for one long lean body, and love made in silence for fear of discovery, and the scent of him that was like an oak copse in summer.

She tried, once, to slip away. Samin heaved himself up and followed her. He waited outside the privy, to which she had to go or be betrayed, and followed her back to the room. He had not followed Alia on any of her many excursions. He was, beyond any hope of doubt, set to guard Joanna.

It would have been easier if she could trust Aidan not to do something mad. Not tonight, maybe. He had that much sense. But if he was kept away from her every night, sooner or later he would break, and then there was no telling what he would do.

When this was over, she would go back to Outremer. Ranulf would try to claim her. She was his wife; there was no escape from that. She did not—God help her, she did not know if she wanted to escape from it. She did not want to be Aidan's wife, even if he would ask it, or expect it. A wife was too much like a servant. She had a duty to her husband's bed. Duty was no part of what was between her and the witch's son of Caer Gwent.

He could be all utterly like a man, warm flesh, swift desire, tears when he grieved, laughter when he was glad. He was as devout a Christian as any other nobleman, though sometimes he forgot and swore by the goddess of his mother. He was no devil, or monster, or creature beyond human ken.

But he was not human. He did not, when he let himself be himself, think like a man. Which was why she was knotted with more than wanting him. She feared him. For him. He was as dangerous as a beast of prey, and as unchancy. And men hunted beasts of prey; killed them, and called it justice, because their world allowed no predator but man.

Be human, she willed him—prayed him. *Think. Remember the danger to me.* Since he would never care for his own.

Maybe he heard. He did not come.

He was wise; and she. But ah, she wanted him.

He had heard her. He saw what safeguards hedged her about. None of them could be proof against sorcery. And yet, was he? He did not even know what it was that he faced: whether demon or mortal magus, or nothing at all but fear in the night.

Nor could he know, unless he saw it. But to see it, he must lure it; and he would not—could not—use Joanna as the bait.

He sat bolt upright. Perhaps he would not need to. He had his own magic. It was by no means without its limits. But perhaps—perhaps—for this it would be enough.

He sank back with a groan. It needed time for the doing. Time he might not be given. He had dallied overlong as it was, letting the caravan carry him in Joanna's wake. This city that had opened like the jaws of a trap, this would be the place where the Assassin made his move; and it might be soon. Half Aleppo knew that the House of Ibrahim's southern caravan had come in. The word would reach Masyaf at winged speed. And then, out of the night, the stroke.

His senses leaped outward in fear. No danger met them. Joanna was guarded; nothing crept in upon her. In the city round about, no malice turned against her.

He did not linger to read what else was there to read, although some of it pricked at his awareness. It was not in him tonight to wander the mind-winds, long though it had been since he had ventured them. He set his strength in the wards and his will on sleep, and settled to endure the night.

* * *

After all his sleepless fretting, he slept well past sunrise. It was Arslan who roused him, looking well and grimly content, and saying as soon as Aidan had opened his eyes, "My lord would do well to rise quickly. He is summoned where he had best deign to go."

Aidan sat up scowling, raking his hair out of his face. "Would my servant deign to explain himself in plain Arabic?"

Arslan grinned, unrepentant. "You're blessed, my lord. The Lady Khadijah wants to speak with you. I don't think," he said, "that she often grants audience this soon."

Aidan knew that she did not. As lady of the House, she stood somewhat higher than a queen, and she knew it. He was up in an instant, into Arslan's capable hands. As the mamluk washed him, he said, "The last I knew, the whole pack of you had been herded into exile."

"So we were." Arslan wrung the cloth into the basin, laid both aside, began to dress his master. "We chose not to accept our banishment. It never came from you, after all. I shall be your body servant, at which I am somewhat more accomplished than the fool who claimed the office. The rest will guard you, taking turn and turn. May I grant them leave, when they are not guarding you, to go about the city?"

"Only if they—and you—promise the utmost of discretion. And leave your livery at home."

Arslan dipped his head. "Yes, my lord."

"Mark you," said Aidan. "No spying; and no rabblerousing. If you see an Assassin, you let him be."

"Even if he is murdering a citizen, my lord?"

Aidan's teeth clicked together. Arslan's politeness was beyond reproach, but his mind was rather too patently his own. "There will be no heroics while we are guests in this city. We would be worse than fools to betray our hand in assaults against slaves, while the master keeps to his own place, free and strong and all too well aware of us."

"Yes, my lord," said Arslan.

He was a master of the opacity of servants, was that one.

But Aidan had better eyes than most. "On your honor," he said, "and on your soul, swear to it."

So compelled, Arslan could not but obey. He was not happy, but his respect for his lord had gone up a notch or two.

Aidan was ready: washed, combed, royally if somberly clad. He did not go armed, although his side was sadly naked without his sword. Arslan followed him. Raihan and Conrad fell in behind.

None of them was admitted to the harem. That was law, and immutable. Aidan went in under the guardianship of a mountainous, soot-black eunuch, hideous as a devil out of an abbot's nightmare, armed with what could only be a captured Frankish sword. His lowering glances promised application of that blade to a salient portion of Aidan's anatomy, if Aidan ventured the slightest step out of the way ordained for him.

Aidan did not intend to stray; nor indeed could he have wandered far. He was taken only to the first court, to a chamber just within it, a dim cupboard of a room divided in half by an intricately carven screen. Foreign though it was with its tiles and its carpets and its shelf of silver vessels rimming the whitewashed ceiling, it reminded Aidan of nothing so much as the reception room of a nunnery. There was even a chaperone in black, heavily veiled, with gnarled and age-spotted fingers laced quietly in her lap.

And with her, near but not behind the screen, a figure whose veil might have been smoke for all it concealed of Joanna.

Aidan was trained in courts and among kings. He did not falter. He did not cry out, or leap forward, or seize her and crush the breath out of her. He entered quietly. Half of the way between the door and the ladies, he bowed a low and courtly bow. "*Ma dama.* You are well?"

Her eyes were lowered, as always when she did not want to betray herself; her voice was muted. "I am well, my lord. And you? Have you rested?"

"Well enough, my lady," he said.

He knew in his skin why she veiled herself against him. Her cheeks were burning. Her breath came quicker than it was used to; he could hear her heart beating.

If he was calmer, it was only because he had a witch's mastery of his body. There were eyes all about, staring, judging, alert for the smallest betrayal. And most intent of all, the ancient woman in her swathing of veils, no more than a shape of shadow with yellow bird-talon hands and eyes as fiercely steady as a falcon's. No servant, this; and no fool.

He would not blanch beneath her stare, though it dared him to defend his discourtesy in greeting Joanna first before her. Let her make of it what she would. He was Joanna's first, any other mortal's after.

He bowed as to a queen, a prince's bow, with no submission in it. "Lady," he said.

The falcon-eyes glinted. The veils inclined a fraction. "Sir Frank," she said.

Her voice was younger by far than her hands. It made him think of Margaret: of velvet over steel. "You honor me with your presence," he said to her, "my lady Khadijah."

Perhaps she smiled. "I do, yes. My granddaughter names you kinsman; the daughter of my granddaughter speaks well of you. And," she said, "I had a fancy to see your face."

"Does it please you?"

She laughed, no crone's cackle but the rich deep laughter of a woman in her prime. "Of course it pleases me! The young moon in Ramadan, indeed. I think I shall not let my daughters see you. They might be tempted from the path of virtue."

"Surely the ladies of your line are not so easily led astray."

"Perhaps not; but they might be induced to look on the men whom Allah has given them, and be sadly disappointed."

"There is more to a man than beauty," Aidan said.

"But never so evident to the eye." She beckoned. "Come here."

He came; he sank to one knee before her, to spare her the

effort of craning up at him, for she was very small. Tiny; astonishing, for she towered in the mind's eye. He could have lifted her with one hand.

She leaned toward him. "Were I even twenty years younger," she said, "I would cast prudence to the winds and take you to my bed."

"Twenty years, lady? Why need you be younger at all?"

She laughed again that wonderful, earthy laughter. "Why indeed, young stallion? Surely you would not be pleased to embrace such a shriveled husk as I am."

"My first lover was past her third score of years, and though time had had its will of her, it only made her sweeter."

"Ah, sir," said Khadijah, "you tempt me. To know again the sweetness of young flesh . . ." She sighed. "No; I submit; Allah wills it. My eyes take pleasure enough. Thanks be to Him Who is ever merciful, that I have them yet. And my thanks to you, O beautiful, that you offer me such a gift. Your God may not reward you, but mine understands a generous heart."

"Is He not all one?"

"Some would say so," she said. She straightened; she met him stare for stare. "Tell me why you have come."

She knew it as well as he, but she wanted to hear it as he perceived it. He told her. Time and retelling had smoothed the raw edges of his grief. He could speak quietly, levelly, without tremor or evasion. Even what most condemned him: that he had had no foreknowing of either death, nor sensed aught amiss, until the lives were long since fled. He had been blind and deaf and dumb, and foolish beyond belief.

"A fool," said the Lady Khadijah, "is one who never knows when he has failed. You failed; you have paid."

"And I continue to pay, and shall, until this war is ended."

"One might contend that your enemy is not the murderer in Masyaf but my granddaughter in Jerusalem."

"Or that it is not even she, but the House for which she sacrifices all that she loves."

"Truly then, I am here, and defenseless, and ripe for your taking."

"I think not," said Aidan.

"Truly."

She was serene, looking death in the face, too long accustomed to its presence to know any fear of it. He bowed to that serenity. "Pride, I can comprehend; and honor; and the defense of what is larger than oneself. But sheer, raw greed . . . that, I will not forgive. And I fear what my world would be, if Sinan had sunk his claws into its kingdom of trade."

"I extend more charity. I think that he sees a fair road to the triumph of his mission and his faith. It is our misfortune that he pursues his ends by secret murder. Is he any better, or worse, than the captain who puts every soul of a city to the sword because their lord has resisted his will?"

"That captain has not murdered my sister's son." Aidan drew breath in her silence. "Yes, lady. As simple as that. I loved him; he was a son to me, and more than a son. Among our people, the sister's child is sacred; he is the closest of kin, the heart's son—the more if one has no son of one's body. For his sake alone I would level Alamut."

"Perhaps," mused Khadijah, "that is what it is to be a Frank. To love one man more than nation or tribe or clan. To see that man's death as the fault of one man, and one man only. To cut straight to the heart."

"Better that than to lop off limbs one by one, as he has done to us. I have been called cruel, my lady. But when I can, I seek a clean kill."

"There is wisdom in that," she said.

He paused, glanced at Joanna. She was mute, listening, clear as water to his sight. She had been amused, if more than slightly scandalized, by her grandmother's frank appreciation of Aidan's beauty; even his confession that he took no account of years in reckoning desire, had almost comforted her. Now she waited for him to say what he must say.

He said it with care, but not with diffidence. "Lady. Would

you advise your granddaughter to surrender to Sinan before he raises his vendetta against the whole of your House?"

"I would not," said Khadijah.

He nodded once. "Have you considered taking the war to him before he brings it to you?"

"We are not a house of war."

"Even when compelled?"

"When compelled, we avail ourselves of the weapons that come to hand."

He sat back on his heels. "Are you telling me that I am that weapon?"

"Did I bid you swear your oath against Sinan?"

"Ah," he said. "I understand. I shall wreak my revenge, and you will reap the profits. And, since I am a western nobleman and therefore no merchant at all, I cannot trouble you by demanding even a sellsword's pay."

"Of course you will not." She was amused, and not at all cowed. "We are merchants, prince, but we are honest merchants. We pay our debts."

"Is there a debt, then?"

"If you succeed," she said, "yes. And you are due at least a guardsman's hire, for bringing our kinswoman safe to us. I think that we can give you recompense beyond your guesting here."

"Such as?"

"What do you ask? Gold? Jewels? Spices? Silks to adorn your beauty?"

"A part interest in certain of your caravans." They both turned to stare at Joanna. She had dropped her veil; her chin was up, her face stubborn. She went on in the same hard clear voice. "Ten years' worth of shares in trade, including the trade with Rhiyana, at family rates of exchange."

Aidan opened his mouth to protest. Khadijah herself prevented him, turning to her great-granddaughter with what could only be relish. "Ten years' shares, for the averting of a danger that might never be more than indirect?"

"Would you rather Sinan had my mother's share, and all that goes with it?" demanded Joanna.

"But—" said Aidan.

Neither paid him the least attention. They were merchants; haggling was their life's blood. And they were bent on making a tradesman of him, if only by proxy.

"You need never touch coin with your clean white hands," Joanna said when it was ended. She was not unduly dissatisfied, although it was evident even to Aidan that she had been outmatched. Two years' share in five caravans and trading ventures, aside from any that went to Rhiyana; of those he was to have five years' share. And with that, full guesting in Aleppo, and provisioning for his venture against Sinan, and mounts and remounts for himself and any who went with him. All to be overseen by the House of Ibrahim, through a steward of Khadijah's choosing and Joanna's approving. He need do no more than accept what was given him, and use it as he saw fit.

It was no more than royalty ever did. He did not know why he should feel as if he had been led on like a child. He who had done what he might with what his lands in Rhiyana could spare and his hosts in Outremer bestow, now had wealth in his own right: more than he could conceive of.

"If," said Khadijah, "you turn Sinan aside from the House of Ibrahim, without setting his servants and his sect against us. Aleppo is an Ismaili city; we live in Aleppo. We would prefer to continue in peace."

"That was not what I swore to do," Aidan said.

"You swore to exact payment for your kinsman's murder. You did not specify the nature of the payment."

"I'll kill him if I have to. What will you do to me then?"

"What can we do, except revoke the bargain? You will do as you must. So too shall we."

He could not quarrel with that. But there was still his pride to think of. "I won't fulfill my vow for your gold. If I hesitate to do murder, it will be for honor's sake."

"Of course," she said. "You are honorable above all. The

gold, if you fulfill the bargain, will be our gift of thanks. Surely you can accept a gift in return for a mighty service."

He looked hard at her. He could discern no laughter, no mockery of knightly scruples.

After a long moment he said, "As a gift, yes, I can accept it. If I am able to do all as you would wish. That, I cannot promise you."

"I understand," said Khadijah. "It is a bargain; it is witnessed. Allah's blessing be upon it."

20

Sayyida stifled a yawn. Hasan was asleep at last on his blanket beside the fountain, flushed with the fever that had kept him awake and fractious through the night; but morning and quiet and the song of falling water had lulled him. She rubbed the breast that he had bitten in his temper, not wanting to touch him and chance waking him again.

She was refusing to listen to fear. How fragile his life was; how many children died in infancy; how easily, how hideously easily, a fever could rise to burn the soul away. Fahimah had wound him with her own blue necklace and its amulets against evil. Mother had prayed. Laila had promised to pray, later, when she was properly purified after her night with Farouk.

None of them had shared the night's vigil. Fahimah had tried, but she was not as young as she had been, and Sayyida had not had the heart to wake her when she fell asleep.

Sayyida's yawn escaped at last, wide enough to crack her jaw, deep enough to feign for a blessed moment the relief of sleep. She opened her eyes from it, to meet Morgiana's.

The ifritah sat cross-legged next to Hasan, looking like a young man of Damascus: slender and beardless, a eunuch, and not one who accepted meekly his condition. The illusion was startling. Maybe there was magic in it; maybe it was only Morgiana in man's clothing, being Morgiana. "He has a fever," she said of Hasan.

Sayyida nodded wearily. "I was up all night with him. He's a little better now, I think."

Morgiana ran a light hand down his back. Sayyida swallowed the swift protest. He neither moved nor woke. Maybe his frown eased a little.

"I can't heal sickness," said Morgiana. "It's too subtle. All the myriad tiny demons . . ." She paused; she seemed to sense Sayyida's incomprehension. She shrugged. "No matter. He was sicker, earlier; I felt it. He's mending now."

Sayyida almost fell over. It was one thing to hope. To know —it was too much, all at once.

Morgiana's strong hand held her up. She leaned against it, glad of it. After a little while she straightened, took a breath. "It's silly. But I was so scared. I love him so much; he's so close still to not being at all."

"Not silly," said Morgiana. "Never silly, Sayyida."

Something in her tone made Sayyida stop and stare. She was different. Not gentler, exactly. She was fiercer, if anything. Woman-fierceness.

She did not look like a eunuch any longer, even in the turban, with daggers. She propped her chin on her fists and glared at the fountain's fall. "Why is it," she demanded, "just why is it that Allah makes us love what we can only lose?"

Sayyida blinked. She was too tired to be profound. She could only say, "We love it because we know we'll lose it; and we see Allah in it."

"That is not an answer. That is a circle."

"I'm sorry," said Sayyida. "I can't think. I keep wanting to fall asleep."

"Sleep, then. I'll watch the baby."

"No," Sayyida said, though she yearned to accept the gift. "Keep talking to me. What's troubling you? Is it the Frank?"

Morgiana bared her sharp white teeth. "Am I that obvious?"

"I don't know. Maybe not. I noticed how you looked at him, the day Ishak brought him to dinner. Maimoun wanted to throw out every dish we had, and buy new ones. Mother talked him out of it."

Morgiana snorted. It was almost laughter. "What would Maimoun have said if he had known all of what the Frank was?"

"What, a king's son? Ishak told me that. I'm not surprised. He looked noble, for an infidel."

"He's a little more than that," Morgiana said. "Did you notice how white he is, here where the sun stains every man black?"

Sayyida was puzzled, but she could answer, "Yes. I noticed. I wondered how he does it. To stay so perfectly pale. Like—"

Morgiana's face was still, waiting for Sayyida to see what a blind man could see. How white it was. At long last, comprehension pierced the fogs of her brain. "Then—he's—"

"His name means *fire*," Morgiana said, dry and deceptively calm. "He is one of two. Two such faces in the world; imagine it. The other is mage and king. He is mage and knight—emir, we would say. He is, for one of our kind, very young. He thinks himself quite old, and wise enough. He knows that he is beautiful. He thinks—I—"

Almost, she broke. She caught herself. "He thinks that I am good to look at. He will not love me carnally. He doesn't know me, he says. And if he knew me—" Her eyes squeezed shut; her fists came up. "O Allah! If he knew me he would hate me beyond any hope of healing."

"Not if he's like you," Sayyida said, "and knows you as I know you. He can't be innocent of blood himself, if he's the warrior he looks to be."

Morgiana laughed. It was horrible, because it was so light and sweet, and so empty of hope. "But you see, it's what blood I'm guilty of. Do you remember the Frank I killed?

That was his sister's son. He has sworn to destroy me and the master who sent me. And he thinks . . . he thinks I may help him find the murderer. He thinks that none of us can harm his own kind."

"You didn't know," said Sayyida.

"Do you think that can matter to a vow sworn? When he knows what I am and what I have done, he will raise all his power against me. He will blast me with his hate."

Sayyida was silent, hunting for words. All the Franks that infested the world, and this should be the one whose kin Morgiana's master had forced her to kill. An ifrit—a Christian ifrit.

She spoke carefully, trying not to be too unkind. He could not help it that he was an infidel. "He'd be a fool to hate you. You only did as you were commanded, under your oath. Surely he's capable of understanding that."

"Does it matter? I did it. The first—I could talk my way out of that. The second was a child. The third, whom my master has this morning commanded me to take, is a woman. I refused. But my oath is strong, and it tears at me. I don't know how long I can hold against it." She held out her hands. Steady as they had always been, unerring with a dagger, now they shook. "He will ask again. And again. Until I do it, or I break."

Sayyida clasped those trembling hands and held them as tightly as she could. "You won't. You'll be strong. He'll learn to see it, your Frankish ifrit. Doesn't his god teach forgiveness?"

"His mother was a pagan. Sometimes it pleases him to remember it."

"Morgiana," said Sayyida. "Morgiana, stop it. You've talked to him, haven't you? What has he said to you?"

"Nothing. Air and wind. I," she said, "have shamed myself utterly. I told him that I loved him."

Sayyida sucked in a breath. "That was . . . very brave." Forward, she almost said.

Morgiana heard it. "Yes, I was presumptuous. I couldn't

help myself. He was there, and looking at me, and beginning —beginning—to incline toward me. I fell like a pigeon with an arrow through its heart."

Sayyida tried to understand. It was all like a story, or a song. She had thought that real people were less passionate than song-people; more sensible. There was always dinner to think of, or the chance of a baby. Though in the middle of it, babies and dinner tended rather to get themselves forgotten.

Morgiana did not look like a princess in a poem. Those were all dark-eyed languid beauties with queenly haunches. But her passion and her despair—those were larger than any life Sayyida had known.

"Does it always strike you so?" Sayyida's tongue asked before she could stop it.

"No!" Morgiana looked less angry than simply wild. "I've never—" She was blushing like any fool of a girl. "I never wanted a man before."

"Never? Never at all?"

The turbaned head shook, short and sharp. "Of course you don't believe me. Who would? I always belonged to the Master of Alamut; since he is always male, and I female . . ." She laughed again, raw and unlovely, like a raven's cry. "What man can touch such a creature as I am, unless I will it? And I never have. I was always—I was cold. Yes. Cold fire, one of them said of me. I was a dagger and a mission, and when the mission failed me, an oath. I was never anything that a man could touch."

"Until you saw the Frank."

"Until I saw one who was like me. Who moved in magic. Who was beauty bare. Then I knew what all the singing meant.

"And he was born to be my enemy."

Sayyida was still holding Morgiana's hands. She kissed them, to stop their bitter, bone-deep trembling. "Sister," she said. "Sister, trust in God. If He brought him to you, surely

He will show him the truth. Are you any less oathbound than he?"

Morgiana pulled free. "Oh, to be so wise! I who am as old as hills, I who walk arm in arm with the Angel of Death, I know nothing of love, except that it is pain."

"Not always," said Sayyida. "Even for you."

"Then pray for me, child. I have no prayer left."

She was never one to linger for farewells. Sayyida stared at the emptied air, and sighed.

As if Morgiana's going had broken a spell, Hasan woke and began to fret. Sayyida gathered him up. For a miracle, he quieted, sucking his fist with an angry ferocity that was like nothing so much as Morgiana's own. Sayyida kissed his hair. It was damp, but his brow beneath them was cool.

Her heart leaped. He *was* cool. She clasped him close, until he squawked in protest. "Oh, love!" she sang to him. "Oh, light of my eyes! Thanks be to Allah!"

It seemed all a part of her joy that she should look up to see Maimoun standing by the wall, staring at her. She scrambled up with Hasan in her arms. "Maimoun! He had a fever, it was so fierce, I was so scared, but now, look, it's gone."

Maimoun said nothing. Something in his face made her stop. Hasan's weight dragged at her. She shifted him to her hip. "What is it? Is there trouble? Is it—is it Father? Or Ishak? Or—"

"No." He said it coldly, more to silence her, it seemed, than to ease her fears.

Maimoun was never cold. Sullen, yes, sometimes. Dour when he encountered someone, or something, whom he did not approve of; because he had been trained, rigorously, to be polite, and politeness was not his native condition. Maimoun always wanted to say exactly what he thought.

It was frightening to see him so still, not even frowning; looking at her as if she had no honest place in his world. "I thought," he said, "that she was lying. Because of Hasan."

"What—" Sayyida was baffled. And, more than ever, afraid. "Who—"

"She envies you," said Maimoun reflectively. "I think she hates you, at least a little. You have a son. She has none."

Hasan began to struggle on Sayyida's hip. She held him more tightly, hardly aware of him, intent on his father. "Are you talking about Laila?"

"Or maybe," he went on as if she were not there, "it honestly is concern for me, and for the family's honor. Even she might be moved to think of such things, under sufficient provocation. Such as"—and now he was not so cold; his breath came faster, his cheeks flushed in hectic patches, as in a fever —"such as that my wife disports herself in our own garden with—with—"

Sayyida heard him in growing horror. But more than that, in anger. Neither was something she was used to. She was— yes, on the whole, she was a placid person, happy with the gifts that Allah gave her, not inclined to rebel against the life He ordained for her, except once in a great while, when Morgiana—

She heard herself say with perfect calm, "Disporting myself, Maimoun? With whom? Or what?"

Maimoun choked on it. "With *what,* indeed. A man, Sayyida—a man, I could almost endure. But *that*—"

"Are you telling me," she asked carefully, "that I am not to entertain friends in my father's garden?"

He laughed. It tried to be light and wild. It sounded merely strangled. "Friends. Oh, friends, indeed. Did they leave him anything when they cut him? Is he better at it than I?"

She drew herself up, heedless of Hasan who had begun to wail. "He?" she asked. "Him? No man but you or Father or Ishak has ever entered our garden; at least, to talk to me."

"No man, no."

"Ah," she said, letting herself understand at last. "You thought—yes, it would look like that, wouldn't it? Especially if your mind was prepared." She shook her head. "You know Laila. You shouldn't let her chaff you."

"Was it chaffing that set you here, locked in passionate embrace with Bahram the eunuch?"

The wilder he was, the colder she became. "So; that's what she calls herself. I never thought to ask."

"Then you don't deny it?"

"What's to deny? Except the embrace. I was only holding her up; and even at that, Hasan was between us."

"You brought my son—into—"

"My son," she said with pointed emphasis, "and my friend, whose name is Morgiana, and who is admittedly rather eccentric, are on the best of terms. I see no objection in it. A woman, after all, should understand babies, for when she has her own."

"A woman? That?" Maimoun folded his arms tightly across his chest, as if to keep himself from hitting her. "What do you take me for? That is Bahram the eunuch, who came this morning for a dagger with a silver hilt. He has a predilection for them. As, it would seem, for men's wives."

Between frustration and plain tiredness, Sayyida almost burst into tears. "She does *not!* She is my friend. She has been my friend since I was a child."

He went white, and then scarlet. "You are lying."

Maybe he lacked somewhat of conviction. She was too far gone to care. "I do not lie. That is Morgiana. Morgiana is my friend. I will not be held guilty of a sin which I have never committed, nor wanted to commit."

Maimoun swallowed visibly, and pulled at his beard as he always did when he was caught in the wrong: as if to assure himself that he was still the man; he was still her lord and master.

As he was, as Allah had willed it. She was finding it very hard to be a good Muslim. She kept wanting to damn all boys and their idiocies.

"Morgiana is my friend," Sayyida's temper said for her.

"Laila is corroded with envy. What kind of man are you, that you believe a known and notorious twister of the truth, over your own wife?"

Maimoun snapped erect. She had gone too far. Soon, she was even going to care. "Hereafter," he said, "hereafter, you will keep to the house; you will attend to your duties; you will not idle your days away in the garden with creatures of dubious gender and still more dubious reputation. Do you hear me, woman? I forbid you to see her. I forbid you to speak with her. I forbid you to hold converse with any but your most immediate kin. Do you understand me?"

"I understand you," she said. Hasan began to howl in earnest. She jogged him on her hip, to small effect. "Will my lord permit his humble slave to depart for the duties to which he has confined her?"

He had to know that he was being mocked; but he was male, and glorious in his lordship over the lowly female. He raised his chin. "Go," he commanded her.

Maybe Iblis had a hand in it. Sayyida could not make herself regret what she had said. Any of it.

Maimoun did not know how right he was, to forbid her Morgiana's company. Morgiana made her think at angles; made her forget that she was woman and wife. She had never disobeyed Maimoun, however strangling-close he kept her, except for Morgiana's sake.

Some things, even her husband was not wise to touch.

He had called her a liar. She had sins in plenty to her account, but lying had never been one of them. Even he should have been able to see that.

"Arrogant," she muttered to Hasan in the stifling room that would, if Maimoun had his way, be her prison. "Pompous. Self-righteous. *Child*. Everything must be his way and no other. The Prophet—may Allah bless him—said that my husband must be my protector. He never said anything of my being my husband's slave."

Hasan, nursing with vigor, took no notice of his mother's troubles.

"No, and what should it matter to you? You're blessed of Allah. You can do and be whatever your soul conceives of. And if it suits your whim to rule your wife's every utterance . . ." She wound her fingers in his hair, tugging very lightly. "You'll not do that, at least. Not if I can help it. *You* will trust your wife; you will let her bear the weight of her own honor. She can, you know. She's a woman, and maybe she has neither faith nor reason, but she does understand plain good sense. If," she said, "she is allowed."

And if she was not, then she would do as she pleased. It was no more than a man did; or a woman whose man had any sense of his own.

It was possible, without being overly conspicuous, to avoid going near Maimoun at all. Since Sayyida grew big with Hasan, and then while she nursed him, Maimoun had slept apart from her, except when he simply wanted to be with her. She did not want to remember how pleased she had been, to see how often he came and lay beside her and did not try to do what men did with their wives: holding her, only, and Hasan warmly content between them. Now, she kept the door shut, and if he knocked, she did not hear. And since Shahin and Rafiq were sufficient to wait on guests, Sayyida did not see need to wait on her father and her husband when they were alone. She had duties enough elsewhere.

She told herself that she hardly missed him. What had he ever done but bind her with caprice, and call it duty and honor?

Tonight he did not knock. He came in as if he had a right to trespass, and not as if he tried to be circumspect about it. Sayyida had her back to the door; she stiffened it. Hasan had been slow to fall asleep. Now that he was quiet, she had no desire at all to wake him for his father's sake.

She felt Maimoun come to stand over her. He smelled of rosewater. She throttled a sneeze.

"I know you're awake," he said.

He knew altogether too much for anyone's comfort. She thought of defying him, but it was late, and she was tired, and her hold on her grudge was slipping. She turned to face him.

He looked almost as contrite as she would have liked, with stiffness over it, for after all he had his pride. He chewed his lip, not quite looking at her. It was too dim to be sure, but maybe he flushed. "How is the baby?" he asked, after a long pause.

"Asleep," she answered. It was not precisely friendly, but neither was it hostile.

He knelt beside her. He knew better than to touch Hasan; he was not ready, yet, to touch Sayyida. Her hand, which had no pride, wanted to wind itself with his, and kiss the square clever fingers, and smooth the scar on the back where, in the folly of his apprenticeship, he had caught a spatter of molten steel.

She kept her hand where it belonged, knotted by her hip. He would never apologize. She did not intend to.

It felt strange, that obstinacy. Light and hollow, and yet immovable. She had never refused to give in before. Not on anything that mattered.

Maybe he would not ask her to. He ventured a smile, a brush of fingers over her hair. "You look pretty tonight."

She could be that, with a little effort. Not now, rumpled and scowling and hollow-eyed with too much Hasan and not enough sleep.

Men had no sense. "You're flattering me," she said. "Do you want something?"

This was certainly a flush. "Maybe I want my wife. Is that too much to ask?"

"It depends on what you're asking for."

"You've been avoiding me."

"I've been obeying you. Keep to the house, you said. Attend to my duties. Talk to no one but my closest kin. None of that leaves much space for lesser things."

"I am a lesser thing?"

"You are my husband. You command, and I obey."

"But I never—" He stopped. "Now see here. If your conduct had been honorable to begin with—"

She rose in a white heat. Because of Hasan, she did not scream, or spit in his face. "When have I ever been anything but honorable? *When?*"

"You are defying me now."

She gulped air. "There. There it is. Honor is whatever you choose to call it. I have none; I can have none: no matter what I do, you tell me that I do it wrongly, and without honor. You don't want a wife, Maimoun. You want a slave."

"At least a slave would pretend to be obedient."

"Oh?" she asked with vicious sweetness. "It's not the truth you want, but pretense? Is it as simple as that?"

His voice rose with his hands. "You know it's not!"

"Hush!" she hissed at him. "You'll wake the baby."

He was remarkably in control of himself: he shut his mouth. After a moment, much more softly, he began, "Sayyida." He swallowed as if it hurt him. "Sayyida, this is ridiculous. We've always got on so well. Why have you taken so against me?"

She stared at him, incredulous. "I, against you? Who was it who started it all?"

Clearly he was trying to be wise, and prudent, and magnanimous. He must have spent days working up to it. "You must admit that that . . . woman . . . is hardly fit company for a young mother of good family."

"She was good enough for me when I was only a child of middling good family."

"That was when you were a child." He reached for her. "Sayyida." Her name sounded rather pleasant, the way he said it. Even when she was ready to hit him. "A man and his wife should live in harmony. No?"

"Yes." His hands were on her, not doing much, simply being warm and solid and inescapably there. She did not know why she should think of shackles. He smiled at her, and she had no power over herself; she felt her lips twitch in response. It was not even that he was a handsome man. He was not. Pleasing, that was all, in youth and smooth skin and clear brown eyes, and in that he was hers.

She sighed a little. Her arms had found their way about him. His solidity was familiar, the way his bones fit beneath the skin, the scent of him under the sweetness of new bath and rosewater. Her heart swelled just so when she held Hasan. Or, no, not quite so. Her body knew very well the difference between her son and her son's father.

They lay down. She did not know which of them thought of it first. When he set hand to the cord of her drawers, she did not stop him. Perhaps she should have. She spared a glance for Hasan, who slept oblivious. Maimoun's face came between; he had the look he always had in these moments, a little strained, a little abstracted, as if he had forgotten that she was there.

If he had meant to extract a promise from her, he never came to it. In fact he never finished what he had been leading up to at all; and she was not inclined to remind him.

When he slept as men did when they had satisfied themselves, cradled on her breast as heedless-heavy as Hasan, she held him and played a little with the curls of his beard, and stared into the dark. Her body was at peace with itself, aching a little, perhaps, but a pleasurable ache. Her mind had shifted not a hair's width. "I love you," she said very softly to the weight on her breast, and she meant it, though she had just begun to know it. "I'll obey you in everything you ask, if only it stays within the bounds of reason. I'll be your wife and your servant, and be glad. But some things, even you can't touch. Some things go too deep."

Some things were too simple. That was all there was to it; all there needed to be.

"Someday you'll understand. You'll see that I can be myself, and guard my own honor, and still belong to you." She paused. "Allah willing," she said.

21

Merchants, thought Aidan sourly. Aleppo was crawling with them. Most seemed to have a hand in Sinan's pocket, or to owe him loyalty of one sort or another. Though every one owed his first loyalty to his own house.

It was hard to be a Frank here, and a nobleman, and a witch. Damascus was alien but enchanting, like the music of the east. There was no enchantment in Aleppo. Its walls closed in like prison walls. The need to wait on provisioning, on the finding of mounts and pack-camels, on the propensity of easterners for taking their leisure about anything that did not seem to them to be deathly urgent, wound him about in coils of frustration.

Only Joanna kept him from riding out alone and bearding Sinan in his lair. He was allowed to see her every day, for as long as either of them could stand it. There were always attendants. The black eunuch, inevitably. Often her maid. Once or twice a veiled and swaddled aunt of impeccable probity. None of them ever said anything. They were simply there, watching, listening with bland patience.

At night she was guarded like a sultan's treasury. He dared not even come to her in dreams.

He prowled instead. About the house; in the gardens. Even in the city, though his old horror of walls and crowding humanity had come back fullfold. It was still better than waiting, endlessly, for the House of Ibrahim to loose him on Masyaf.

Or for his own will to muster itself to leave Joanna.

There was the truth. He could not bear to leave her. Even

the maddening little he could have of her, here, where her kin stood so strongly on guard over her life and honor.

One more day, he told himself, more than once. One more day, he would tarry. Then he would go, and be damned to them all.

He was thinking of it as he came back to his chamber after a wretched few moments with Joanna. She had been unwell, pale and tired, a little green about the edges; and unwontedly sharp with him when he asked if she were ill. Her denial was nothing short of fierce. But worse than that was her visible and palpable rejection of him: of the touch he ventured, guards be damned; of the touch that was more than touch, of which none but she could know. All she wanted of him was his absence.

He was too shocked to do aught but give her what she wanted. Too shocked at first even to be angry; still less to wield his power, and discover what had turned her so against him.

The anger was beginning to rise now. He turned in the room, swirling the Bedu robes she was so fond of. Arslan was nowhere about. This morning's guardhounds, Tuman and Zangi, had prudently drawn off to the balcony. A moment more and he would throw off sparks.

Someone was at the door. A servant, with a summons. He was wanted. He must come. And yet, the man said with eyes and tone and face, he should not.

Because it was not anyone in the House who desired his presence. It was the atabeg, the regent of Aleppo. The one who had set the Assassins on Saladin. The ally of Sinan.

His messenger had ample escort. Nubians, huge and demon-black, bristling with steel. No less a force than Karim endeavored to hold them off.

Aidan greeted them with his sweetest smile. "I am wanted?" he inquired.

His mood had lightened marvelously. Even when it was made clear that he was to come unarmed and unattended.

Even when they searched him to be certain, and were neither gentle nor respectful. They could not object to his leaving his weapons with his mamluks, although they would have liked to. It was the mamluks who raised the protest, which he quelled with a single level glance.

He was not bound. But, they made it very clear, they would do what they must, to keep him from escaping.

He had no such intention. Here was danger; it worked in him like wine. Karim thought him bereft of his senses. So he was. He always had been.

His guards knew only that he was wanted; it was not their office to wonder why. But he could guess. He had made no effort to proclaim abroad who he was, and where he had come from, and why he was here, but neither had he made a secret of it. Any spy worth his wages could have discovered that the House of Ibrahim harbored a Frank sworn to bitter enmity against the Master of Masyaf.

They set him on a mule, which was not a compliment: it was a small mule, and headstrong even for its kind. He could do little to lessen the length of his legs, but he could come to an accommodation with the beast. It carried him with only the essential minimum of disgruntlement. He hooked his knee over the pommel and took his ease, and let the atabeg's servants conduct him to the citadel. His insouciance, he was pleased to see, was fraying their tempers alarmingly.

"Franks," one of them muttered.

Another spat, just aft of the mule's tail.

He showed them his fine white teeth. He let it dawn on them that it was not a human smile. There were too many teeth, too white and too long and too sharp.

If the citadel had been a few furlongs farther than it was, he might have had the atabeg's dogs in a truly splendid state. For, once they had counted teeth, they would take note of the cast of a face, the pallor of its skin, the gleam of its eyes. And what those eyes were . . .

As it was, their own eyes were rolling white, and they were

beginning to remember older gods than Allah. They came up the last of the steep winding way, breathing hard with more than exertion, and surrendered him with heartfelt gladness to the guard of the citadel. Turks, all of those, in black livery. He went as quietly as a tiger on a chain. Fear might have been wise, or apprehension at the least. But he was not a wise creature.

He was made to wait, and wait long. He suffered it in patience. This was battle, and in battle he knew how to stand fast. He amused himself in watching people come and go through the anteroom in which he was set. Most, seeing the robes, took him for a desert tribesman. Some wondered at the guard about him. A bandit, they concluded; a criminal brought to justice. He took them aback with a smile, lounging where he had been bidden to sit, composing a satire on the Master of the Assassins. That most deadly of bardic arts fitted itself surprisingly well to the eastern modes; and Arabic was God's own gift to the connoisseur of curses.

He had not been so light of heart since the tournament in Acre. A battle, that was what he had needed. The prospect of an open adversary; the sweet savor of danger. It was all about him here. He almost regretted that he had not worn his robe of honor. Saladin's name was not spoken with love in this place. A man who wore it on his sleeve might find all the fighting he could wish for.

"What are you singing?" someone asked.

Aidan turned his head. One bold soul had pierced his wall of guards. A very young one. Baldwin's age; Thibaut's. He looked, mercifully, like neither of them. He was a Turk, handsome as they would reckon it, plump and soft to Aidan's eyes, dressed as plainly as a servant. But no servant would carry his head at that arrogant angle.

"What are you singing?" he repeated, clear and imperious.

"Scurrilities," Aidan answered him, "hardly fit for young ears to hear."

"And who are you, to be the judge of that?"

"Who are you, to question me?"

The boy's narrow eyes went wide. No one, it was readily apparent, had ever dared to address him so. He tossed his oiled braids. "I am the Prince Ismail. Who are you?"

"Ah; so you're a king's son, too? That makes two of us."

"How can you be the son of a king?"

"As easily as you," said Aidan.

"You are insolent," Prince Ismail said, as if he must say it in order to believe it.

"I only give back what I am given. It's a failing, if you like. I suppose I was badly brought up."

"I think you were," said the boy. "Why won't you tell me your name?"

"You haven't given me the chance. My name," said Aidan, "is Aidan."

"What kind of name is that?"

Aidan laughed. "What kind of name is Ismail? I come from Rhiyana, where everyone has a name like mine. I have others that may suit you better. I'm Lathan, for my father, and Gereint, for my father's brother, and Michael, because I have to be called something that sounds Christian, and—"

"You are a Christian?" A horned devil, he might have said, in that tone.

"I'm worse than that. I'm a Frank."

Aidan had not thought those eyes could widen any further. They were almost round, black and shiny as olives, and completely unafraid. "A Frank." Ismail let his breath out slowly. "So that is what a Frank looks like. Your hair is the wrong color. It ought to be yellow."

"Rhiyanans are dark. We're black Celts, you see. It's true Franks you're thinking of, and Northmen. We're the old people, the folk they tried to drive into the sea."

That meant nothing to a Seljuk prince whose cousins still rode wild in the outlands of the east: the drivers, and never the driven. He looked at Aidan as one looks at an exotic beast in a cage, and sighed in pleasure. Clearly he had not been so well diverted in time out of mind. "Now I see why you have no manners. You know no better. You should learn, if you want to leave here with a whole skin. My atabeg is very strict."

"Maybe he makes exceptions for princes."

"But you see, you aren't a real prince. Real princes are civilized."

"Truly?" Aidan asked. "Is that what it is to be civilized? To be rude to strangers?"

"You're mad, I think," said Ismail, as if it explained everything.

"My thanks," Aidan said.

"Mad," Ismail repeated. He leaned closer. "Why are your eyes like that?"

Aidan veiled them, unthinking; but his will opened them wide. He smiled. "I was born so."

"Are you human?"

"No."

Ismail nodded as if he had expected it. Aidan was sure of it then. The boy was simple. No idiot, certainly, nor by any means dull-witted, but something in him had not grown as it should. He knew, from training, when to be wary, but it made no mark on him. He regarded Aidan in open and fearless fascination. "Franks are very strange," he said.

"I'm strange for a Frank."

"You must see well in the dark."

"Quite well," said Aidan.

"I should like to be able to see like that," Ismail said. "Can you do magic, too? My nurse used to tell me that Franks are sorcerers, and that they take their powers from Iblis. Are you a slave of Iblis?"

"Certainly not," Aidan said, but without heat. "The last of my names is for the archangel who defeated him. I'm not likely to bow down before him."

Ismail was disappointed. "People always talk about magic, but nobody ever does any. Sometimes they pretend, but I can see. It's all a trick."

"Not all of it," said Aidan. "I didn't say I couldn't do any. Only that I have no pact with the devil."

"But that's where it comes from."

"Not mine."

Ismail eyed him, wanting to be convinced, unwilling to be gulled yet again. Aidan gave him a handful of fire.

"Ismail!"

The voice was high, but it was not a woman's. Ismail looked round sullenly but with trained obedience. The creature who swept down upon him was as attenuated as a Byzantine angel, sweet-scented as a woman, bearing the remnants of what might have been remarkable beauty. But it was all stunted and soured, like a frostbitten fruit.

It was not the atabeg. After the first shock, Aidan saw that clearly enough. He quenched a sudden surge of pity. For Ismail; for the people whom Ismail had been bred to rule.

The eunuch snatched his charge away, sparing Aidan only a single, outraged glance. Ismail seemed to lack the will for resistance. All his self was bent upon the fist which he pressed to his heart, and to the cool strange fire that quivered in it. It would fade, but not for a while. And he would always remember that he had had it; that he had held magic in his hand.

As the boy disappeared through an inner door, Aidan's own summons came at last. He did not think that the coincidence was intentional. The child had escaped his wardens and wandered out of his accustomed bounds. Aidan hoped that his punishment would not be too cruel.

For his own, he cared little. He rose as the chamberlain beckoned, his guards rising with him, their glances as darting-wild as the Nubians' had been. They had heard his colloquy with Ismail; some had the wits to understand it. He smiled at them and followed in the chamberlain's wake.

The regent of Aleppo was, like Ismail, a Turk: amply and impressively fleshed, but solid for all of that, and strong. There was a sword across his knees as he sat in his hall of audience; the hand that rested on its hilt bore the calluses of a swordsman.

And yet the weapon itself was almost too rich for the wielding, crusted with gems and gold. Likewise the atabeg. His splendor put even Joanna's Uncle Karim to shame; Aidan's eyes were dazzled. One jewel alone, the ruby that burned in his turban, could have purchased a respectable fief in Francia.

It said something for the man, that Aidan had seen his splendor second, after his face and his warrior's hands. And only after all of that, did Aidan recall the significance of a Muslim without a beard. Gumushtekin, like Ismail's nursemaid, was a eunuch.

His voice might have been a light tenor: male enough, and deep enough, for the purpose. His eyes held none of the mute endurance which Aidan had begun to regard as the mark of his kind. They were clear, hard, and subtly bitter, facing this world which had robbed him of his manhood, and daring it to master him. Indeed, he had mastered it. He who could have no sons of his own, was father in all but fact to the rightful Sultan of Syria. And if that sultan lacked aught of will or wit, then Gumushtekin would supply it, and rule as he chose in the child's name. Higher than that, no eunuch might hope to rise.

Aidan shivered. There were no eunuchs in Rhiyana. He was too keenly aware, now, of how delicate a creature a man was, how easily he could be unmanned.

Perhaps Gumushtekin comprehended Aidan's discomfiture. Having dismissed all but two of the phalanx of guards, he seemed to forget that he had summoned the Frank, and turned back to the attendants who waited upon his pleasure.

That, Aidan could understand, and easily contend with. He sat unbidden, at his ease, letting his eyes take in the beauties of the chamber. Its tiles were gold and blue and sea green; its pillars were like young trees wound with vines; high on its walls flowed a *sûrah* of the Koran, wrought in black and gold on silver tiles. He puzzled it out, word by word.

The atabeg was well versed in calculated insolence, but Aidan was older than he, and wilder. It was Gumushtekin who spoke first; it was Aidan who took his time in replying, who in fact did not hear or heed him until one of the guards raised a hand to strike. He flexed like a cat before the blow, eluding it with fluid ease, lowering his eyes and his mind to the mortal man who had brought him here. The guard let his hand fall, flinching, though Aidan had not even glanced at him. Aidan's eyes were on the atabeg. He raised a brow, and waited.

Gumushtekin smiled thinly: a tribute to a master of his own art. "You are, I presume, the Frank with the outlandish name, who suffers himself to be called Khalid."

"I am Aidan of Caer Gwent."

"Just so," said Gumushtekin. "You are also, therefore, the servant of the leper king, and the spy of the usurper in Damascus."

Aidan smiled very slightly. "I allow you your interpretation of Saladin's position, but pray allow me a little of the truth. I'm no spy."

"You would be a fool to admit it," said the atabeg. He clapped his hands.

A new company of guards conducted new prisoners into the regent's presence. Three of them. Even beneath bruises and battering and one gloriously swollen eye, Aidan knew them. Arslan was the least sorely wounded and the most nearly contrite as he met his master's stare. The Kipchaks grinned broadly; Timur revealed a gap where a tooth had been.

Aidan rose slowly. The grins lost somewhat of their luster. Arslan had the grace to pale under his bruises. "Well?" Aidan asked them.

They glanced at one another. Even Arslan seemed disinclined to begin. It was the atabeg who said, "These gentlemen have waxed somewhat heated in their defense of your honor and that of your master in Damascus."

"And why not?" cried Timur. "People were spitting on our sultan's name, my lord, and calling him a liar and a thief. We sat still for it, my lord. But then they called you a skulking Frankish dog. Were we to endure that, my lord?"

"He forgot," said Ilkhan by way of explanation, "and let out our old battle cry." He glanced at Gumushtekin. "The one that refers to his lordship's . . . attributes."

Or lack thereof. Aidan drew his brows together.

"That brought the watch," Timur said. "Ilkhan lost his temper. He started singing the song we used to sing when we were riding herd on the siege engines outside Aleppo. They recognized it, of course."

"And hauled us in," said Ilkhan. "They think we're spies. Now, I ask you. Would any spy be as obvious as that?"

"They were," said Gumushtekin, "in a shop which is known to sell wine."

Timur grimaced. "It's horrible," he said. "Worse than Egyptian beer."

Aidan regarded them all. His eye fixed on Arslan, who alone had said nothing. "And you, sir? Where do you come into this?"

"Late," answered Arslan, "and unavailing. I found the battle in full fly; I was netted with the rest." He bowed his head, which had lost its turban. "My fault, my lord. I should never have let these two off the leash."

Aidan did not try to deny it. Nor did he voice a rebuke. Arslan did not need it; the imps would not heed it. And Gumushtekin was waiting, silent, clear-eyed, and dangerous.

"Spying," said Aidan, "is not our purpose here."

"Perhaps not," the regent said. "But sedition may be. You are a Frank; you come from Jerusalem, you tarried in Damascus. These mamluks who proclaim themselves to be yours, have ridden under the upstart's banner. Why should you not undertake at your leisure to search out our secrets? Both Damascus and Jerusalem would pay you handsomely."

Timur laughed. His voice was barely broken, and sometimes it slipped; he sounded like a child. "Oh, sir! You don't know my lord at all. He's a Frank. He'd die before he'd dirty his fingers with money."

"He'd die before he thought of it," Ilkhan put in. "He's horribly impractical. It would never occur to him to sell anybody anything."

"Spying is for commoners," said Arslan. "Our lord is a prince."

Aidan broke in on their chorus. "My lord," he said to the atabeg, "would you trust these young idiots with anything that smacked of a secret?"

Gumushtekin's lips twitched. Very much in spite of himself, he was amused. "I might not. But you are not I."

"Nor am I that magnitude of a fool."

The ruby flamed as the atabeg inclined his head. "Perhaps you are not. But the reputation of your race, and the inebriation of your servants, would argue against it."

Timur squawked in outrage. "We never got as far as the wine!"

Arslan was quieter. "Are you calling our lord a skulking dog of a Frank?"

"That might not be wise," said Gumushtekin, "even if it were true." He turned his gaze on Aidan, the laughter in it like light on deep water; and dark things moving beneath. "I speak no word of dogs or of fools. But of skulkers . . . Do you deny that you serve the upstart in Damascus?"

Aidan sat again where he had been, cross-legged on the carpet, and let them all wait. When every eye was on him, every mind leaping with impatience, he said, "I serve myself, and my given word. That I have been known to the Lord Saladin, I will not deny; nor that he has looked on me with favor. But I have never been his servant."

"Yet you came from him to us; you made no secret of it."

"Should that not prove that I tell the truth? I am kin to the House of Ibrahim; I came here with its caravan, as guard to my kinswoman, who has come to sojourn among her mother's people."

"It is said," said Gumushtekin, "that you are more than kin to her."

Aidan clenched deep within, but his face was calm. "In strict fact, I am rather less. Her mother was wife to my sister's son." He smiled his sweet deadly smile. "Are you going to condemn her too as a spy?"

"I condemn no one," said Gumushtekin. "I merely seek the truth. It is not common for a Frank to enter our city; still less for him to enter it companioned by a troop of our enemy's mamluks. Surely I can be forgiven a modicum of suspicion."

"That depends on what you suspect."

The atabeg shifted his bulk. A servant sprang to aid him; he accepted a cushion, frowning, his mind fixed on the prisoner before him. "I suspect danger to my city and ill-will toward the lord in whose name I hold this office. All that you are, proclaims you enemy."

"So I am," Aidan said. "But not to you, unless you hinder me."

The black eyes narrowed. "You dare to threaten us?"

"I tell you truth. I am a hunter, lord atabeg. My quarry is none of yours, nor shall I linger long in your domain."

"What do you hunt?"

Aidan showed a gleam of teeth. "Assassins."

The air chilled and tautened. Gumushtekin was still; and Aidan, in the center of it.

Aidan let his eyes wander, as if idly, in the silence. There was more than fear here, or even hate. There was a sharpening of awareness; a fixing of will upon him, a taste on the tongue like cold steel.

His body eased, secure in its element. He smiled with lazy pleasure. "There are," he said, "three of them here."

Gumushtekin's jaw flexed. He had been aware of one.

Aidan smiled wider. His eye found each. The one who was obvious: the youth in white that here was the color of death, with the eyes of a dreamer or a madman. The two who had been hidden: the chamberlain in his silks and his servility, and the guard who was closest to the atabeg's person, most cherished and most trusted of his servants. Aidan inclined his head to the last. "Tell your master," he said, "that I shall come to demand an accounting. For my kinsman; for the child who died untimely."

The guard stood unmoving, but his fist clenched on the hilt of his sword. In his eyes was death. He had been betrayed; he had failed of his duty. He would die.

"No," Aidan said, purring it. "Not until you have been my messenger." He gathered power in his hand and held it, lightly, straining against the bonds of his will. The guard could see it. His fear was sweet. Aidan set a single word deep in him, where no power of his could cast it out: "Go."

He went. The others watched, mute.

The atabeg was sorely shaken. He was like all the rest: he never truly comprehended the power of Alamut, until he saw it bare. His guard, his mamluk, his cherished possession, whom he had raised from a child, had never been his at all. So close, the Assassin could come. So easily.

He would not have been mortal if he had loved the one who stripped him of his complacency. He was lord enough, and king enough, not to call in the executioners. He said, "You are no friend to me or mine."

"No enemy, either," Aidan said.

"There is nothing between."

"My lord is entitled to his judgment."

Gumushtekin's lips were thin for a man so richly fleshed. They thinned to vanishing; he drew himself up. "I might best serve my city and my lord, by handing you over to our ally in Masyaf."

"You might. You might also win the open enmity of Jerusalem, and bring Damascus down anew upon you."

"Do you matter so much in the high places of the world?"

"Let us say," said Aidan, "that I'm an excellent excuse."

The atabeg did not believe him. Not quite. But the seed of doubt was large enough to give him pause. "Shut up in my prison and held for ransom, you would bring down no army upon us. Dead, you would cease to trouble us at all."

"I doubt that you can hold me. I doubt very much that you can kill me."

It was the simplicity of it that caught Gumushtekin and held him speechless. It was not even arrogance. It was merely the truth.

"Let me go," said Aidan, gently, quietly. "Give me my servants and leave their punishment to me. I can promise that it will be just, and that it will not be light. And that I shall execute it well beyond the bounds of your city."

Gumushtekin had no words even yet. He barely understood what Aidan offered. Aidan said it again. "You have no need of me here, whether alive in your dungeons or dead on your scaffold. Let me go, give me my mamluks, and I will leave your city. I give you my oath that I will betray none of your secrets; for truly I am no enemy of yours, but only of the spider in his web in Masyaf."

"You were better dead," said the atabeg. But slowly. As if he had begun to doubt it.

He was thinking, clear as a shout, of his alliance with Sinan. Of promises given and received. Of two trusted servants who were not his own; and one who was openly Sinan's, who seemed now no more than a feint.

Aidan let him think. He gnawed his lip. He looked without love at the dog of a Frank who so troubled his peace.

He said, "Very well. You live; you go free. I banish you from my city. If after tomorrow's sunset you are found within these walls, your life is forfeit."

"And my mamluks?" Aidan asked.

"They share the ban."

They were not remarkably cast down. Aidan brought them to heel with a glance and a toss of the head; they came willingly, the Kipchaks with a hint of a swagger that drew growls from the guards and a hiss from Arslan. The latter had the greater effect.

Aidan, oblivious as a prince should be to his servants' infelicities, bowed to the atabeg in Frankish fashion. He voiced no thanks. When he turned to go, there was outrage, that he should turn his back on the lord of the city. He stared it down. Coolly, with his mamluks in his wake, he left the regent's presence.

22

After Aidan had gone, Joanna sat unmoving, hardly thinking. Not daring to think. The roiling in her middle threatened to become all of her; bile seared her throat. She choked it down.

It was easier for him. He could go out. She was not allowed. Her every movement was watched and guarded. His presence every day was a torment: to have him so close, within her arms' reach; to knot her hands in her skirt, to keep from clutching him. She might have touched him. Easily. But she dared not. For if she did, she knew that she could not let go.

Or that she would claw his eyes out.

She knew where he slept: he had told her. He had not been fool enough or mad enough, yet, to enter the harem and snatch her away. That he had thought of it, she knew very well. It was in his eyes when he looked at her. It was in his persistence in coming back, day after day, although he took no more joy in it than she did.

It was flattering, somewhat. He was not tired of her.

Yet.

When she told him what she had to tell him . . .

She rose slowly. Her maid and her guard rose with her, watching her. She wanted to scream at them, to thrust them away from her. She set her teeth and advanced, at a dignified pace, toward the privy.

* * *

The day dragged itself through what had become its pattern. She remembered little of it. She had duties, which she did. None lingered beyond the doing.

She knew that Aidan had been taken away to the atabeg. She could not make it mean anything. He would come back unharmed, and scarcely inconvenienced. No mere mortal lord could be a match for him.

And, damn him, he knew it.

In the House of Ibrahim, they took the nightmeal after the sunset prayer: the men first, the women after, when the men had eaten their fill. Tonight Joanna had no appetite; as she had taken to doing, she retreated to the garden, to feel the cool of the evening, to breathe sweet air. She never lingered long: only until the flies had found her. Even so, it was almost enough.

It was a long, scented, fly-stung moment before she realized that she was alone. The women all lingered over their dinner. Samin the eunuch, for what reason God knew and she hardly cared, had not followed her.

She had waited, hoped, prayed for this. She glanced about. Nothing human stirred. She darted toward the wall, and the gate which she knew was there, deep hidden in greenery. There were thorns, which she had not expected; she cursed as they sank claws into her. But the gate was as it had always been, small, weathered, its latch long broken and never mended. She slid through it, not easily for all the vines that wove about it, but the other side was clear, facing the back of a little pavilion. No one lingered there or anywhere that she could see, or that she could hear through the pounding of her heart.

She went slowly, pausing more than once to remember where she was. Dusk made it all different. There was jasmine where she remembered roses, and the pomegranate tree that had shaded the path was gone.

She found its stump by stumbling against it. She stopped. This was idiocy. She should go back where she belonged. She was not sure that she wanted him. What if he did not want her?

Then be damned to him. She knew the way surely, now. Round the rose arbor, past the fountain, and there was the loom of the house, the glimmer of white that was the rail of its gallery. Painted iron. They said that witches and nightfolk could not abide it: it seared them like fire.

They knew nothing of this one, with his predator's eyes and his affinity for fine steel.

She was not the hoyden she had been, but she could still climb a trellis, particularly in eastern trousers. It groaned under her weight, but held. She grasped the rail and hung there, and paused to breathe. The muezzin's wail nearly made her lose her grip.

It was safety. They would still be away from their sleeping places, all the younger uncles and cousins who were housed here: lingering over their dinner, praying together there or in the mosque, many of them ready to go out afterward in search of the night's pleasures.

She pulled herself up and over the rail, and nearly fell. One of Aidan's hellions grinned at her: Raihan the half-Frank, whose dour face was only for strangers. He offered his hand. She took it, and let him steady her on the tiles. He let go quickly.

He knew. They all did. And she was in no mood for pretending at secrets. "Is he there?" she asked.

Raihan shook his head. "Not yet, lady."

Her heart chilled. "He's—still—"

"Oh, no, lady!" he said with swift solicitude. "He came back hours ago. He's at dinner."

Of course. Where else would he be?

It was only Raihan on guard, alone and glad of the company. Joanna left him at his post by the door, and went in slowly. There was a lamp lit, illumining a room that might have been anyone's, small and bare. The mat was spread, the coverlet arrayed on it, a robe laid out. Aidan was the wonder and the despair of the harem, tall as he was, needing garments new and not made over from the common stock. The cousins liked to giggle over the length of them, and wonder aloud if all of him was likewise endowed.

She settled on the mat. When sitting wearied her, she lay down. The flutter in her middle lessened. The edge of fear receded: fear of the Assassin, fear of being discovered here, fear of the hunt that would, inevitably, catch her. Aidan would find her first; he would defend her. If she did not tell him yet. If—

She must have slept. She closed her eyes for a moment, and when she opened them, he was there, sitting on his heels, watching her. His face wore no expression at all.

Then he smiled, and she had no will left. She was on him, clinging to him, drinking him in until surely she would drown.

Even he had to come up for air on occasion; and she was mortal. When she pulled back, she was in his lap, and he was laughing in delight. She was grinning herself, even though she wanted to hit him. Because—

No. She must not think of that. Think of him; of the light in his eyes, making them strange; of the warmth of his body, the strength of his hands, the joy in him that she was there, escaped, free. How great it was, she could well see: his robe was light, its belt lost somewhere in their greeting, his shirt and drawers of silk, concealing nothing of consequence.

"I was going to come to you," he said, "if you hadn't come to me first."

She hardly heard him. "I should go back. They'll be looking for me."

"Not now."

She stared at him.

He smiled. "Yes," he said as if she had spoken. "I've added a touch or two of my own. You've decided to sleep in the garden, where it's cool and quiet. Your maid is watching over you."

Dura, who was terrified of Aidan, who endured him for love of her mistress. Joanna frowned. "Will it work?"

"Until dawn, it should. I'll go back with you. We won't be seen."

She wished that she could be as sure of it as he sounded. She had been mad to venture this. She had been worse than mad. With a little more time, she might have cured herself of him. Now the sickness was worse than ever. The thought of dawn, of leaving him, of going back to her cage and her fears and her wretched few moments of his presence, tightened her fingers on his arms and wrung from her a gasp of protest.

"I wish," she said fiercely. "I wish we could run away and never come back."

"We can," he said. "When I've fulfilled my oath."

She stiffened. "Yes. There's always that. Isn't there?"

"Only a little while longer," he said. "That's all. Then, if you want it, we'll go. The world is wide. I'd joyfully span it with you."

Her tension eased not at all. "What if I asked you to forget your oath? To take me now and carry me far away, and thwart the Assassin as he'd never expect. Would you do it?"

He barely hesitated. "I can't." It was gentle, but there was no yielding in it. "I've made too many promises, set too much in train."

Understanding flooded, blinding her. She thrust herself away from him and stumbled to her feet. "The atabeg. He called you to him. You made a bargain."

Aidan nodded. "He banished me from Aleppo. He thinks I'm a spy; I may have dissuaded him, but my presence does nothing for his peace."

She drew a breath. Suddenly she could have laughed, or wept, or shouted aloud. She asked with barely a tremor, "When do we leave?"

"I," he said, "must be gone by tomorrow's sunset."

"We're going to have to be quick, then, or we'll never be

ready. If we begin now—Grandmother should know, and Karim—"

"They know," he said. His voice gentled. "I am going, Joanna. You will stay here."

"And be killed the moment you leave?"

He checked for the fraction of a breath. "I'll lure the Assassin away, as I deceived your kin tonight. When we're far from here, I'll face him and cast him down. He'll never come near you."

"How do you know?" she demanded. "How do you *know?*"

"Joanna," he said with mighty patience. "Think. If you are riding with me, on such a ride as this will be, what can you do but chance being killed if my vigilance fails again? Here at least you are with kin; you have duties; you are safe, and loved, and needed."

"And you need not fret your mind over me."

"I'll always do that, no matter where you are. But if you're here, I'll fret less."

"I don't want to stay," she said. "I won't. I've had enough of being locked in cages while you fly free."

"Even to save your life?"

"My life is no more or less safe whether I go or stay. My sanity is another matter."

He was, when it came down to it, male. He refused to understand. "You can't go."

"I will. Lock me up if you like. I'll break free. I'll follow you on foot if I have to. I'm not staying in this city without you."

He sucked in his breath. She flung herself at him, bore him down. He did not try to fight her. She sat on him, searing him with her temper. He winced. "Lady—"

"I'm going. If you want to lure the Assassin, what better bait than my living self? And no need to wear yourself out in working your magic from so far away."

His face was set, stubborn, but his eyes betrayed him. Oh, yes, he wanted her. He might not find it as easy as he pretended, to leave her behind.

She kissed him. Lightly at first, defiantly. He stiffened against her; then, all at once, he kindled. Even in her anger she laughed, for he was splendid, and terrifying, and he belonged to her. She commanded him to love her. He was her servant: he obeyed.

After the storm, the calm. The jangling tension that had awakened Aidan to Joanna's presence even in the garden, had eased. She was as beautiful as she had ever been, lying beside him, warm and richly pleasured. Her face in the lamplight had lost its hard edge of discontent, her eyes dark and soft, her mouth loosed from its taut line. He kissed it. She tangled her fingers in his hair and smiled. "You are beautiful," she said.

"I was thinking the same of you."

She shivered slightly, with pleasure. His voice could do that to her, even when she would not believe what it said. "Do you really find me bearable to look at?"

He shook his head between her hands. "Madam, you are not even modest. You are blind, and obstinate, and—yes—beautiful."

She untangled one hand to run it down from his temple to his jaw. "I see," she said. "You're behind your face. You don't care how unlovely we all are beside you."

He silenced her with yet another kiss. "Then it's only my face you love. If I were ugly, you'd never deign to look at me."

"That's not true!"

He laughed at her indignation. "That's no more than you're saying of me. I'm not mere mindless beauty, *ma dama.*"

"Of course you're not." She glared at him. He smiled back. She yielded slowly. "You know what you look like."

"I can hardly help it." Nor was he minded to dwell on it. He smoothed the frown from her brow with a light finger, and followed it with kisses, down the taut lines of her face, past her chin to the sweep of neck and shoulder, round the fullness of her breasts. Her heart beat light and swift beneath the warm soft woman-skin. His awareness sank beneath it, spreading slowly through her as he moved downward again, over the curve of her belly to her navel, that poets here would call the jewel in the goblet. He laughed at the thought, a small explosion of breath: a shiver of pleasure for her at the warm brush of it. Her hips flared wide and deep between his hands. Her buttocks filled them to overflowing. He descended to the secret places, dizzy with the scent of them, his power flowing in and through them, filling them. But not his body, not yet. The waiting would make it sweeter. His kisses circled their smoothness—alien even yet, that eastern art of razor and of stripping-paste, but exciting in its strangeness. His mind traced the paths within. *They* were all familiar, all perfectly a woman's.

He paused. Familiar. Surely. But—

It was nothing. A moment's distraction. The call of a nightbird in the garden.

It was there still. Familiarity grown unfamiliar.

Grown, and growing.

He lay utterly still. The fool in him, which was a very large part of his self, denied it; called it delusion. That fleck of awareness which saw only truth, called it what it was.

Joanna stirred, sensing the wrongness in his silence. "What is it? Do you hear something?"

His head shook. He laid it on her belly. Now that he was awake to it, it burned in his mind's eye: not mere soft skin and sparking pleasure, not a path to his own delight, not simply the center of this creature who was Joanna, but woman, and womb.

And in it . . .

He could have sung for joy. He could have killed them both.

No. Not both. All three.

There was no doubt of it. None at all. What grew in her had been growing for perhaps a pair of months. They had left Jerusalem almost a season ago. She had had no other lover,

nor wanted one. And she had not had congress with her husband since before her son was born.

He raised his head. She met his eyes. She saw that he knew.
Her fear rose; it smote him to the heart. That she could be
afraid of him, because she had conceived. And had he not had
as much to do with it as she?

She read his anger at her folly, as anger at her condition.
She struck out at him with hands and voice. "Yes. Yes, I'm
pregnant. Yes, it's all my fault. Yes, I didn't want to tell you!"

He evaded her hands; he pulled her to him, holding her
though she struggled, stroking her until she surrendered,
breathing hard, hating him for being so much stronger than
she. For being male, and desirable. For getting her with child.

"Why were you afraid to tell me?" he asked her, as gently as
he could. "It's mine, too."

"That's why."

He puzzled out the logic of that. Understanding appalled
him. "You thought I'd stop loving you? You thought I'd abandon you?" He shook her hard. "What do you take me for?"

"Male."

He let her go. He rose; for if he stayed, he would do something regrettable. In his swift pacing he came up against the
wall. He leaned against it, letting its coolness sink into him.
He was shaking.

He spun. She was sitting up, watching him with eyes wide
and burning dry. Her hair tumbled over her shoulders and her
breasts. One hid in the mass of it; one peered coyly out, white
breast, pink nipple, lovely and maddening. Now that he knew,
he saw what bloom was on her, not of a woman with a lover,
but a woman with child.

"I suppose," she said, "that you are kind to all your women.
And your bastards."

He flinched from the venom in her voice. "I have none."

"That you know of."

His fists clenched. "I have none. Nor ever have had. I had
thought that I could not. There are ways to tell, if one is like

275

me, or like my brother; and I was never . . . potent . . . in that way."

"Potent enough," she said.

"But I *shouldn't* be!" He reined himself in before he ran wild. "If I had known that I could—if I had thought that I would—"

"You would have resisted me?"

"I would have been more careful."

She shook her head. "Then you're wiser than I. I never even thought."

"I can't understand," he said, "why, all at once, I should be . . . I should be able . . ." He stopped. "Maybe—maybe I was only—as boys are. Sometimes. If they kindle early. Able to love, but not to beget. But now . . ."

"You hardly look like a boy to me."

"I'm not a man, either." He said it again, slowly. "I'm not a man. I'm not human. I don't even know how different I may be."

Her hands went to her belly. Her eyes were wild. "Then—this—too—"

It was not fear that leaped in her. It was a white, mad joy. It brought him by no will of his own, drew him down before her; but his hands would not reach, to touch her. "It is." He had not willed that, either. But it was true. Now his hand would yield to his will. It laid itself over hers, where the spark was, the seed of life that would be another of his kind.

She drew a long slow breath. Suddenly, as if his touch had had power in it, she was calm; she was herself. "This is going to be very complicated."

He laughed, half in pain. "What's complicated? I'll be done in Masyaf before you begin to swell. Then we'll go away. We'll have our child together, somewhere where we'll be safe and protected. I'll never take it from you."

"Will you swear to that?"

Of course she did not trust him. She had reason. It did not hurt the less for that. "I swear."

She eyed him steadily, under her brows. "Ranulf said it, too. The next one, I could keep. He may even have meant it."

"No doubt he did."

Her lips twitched: less smile than grimace. Her hands turned to clasp his. "I want this baby, Aidan. Never doubt that. For all that it may do to me, for all that it may cost . . . I want it."

"And you wonder why I love you."

"I know that. You like a challenge."

Her heart was lighter now: free, glad, almost antic, now that fear was proven folly. She pulled him up and spun them both about, laughing. "Oh, my lord! Oh, my love!"

He bent his head to her kiss, laughing with her, soft and deep. *"Ma dama,"* he said.

23

The black eunuch was dead. He had lunged upon Morgiana, and she had struck harder than she meant, and his neck had snapped. It was of a piece with all the rest of this accursed day. If he had stood still for her ensorcelment, he would be deep asleep but very much alive, hidden in the space beneath the blue pavilion, and she would bear one less burden of guilt.

Her oath was burden enough, and more than enough. Sinan had invoked it yet again, compelled her with it, even dared to threaten her. "Do as I bid," he had said to her, "and remember well. There are oaths more potent than that which you have taken on yourself, and bindings stronger than this near-freedom of yours. I have your name set within the Seal of Suleiman. Do not tempt me to invoke it."

She told herself that she did not care; that she was stronger than his mere human magic. But the twisting in her vitals was fear. He held her name, her oath, even her self if he were so minded. He would not spare her for pity or for mercy.

He had tried to feign both. "Take this last sacrifice," he said with what he dreamed was gentleness. "It is only a Christian, a Frank. And when it is taken, come back to me. Perhaps then I may loose your bonds."

Perhaps. Her lip curled. She knew the royal *perhaps*. It was tantamount to *never*.

The eunuch's body was hidden beneath the pavilion. Time and men's noses would uncover him, but not until she was long gone.

The Frank had been in the garden when Morgiana came. No longer. Her scent led not toward the house but away from it, toward the wall. Morgiana raised her brows. So: she would escape? Wise woman. It was a pity that her hunter was not human, to be foiled by human sleights. And that that hunter, under the chains of her oath, could not let her go.

The scent was growing cold. It had taken an unconscionable while to subdue the eunuch, and then to dispose of the carrion. Iblis had beset her with a gaggle of chattering women, and a dog that barked and howled until she silenced it with power, and a child playing with a ball and a stick. She had not been under bond to kill any of them; therefore she would not. Now the garden was empty and she was free to hunt, but her quarry was gone.

Morgiana found the gate, and the thorns. She could admire the Frank. For such a large woman, she left a remarkably slender trail.

And an interestingly direct one; and not toward the outer wall as Morgiana might have expected. Had she a lover, then? One of her kinsmen; or maybe one of her ifrit's mamluks who were so notorious in the city. One of them was born a Frank, and not ill to look at.

It was not he on guard where the woman's scent led, but one fairer by far to eastern eyes, a slender dark beauty like an

Arab stallion, with a stare as startling as it was startled: water-blue, gem-blue, sky-blue. He heard nothing of Morgiana's passage up the trellis, nor felt aught of her presence, until he crumpled into her arms.

The door was shut, but she heard them clearly enough. Voices: a woman's and a man's. They spoke Frankish, which she did not trouble to make sense of. She knew the sound of lovers at war. She set hand to the door. Confident, they were: it was unbarred. She eased it open.

The lamplight flickered, dazzling her eyes after the dark of the night. They were shadows, two tall dark shapes twined about one another. They had, it seemed, declared a truce. The woman laughed, half mirthful, half reluctant.

Morgiana's dagger was in her hand, new and keen and eager for blood. Maybe—maybe, after all, she would not use it.

It was revelation, that opening of her mind, that awakening of subtlety. Nothing in her given word had stipulated that she must slay the woman tonight, least of all with her lover as witness. Perhaps it would be enough to frighten her, and to betray her transgression to her kin. Sinan had demanded a sacrifice. He had not specified that it be in blood, although he had certainly meant as much. This woman's honor might be enough, and the honor of her house.

Sinan might even accept it. He was a subtle serpent himself, and he was no fool. What might it do to the woman he wanted, that her daughter disported herself with a man not her husband?

The air was heavy with the scents of passion, musk and sweat and the rank sweetness of a woman in heat. Morgiana's nostrils flared. There was an ache between her own thighs, a trembling in her body. She had spied on lovers enough, and killed when weariness cast them into sleep, but none had aroused her as did these two. Perhaps it was that she had never been commanded to slay the woman and not the man; and that she had no desire to kill at all.

They spoke, laughing. The woman's arms were about her lover's neck. His head bent to the kiss. *"Ma dama,"* he said.

Morgiana froze. She knew that voice. She had been refusing to know it. And the face that lifted, all besotted, all rank with the stink of mortal flesh.

She moved without knowing that she moved, as a cat will, flowing from shadow to shadow.

The woman locked legs about her lover's middle and mounted him, there, with abandon that would have put a whore to shame. His breath caught in startled pleasure. He laughed low in his throat. His arms were full of her. His mind held nothing that was not she.

Morgiana's lips drew back from her teeth. She had never hated. She had never had cause. The deaths she dealt were justice only; execution.

Aidan sensed the strangeness in the air, even in the surging of pleasure that was Joanna's as much as his. Her weight bore him back and down in a sidewise tangle; but light, light, for his power made the air a bed for them. She never knew, nor cared. She buried her face in his shoulder, drunk on his scent, riding him with mounting urgency. It carried him, even as he looked through the tousle of her hair, into eyes that burned green.

He could not, in the moment's shock, remember shame. Half of him was Joanna's. Half knew the lure of his own kind, the beauty of that pointed cat-face, that fall of wine-red hair.

His eyes knew the gleam of steel. Knife, in her hand. But why . . .

He saw the madness in her eyes. He knew.

Worse than fear was grief, and desperate denial. *No,* he tried to say. *No. Not you.*

I. Her voice, cold and clear.

No, he said again.

Yes. She was in the air: death, winged, with steel. Hate rode her.

He thrust against too-yielding air, struggled to turn, to shield Joanna. The utmost edge of bitter blade seared his side.

Joanna gasped, stiffened. Her agony resounded in his mind. She convulsed in his arms.

She was deathly heavy. He gasped for breath that would not come, trapped as beneath a weight of stone.

She shifted; but it was no movement of her own. Morgiana bent over him. Her face was a mockery. Stark with fear for him. Reaching to touch, to be certain that he lived.

Assassin. Murderer of children.

Her throat in his hands was a wonderful thing, as delicate as a flower's stem, and hardly more difficult to break.

She was still, unresisting. She would let him kill her. It was the way of her faith. To kill for the Mission; to die for it. It was just, that he should be her executioner. He who was of her own kind. He whom she loved.

He flung her away in a passion of disgust. She lay where she had fallen, eyes wide, fixed on him, as devoid of humanity as a cat's. No more than a cat did she know remorse for what she had done. Regret, yes, that she had not killed with the first blow, without pain.

He turned his back on her and knelt by Joanna. The Assassin had cast her aside like a broken doll. The dagger lay hilt-deep in her side. The point of it just pricked the heart itself; blood welled about it where blood should never be. He knew. He could see. He had no power to stop it.

Her breast heaved. The hilt pulsed, swifter, swifter. Her hands clawed at it. He caught them. They fought him. She did not know him. She knew nothing but agony.

He turned his head. The Assassin had not moved. "You," he said, though it choked him. "Have you healing?"

She did not answer. He could see how it tore at her, the tenderness with which he regarded Joanna. And he was glad. She had destroyed all that he loved. Now let her know the pain he knew. Now let her suffer as he suffered.

Her face twisted. He laughed, cold and bitter. With a sound like a hawk's cry, she fled into the night.

No matter. He would find her. And her master. And make them pay.

He was perfectly calm. Joanna was dying. What he would do, must do, would kill her truly; or it would free her to heal herself, since he could not heal her with power. He grasped the hilt. If he prayed, there were no words in it. Only the dagger, and the heart fluttering bird-swift, and blood that for her now was both life and death. With utmost care he eased the dagger out of her breast.

The dam burst. A trickle, at first, runneling down the grooved blade; then a sudden flood. Human instinct cried to him to stop it. Instinct that was not human held him fast, the blade half-drawn, half-sheathed in living flesh; sight that was never of human eye, saw the emptying of places that should never have been filled. The great fist of the heart unclenched, freed again to beat.

He could not heal, but he could hold: draw the blade at last and bind the wound, and wipe away somewhat of the blood, and all the while hold back the tide that would fill her anew unless, until, healing grew stronger than wounding. He wrapped her in his own robe against the cold of shock. He remembered to find his drawers and don them. Then he raised her.

The harem's gate opened before him with no hand upon it. There was resistance. He took no notice of it. He had no slightest care for their laws or their proprieties. A chamber emptied for him. He laid her in it. He said, "A physician. Fetch one."

People hovered, expostulating. He should not be here. He was not allowed.

He sat on his heels and let the storm die of its own futility.

The doctor came: a woman, and, beyond a single swift glance, undismayed by his presence. She cleared the room with a word. Her apprentice, a young eunuch with a face as Byzantine as her own, laid down her box of medicaments and waited for her to command him.

It was swift, for Joanna's life's sake, and yet it seemed slow, like a dance: no move wasted, none enfeebled with haste. Aidan found the dagger in his hand. He did not remember taking it up, or bringing it here. He knew Farouk's forging, Maimoun's artistry in the hilt. Of Morgiana's presence there was nothing. Of Joanna's blood there was far too much.

Someone was speaking, tracing the path of the blade through her body, naming what he had done to draw it, and how, and why. It was a man's voice. His own. The physician's incredulity stung like salt on a raw wound. But she had eyes, and fingers nigh as gifted in seeing, and she could see what was clearly evident: that here, where should have been death, was life beating strong. She did not pause to question. She bent to the task which he had left her.

Aidan looked up from it into a stranger's face, but eyes which he knew, dark and clear and young amid the wrack of age. The Lady Khadijah had laid aside her veil; she leaned on a stick, but lightly, with no tremor of hand or body.

She beckoned. Aidan did not choose to disobey. He would not leave the room, but she was content to pause by its inner door, through which breathed the coolness of water, the fall of a fountain in its own courtyard.

She sat there on the threshold, on a mat from which he dimly remembered startling its occupant. A sharp gesture brought him down beside her. "Now," she said. "Tell me."

There was little that she did not know, or suspect. And there was no softness in her. He gave her the truth. "My lady was with me. The Assassin found her there, and struck."

"So I can see," said Khadijah. Her eyes were not on Joanna, but on Aidan.

He glanced down at himself. He was clean enough, except for the hand that had held the dagger. With some small surprise, he remembered the burning kiss of the blade. A long cut, hair-thin, seamed his side. It barely bled. It stung a little; he quelled it, and forgot it anew. "Did you know, my lady, that the slave of Masyaf is a woman?"

Khadijah nodded slowly. "Ah," she said. "The ifritah. I had feared it; I had prayed that it might not be so."

"You knew?" he cried. "You knew, and you never told me?"

"I was not certain," she said. "But yes, I knew of her. She is old and she is strong, and she has never failed of her kill."

"Until now."

"Pray Allah," said Khadijah. "It is a measure of Sinan's desire, that he has unsheathed this most deadly of his weapons."

"If I had known," Aidan said. A cry was rising up in him; he battled it down. "I saw her. She followed us. She spoke to me. She named me for what I was: Khalid, *Foreigner*. I took her for one of my own people. I never dreamed that it would be she —who—"

"You are not the first man whose fatal weakness was a woman. Or two."

His face flamed. "If there is any dishonor, it is mine alone."

"And the child, too: that is yours?"

The blood drained from his face. "How did you know?"

"Women do," she said. She sighed. "I had been fool enough to hope . . . No matter. I am not a man of this House, to defend its honor with steel. My own defenses all too evidently failed. Do not trouble to lie to me. I know which of you sought the other."

"An hour later, and it would have been I who sought her."

"Doubtless. An hour later, and she would have been dead when you found her."

It was not approval. But it was absolution, of a sort. He bowed to it. "Then you will not punish her."

"Has she not been punished enough?"

His hands ached. They were fists, the nails digging deep into the palms. "It is I who should be punished, and I who will exact her blood-price."

"You take much upon yourself."

He smiled almost gently. "But you see, no one else can. Now at last I know what I face. Now I can hunt in earnest."

It was not in her to shiver, but she nodded once. "You will go soon."

"Now."

"Nothing is ready," said Khadijah.

"There are horses," Aidan said, "no? There is food, water, the wherewithal to carry them."

"Your guides—your caravan—"

"I can guide myself. A caravan would only slow me." He paused, drew a breath. "Lady. I lingered not for prudence nor for any bargain, but for my lady. A weakness, yes, and fatal. If I fail again as I have failed in all my vigilance since I came over sea, then perhaps God will have mercy and slay me for my folly."

She looked long at him, and deep. She saw what he knew very well. He was quiet. His mind was clear. He knew precisely what he did. And he was quite mad.

He rose and bowed low, as low as a Frank and a prince might ever bow. He did not speak. What promises he might have made, she knew as well as he: which of them he had a hope of fulfilling, and which were hope only, well beyond the edge of sanity.

The Greek physician had come to the end of her ministrations, for the moment. Joanna lay on the mat, less unconscious now than deep asleep. The thin deep wound was bandaged, a reed in it still, and a bowl to catch what might yet flow forth; all the blood that there had been was washed away. He bent to kiss her, not caring who saw, and turned from her.

Again he passed through the house. Again no one stopped him. This time no one tried. His room was empty, except for memory. No guard, no mamluk, not even a servant. He dressed himself carefully in the alien garb that had become familiar: Bedu robes, fresh-cleaned but bearing the ineradicable stamp of dust and sun and desert spaces. He would bring them home again, and with them his sword, and two knives. One of his own forging. One christened with Joanna's blood.

He was a fine fierce sight, returning the way he had come, looking the desert bandit for whom the idlers in the atabeg's chambers had taken him. He would give them something to talk of.

Little had changed in the harem, save that it was quieter, less like a henhouse with a hawk in it. The hawk's return met with greater calm and fewer faces. He did not care. There was only one face he wanted to see, and hers would never be veiled for him.

She was awake, which he had not dared to hope for. The healer's eunuch looked up from coaxing a potion into her— wine, heavy with spices and something dark, sweet, redolent of sleep—but did not pause. His eyes were enormous, like the eyes of a saint on a mosaicked wall, and utterly quiet. One could drown in that quiet.

Aidan flung himself free, sparking fire-gold. The flare of it was still on him as he knelt by Joanna's side. She frowned up at him. "I'm a coward," she said.

She could still startle him, even into laughter: laughter with tears in it, for she was alive and scowling and being unpredictable.

"I am," she insisted. "One little bit of pain and I ran away, right into the dark."

"So would any wise creature," he said.

She shook her head, slightly, for it hurt to move at all. "I made myself come back. It was a long way. I saw you like a flame in the night. You guided me. I was never lost while I had you."

The tears were running down his face. He could not even curse them.

She saw. She tensed, tried to rise. He caught her before she tore herself anew. She did not feel it. The drug was working in her; she fought it with desperate ferocity. "The baby! Have I lost the baby? Why are you crying? Have I—lost—"

A cold, clear, Greek-accented voice cut across her outcry. "You have not. But you will, if you go on with this foolishness. Lie down and sleep."

It was not in Joanna to obey anyone without a struggle. She lay down, but the hand under her cheek was a fist, and her eyes, though clouding, were fixed on Aidan's face. "Why are you crying?"

"Because I love you."

She took that with her into sleep. The smile broke free when all her defenses had fallen; she never knew it, or needed to know. He kissed it, and her brow, and her nape beneath a tidier braid than she herself would ever weave. His hands stretched over her, edged with fire still. He made it his gift to her. He poured it forth without heed to the cost. It would not heal her, not of itself. But it would make her strong, be light and warmth to her when the dark crowded close, guard her and defend her against the demons of sickness.

His hands fell slowly to his sides. The room was dim, the fire gone from him. Joanna had it now, all that he could give. He had never given so much. He was dizzy, as if it had been blood and not power that he shed. He smiled. She would not die, now. She or the child they had made.

The Greek woman watched him with knowledge, with understanding, but with only a flicker of fear. "You could have killed her," she said.

"But I did not."

"No credit to your wisdom. I know what you are, spirit of fire. Have all your years never sufficed to teach you sense?"

"I'm a very young daimon." And he felt it, now, here, before this mortal woman and her apprentice who would never be a man. Youth was no strangeness to him who would never grow old, but he had forgotten what it was to be a raw boy, untried, untested, with an enemy before him who was none of those.

And he had emptied his power to give Joanna life.

He straightened. He mustered a smile. Child in power he might be, but his body was a man's, and it knew war.

Joanna slept in her armor of light. He left her and her dark-eyed guardians, and went to claim her blood-price.

V

MASYAF

24

There were torches lit in the outer courtyard, horses stamping and fretting, even a roar of disgust from amid a huddle of laden camels. Aidan took it all in with mild surprise. That his mamluks would follow him, he had expected. He had not thought to find an expedition fitted out as if for a raid in the desert.

Karim came toward him, as fussily elegant as ever, with his curled and perfumed beard and his towering turban. He looked unhappy, but that would be for appearance' sake, and in remembrance of Joanna. Under it, where Aidan's blunted power could just perceive, he was richly content. He had had an impossible task, he had fulfilled it, he was well rid of this disturbance in his household; and he had paid less for it than he had expected.

He regarded Aidan without hostility, if with no great liking. "I regret," he said, "that we were unable to provide you with all that we had agreed upon. Guides, the full complement of baggage camels, doubled remounts . . ."

"No matter," said Aidan. "I see two horses for every man, and camels enough. Guidance I do not need. I know where we go."

"And do you know where it is safe, and where the tribes have forbidden passage?"

"God will guide me," Aidan said.

No good Muslim could express doubt at such a sentiment. Karim, trapped in piety, escaped to duty. "I have told the chief of your mamluks what I know of the road and its dangers. You would do well to ride warily, even where the land seems most quiet. He whom you hunt is not above using the tribes as his weapons; and they are much given to raiding for the love of it."

"Then I'll have to oblige them with a battle, won't I?"

"Youth," said Karim, "is a wonderful thing." A man could die in battle, his eyes said. And this one had dishonored his kinswoman and his House; and Allah was just as well as merciful. If it was a prayer, it was a very subtle one.

Aidan smiled at him. "It's hardly youth, sir. I was bred to oblige my enemies as my friends."

"God help your friends."

An unguarded utterance. Aidan saluted it, even as he turned to find his grey gelding waiting, Arslan at its head, somewhat owl-eyed but holding back hard on a grin. Others had not so much self-restraint. Under his eye the grins vanished, but there was no quelling the high fierce joy.

He knew it himself. It was black and scarlet, like fire in the dark. He swung lightly into the saddle. "I shall come back," he said, "to see the end of our bargain."

It did not cost Karim excessively much to murmur, "Allah grant." Then, because he was an honorable man, and because he saw no profit in vindictiveness: "May God prosper your venture."

Aidan bowed in the saddle. His hellions were waiting. He flung them into flight.

The city was closed up until dawn, but the House of Ibrahim had influence at a postern gate. Once that was past, none of them looked back at the bulk of shadow and starglimmer that was Aleppo. Part of Aidan's heart was in it, and most of his power, and some of his soul if he had any. But all of that, he bore with him in memory. His eyes were on the road ahead.

It was five days' journey to Hama on the Orontes, riding at a comfortable pace; three days then at lesser speed and with an eye toward ambush, to Masyaf. To Aidan on this first night, as the stars paled into dawn, it seemed as distant as the moon. He had come so far, for so long; he had lost the power to see an end to it.

The mamluks were Muslim to a man, and orthodox. Even

Conrad with his fair Viking face bowed five times toward Mecca between each dawn and night: at first light, at sunrise, at noon, at sunset, before sleep. They were as regular as monks, and as persistent.

They were also expeditious. Aidan had to admit that. And sensible: they always took advantage of the opportunity to rest the horses.

After the sunrise prayer, the first day, they ate and rested. It was not properly a camp: they pitched no tents, but settled in a stony hollow not far from the road, where there was a little rough grazing for the camels. Most slept. Strong they might be, and hellions they certainly were, but they were young creatures, and they had had no sleep in the night.

Aidan, for whom sleep was more habit than necessity, wandered among the beasts. His gelding came unsummoned, to blow sweet breath in his hands and coax from him the bit of dried apple he carried in his sleeve. He laid his cheek against the warm smooth neck, rubbing the nape where horses always loved to be rubbed, empty for a little while of thought, sense, self.

A light step brought them flooding back. He turned, slowly enough as he thought, but the other started. It was Raihan, grey and haggard, wild-eyed as if he had remembered, all at once, what his master was.

Aidan tried to calm him with a smile. He never saw it. He was down in the dust, groveling as easterners were given to doing, babbling in no language Aidan could make sense of.

Slowly it came clear. "I saw your lady come, I greeted her, I stood guard until you came. When you were there, I watched by the rail. And when I remembered again, I lay there as if I had been asleep, and your chamber was empty, and all the word was that the Assassin had come and struck and gone. My fault, my lord, my grievous fault. I failed in my vigilance. I should die for it."

Aidan dragged him up and shook him until he stopped

babbling. "*You* should die? She was in my arms when she was struck. How would you have me pay for that?"

Raihan swallowed audibly. His hands worked, clenching and unclenching. "But, my lord. You were distracted."

A bark of laughter escaped, for all that Aidan could do. "And why was I distracted? No, Raihan. I won't punish you. You were bespelled by a demon of great power and cunning. I was merely and unforgivably a fool."

"My lord!" Raihan protested, outraged.

"Go and sleep," Aidan said. "We've a long ride before us."

Raihan drew a breath as if to object, but Aidan's eye was steady. He went away slowly, found his place, lay in it. His sigh was loud and much oppressed; but he seemed a very little less wretched than he had been.

His guilt would pass, if not swiftly. Aidan did not know that his own ever would.

When the day's heat had begun to abate, they took the road again. There were few travelers upon it. A shepherd crossing with his flock; a caravan wending its way to Aleppo. The land was quiet, bare brown desert with here and there a glimmer of green. Where green was, people were, villages huddled about a spring or a trickle of river.

They camped well after dark, under a waxing moon. Even the tireless Kipchaks were all but asleep in the saddle. Aidan saw them settled and a guard mounted. He took the first watch himself. They did not like it, but he had no use for sleep. His power was still an emptied cup, although the first trickle of its renewal brightened the edges of his mind. He watched with eyes and ears and nose, as any earthly beast could do. He prowled the edges of their circle. He waited for the slow hours to pass.

He could leave them all and go on alone. But they would follow; while he had no power for aught but gleaning the thoughts of one who stood within his arms' reach, he could neither fly beyond their compass nor defend them against the demon from Masyaf.

He snarled as he paced. That one. Morgiana. Monster of his own kind. Blind groping beast without heart or soul, only hate, and lust that she called love. Was that the essence of what he was? Without human raising, human taming, to be no more than a wolf or a panther. An animal. A killer without measure and without mercy.

And he had thought her beautiful. He had wanted her; dreamed of her. While she lied and laid traps for him, and lured him to destruction.

He spoke to the air. "Morgiana. Morgiana, hunter in the night. I know you now. I come to you."

If she heard, he had no power to know. She did not answer.

There would be time and to spare for that. In Masyaf; or, if her steel was swifter than his wrath, in hell.

Aidan did not know when it dawned on him that he was off his reckoning. His mamluks seemed to find nothing amiss. The cup of his power, filling slowly, tried to persuade him that this road was the proper one, the road to Hama from which he must seek that to Masyaf. It was leading them south and west by sun and moon.

Yet beneath that surety was deep uneasiness. His mother's haunted Broceliande was just so, subtly treacherous, with a taste on the tongue and a quiver in the skin that spoke of magic. They were being led, and led astray.

He knew it surely on the day when, swiftly as they had traveled, they should have come to Hama. Where before them the wide barren plain should have opened to the winding of the Orontes, was naught but dust and sand and stones. The road stretched away into it, empty and mocking, with a dance of heat-shimmer on it.

They were not in difficulty, yet. They had avoided the larger towns, but in the last of many nameless villages they had filled their waterskins and watered their camels well. Aidan's prudence. The others had thought him a fool, close as they were to river and city, to prepare as if for the deep desert.

He bade his gelding halt. It ran the reins through his fingers, lowering its head to rub an itch in its foreleg.

Arslan rode up beside him. "Do you see something, my lord?"

"Nothing," Aidan answered. "Nothing at all."

Arslan raised a brow. He had taken to doing that of late. Aidan felt his own go up as he realized where the boy had learned it. "My lord?" Arslan inquired.

"I see nothing," Aidan said. "I ought to see Hama, or at least its river."

The others came up, drawing in as close as their horses would allow. Timur's mare, as always, squealed and kicked at his brother's beast, which, as always, had taken advantage of the halt to make overtures. That it was a gelding seemed never to have dawned on it.

Ilkhan slapped its neck. "Idiot," he said to it. And to Aidan: "We can't see Hama. It's down in the river's furrow."

"So, then: where is the river?"

None of them could answer that. Most seemed not to want to. "We've been slower than we thought," said Dildirim.

"Or taken a wrong turning," Conrad said.

Andronikos frowned. "Do these look to you like the hills near Hama?"

"What should they look like?" Arslan demanded. His voice was sharp.

He frowned down the road. His frown darkened to a scowl. He cursed in Turkish, short and foul. "Allah!" he answered himself. "Not like these. Where in God's name are we?"

"South of Aleppo," said Timur.

Even he could quail before their massed glares.

"I would rather know why than where," said Andronikos. And when the glares shifted to him: "If we know why we went astray, we can guess where we are."

Greek logic. It made no sense at all to a Saracen. To a

Frankish he-witch, it was eminently sensible. "As to why," Aidan said, "I can tell you easily enough. We were bespelled." He met their stares. "Yes, even I. I'm not invincible."

They protested, loudly. He waited until they tired of out-shouting one another. Then he said, "We'd best search out a camping place. We'll need rest, and quiet, to think our way out of this."

They found a place that would do well enough, a low hill topped with the ruins of a very old fortress. One wall rose still almost camel-high; the paving there was solid enough, and there was browse about the hill for the camels, although the well had long since gone dry. As always, Aidan's presence was proof against snakes and scorpions, and even the flies hesitated to come too close. He was not supposed to know, but his mamluks drew lots for the place closest to him; every night there was a different drowsing warmth at his back.

Tonight, it seemed, Andronikos had won the toss. As the last blaze of sunset faded from the sky, he sat on his heels beside Aidan, sniffing the savory scents that rose from the cookpot, prodding the camel-dung fire with his scabbarded sword. Arslan, whose rank entitled him to a nightly place at Aidan's right hand, stirred the pot abstractedly. It was a deep trouble in him, that they—even they—had fallen prey to a spell. Aidan's arm about his shoulders hardly comforted him.

They ate in near-silence, with none of their wonted boister-ousness. Their eyes kept coming back to Aidan. Clearly, if thinking was needed, it was his place to do it.

His appetite, never remarkable, died altogether. He choked down a last mouthful, and licked the grease from his fingers. He knew what he had to do. He did not know that his power was enough for it.

They all slowed to a halt, staring. He growled at them. They flinched, but they did not stop staring. "God's bones!" he burst out. "Was there ever such a pack of goggling idiots?"

"No," someone muttered.

He laughed, sharp and short. "Come, then. It's not thinking that we need to do. Not quite yet."

As he spoke, he drew back somewhat from the fire, smoothing dust and scattered stones from the pavement. Where the
fire was, it sank into a hollow, but that before him was level
and unbroken. He drew a long slow breath, contemplating it.
The fire in him burned low, but it burned. His mamluks'
intentness fed it. With great care he gathered it, cupping it in
his palms. It flickered; he breathed on it. It steadied. He set it
on the pavement. It shone like a jewel made of light, ruby in
its heart, moonstone about it. He spread his hands above it. It
melted and flowed. His will shaped it and gave it substance;
made it an image of the world. The east of it swelled and grew
and filled the circle between himself and the fire.

There was Aleppo, bone-white city with the lofty jut of its
citadel. There, Damascus, green jewel in the desert. And
there, Jerusalem, heart of the world, the Dome of the Rock a
minute golden spark. Lesser cities came clear one by one as he
named them. Shaizar, Hama, Homs, down the meander of
the Orontes. Antioch, Tortosa, Tripoli, westward and sea-
ward. And between them in the mountains of Syria, Masyaf.

He swayed; his eyes dimmed. The image wavered as beneath
a ripple of water. Its edges were clear. Slowly he traced the
line between: the shape of the power which flowed out of
Masyaf. Its limit followed roads where it could, feigned them
where it must, leading his eye as it had led his body. South
and west, yes, but wide of the mark, into the desert. Hama
was a long day's journey west. The Orontes, they would come
to, but south of Homs, on the shores of its lake. Then, if they
would, into the mountains, but never to Masyaf; road and
power would cast them up in Tripoli, among the Franks.

It was a gentle enough magic, subtle and marvelously
skilled. It revealed him for what he was, a heedless child,
wasteful of the power that was his; prodigal of it when he
should be sparing, shutting it in walls when he should let it fly
free.

He knew no better. His wars had always been human wars; power had been a game, a gift to use because he had it, never because he had deep need of it. He had never trained it as he would a horse or a hound. He had let it train itself, as he needed it, or for his own pleasure.

It was very late to lament his folly. He was walled off from Masyaf; he had neither the strength nor the skill to break down the wall.

But he was oathsworn. He must go. He must break the wall.

Or skirt it.

Or burrow beneath it.

He blinked in surprise. He was lying on his side; he did not remember falling. The image was gone. But it was burned in his memory. He knew where they were, and where they could go. He tried to say it; he could not find the words in Arabic. All his senses were blunted as they had been when he poured his power into Joanna. He was empty, again. He should learn to be wiser.

Later.

Sleep, now. His mamluks wrapped him in blankets—their own, too; he could not speak to upbraid them for it. They heaped about him like puppies. Warmth spread through all of them, and sleep, and blissful certainty. He was their lord. Whatever he set out to do, he could not fail.

He could happily have throttled the lot of them.

25

It was possible, Aidan discovered, to skirt the edges of the ban, pressing as close to it as its limits would allow. It was like a blankness on the right hand, an inborn incapacity to turn toward Masyaf. Sometimes he tried. He always found himself wandering far out of his way, waking slowly from the conviction that he was on the right road.

They rounded the Lake of Homs and forded the Orontes, and began to angle northward. Aidan's power was waxing, as if the long days of feeling out the borders of the ban had honed and tempered it; he could not turn fully toward Masyaf, but he could edge closer to it.

They were in Frankish lands now, in the County of Tripoli. To Aidan it mattered little. Half of him centered on the grief and wrath that drove him; half, on walking the narrow line between the Assassins' ban and the free earth. There was nothing left to care whether he ate or slept, rode or rested, trod land under Muslim sway or under the shield of Christendom. His mamluks were more in awe of him than ever; that, he could sense. They also thought him quite lost to reason.

As, truly, he was. Often his sight of the world faded, and he saw Joanna where the Assassin had cast her, and the land as his power had limned it, and the ban as a ring of fire. But he who himself was fire, had begun, by inches, to bend it.

On a day without number or name, under a sky as grey as his perception of all that was not the ring and the ban, he snapped erect in the saddle. His mount bucked to a halt. His escort tangled about him.

There was no living will behind the ban. It was wrought by living power, to be sure, but once wrought, it sustained itself: like the wards which he knew how to raise, but far greater. It was a pity, he could reflect, that such a master of power should be so vicious a beast.

But there was something he knew, which she well might not. Wards without constant living guard could be passed. Not easily, not simply, but it could be done. Once he had passed through, if he was skillful, and strong enough in power, the wall would rise again, but he would be within it, and perhaps beyond the ken of the power that had raised it.

He smiled slowly. He was terrifying his poor lads; but it was nothing that they would understand. He touched his nervous horse to a walk, soothing it with hand and voice.

They were going almost due north on a road that had been old when Rome was young; but Rome had leveled and paved it, and it had endured a thousand years. The ban wanted to nudge them westward; Aidan clenched his mind against it, turned his thoughts from the end of the hunt, focused them only on what was directly before him. The tautness eased. He eased with it, almost into a drowse.

Hoofs clattered on stone. Aidan tensed anew. Timur, who had ranged ahead, careened over the hill and skidded to a stop. He was all but dancing in the saddle. "Riders! A whole army of them. In armor. With lances."

"Franks?" Aidan asked, although he knew.

"Franks," said Timur.

The mamluks drew together. One or two drew swords. The Turks reached for their bows.

Aidan stopped them all. "No," he said. "No fighting."

It was slow, for some of them. They had forgotten what their master was.

He took the lead, with Arslan in the rear to ensure that swords stayed sheathed and bows unstrung. Not hastily, not slowly, they mounted the hill.

Riders, indeed. Riders in black, with white crosses on shields and shoulders. A pair of Knights Hospitaller with novice-squires and a company of men-at-arms. They had seen Timur: they were in marching order, the knights helmed for battle. At sight of Aidan, the knight who led raised a hand. The Franks halted, barring the road.

Aidan brought his own company to a halt, mildly startled and beginning, dangerously, to be amused. If his mamluks had forgotten that he was a Frank, so had he forgotten how he would seem to a knight of Outremer: a Saracen in a pack of Saracens, he in Bedu robes, they in their scarlet livery, as exotic as a flock of cock pheasants; and arrogant with it, to ride armed on the open road where the Frank was lord.

The Hospitaller called out in appalling Arabic, his voice booming in the still air. "Who are you? Why are you riding here?"

Aidan rode forward, waving his mamluks back. They obeyed, ready to leap at the slightest hint of threat. The Franks tensed. He kept his hands well away from his weapons, his face quiet, his laughter tight bound behind his eyes. He spoke in his most exquisite *langue d'oc,* as sweetly as ever he had wooed his lady in Carcassonne. "A good day to you, reverend brother, and to all your company."

If the Hospitaller was shocked to find knightly courtesy in a wolf of the desert, he did not pause to indulge it. He shifted to his native tongue with evident relief. His accent was no purer than Aidan's own. "A day is only as good as the man who lives it. Who are you, and what business have you in our lands?"

"I am," said Aidan, "a middling fair Christian and a knight of the west who hopes to become one of Jerusalem, and if I trespass, I pray you forgive me. I had thought this road open to any who has need of it."

"That depends on the nature of the need."

Aidan smiled. "Have no fear, reverend brother. It's nothing to do with you or yours."

"You can hardly expect me to believe that."

They were all, spokesman and silent company, glaring at Aidan's escort, which glared back with fine fierceness.

He smiled wider. "Ah," he said. "I see. Your pardon, sir. These will do you no harm. They are mine; they'll do as I bid them."

"Since when," the Hospitaller asked acidly, "has a pack of Saracens done the bidding of a Christian knight?"

"Since the sultan in Damascus gave them to me," Aidan answered.

A mutter ran through the ranks.

Aidan stiffened at the import of it. "Recreant, you think

me? And have you yourselves never entered alliance with the House of Islam?"

"You would," said the Hospitaller, "do well to come with me. If you are indeed all that you say, then you may offer proof to those better fit to judge than I."

And if not, it was clear, he would be dealt with as he deserved.

He glanced back. His mamluks watched, beast-taut, beast-wary. Only one or two of them could understand what had been said, but they all knew tones and faces, and they knew hostility when they felt it. The Hospitallers waited in patience that bade fair to break, and soon. Behind, where they would take him, was their castle.

It lay within the ban, near a road that ran nigh straight to Masyaf. Aidan considered the weight and number of human minds about him, and the power that was in them to veil his strangeness. It might, just possibly, be enough.

He sent a prayer of thanks to the good angel who had set the Hospitallers on his path, and said, "I would be pleased to accept your hospitality."

They took it for irony. He lacked the will to enlighten them. He let them fall in about his smaller company, holding his hellions back from the edge of violence, ruling them with word and glance. Timur was bold enough to say what they all thought, fiercely, just above a whisper: "But we're *prisoners!*"

"Guests," said Aidan, princely certain, "and allies."

None of them believed it. But they held their peace. They had not been disarmed, which they should have noticed. They were simply prevented from going anywhere but where the Hospitallers led.

And that was full upon the ban, blind to it, unmoved by it. Aidan, trapped in their midst, could not escape it. He was a straw in a millrace; and no matter that he willed to pass the wall. All the force of his power was not enough, even quelled, even buried deep in human minds, even damped almost to oblivion. He was not strong enough. He was not skilled enough. He would break. He would bolt. He would—

Just precisely when he knew that he could not endure it, when it seemed that his brain would boil in his skull and his blood turn molten in his veins, the wall stretched and wavered and, for the flicker of a moment, broke.

He was past it. He swayed heavily against the pommel of his saddle, and clung there for a long moment, dizzy and sick.

His warriors were staring, beginning to be afraid. He drew himself up with an effort, composed his face. Behind them all, the ban had restored itself. Nothing came hunting; no sign in earth or sky betrayed that the wielder of the wards had marked their breaking.

He laughed as much for defiance as for joy, and touched his gelding to a canter.

He would happily have shed his escort and taken the straight road to Masyaf, but some last remnant of circumspection kept him where he was. Night was coming; his horse was tired. As, for a very surety, was he. What matter if he rested in camp or in a Hospitaller stronghold?

To Arslan and his companions it was Hisn al-Akrad, Castle of the Kurds; but to the Franks who surrounded him, Krak des Chevaliers, Krak of the Knights, that warded the marches of Tripoli. It loomed on its crag, wall and tower, rampart and keep, vast and impregnable. Nothing in the west could match it; in the east, none that Aidan knew.

It was beautiful against the pitiless sky, beautiful and terrible. But Aidan could have no fear of it. It was not Masyaf.

His mamluks tried to imitate his calm. Even through the vast echoing gate. Even in the courtyard which could have swallowed a whole castle in Francia, where they must leave their horses and, at last, surrender their weapons. Aidan let a grim-faced sergeant disarm him and search him, saying with hard-won lightness, "Mind where you put these. I'll be wanting them back."

"That's for the castellan to say," the sergeant said. He handed Aidan's daggers and his sword to a lay brother, and turned toward his commander. "He's clean, sir."

The knight nodded. His helm was off, his coif on his shoulders, baring a weathered, ageless face, greying hair cropped short round the tonsure, beard grown long after the custom of the warrior monks. Here in his own place, among his own people, he could ease a little, allow himself to wonder if perhaps, after all, this oddity of the road spoke the truth. "You'll come with me," he said, still giving no honor and no title, but offering no enmity, either.

Aidan did not move. "Alone?"

The knight frowned slightly. "One other, then."

"And the rest?"

The frown deepened. "They'll be looked after."

"As guests?"

Aidan walked a thin and dangerous line, and he knew it. But it seemed that the Hospitaller saw no profit in anger. "As guests," he said. "Until you are proven otherwise."

Aidan inclined his head to courtesy. In Arabic, to his mamluks, he said, "I'm going with this man. You are guests; conduct yourselves as such, or you'll answer to me. Raihan, you come."

He was aware, as they were, that his words and their obedience were watched and weighed. For that, they bowed all together, with grace and pride and no little defiance, and went where Hospitaller servants led them. Raihan stayed, wanting to cry his unworthiness, but too proud to do it before so many Frankish faces. Aidan laid an arm about his shoulders and grinned at him. "Well, younger brother. Shall we show these people what we're made of?"

That stiffened his back for him. He would never forget that he had failed of his guard when he was most needed, but he was learning to forgive himself. Aidan smiled, satisfied. He let the boy fall back to the guardsman's place, a pace or two behind, and followed their guide into the inner places of the castle.

Eastern custom held even here, where God's knights stood guard against the Saracen. Although the austerity of bare stone and dim-lit passages was all of the monastery and the west, there were signs of a gentler world: a carpet, a hanging, a chapel with an altar cloth of Byzantine silk. Aidan was offered a bath, food and drink, fresh garments. That they were a test, he well knew. He greeted the wine with heartfelt joy, warned Raihan from the pork roasted in spices, left him to choose bread and mutton and clean water. But Raihan had let the servant dress him as a Frank, taking a wicked pleasure in it, which he shared with his master. Aidan had seen young lords in Jerusalem who wore cotte and hose less convincingly than this, and with less grace.

When they had eaten, they began to test the limits of their freedom. They were not, it would seem, either prisoners or guarded, unless the silent and ubiquitous servant counted as such. Raihan tried the door; the servant watched him carefully, but made no move. Boldly then he strode into the passage. His steps receded, light but firm, and no hesitation in them.

He came back with escort. A Hospitaller knight, again, but not the one who had brought them to Krak. At first Aidan did not know him. It was a long black while since a knight of the Hospital had come to see Gereint laid in his tomb.

He paused just within the door, with Raihan ahead of him, black-browed and forbidding. Carefully, in Arabic, he said, "Lord prince. I thought it might be you."

"Brother Gilles," Aidan said, smiling in spite of himself. "You were expecting me?"

The Hospitaller eased visibly, and met smile with smile. "Not, perhaps, in such company."

Aidan laughed aloud. "I'll wager not! I was shocked that your order would treat with Saracens. And here am I, master of a pack of them."

"That's a story I'd be pleased to hear," said Gilles, "if you were minded to tell it."

"It's simple enough," Aidan said. "I learned the virtue of necessity. The Assassin has been my teacher; the sultan, my fellow scholar. He gave me what his own necessity forbade him to use. I was," said Aidan, "taken aback, to say the least."

"No more than I, when I heard that one had come who could only be yourself, but in the guise of a Saracen emir. That's a long summer's journey, even for the Prince of Caer Gwent."

"It has been . . . very long." Aidan had not meant to sound so deathly weary. "Thibaut is dead. Did you know that?"

Gilles nodded somberly.

"A little while ago, in Aleppo, his sister was struck and nearly killed. That she lives is no credit to my guardianship. But I have seen the face of the Assassin. I may even, however feebly, have left my mark on her."

"Her?" Gilles wondered, visibly, if Arabic had failed one or both of them.

Aidan bared his teeth and spoke in the *langue d'oc.* "Yes, Brother. A woman. A female, at least; a she-demon with a silver dagger. Haven't you heard of the Slave of Alamut?"

"A legend," said Gilles: "a terror of the night."

"A very real one. I hold two lives to her account; the third, God willing, will be the death of her."

Gilles said nothing.

"Yes," said Aidan. "Yes, she is like me. My folly, that I would not believe; that I saw her, and knew her, and never dreamed that she would be the death that stalked me." He was breathing hard; his hands were fists. Grimly he mastered himself. "She is older than I, and stronger. She guards her lair well; for long and long she has kept me from it. And yet, perhaps, God has remembered me. He sent your brother in the cross to find me, even as I contemplated battering down the walls of magic with which she barred the road to Masyaf.

Alone I was never strong enough. In the company of your brothers, warded by their humanity, I passed the wall. Now I am within it, and the way is clear. I owe you and yours a mighty debt for that."

Gilles took time to comprehend all of that: time which Aidan was glad to give, for it freed him to sink down, weary beyond desperation. At length the Hospitaller said, "There is no debt but what is God's. I offered you what aid the order may give; it was offered freely, without price. Even, in the test, without our knowing that we gave it."

"And yet it was given. I shall remember." So he had said before, in the courtyard in Aqua Bella, ages ago in the soul's time.

"You expect us to let you go," said Gilles.

Aidan raised his head. The Hospitaller flinched from the light in his eyes. "Can you hold me?"

"Mostly likely not," Gilles said. "Yet for your life's sake, we might try."

"No," said Aidan. "You fear that, after all, I may kindle a spark that will sear even you in your castles on the marches of Islam. What surety can I give you, that in this I hazard myself alone?"

"Yourself, and twelve mamluks of the Syrian sultan."

"They are part of me. I guard them as myself."

Gilles drew a slow breath. "I am not the ranking officer here. Simply a brother of the order, who thought that he might know an answer to the riddle of the Frank who seemed a Saracen. The castellan is minded to keep you here under guard until you should prove yourself no threat to us or to our castle. I can speak for you, but I must tell the truth. I think that you go to your death."

"That will be as God wills. I have no great desire to die, you may believe that. The death which I desire is another's altogether."

A knight of the Hospital could indeed believe that, and

understand it. But Gilles, who was monk as well as warrior, said slowly, "Revenge is hardly a Christian sentiment."

"Then my confessor shall hear of it when I am done."

Gilles shook his head in wry surrender. "A very perfect prince, and Christian enough for the purpose. Have you quite corrupted your Saracens?"

"Not noticeably," Aidan said.

They watched Raihan, who, forgotten, had begun his sunset prayer. After a moment Gilles said, "Will you hear vespers with us?"

Aidan bowed acquiescence.

He had not heard an office of his own faith since he crossed the Jordan, nor stood and knelt and prayed in the company of monks in time out of mind. They were all men here, all deep voices in the chanting. No women, ever; no boys. Those had no place on the sword's edge.

This was an army in the midst of war. And yet the words were the same as they had ever been, words of rest and of peace.

Aidan took no comfort in them. He had gone too far; he had suffered too much. For him there would be no peace until the Assassin was dead.

The Hospitallers ended their worship and withdrew from the chapel. Aidan remained in the stall to which Gilles had guided him. Gilles had gone out with the rest. A young brother extinguished the candles one by one, all but the vigil lamp over the altar. Aidan, in the shadows, he seemed not to see. He bowed low to the altar, straightened, yawned audibly, and departed.

In a little while a shadow crept by inches through the door. A sneeze betrayed it: the shock of incense to unaccustomed senses. It slid along the wall, desperately uneasy in this alien holiness, but needing its master's presence. On the edge of the stalls it hesitated. Aidan made no move. It darted, silent and sudden, and dropped panting at his feet. Raihan's eyes stared up at him, startlingly pale in the dark face, and all but blind where Aidan's eyes saw but dimmed daylight. He trembled against Aidan's knees, hating this place, but determined to stay in it. "I went," he whispered. "I went to see where the others are."

"Are they well?" Aidan asked, not loudly but not particularly softly.

"They would be, if they could be with you. But they're obedient. They wait for you to command them."

"Soon," Aidan said. He leaned back in the stall and closed his eyes. When he opened them, Gilles was there, and the knight of the road, and a third who was older than either: a lean, weathered whipcord of a man, whose black Hospitaller habit sat on him like well-worn mail. All soldier, this one, and yet all God's; no gentle cloistered monk, but a warrior of the faith, as fixed and firm in it as any Muslim.

Aidan rose to accept the blessing of the castellan of Krak. He staggered a little, rising. The ban had taken greater toll of body and power than he wanted to know.

None but Raihan seemed to see: his shoulder was there, unobtrusive, bracing where it was needed. Aidan rested very lightly on it before he knelt for the blessing.

As the castellan gave it, he said, "You are welcome to Krak, lord prince."

Aidan inclined his head. "Reverend father."

"Gauthier de Tournai," said Gilles.

Aidan's head bent again.

The castellan looked up at him, measuring him against what had been said of him. "I see you haven't gone completely infidel."

"I'm not likely to," Aidan said, "reverend father."

The castellan nodded. "The king will be glad of you, if you live to serve him. You won't reconsider?"

"Not until my vow is kept."

"Even if it kills you?"

"Would you do any less?"

"No," said the castellan. He drew himself up. "I have no authority to prevent you. If you were to ask my counsel, I would see you returned to Jerusalem and sworn to the king's service. Since my brother here gives me to know how little I can hope for that, then I can do no more and no less than set you on your way."

"My thanks," Aidan said, meaning it: more than the castellan knew. But Gilles understood. He smiled behind his superior's back, widely enough to encompass a battle hard fought but well won.

"You may stay," said the castellan, "as long as it pleases you, and leave when you will. You are the guest of the Hospital; what aid we can give, you may have."

"I ask only a night's lodging for myself and my following, and your prayers."

"You have both," said the castellan.

Aidan swayed. It came on like that, sometimes: power taxed to its limit and then beyond it, turning his body traitor.

This time Raihan was not swift enough, or invisible enough. Gilles caught him through the mamluk's glare. "You're ill," he said.

Aidan shook his head, too hard: he nearly fell. "Only need sleep," he said. It sounded odd. He tried to say it again. "Sleep—need to—"

They carried him to bed. He had no strength to fight them. Most of them went away, but Gilles lingered, frowning down at him. "If she is too strong for you already, how do you hope to face her in open battle?"

Aidan's tongue at least was his own again, now that his body was at ease. "Do I have a choice?"

"Probably not." Gilles sighed. "Will you be shriven, at least, before you go?"

"Have you the authority to do it?"

"I, no. I've taken only monk's vows."

Aidan closed his eyes. "Then I'll live in sin for yet a while."

"I should be scandalized," Gilles said.

Aidan smiled in the dark behind his eyelids. "Brother, I am a scandal. Would you have me confess to a stranger, how very much of one I am?"

"Under the seal of the confessional, what harm can it do?"

"Enough," Aidan said, "and little enough good. Let be, Brother. I am what I am. I do as I must. We'll fight the infidel yet, you and I."

"God willing," said Gilles.

Aidan laughed, though he was fast falling into sleep. "You sound like a Saracen."

"Sometimes even an infidel may perceive a little of the truth."

"As God wills," Aidan said, smiling still. "He will, Brother. Only wait, and see."

26

All of Sayyida's men were fed and settled into the day: Father and Maimoun in the smithy, Hasan with Fahimah who was minded to spoil him for an hour. Sayyida, freed and oddly incomplete, went to tidy the room she shared with Maimoun. She smiled a little as she went. He had promised to come again tonight, and he had all but promised to let her go out to the bazaar in a day or two. Subtlety, that was what he needed. Allah knew, it had taken her long enough to discover it.

The tiny cell of a room was blind dark. She made her way deftly through it to fling open its window, and paused, savoring the warmth of sun on her cheeks.

A whisper of sound brought her about. Someone huddled on the mat: white and scarlet and sudden, astonishing crimson. Sayyida named it in surprise and pleasure. "Morgiana!" Then, less joyfully: "Morgiana. What in the world—"

She was wound in a knot, trembling. Sayyida touched her shoulder. She knotted tighter. She was weeping. Sayyida gathered her in and held her.

She stilled; in shock, it might have been. Had she ever wept? Had anyone ever given her plain love, with no price on it?

Her body loosened from its knot. She raised a face that, even blurred with tears, was beautiful. It was a long moment before Sayyida comprehended what was beneath it. Her throat was livid, swelling almost as Sayyida stared. Her voice was a raw whisper. "I wasn't supposed to come here."

"Who told you that?"

Her head shook, tossing. She struggled upright. Her hair tangled in her face; she raked it back. Stopped. Stared at her hands. There was blood on them, not much, but enough; drying, beginning to crack. She shuddered. "Clean. Must be —clean—"

There was water near, for washing in the morning, before the prayer. Sayyida brought the jar to the mat, and gently, persistently for Morgiana kept trying to recoil, sponged away the blood. It had a scent, faint yet potent, like earth and iron.

"Heart's blood," said the battered remnant of Morgiana's voice. "But not . . . not lifeblood. I failed. I, who have never failed of a kill." She tried to laugh; it was hideous to hear. "For once it was clean hate and not cold murder. For once, I truly wanted a life. And Allah took it from me."

"It looks," said Sayyida, "as if He had help." With a clean cloth and the last of the water, she began to bathe the tortured throat. Those were brands on it: finger-wide, a little narrower than her own, but much longer.

Morgiana's fists struck cloth and hand aside. "Let me be!"

Calmly Sayyida came back. "Don't shout," she said. "You'll ruin your voice."

Morgiana hissed, but when she spoke, it was in a whisper. "Allah had nothing to do with it. It was not even Iblis. It was a Frank of my blood, and I taught him to hate me."

"A Frank?" Sayyida paused. "Your Frank?"

The ifritah's lip curled. "Never mine. He belongs to a great cow of a giaour. A mortal woman, a Christian's wife; but no wife of his."

Sayyida needed a moment to make sense of that. "You found him in bed with someone else's wife?"

"I found my master's quarry dancing the old wicked dance with her guardsman, who is no more a mortal man than I am mortal woman. I struck as I have never struck, in hot hate, and it blinded me. I smote awry. And now he knows me, and he hates me, and he has flung all his heart and power into the saving of his doxy's life."

"He tried to kill you."

She laughed again, choking on it. "Not—not kill. Nothing so merciful. He cast me out." Tears streamed from her eyes, through the horrible, strangled laughter. "He hates me. But I —but I—I want him more than ever."

"Some women are like that," said Sayyida. "They need a man who can master them."

Morgiana stiffened. "I am *not*—"

"Don't shout."

She drew a shaking breath. Her eyes were cat-wild. "I—do —*not*—need a master. I need *him*. Do you think I'm glad of it? He wants my blood. He fancies himself man and prince. Infant. Child. This"—her fingers brushed her throat—"this is a youngling's trick. If he were a man, he would have finished it."

"Thank Allah he didn't, then." Sayyida frowned. "You're going to need more than water on this."

"I need nothing."

Not all grown infants, Sayyida reflected, were male. "You stay here, and stay quiet. I'll be back directly."

For a miracle, Morgiana was still there when Sayyida came back, curled on the mat, white-faced and silent and exquisitely miserable. She submitted quietly to salves and compresses, and to the soft wrappings with which Sayyida bound them. She had emptied of rage. "He's hunting me now," she said. "He thinks I've laired in Masyaf. Wise fool. Shall I indulge him? Shall I go back, and let my master command me to kill him? I could, I think. An oath is a wonderful, terrible thing."

"You'll stay here," said Sayyida, "and try not to think about killing. Here, I've brought you something cool to drink, and in a little while, when you want it, you can eat."

Morgiana did not want the sherbet, but Sayyida coaxed it into her. She lay back after, a little less wretched, and beginning to nod. "I can't stay," she said in her rough whisper. "My master—I haven't told him—"

"Your master can wait. Sleep. You're safe here."

She laughed: a brief gust of breath. "Safe. Yes, I'm safe. Who can touch me? Who can slay the Angel of Death?"

"Hush," said Sayyida, alarmed.

Morgiana shook her head and yawned, delicately, as a cat will; startling herself with it. "Don't be afraid. We know one another well, he and I. Aren't I the most faithful of his servants?"

"Not here," Sayyida said.

"No. Pray Allah, never here." Morgiana's eyes squeezed shut. Tears welled from beneath the lids; she turned her face away, angrily.

She cried herself to sleep. Sayyida stayed with her, saying nothing, stroking her hair with a gentle hand.

When her breathing slowed and steadied at last, Sayyida drew back. She would sleep for a while: there had been a draught in the sherbet. It was a mark of Morgiana's trouble that she had not tasted it.

Sayyida smoothed the coverlet over her and rose, sighing a little. She would never think of questioning Allah's will, but this was a burden. She did not know that she would be able to bear it. Maimoun would be furious: just when she had begun to work him round to seeing sense.

Allah would provide. He would have to.

To be sure, He began it well. Fahimah was alone, at an hour when all the women usually gathered to ply their needles. Hasan slept, flushed and deeply content.

"Ah, the darling," said Fahimah as Sayyida came to stand by them. "He played as hard as he could play, and then, out he went, as sweet as you please."

"Someday I'll understand how you do it," Sayyida said. She reached toward the basket of mending, hesitated. "Where are the others?"

"Your mother has a headache," said Fahimah. "Laila took Shahin to the bazaar. There's a new caravan come in."

Laila always knew when the caravans came. She seldom remembered to tell anyone else.

For once, Sayyida was glad. She dropped down in front of Fahimah and took the plump hands in hers, thread and needle and all. Fahimah smiled, startled and pleased. "Little mother," Sayyida said. "Fahimah, can you help me?"

"You know I always try, child."

Sayyida swallowed hard. This might not be a wise secret to share. But she could not keep it alone. It was too heavy. "Fahimah, Morgiana is here. Maimoun has forbidden me to see her. But how can I turn her away? She's hurt; she needs me. I can't cast her out."

Fahimah wasted no time in trivialities. "Hurt? How?"

Sayyida bit her lip. "Someone tried to kill her. But it's not that," she said hastily. "That's easy enough to mend. It's . . . she loves him, and he wants her dead."

"Did she try to kill someone he loves?"

Sayyida gaped like an idiot.

Fahimah shook her head. She looked no more clever than she ever did: a round, comfortable, faintly silly woman, whom one went to when one wanted ease or comfort or unquestioning acceptance. She said, "Allah gives every woman the man she deserves. Even the Slave of Alamut."

"You *know?*"

"Little one," she said, "my wits aren't the quickest in the

world, but sometimes they don't need to be. When I married your father, he gave me some of his secrets to keep. This was one of them."

"Then you can help?"

"Let me see," said Fahimah.

"Ah, the poor child," she said, bending over the sleeping Assassin. Between them they had carried her to the room that was Fahimah's, washed her and clothed her in Laila's castoffs, and taken her bloodied garments to be burned. Asleep, with her astonishing hair tamed in a braid, she seemed all harmless, too young and slender by far to bear such a burden of death.

"Not so poor," said Sayyida, "and not such a child." Hasan yearned out of her arms; she yielded abruptly, and let him curl in the hollow of Morgiana's body. He seemed to know what was expected of him: he was quiet, and although he could not resist the wine-red braid, he contented himself with nibbling on the end of it. " 'Giana," he said distinctly. " 'Giana."

Sayyida clapped hands to her mouth. Fahimah was less restrained. She swept him up. "His first word, Sayyida! His very first! Oh, the little prince!"

The little prince showed clear signs of his displeasure. " 'Giana!" he demanded peremptorily.

" 'Giana," Sayyida sighed, as Fahimah returned him to the place he wanted. "His first word, and I can't even tell his father."

"There will be others," Fahimah comforted her. "Come now, stay with him, and I'll see to everything."

"But—" Sayyida began.

A frown was so rare a sight on that gentle face, that it quelled Sayyida utterly. She bent her head; Fahimah nodded, satisfied, and went to do Sayyida's duties as well as her own.

At least Sayyida could keep herself busy: she had brought the basket with her, and enough needlework in it to last out the month. She settled to it with the patience that every woman learned, if she was wise, long before she put on the veil.

Morgiana slept through the day and into the night. Sayyida worried, for she had not meant to give so large a dose, but it seemed a natural sleep. She breathed easily; her face was no paler than it ever was. Sometimes she stirred, to lie on her side or to shift a cramped limb. When Fahimah came to change the guard, she was calm about it. "She'll wake when she's ready to wake. Go to your husband, child."

It seemed that Sayyida was always going or staying at someone's bidding. She left Hasan, fed and drowsy, where he so obviously preferred to be, and arranged her expression for Maimoun.

He suspected nothing. He wanted to talk about an idea he had had, a new way to work a pattern in a dagger's hilt. It was interesting, she granted that; she did her best to listen and make the proper noises. She even saw a way round a problem; he was lavish in his praises. She was glad when the flood of talk began to ebb. He was eager for her tonight, but he was trying: he went a little slower, the way she liked it, and a little gentler than his young male urgency might have called for.

For a little while, she let him carry her out of her troubles. But he was sated too soon, as he often was, and then he was asleep. And she was alone beside him, her body like a note half-sounded, her mind cravenly glad that it was over. She found herself wondering what it would be like to share a bed with an ifrit. He would know everything she felt, everything she wanted. Would he fall asleep as soon as he was satisfied, and leave her to lie awake?

She shook her head, annoyed at herself. There was another side to that coin: no solitude when one wanted it, and no secrets. She could never have hidden Morgiana from a demon lover.

* * *

The second day was harder. Laila was home, and needed art to elude. Mother, recovered from her headache, wanted to be catered to. Hasan was fretful; Sayyida went in imminent dread that he would try his new word on someone injudicious.

Allah offered one small mercy, if mercy it was: when Morgiana regained her senses, Sayyida was there. She woke cursing the light and her pounding head; her voice was a croak. It must have been agony to swallow, let alone to speak. Somehow Sayyida got a cupful of coolness into her: plain water, this time, and after she spat the first mouthful in Sayyida's face, she seemed to recognize it. She drank thirstily; when the cup was empty, she leaned back on Sayyida's arm, glaring. "Never," she whispered. "Never dose me again without telling me. I'm not like a human woman. You could have poisoned me."

"But I didn't," Sayyida said.

"No thanks to your leechcraft. How long have I been asleep?"

"A day and a night," Sayyida admitted.

Morgiana staggered up. She promptly fell down again, dragging Sayyida with her. The second time, she moved more slowly, and settled for sitting up, holding her head in her hands. With great care she let it go. It seemed to stay where she bade it; she drew a long breath. "Beard of the Prophet! Girl, if I loved you even a little less, I would have your hide for this."

"Go ahead and take it. Maimoun can have the leavings."

Morgiana seized her. Even weakened with sleep and the drug, her hands were cruelly strong. "Has he made you suffer for me? Tell me!"

"He doesn't even know you're here. Nor will he, until we're most properly ready. Can you play an indigent cousin whose husband has set her aside? You'll have to wear a veil when he's likely to be near, and cover your hair."

"What good will that do? The women will still know me."

"They'll get enough of the truth to keep them quiet. Fahimah already knows everything."

Morgiana shook her head. "I have to go. My master is waiting. The hunt is up. It won't touch Masyaf, I've long since made sure of that, but the Frank may be stronger than I think. I've dallied here more than long enough."

"Can't you do what you need to do from here? You told me about guard-magic. It's nothing that calls on you to be in your master's clutches." Morgiana's grip loosened; Sayyida took her hands. "Stay at least until your throat stops hurting."

"I can't."

"A day, then. Or two. Hasan said a word yesterday. It was your name. Don't you want to hear it for yourself?"

Morgiana knew blackmail when she heard it. She scowled, but she said, "A day. No more. To get over the poison you dosed me with."

That would do, for a beginning.

"For an ending," said Morgiana, snatching the thought from her head. "Now. Where is this eloquent son of yours?"

27

Aidan left Krak in the early morning, rested if not entirely hale, and fixed on his course. Gilles rode with him as far as the border of the Hospitallers' lands, as much for a surety should they meet with Hospitaller scouts, as for the company. The black robe and the white cross stood out oddly amid the mamluks' scarlet, but he rode easily, trying his Arabic on Aidan's hellions and winning them over with skill that even the prince could admire.

At the border between the Hospitallers' lands and those of Masyaf, stood an ancient milestone, the name of a forgotten procurator carved on it, too dim and ageworn now to read.

Gilles drew rein beside it. The others paused, spreading a little, watchful. "Lord prince," said the Hospitaller. "Won't you reconsider even yet? Yonder madman has done the Lady Margaret all the harm that he can do."

"No, Brother," Aidan said. "That, he has not. Her daughter has a son in fosterage near Acre."

"But surely, an infant—"

"He didn't stop at a child or a woman. Why would he hesitate to kill a baby? Or worse. Take him; keep him. Raise him an Assassin."

Gilles smote his thigh with an armored fist. "Devil take you, man! The Sultan of Syria with all his armies couldn't even begin to break the power of Masyaf. And here are you, with a dozen half-grown boys and a string of skinny camels. He'll eat you alive."

"He might not," Aidan said. "He might let me in, to see how amusing I can be."

"And then?"

Aidan shrugged. "And then God will guide me. Or the devil, if you will. You forget what I am."

"I remember what he has of his own."

"She is flesh and blood, even as am I." He flexed his fingers before the Hospitaller's face. "These have left their brand on her already. Who's to say that I won't finish what I began?"

Gilles was silent for a long moment, eyes steady on Aidan's face. At last he raised his hand and signed the cross. "God go with you, my friend, and bring you home again."

Aidan bowed beneath the blessing. "God keep you," he said, "my friend."

He looked back once before the road bent, raising a spur of rock between. Gilles sat his patient horse by the milestone. His helm was on; he was a shape without a face, a knight of stone and steel. Aidan lifted his hand. The mailed arm went up in answer. Aidan turned away from it, toward the Assassins' country.

* * *

It was not so very far from Krak to Masyaf. A horseman could ride it in a day, if the need were great enough. Aidan did not choose to. It was not wholly cowardice. He was less strong than he wanted to be, and more prudent than a good madman ought to be. The way grew steep as they advanced, a narrow mountain track, now passing between high walls, now careening on the edge of the cliff. He kept a careful pace, his power stretched as much as it would allow, to warn of ambush.

With the approach of evening, he called a halt. The track widened briefly, and leveled enough for a camp; there was little forage, but the camels could make do with what there was. They pitched a rough and fireless camp, with a guard posted on the summit above them: Dildirim, who had drawn the short straw. He took it in good part, and he had the spare blanket, for the wind was blowing cold. "But mind you don't get too comfortable," Arslan warned him. "If you sleep and we come to grief for it, I'll dine on as much of your liver as the Assassin leaves behind."

Aidan, out of human earshot, swallowed a smile. It ended in a grimace. He should have tarried longer in Krak. He could admit it here, to no one but himself. A day, only, would have restored his strength.

Another night's sleep would do well enough. He rolled himself in cloak and blanket. The warmth against his back was Timur, the warmth at his feet Ilkhan. In a little while, Arslan came to warm the rest of him.

They were amply wary, for innocents. Morgiana, a shadow in the shadow of a stone, reckoned their disposition. He was in their center where a prudent commander should be, burning brighter in her eyes than the fire which they had been too wise to kindle, but dimmer than she remembered. So, then: the ban's crossing had had its price.

It had brought her from Damascus at last, out of too long an idleness. Sayyida and Fahimah between them had hidden her from Sayyida's pompous fool of a husband, whose only virtue was that Sayyida loved him. But for that, Morgiana would long since have taught him proper respect for his wife.

When this was done, she would begin his lessoning. Gently, if her temper held. There was, after all, Hasan. A boy should have a father, however sadly flawed.

A second shadow swelled her own. "All are ready," it breathed in her ear.

She stayed it with her hand. Lean wolf-bones flexed under her fingers, stiff with fear of her. She smiled mirthlessly into the dark. Yes, let him be afraid. Only let him serve her, and do as she bade.

Her fingers tightened, sprang free. "Now," she said.

Aidan started awake. It was deep dark: the dark before dawn. Even the wind was still, the stars burning cold in the vault of the sky. And yet, there was something . . .

Arslan stirred against him. He laid a hand over the boy's mouth; they lay still, eyes wide, ears straining.

It was too quiet.

The horses; the camels.

Gone.

Aidan eased his sword from its scabbard.

The night went mad.

They were not Assassins. Aidan did not know why, but he needed to be sure of that. They were Bedouin, wolves of the desert, abandoning stealth to shrill their wild war-cry. It flung the mamluks out of sleep and onto their weapons; it roused the camp to battle. No time to gather for defense, no space. Arslan struggled to set himself at Aidan's back; the tide, relentless, swept him away.

They walled Aidan in spears. He hewed at them; they only grew the thicker. They pressed him close. They pricked him, hampering his sword-arm. He thrust the blade into its sheath and seized a spear, hurling its astonished wielder over his head.

Another kept his wits about him. Aidan froze. A spearpoint rested on the most tender of places. A white wolf-grin gleamed beyond it.

Aidan shattered that grin with the haft of the spear.

But the spearman had a dozen brothers, and each of them seemed to have a dozen more. None of whom would give Aidan a proper battle. Only prick, and prick, and prick, and circle, and sunder him from his mamluks.

Whom he could not find. Not one. Not with eye, not with mind.

Mind.

He forgot the spear in his hand and the spears that hemmed him in. He cast wide with voice and power. "Bitch! Murderer! Coward! Come out and face me!"

His tormentors fell back. He hardly saw. "Assassin! I know your stink. Come out of your lair!"

Nothing. No sight, no sign of her. He howled until the mountains rang. "Morgiana! *Morgiana!*"

The mountains came down, and the night with them.

The circle of Bedouin drew back, blinking in the grey dawn. Some of them were down. At least one was dead.

Morgiana spurned the dead man with her foot, and knelt by the one who had killed him. Very much alive, that one, but stunned: the butt of a spear had felled him even as he woke the echoes with her name. She spelled him deeper into darkness, only then daring to touch him, to lay her palm against his cheek. He was thinner than she remembered, the skin stretched tighter over the fine strong bones. "I shall teach you not to hate me," she said to him.

Her wolves watched with edged fascination. She wheeled upon them. "Take him up. Bind him as I tell you." And when they did not leap to obey: *"Now!"*

They moved quickly enough, once they had begun. Even

their kind could be wary of trespassing in the Assassins' domain; and they were deep in it. They bound the Frank with cords both soft and strong, and set him on the best of their camels. She rode behind him, steadying him. He was warm in her arms.

The Banu Nidal gathered the wounded and the dead, and swept the field clean. The greater part of them gathered their beasts and their booty and departed where Morgiana bade them, making all the speed that they might. A small company remained under her eye, but those were the best of them, their sheikh himself and the pack of his sons. Their way was the swifter and the more secret. They took it at racing pace, under a glamour that made of them a shadow and a shimmer.

The tribe camped on an oasis which was their secret, a green haven in circling mountains. The roads of trade and war ran closer to it than travelers knew, but the entry was narrow and hidden and most well guarded.

They rode down it in the last light of evening, stretching their weary mounts into a gallop, shrilling their victory. The guard of the pass let them through with a shout. In the field below, the tents emptied: women, children, a few sullen boys left behind to guard the camp. Old men, there were none. Men of the Banu Nidal lived only as long as they could fight.

Morgiana saw her prisoner laid in a tent beside the sheikh's own, on the tribe's best rugs and blankets. "This is mine," she said, "and I will drink the blood of the tribe, if I come for him and he is gone."

The sheikh nodded. "We can make sure of that," he said. He knelt and thrust up the dusty robe, and drew his knife. "Hamstrung, he'll do no running, but he'll be sturdy enough for aught else you wish. Or a quick thrust, here, in the heel, and a cord through it—"

She knocked him sprawling. "You shall answer to me with your own body for every drop of his blood you shed. That"— she slashed his bony chest with his own blade—"is for the word of his maiming. Keep him close and keep him safe, and cherish him as you cherish yourself, for his life shall be as yours." She held up a vial. "He will sleep for yet a while. When he wakes, dose him with this. But gently! If he sleeps too deep, or dies of it, I will see that you pay."

The sheikh took the vial in a hand that would not stoop to tremble. He feared her: he was no fool. But it was a clean fear, the fear of the wolf for the rival who bests him. He bowed to her will, but he did not lower his eyes. "I will guard him as myself."

She nodded, once, and turned her back on him. She paused to draw down Aidan's robe, and to brush his cheek with her fingers. In the space between breath and breath, she was gone.

Aidan wandered in a dim strange dream. He saw the camp on the mountain, and it was all broken and scattered. His mamluks were gone out of his knowing; the horses, the camels, his beautiful sword, all gone. Beyond grief was rage and loss and bitter helplessness.

The dream blurred. He lay in a woman's arms on a lofty, swaying bed. Her touch was gentle, her body warm and supple against him; her scent was wondrous sweet. Somewhere in the light, he knew that there should be hate. Here was only peace.

He clawed his way out of that peace, through a long dark and a longer twilight. His body was a shape limned in ache. Twilight shaped itself into mortal dimness: dark walls that shifted with the wind's song, air heavy with manifold stinks, man and goat and camel and ancient smoke all mingled. He gagged on it, and gagging, knew that he was awake.

He lay on musty carpet in a tent woven of goat's hair, bound hand and foot, with the throbbing of a blow in his head. Of the stroke he knew nothing. He had gone to sleep among his mamluks. He had—waked? Fought?

Yes. Fought. Now, too clearly, he was captive. But not in Masyaf. The wind's song was a song of open places, with voices in it, and the blatting of goats, the clatter of hoofs on stone, the roar of a camel.

His power stretched stiffly, but it stretched. He knew a moment's bitter amusement. So, then. He had had his night's sleep, however ill his body had taken it. He touched minds; a mind, more open than others, because it was younger and somewhat simple. Desert, oasis, camp. Banu Nidal: Bedouin, deep-desert tribesfolk, bound in service to Allah and to a demon of the air. The men were out raiding—resentment, at that; one should go, one was old enough, one could string one's father's bow—but the strongest had come back with the demon, and a morsel for the demon's dinner.

The morsel lay on his side in the tent, ascertaining that his bonds were cleverly tied. He could move with fair freedom, even sit up, but the knots were all out of his reach.

Sitting up was a mistake. His stomach, empty, did its best to heave itself out on the carpet.

The spasms passed too slowly, leaving him in a knot, shaking, running with cold sweat. For a long while he could do little more than breathe.

And, in spite of himself, think. Who the demon was, he could well guess. Time enough yet to wonder why she had brought him here and not to her master in Masyaf. Maybe they had had a falling-out. Or maybe she wanted to carve him into collops for her own, sole pleasure.

She was not here. That, he was reasonably sure of. He was being kept until she deigned to claim him.

The guard in front of his tent had heard his convulsions; but it was a bold man who meddled with the demon's prey, and this one was no paladin. Soon enough, someone else came to the guard's call, no bolder perhaps, but more mindful of the demon's will. *Unharmed,* the newcomer's mind jabbered. *Unharmed, or she dines on my liver.* Beneath it: *If he dies while we leave him unmolested, how can she blame us?* And, to that: *Easily. Oh, easily.*

Light stabbed him. A shadow blunted it. The reek of human and of goat nigh overwhelmed him. The mind babbled on. *Awake. Iblis take him! Food—water—the vial, as she commanded—* Inspiration struck; relief loomed huge. *Woman's work, that. Let a woman pay, if he takes ill.*

"Yes," Aidan said sweetly. "Let her."

The man fled.

He was not so timid in ruling his women. But the one who came, came of her own will, brandishing her bruises like a banner. She was a strong man's woman; she walked with pride, queenly erect even in the confines of the tent.

She wore no veil: strange after so long in Islam, to see a woman's naked face. She was hardly a beauty, and the desert had aged her well before her time. No doubt her husband had thought of that in allowing her to play nursemaid to the demon's prey.

He should have recalled that even unbeautiful women had eyes. Aidan was hardly a feast for them, bound and battered as he was, but she was accustomed to worse. He made her a gift of his most limpid smile.

She set down what she carried: a round of flat bread bearing a handful of dates and a bit of cheese, and a skin of what must surely be water, and a wooden cup. She was keenly aware of his beauty, but she was a damnably sensible woman. He was beautiful; Morgiana was terrible. It was a simple enough choice.

She helped him to sit up, this time with no worse consequence than a moment's dizziness. He was not, it was clear, to be unbound, even to eat. She fed him with visible enjoyment, bite by bite until he would take no more, and held the cup to his lips.

His nose wrinkled. Ancient goatskin, salt and sulfur—water of the desert as it too often was. But beneath it, something else. Darkness, and sleep.

His throat burned, crying for water. His will hardened against it. He fell forward. The cup flew from her hand, scattering its burden of sleep. He lunged upon the waterskin.

She snatched it away. "Ah," she said laughing, "a clever one! What would you give for it?"

"A smile," he said.

Her head tilted. "I already have that."

"If you already had a gold bezant, would you refuse another?"

"If I knew I could get something better."

"What would that be?"

Her eyes danced upon him. She was not so old; nor must she have been so unlovely, when she was young. "My husband is a terrible man, but She is more terrible than he. If you kiss me, what can he do but rage?"

"He can beat you."

She shrugged. "He hits me. I hit him back. Sometimes I win. Sometimes I let him win." She dangled the waterskin, enticing. "Are you thirsty, O my gazelle?"

"For your kisses, O my fawn."

She gave him both, with rich pleasure, and left him the waterskin: a gift more precious than gold. "Pretend," she advised as she left him. "Sleep. Him, I doubt you can buy with kisses; and She is not to be bought at all."

What she thought of Morgiana, he hardly needed power to see. She would reckon it a fair exchange, if she paid in pain to thwart the demon. But even she would not go so far as to set him free.

He lay where she had left him, flexing his wrists in their bonds. They were most well knotted.

No one, he noticed, had considered the most human consequence. Perhaps they expected him to soil himself. He was not ready to do that, yet.

Submission, he never thought of. The longer he lay, the surer he was, that he was not watched by other than mortal means. He was supposed to be deep in drugged sleep, mindless and helpless until she came for him.

He had an oath to keep, and a debt to pay: greater now by

the worth of a dozen mamluks. This captivity was no part of it.

His captors did not know what he was. She had not seen fit to tell them.

He began to smile.

28

Sayyida burrowed in the depths of the clothes press, winnowing outright rags from clothes that could be mended from what needed no mending at all. Laila always relegated to rags what she was tired of, no matter its condition; Sayyida had already found a veil of peacock silk with gold thread in it, that would do very well for when she wanted to look pretty for Maimoun. She wrapped it about her neck and dug deeper.

"This would suit you," someone said.

Sayyida erupted from the press. Morgiana held up a plum-colored gown. It clashed hideously with her hair.

By slow degrees Sayyida's heart stopped hammering. She took the gown in fingers that still shook a little, and drew a long, steadying breath. "I wish you wouldn't do that," she said.

The ifritah laughed. Her throat was a patchwork of greening bruises, but her voice was her own again, only a little huskiness left. She looked as if she would have liked to dance.

No sooner thought than done. She swept Hasan out of the tangle of castoffs and whirled him about, to his manifest delight.

"You're in good spirits," Sayyida observed, a little sourly.

Morgiana's grin was all mischief. "Oh, I am. I am!" She hugged Hasan to her and kissed him resoundingly on both cheeks. "Do you know what I've done?"

"Something appalling," said Sayyida.

"Oh, yes. It is that. I haven't even killed anybody." That sobered her a little. But her secret was too much for her. She held it yet a while, as if she could not bear to let it go. Then: "I have him now."

"Him?"

"Him!" She bounced; there was no other word for it. "My Frank. I caught him before anyone knew what I did, and took him away. He's safe now, till I'm ready to claim him."

Morgiana acting like a silly chit of a girl was a revelation. Sayyida tried to bring a little reason into the proceedings. "Does he have an opinion? Or aren't you letting him have one?"

"He will. When I'm ready." She laughed again, almost— Allah help them all—a giggle. "Do you remember how you almost poisoned me? I borrowed the bottle. He'll sleep till I want him to wake."

Worse and worse. "And then?"

"He wakes." She waited; Sayyida failed to extol her brilliance. "You don't see. He wakes, in the place I've readied for him. He'll be wild, I know that. But I'll tame him. From hate to love is no distance at all; and we belong together. He's a child, but he has the beginnings of sense. He'll see what has to be."

"You," said Sayyida, "are stark raving mad."

Even that could not touch Morgiana. "You are mortal," she said. "You think in mortal ways. He and I—we are of the same kind. He will remember that. He will come to see as I see."

"May Allah will it," Sayyida said.

Sayyida wore the veil and the gown that night. Morgiana was delighted to help her: to wash her hair with a little of Laila's henna and put it up with a clasp that Maimoun had made himself, silver set with turquoises; and paint for her eyes, and even a whisper of scent. She had not felt so close to beautiful since her wedding.

Maimoun was late in coming. That was nothing to fret

over: he was dining with a friend or two, and they liked to pass the night in playing backgammon. Maimoun would stay a while, for decency: a man should not seem too eager for his wife.

She waited alone. Fahimah and Morgiana had Hasan. She thought of going to fetch him, for the company, but it would hardly do for Maimoun to come back while she did it. She wriggled in her unaccustomed splendor, and tried not to rub the kohl from her eyelids. If he did not come soon, she was going to stop feeling splendid and start feeling silly. What was she doing in paint and scent and hennaed curls? She was plain gawky Sayyida, no more a beauty than she was a sultan's bride.

She knew his step: solid, like him, and a little self-important. It shook her out of her half-drowse, drew her up at the angle Morgiana had told her was her best, tensed her as it always did these days, since she had secrets to keep.

Outside the door, he hesitated. She held still. Sometimes his friends had wine, which she was not supposed to know about. But she always knew, because he moved more carefully and talked more freely, and his breath smelled of mint.

He came in slowly. His brows were knit. Her nose caught neither wine nor mint, but something sweeter. It reminded her of . . .

She was wearing it. Laila's perfume.

No. He would never do that. Not with his master's wife.

His eyes fixed on her face. He never saw the veil at all, or the gown, or even the kohl that made her eyes almost beautiful. He said, "You've been hiding something from me."

She opened her mouth, closed it again.

"I told you," he said. "I told you not to see her."

She could lie. She could deny. She could scream at him. She said calmly, "Who told you she was here?"

"Laila."

It was out before he thought. He flushed.

"That," she said, "was treachery."

His flush deepened to crimson. "You admit it?"

"I won't lie." Her hands shook; she knotted them. "I didn't have any choice, Maimoun. She was hurt; she was sick. She had nowhere else to go."

He advanced on her. "I forbade you. You defied me. How dared you? How *dared* you?"

Her back struck the wall. She did not even remember moving. She had never seen Maimoun like this. "Maimoun! Won't you listen? She's a friend. She came to me; she needed me. How could I cast her out?"

"I told you not to see her."

He bulked over her. She tried to get up; he pushed her down. She would not cry—she would not. "Why? Why do you hate her so much?"

"She is a horror. She has killed more times than anyone can count."

"Who told you that?"

He would not answer.

"It was Laila, wasn't it? You know how little she loves me."

"Sometimes she tells the truth."

"You don't even *know* the woman!"

"Woman? Woman, is it? I know whose slave she is. I know how she has cursed your family. I know it all, Sayyida. You thought you could keep it from me, didn't you? All of you." He sneered. "Bahram the eunuch. Bahram the unmanned, with a passion for silver-hilted daggers. You made a fool of me."

She clutched his coat. "Maimoun! Stop. Please, stop."

He tore her hands free. "No, I won't stop. You wouldn't stop harboring her, even when I expressly forbade you."

Something snapped. She did not want it to. She tried to hold it together, to keep her voice from shaking. "She needed me. I've known her since I was a baby. I couldn't turn her away."

"She needs nothing and no one. You chose. You chose her, and you defied me. What else have you done? Where have you gone? Whom have you seen? Spoken to? Slept with? Is even my son my own?"

"Maimoun," she said. "Don't."

He hauled her up. His spittle sprayed her face. "Don't! You command me, woman? You laugh in my face? Go on. Tell me the truth. Tell me how you scorn me."

"I don't."

"Liar."

Her breath caught: a sob. "Don't call me that."

"I'll call you anything I please."

She could not hold it in any longer. She was sorry. She did not want it. But it was too big; it was too strong. It was rage.

It came softly, softly. "You will not," it said to him.

He shook her, rocking her head on her neck. "I will. Liar." Shake. "Liar." Shake. "Liar!"

Her hand tore free and smote him with all the force of rage and grief and betrayal.

He clubbed her down.

"That," said a voice as soft as the voice of Sayyida's rage, "was not wise."

At first he seemed not to hear it. He gaped down at Sayyida, as if he could not understand how she had got there, sprawled at his feet. She stared up. What opened in her, she knew with cold certainty, was hate.

Morgiana stepped between them. She was in white. She looked like a flame before Maimoun's dark solidity; there was nothing human in her. Hasan clung huge-eyed to her neck.

Maimoun's face had been crimson. It went as white as Morgiana's coat.

She took no notice of him at all. "Shall I kill him?" she asked.

Sayyida swallowed painfully. Her lip was split; she tasted blood. "No," she said. "No, he's not worth killing." She paused. "You haven't done anything to Laila, have you?"

The ifritah smiled with terrible contentment. "No. Nothing. Except . . ." Her voice trailed off.

"What did you do?"

Her apprehension made Morgiana laugh. "Nothing criminal, I trust. I simply laid a wishing on her. To her husband, she must speak the truth, and only the truth, as she thinks it, without embellishment. It was," she said, "illuminating for all concerned."

Sayyida could not laugh. She did not think that she would ever laugh again. But she mustered a smile. "I can imagine."

Morgiana's eyes sharpened; she leaned toward Sayyida. Her finger brushed the throbbing lip. She hissed. "He struck you."

It was nothing, Sayyida was going to say. Not for love of Maimoun. Simply because she did not want any human creature to die on her account.

But he spoke first, blustering, blind to any good sense, seeing only that he was male and this, even this, was female. "Yes, I struck her. She is my wife. She is mine to do with as I please."

"She is?" Gentle, that. Maiden-soft, maiden-sweet. Deadly dangerous.

He heard only the softness. His chest swelled. "She is." He held out his hands. "Give me my son, and get out."

Hasan's face was buried in Morgiana's shoulder. She looked from him to his father. Her nostrils flared. "What will you do if I refuse? Hit me?"

"A beating would do you good."

"You think so?" She was all wide eyes and maidenly astonishment. "You really think so?"

Even he could hardly be as great a fool as to be taken in by that. He paused, eyes narrowing. She laid her cheek against Hasan's curls. One arm cradled the child. The other settled about Sayyida's shoulders.

His hands came up. One, a fist, wavered between the women. The other snatched at Hasan.

Morgiana recoiled. Sayyida leaped. Which of them she

meant to defend, she never knew. His blow, too well begun, caught the side of her head and flung her against the ifritah. Morgiana cried out. Sayyida tried to. "No! Don't kill. Don't kill—"

Silence.

Sayyida sat down hard. Her rump protested: it knew stone. Her head reeled, not only with the blow.

This was no room she knew.

She clutched. Yes, stone. A carpet over it, rich and jewel-beautiful. Lamps in a cluster; hangings of silk, flame-red, flame-blue, flame-gold.

Morgiana, white and crimson and fierce cat-green, with Hasan staring about in grave astonishment.

Sayyida held out her arms. He filled them; she held him tight and tried not to shake. Very, very soon, she was going to break into screaming hysterics. "Where," she managed to ask. "Where are we?"

"Away." Morgiana knelt in front of her. "This is my place, my secret."

"Is it where you go, when you go away?"

"Sometimes."

Sayyida clung to Hasan and rocked. She was cold; she was all bleak inside. More had broken tonight than her patience. "You didn't—you didn't kill him. Did you?"

"You told me not to." Morgiana hesitated. She looked—of all things, she looked uncertain. "I left him goggling and yelling for you to come back."

Sayyida's heart clenched.

"I can take you," said Morgiana. "If you want it."

"No." Sayyida had not meant to say it. But her tongue had a will of its own. "No. He called me a liar. He grants me no trust and no honor. He cages me. I won't go back to that."

"I won't make you."

Sayyida thrust words past the knot in her throat. "Will you let me stay here?"

"As long as you need," Morgiana said.

Forever! Sayyida almost cried. But she was not as far gone as that, even yet. "For . . . for a while," she said. "Until I know what I want. If you don't—"

"How can I mind? I brought you here."

Sayyida laughed, because if she did not, she would burst into tears. "It's like a story. The princess in distress, swept away to the enchanter's castle. Do all stories come down to as little as this?"

Morgiana touched the mark of Maimoun's fist. "Not so little," she said.

The tears came then, for all that Sayyida could do. Morgiana eased the whimpering Hasan out of her arms. She lay on her face and wept herself dry.

When Sayyida set her mind on something, she held to it, though it tore her to the heart. She would not hear of her family; she would not speak of what had happened. She settled in Morgiana's lair, with the baby to keep her busy, and a thousand small tasks such as Morgiana would never think of, still less find worth doing. They did, Morgiana admitted, make a difference, albeit a subtle one. Sayyida claimed a corner of the hall for herself and Hasan, heaped rugs and cushions there, and tried to keep in it the toys and baubles that Morgiana brought for the baby. In the lesser cavern, where was an ancient and blackened hearthstone and where the roof made itself a chimney to the distant sky, she established her kitchen. The rest she kept clean and tidy; she exiled the lizards and the spiders to a quarter near the cavemouth, and the mice with them, since Morgiana would not hear of their expulsion.

Morgiana had no delusions about her prowess as a housewife, but before a master of the art, she felt keenly all that she lacked. It dismayed her a little. It amused her considerably. She was—yes, more than anything, she was pleased to have these interlopers here, living in her secret place, changing it to suit their pleasure.

She had, she realized, been lonely. She lay on her mounded cushions, with the wind blowing cold without and the lamps flickering warmly within, and watched Hasan play on the floor. His mother sat near him, her smooth dark head bent over the coat which she was making for him. There was always a darkness in her now, a hard cold knot of obstinacy, but her surface was placid, even content.

She looked up and smiled. Morgiana smiled back. Neither said anything. They did not need to. That was friendship, that silence.

Much later, Morgiana woke. Hasan slept peacefully. Sayyida seemed to, but beneath the stillness, the tears flowed soft and slow.

It was time, Morgiana knew, to wake again from being to doing. Sayyida was in as much comfort as she could be. When Morgiana left, she was in the innermost cave with Hasan, availing herself of its great treasure: the hot spring that welled into a pool side by side with one both cold and pure.

Morgiana smiled and stepped *round* and *through,* into another air altogether.

The Banu Nidal were in ferment. Half of them seemed to be trying to break camp; half, to be milling about aimlessly, wringing their hands. The sheikh stood in their midst, holding the rein of a spent and trembling camel.

He did not even start when Morgiana stepped out of the air, although his face went a little greyer. He nearly fell as he went down in obeisance.

She pulled him to his feet with rough mercy. There was, she noticed, a wide and silent circle around them, widening as the moments passed. People seemed unusually intent on making themselves scarce.

"I am to blame," the sheikh said. "Mighty spirit, daughter of fire, the fault is entirely mine. Take me and welcome, but spare my people."

She was slower than she should have been: she had only

begun to understand. Her power darted, proving it. She seized him by the throat. *"Where is he?"*

He gasped, gagged. She loosened her fingers a fraction. "Great lady, we do not know. We have been hunting him. But nowhere—nowhere—"

Someone thrust in between them: his senior wife, fiercely defiant. "You never told us that he was a son of Iblis!"

Morgiana drew back a step. It was not a retreat.

Nor did the woman read it as such; but it fed her courage. "You should have told us," she said. "We guarded him exactly as you commanded, as the mortal man he seemed to be. How were we to know that he was no mortal at all?"

It was new, and strange: to be put to shame by a human woman. Morgiana was, for the moment, beyond anger. "Tell me," she said.

She gained it in more than words. Evening; the sunset prayer past, the women bent over the fires, scents of the nightmeal hanging heavy in the air. The guard was vigilant by the prisoner's tent, and prudence had tethered the bull camel behind where a clever captive might think to escape.

He strolled out past the stunned and helpless guard, dangling the cords in his hand. One of the sheikh's sons leaped to seize him; he spoke a word, and the boy stood rooted, staring. He went straight to the sheikh and bowed, and thanked him graciously for his hospitality.

"And then," said the sheikh's wife, "he spread wings and flew away."

Morgiana saw it as they had seen it. He was never so tall as they imagined, his face never so white a splendor, but the mantle of fire was power for a surety; and the wings that he spread, part shadow and part glamour, with a shimmer of red-gold fire.

The Banu Nidal wasted little time in gaping after him. They took to their camels and set out in pursuit; but he was too swift, and he left no earthly trail. She, who could have tracked him with power, did battle in Damascus on Sayyida's behalf, and dallied thereafter, complacent in her lair.

The Banu Nidal waited in dread of her silence. They could not know how she flogged herself. He was young; he was a fool; he was certainly mad. But he was ifrit to her ifritah, and she had committed the worst of sins. She had underestimated him.

She whirled in a storm of wrath. The tribesfolk fell away from her. Their terror did not comfort her. She spread wings of blood and darkness, and hurtled into the sky.

29

The warden of the gate of Masyaf looked out upon the morning. The mountains marched away before him, bleak and bare. Below lay the fields that fed the castle, fallow now with the harvest's ending but bearing a memory and a promise of green. They had suffered in the sultan's war; wind and the autumn rains had begun to blur the remnants of the siegeworks.

He would not come back. Allah, and Sinan, had seen to that. The warden murmured a prayer of thanks, secure in his faith and his righteousness. Was he not the guardian of the Gate of Allah? Was he not assured of Paradise?

A black bird flapped down amid the stubble of a field. It was very large and most ungainly, staggering and struggling as if it bore a wound. And yet there was no archer in the fields, nor had any shot from the walls; and the bird flew alone.

It blurred and shifted in the watcher's sight. Large, indeed. Man-high, and a tall man at that. Its wings shrank to tattered robes. It raised a white face, eyes enormous in it, black-shadowed; black hair in a wild tangle, black beard, nose curved fiercely and keenly enough but patently no bird's.

Even yet, the warden hesitated to call it human. Human-shaped, certainly, and male beyond a doubt. But as it struggled toward the castle, it grew more strange and not less.

It—he—was quite evidently and quite starkly mad. The steepness of the slope drove him to his knees. As often as he fell, he dragged himself erect again, inching toward the gate. His robe was torn; blood glistened on it. His face was serene, even exalted.

The gate was shut. He swayed on the edge of the ditch, smiling. For an instant his eyes seemed to meet the warden's, though that could not be: the warden was hidden in the shadow of the battlement. He raised his long white hands, still smiling, and smote them together. The gate rocked; stilled.

The faintest of frowns marred his brow. Had he expected the gate to fall? His eyes rolled up. Gently, with dreamlike slowness, he crumpled.

The warden would have left him to die, if he was capable of it, but the Master would not have it. They brought him in and tended him. He was filthy, battered, worn to a shadow; he desperately needed water and sleep. But he was in no imminent danger of death. They saw that he was no Muslim. They surmised that he was no mortal.

Sinan contemplated him with great interest and no little wonder. The physician offered him the proof: the eyelid lifted, the eye rolling senseless but, when the light struck it, performing its office. A grey-eyed man who was no human man.

The Master of the Assassins could not wait by a stranger's bedside, however intriguing that stranger might be. He posted guards and bound them with his commands, and returned to duties more pressing, if never so intriguing.

Aidan woke in rare and perfect clarity. He knew where he was. He knew, and guessed, how he had come there. He knew that he was nothing approaching sane.

The bed was hard but the coverlets warm and soft. He was clean; his bruises ached, his cuts stung, but gently. Worse was the ache of his sore-taxed power. He had demanded all that it could give, and then as much again. And it had obeyed him.

It throbbed like a wound. Even to shield it was pain.

He did not care. He was in Masyaf.

He sat up gingerly. Muslim modesty had clothed him in shirt and drawers; they were plain but well sewn, and they fit not badly.

The chamber was small but not ascetic: walls of stone softened with silk, a good carpet, even a window. The door was barred, with a seal like a star set in the lintel. The window looked out upon a precipice.

There was a low table, and a jar, and in it clean water; beside it a plate of cakes, a cheese, a pomegranate. He remembered an old lesson among the monks, and smiled.

Under the window stood a chest of cedarwood, beautifully carved. There were garments in it: white and, like his shirt, plain but of excellent quality. Assassins' garb. He put them on. The room was cold and he was mad, but he was no fool, to refuse warmth when it was offered.

He ate, drank. The cakes were Assassins' cakes; they were good to the taste, without blood to taint them. The pomegranate spilled its jewels, staining his fingers scarlet.

He raised his eyes to the man who stood in the door. He did not know what he had expected. An old man, yes. Old and strong, worn thin with years of austerity. His beard was long and silver, his eyes dark and deep. Perhaps it was not beauty that he had, but it was a strong face, cleanly carved, a face out of old Persia. His kind had waged war against the west for twice a thousand years.

There was no softness in him. Mercy and compassion, his face said, were for Allah. He, mere mortal man, could not aspire to them.

He came unarmed and alone. Wise man. Guards, blades,

violence, Aidan could have met in kind. This fierce harmlessness held him rooted.

"I have had your message," said the Master of Masyaf.

Aidan had to pause to remember it. "And the messenger?" he asked.

"Dead," said Sinan. *Of course,* his tone said.

Aidan could not prevent himself from regretting that. A little. His quarrel was with Sinan, and with Sinan's tame demon. "A pity," he said. "He was useful."

"Not," said Sinan, "once he was unmasked." He regarded Aidan with the shadow of a smile. "Come," he said. "Walk with me."

He was not without fear. Aidan scented it, faint and acrid. But Sinan would be one who reveled in terror; whose greatest pleasure lay in defying it. He walked as a man walks who thinks to tame a leopard, not touching Aidan, not venturing so far, but walking well within his reach. He was a middling man for a Saracen, which was small for a Frank, and thin; Aidan could have snapped his neck with one hand.

They walked seemingly without destination, wandering through the castle. It was small after Krak, but the feel of it was much the same: a house of war, consecrated to God. Its people moved in the silence of those whose purpose is known, and firm. They greeted Sinan with deep reverence and his companion with brief incurious stares. One did not ask questions here, or think them; not before the Master. What they knew or guessed, they kept to themselves.

Sinan said little, and that to the purpose: the use of a chamber, the choice of a turning. We have no secrets, his manner said. See, it is all open, no hidden places, no shame kept chained in shadow.

Yes, Aidan thought. Sinan needed no secrets here. Those were all in the world without, among his spies and his servants.

The garden was fading toward winter, but in its sheltered places the roses bloomed still. Under a canopy of white and scarlet, Sinan sat to rest. "Is it true," Aidan asked him, "that in Alamut the roses never fade?"

"Would you like it to be true?"

Aidan bared his teeth. "In my city there is such a garden. But she who tends it is no mortal's slave."

Did the Assassin tense? His face wore no expression. "No slave in Alamut has such a power."

"And in Masyaf?"

The thin hand rose, plucked petals from a blown blossom, let them fall. "In Masyaf, death and life pass as Allah has ordained."

"Or as you choose to command."

"I but serve the will of Allah."

"You believe that," Aidan said. He was not surprised. A cynic, or a hypocrite, would have been less perilous.

"And you? What do you believe?"

"That Allah is a goodly name for one man's avarice."

Sinan was unoffended. "So? What do you call your own?"

"I have none. My sins are pride and wrath. I call them by their names."

"Proud," said Sinan, "indeed." He cupped a single blood-red petal in his palm, regarding it gravely. His eyes lifted. "What would you have of me?"

Directness was an artifice, in a Saracen. Aidan showed him directness bare. "Surrender."

A lesser man would have burst into laughter. Sinan said, "Is there perhaps some doubt as to who is in whose power?" He gestured: a flick of the fingers. Out of the coverts and shadows of the garden and round its corners stepped men in white. Every one bore a strung bow, every arrow fixed unwaveringly on its target.

Aidan smiled. "Oh, no," he said. "No doubt at all. You asked what I would have. My heart's desire would be your life, but that would not bring back my kin. I would rest content with your surrender; with your solemn oath that you will

cease to torment the Lady Margaret, and the payment of reparation for the lives which you have taken."

The Master of Masyaf looked at him with the beginning of
respect. "Ah, sir. I see that you are a civilized man."

"Hardly," Aidan said. "The price I set will not be low. And
you must abandon forever any hope of gaining power in the
House of Ibrahim."

"There are other houses."

"Merchant houses. And merchants have no love for would-
be kinsmen who resort to the crudity of murder. No," said
Aidan. "With your tactics in this battle, you have lost the
war."

"That supposes that I intend to surrender. What if I should
simply seize the lady and compel her?"

"She'd die first," Aidan said. "And you might find that I am
a larger obstacle than I look."

"Large enough," said Sinan, measuring his inches, "and
strong, certainly. Yet Allah has made your kind subject to certain compulsions." He took from his coat a small thing: a
circle of iron on a chain, engraved with a star of six points,
written about in Arabic and in what must surely be Hebrew.
With a small shock of recognition, Aidan recalled the carving
in the lintel of his cell.

"The Seal of Suleiman," said Sinan, "with which he bound
the races of the jinn. I have set your name in it."

"But," Aidan said, "I am not a Muslim."

"Nor was Suleiman."

Aidan plucked the Seal out of Sinan's hand. The archers
tensed, but none loosed an arrow. He turned the thing in his
fingers. There was no power in it but the cold stillness of iron
and the heat of human wishing.

He weighed it in his hand. Weighing pretense; weighing the
usefulness of the truth. Sinan did not know that he had, for
the moment, no more power than any mortal. Until it had
restored itself, Aidan had nothing but his wits and his bodily

strength to sustain him. That, and the fear his kind roused in human men.

To let Sinan think that this bauble and not Aidan's own weakness bound him . . .

Aidan dropped the Seal in Sinan's lap and sighed. "So. You have me. Are you going to bargain with me?"

"Perhaps. A slave is useful, but a free man who works for his wages has greater will to do well. Suppose that you, in yourself, could turn my mind away from the House of Ibrahim. Would you do it?"

"I won't kill for you."

Sinan smiled faintly. "Do you think that that is all I could wish of you?"

"What more is there?"

"How can I know that, until I know more of you?"

"What is there to know, save that I am what I am?"

"But that," said Sinan, "is hardly simple; and, open secret though it may be, it remains a secret. All that is known of you is rumor and whisper only, save what any mortal man may claim: rank, wealth, prowess in the field. I need none of those. From pride and wrath I might profit, if they were turned to my purposes." He stroked his beard slowly, reflectively. "It is early yet for bargains, or for the trust which must seal them. Yet I tell you this. If you would give yourself to me wholly, for a term which I shall set, then I would consider the granting of your demands."

"Only consider them?"

"I should have to know that I may trust you."

Aidan stiffened.

"We know Frankish faith," said the Assassin. "An oath sworn to an infidel is no oath."

Aidan did not spring. Nor was it the archers who restrained him. Pride, indeed; and wrath. But if he was a young demon, he was old in the ways of humankind; he knew baiting when he suffered it. He bared his teeth in a fanged smile. "That may be. But the oath I swore to win recompense, I swore to my sufficiently Christian self."

"You will be given ample space for proof." Sinan raised a hand. Two of the archers lowered their bows and came forward. Big men, those; giants among the Saracens. One was taller than Aidan, and easily thrice as broad.

"You will wish to rest," their master said, "and to reflect on what we have spoken of." He nodded to the guards; they took station by the prince, one on either side.

Aidan looked from one to the other. Neither would meet his glance. He raised one shoulder in a shrug, turned on his heel. They wavered transparently between dragging him back and letting him go.

He walked calmly toward the gate. Sinan did not move to call him back. The guards hastened in his wake.

The choice should have been easier than it was. Either Aidan would surrender himself for his oath, or he would defy Sinan and win his vengeance by another path. He could kill if he must, and though he die for it. Certainly he would have the life of Sinan's instrument, the liar, the traitor to her kind.

It should have been simple. Better defiance and death than servitude. Yet he could not make the certain and inevitable choice. His mind kept wanting to be subtle. To enter the Assassin's service; to make himself indispensable; to displace the she-devil. And then, when she was well out of favor and he deep in it, but with his term of service drawing to its end, to destroy them both.

He knew that it was not in him to be so subtle for so long. He was no intriguer, and he was no man's slave. But the voice behind his eyes refused to be silenced. *Defy him, and perhaps he strikes again at Joanna. Certainly he will move on her son. The lady will surrender then: even she cannot resist such persuasion. But if you seem to yield, if you win from him a promise to make no move while you prove your good faith, what have you lost but your impatience?*

"My self-respect," he snapped, stalking the length of his prison and back again. "My life, when I break. As I must. Then he will be all the more implacable in persecuting my kin."

You may be stronger than you think.

He snarled, flinging himself down on the mat. He was trapped. He could admit it. He had thought of nothing but reaching Masyaf. Now that he was here, he had no plan and no sensible purpose.

He was captive, emptied of magic, robbed of his mamluks, stripped of his sword, all in the Assassin's power. He was not even certain that he could play for time until his power came back. And if he could, what then? There would still be Sinan, and Sinan's demon, and their debt of death.

Perhaps he should kill them both, and let the consequences settle themselves. Killing was simple; it was final. It put an end to all one's waverings.

He cast off the garments that reeked of Assassins, and lay naked in cold that could not touch him as it touched a mortal man. He shivered once, in memory of his father's blood. But the fire burned strong in him. He wanted Joanna, suddenly: not for lust, not so much, but to fill his arms; to be warm against him, and to love him, and to be woman to his man. He had left her in a madness of grief, abandoned her in her pain. What must she be thinking of him now?

If she was wise, she would be hating him.

He lay on his face. His eyes wept, independent of the rest of him. Only a little; only briefly. He sighed and lay still.

His back prickled. There were sounds enough without, from the keen of the wind to the distant echoes of human presence. Within, the silence was absolute.

He was not alone.

With great care he turned on his side. She was there: the Assassin. Staring. He gave her an ample eyeful. She blushed; her eyes flicked away. He sprang.

For a blackly joyous instant he had her. But she was air and water; she flowed out of his hands. And she laughed. Soft, light, infinitely mocking. It drove him mad.

30

Sayyida added a pinch of cardamom to the pot and stirred it, frowning slightly. It needed something still, but she could not think what. She reached with absent competence to pluck Hasan out of the rice bin. He came up screeching, abruptly cut off as he caught sight of something over her shoulder.

Morgiana was gone again, as she often was—fetching something new, no doubt. Now, it seemed, she had come back. Sayyida turned to see what she had brought.

New. Indeed. And a great deal of him, too: that was clear to see. Morgiana was ruffled, and there was a bruise coming out on her cheekbone, but she was smiling. He was deeply and limply unconscious, cradled in her arms like a vastly overgrown infant.

Part of Sayyida stood back appalled. Part—the part that ruled her body—set Hasan down and ran to help the ifritah.

Between them they laid him in the mound of cushions and coverlets that served Morgiana for her bed, the divan being too small to hold him. Sayyida could not help noticing how well-formed all those inches were, and how surprisingly light. She was almost sorry to cover him decently with drawers from Morgiana's store, and a thick soft blanket.

He seemed to be fighting the spell—for it was that, Sayyida was sure. He stirred; his brows knit; he tried to speak. Morgiana touched his forehead. He stilled.

She sat on her heels, watching him. Sayyida sat and watched her. Yes, she had a new bruise, and her hair was tangled, and there was a rent in her coat. "Did he do all that?" Sayyida asked.

Morgiana shook herself. "He? Do?" She seemed to come to her senses, a little, but she did not take her eyes from his face. "Yes. Yes, he fought. So simple; so cleanly mad."

Sayyida caught her breath. "Mad? And you brought him here?"

"Where else?"

"But," Sayyida said. "He's dangerous."

"I can control him."

Sayyida looked at the last fading marks on her throat; at the new one on her face.

Morgiana flushed faintly. "My misjudgments, both. He's a surprisingly gentle creature when he's not pricked to madness. And he has reason, as he sees it, to hate me. I'll tame him slowly."

"If he doesn't tear you apart first."

"He is not a wild beast."

Sayyida shut her mouth tight. The Frank lay between them, oblivious. His face in sleep was no more human than Morgiana's. She could not imagine why she had thought him pretty, or even handsome. He was too starkly alien to be either.

"Magic," Morgiana said. "When he is with humans, he pretends to be like them; he puts on a mask, a glamour. But he squandered his power. He has none, now, but what makes him inescapably himself."

"None? No magic at all?"

"It will come back. If he lets it. It's like a spring that flows into a pool. He drank the pool dry; it needs time to fill again."

This was altogether out of Sayyida's reckoning. She took refuge in Hasan, who advanced on the Frank with clear and present purpose. She caught him and held him, over his objections; but he agreed, on reflection, to sit in her lap and stare.

Morgiana stood over them. Her hand rested lightly, briefly, on Sayyida's hair. "Don't be afraid," she said. "He'd never harm you. Why do you think he hates me? I killed a human child, and tried to kill a human woman, and sundered him from his servants."

Her voice was frightening, because it was so calm, telling the truth without adornment. It was a very little bitter, a very little sad. But it refused to despair.

"I'll teach him the truth of me," she said. "Watch and see."

Aidan swam up through deep water to a dream of remarkable simplicity. A savor of cooking; a woman's voice singing, clear and light and tuneful. For a piercing instant he was a child again, a small half-wild thing in the house of a forest witch, with no knowledge or understanding of courts and palaces; nor even that he had a father, still less a father who was a king. Almost he reached for the other half of him, the brother who had slept twined with him in the womb.

His hand knew that it would find only emptiness. His body remembered itself. It was warm, in comfort. Except for the lively weight on its chest.

He opened his eyes. Brown eyes stared down, set in a very young face. "Kha," said their owner. "Lid." The child bounced, grinning. "Khalid!"

Aidan struggled to reclaim the breath that had been pummeled out of him. It was a real weight, and a very real infant—manchild, he could see: it wore a string of blue beads about its neck, and nothing else. "Khalid!" it cried jubilantly. "Khalid!"

It swooped upward. His lungs, freed, gulped air. A young woman stared down at him. She had the child's round brown eyes, though not his round brown face. Hers was thinner, almost sharp. She blushed suddenly and covered it with a corner of her headcloth.

He had already deduced that she was a Saracen. He could see that he was not in his cell in Masyaf. Not at all. That Morgiana had something to do with it, he could guess. "Did she kidnap you, too?" he inquired.

Veiled, the girl was bolder. She shifted the baby to her hip, whence he regarded Aidan with joyful intentness. "She's my friend," the girl said.

Aidan was speechless.

The girl scowled. "It is possible, you know. That she could have a friend. What do you know of her?"

"That she kills," he said.

"Are your hands clean of blood, then?"

He sat up. His cheeks were hot. It seemed to be his curse, to be put in his place by veiled and proper Muslim women.

This one recoiled a little as he moved, setting her body between himself and her baby. She was afraid of him. Mad, she was thinking. Dangerous. And a Frank.

His power was coming back.

He sat still. She eased slowly. "I'm sorry Hasan woke you up," she said.

"I can think of worse things to wake to."

Her eyes warmed into a smile—slow, at first; unwilling; but irresistible. "My name is Sayyida."

He inclined his head. "Aidan," he said.

"Are you hungry?"

He was. It surprised him.

She did not trust him, not yet: she took Hasan with her, and came back balancing him on her hip and a platter on her head. He barely paused to admire the feat. Her veil was secure now, but he saw the blush beneath it as he rose to take the platter. He could not help smiling, which made her blush the fiercer.

She would not eat with him. A woman should not, and he was an infidel. But Hasan knew no such compunction. She had to let him go to wait on Aidan, and he dove straight for Aidan's lap. She dove after him, but halted.

"I won't hurt him," Aidan said gently.

She looked down. She was angry, a little, but not at him. "She said you wouldn't."

His teeth clenched. "And you'll take her word for it."

"I've known her since I was as young as Hasan."

"And me, you don't know at all." He made himself relax, reach for a loaf of the flat eastern bread, dip it in the pot. Hasan eyed it hungrily. He divided it, fed half to the child, who took it as no more than his due. He nibbled his own half. "This is good."

She laughed as if she could not help herself. "Yes, I can cook! But don't tell my husband. He thinks that's beneath a woman of good family." She stopped; she seemed to realize what she had said. She rose abruptly and strode through the vaulted hall that was, he saw now, a cavern.

He did not follow her. Hasan wanted more bread. Aidan gave it to him, wanting to laugh, not quite sure he dared. Here he sat in a cave decked like a sultan's harem, brought hence by magic, with a baby in his lap, and its mother suffering the most common of woman's afflictions: a husband with whom she was at odds. He wondered if he was expected to console her.

That was unworthy of either of them. He ate to quiet his hunger, sharing with Hasan. By the time they had finished, she was back, daring him to ask why she had been crying. He asked, "Am I allowed to explore?"

She was tensed to cast his curiosity in his teeth. She had to stop, breathe deep, shift her mind in this unexpected direction. "I don't think I can stop you." She paused. "Are you up to it yet?"

"I don't think I've ever felt better." And it was true. He was fresh; he was strong. His power was the barest trickle yet, but it was swelling.

She did not believe him, but she was sensible: she did not try to quarrel with him. She did insist that he dress—cover himself, as she put it. The clothes she brought were robes of the desert.

His own, cleaned and skillfully mended. But not his weapons. Of course: he would not be allowed those.

There were three linked caverns: the great hall; the small chimneyed chamber which served as a kitchen; the wonder of jeweled walls and flowering stone, with its gently steaming pool. He barely lingered even there. His mind turned outward.

It was morning; his bones knew it. Night's bitter cold was all but gone; the heat of the day had barely begun. All about was desert: sand and stones and sky.

And power. He traced with his own the circle of the ban. It was smaller than that about Masyaf, and stronger to measure. Its meaning was perfectly distinct. Yes, he might explore: for a fair distance, in human paces. But escape, he could not. Not even upward. A more perfect prison for one of his kind, he could not have imagined.

He scaled the crag above the narrow mouth of the cave, welcoming the effort, the toll it took on hands still torn from the crawl to Masyaf. At the summit he dropped down, arms about his knees. The sky was impossibly wide. Away below stretched a ruin of tumbled stones. Earth had covered it, time beat it down, but it was still visibly a work of men's hands.

"That was a city once," the Assassin said behind him.

He did not leap. He did not even turn. "Persepolis?"

"No. This, Sikandar never burned; he built. They say he made it for his hound, because it died here."

"Alexander was mad."

"Surely." Her shadow touched him; he shuddered away from it. "You are hardly being reasonable, my lord Khalid."

"Is there any reason in murder?"

That drove her away. He waited a long while; she did not come back. He descended slowly.

The caves were empty of her. Sayyida did something peaceful and womanly in a corner. Hasan wanted to be entertained. Aidan obliged him.

For all her courage and her forthright tongue, Sayyida was shy. Maybe if he had been a woman she would have opened to him sooner. As it was, she went veiled, and she slept in the kitchen, which she had not been doing before he came. He could not persuade her to share the hall with him, even with its length between them. "It's not decent," she said.

But she did not shun him in daylight, and she talked to him freely enough.

"You're the swordsmith's daughter?" he cried when it came together into sense. "Ishak's sister?"

She nodded. She was amused.

It was logical, in its own fashion. Morgiana's friend would bear some relation to cold steel.

"Then it was you who watched us, that day when I was your father's guest."

She nodded again. "I saw you on the street, too."

"I thought your husband didn't let you go out."

"He didn't."

Aidan said nothing to that. It was delicacy, and prudence.

She did not carry it on then, but later she did: talking of the young smith with no family, whom her father had made his apprentice, and to whom he had given his youngest daughter. "Not," she said, "that he left me out of it. I could have refused. But I liked Maimoun well enough, and I admired his artistry. I thought he'd make a good father for my children."

There was more to it than that; or there had come to be. "He should trust me," she said. "He should let me make my own choices."

"That's hard for a young man," Aidan said.

She eyed him sidelong. He grinned at her. He looked younger than Maimoun, and he knew it. She unbent into a nod. "Yes: you would know, wouldn't you?"

"It's arrogance, you see. To be a man at last, with all a man's power and pride. What's a woman's will, to that?"

"Implacable." And she sounded it.

"So he has to learn. It's no easy lesson: that he's a man, and strong, but he's not invincible. That sometimes he has to yield."

"He can learn it without me. I'll not be beaten for his edification."

"I'll wager he's sorry now."

"I hope he is." There was rare venom in her voice. She held grudges, did Sayyida.

A beast could go mad in a cage, even one as wide as this. A witch's whelp, on the other hand, could go sane.

He did not want to. Sanity was perilous when one had a hate to nurse. It kept finding reasons for abominations, and excuses for the inexcusable. It made him forget grief and remember the warmth of a body against his own; a body that was made for him.

And it looked at Sayyida, and at her son, and could not reconcile the Morgiana they loved with the Morgiana he hated.

Sayyida was hardly blind to what Morgiana was. Better even than Aidan, she knew it. Yet she called the demon friend, and thought of her as a sister. Hasan adored her. In his mind she was a wonder and a marvel, a great shining creature with the most wonderful hair in the world. He thought of Aidan as a part of her. One as tall as the sky, who could sing by the hour, and who taught him new words to make his mother laugh and clap her hands and call him her little king. Who took him out in the wide world, and showed him birds and beasts and rooted things that grew valiantly in the waste; who, one glorious morning, flew with him up to the very summit of the ban.

Aidan came down to find Sayyida in a white fury. "Don't," she said, shaking with the effort of saying it quietly. "Don't you ever—ever again—"

"I didn't mean to frighten you."

She snatched her son out of his arms. "No. You didn't. Did you?"

"Sayyida. I didn't think—"

"Men never do." Her scorn was absolute. She turned her back on him. He stood abandoned, in remorse and in growing indignation.

"Women never understand!" he shouted after her.

She stopped, spun. "Women understand too much!"

"Maybe they do!"

There was no door to slam, but she managed very well without. He flew to the top of the rock, to spite her, and crouched there, brooding on the unreasonableness of women. She was down below, brooding on the idiocy of males. They were carrying on, one of them thought—he was not even sure which—exactly like kin.

It did not appall her. He . . . he wanted to laugh, which was deadly to his dudgeon.

He turned his face to the sky. "Now I see," he said. "You'll soften me with this girlchild; you'll seduce me with her baby. Then you'll find me tamed and gentle, and ripe for your taking.

"But I won't," he said. "I won't give in to you. You murdered my kin. God may forgive you. I," he said, "will not."

31

When Morgiana came back from wherever she had been, she found a scene of striking domesticity. Sayyida sat on a cushion, plying her inevitable needle. Aidan was on the floor with Hasan. The baby wanted to walk, but he could not quite find his balance. And there were greater fascinations in his companion, whose hair, long uncut, hung down enticingly, and whose beard begged fingers to tangle in it. His mother rebuked him, but she was trying not to laugh. Aidan did not even try. He unraveled the impudent fingers and pretended to gnaw on them. Hasan whooped with mirth.

Sayyida saw her first. Morgiana set a finger to her lips. Even with the warning, Sayyida could not keep her laughter from fading into apprehension.

Aidan was engrossed in the game. It was Hasan who betrayed them with a cry of gladness. " 'Giana!"

Very slowly Aidan lowered Hasan's hands from his cheeks, and drew himself up. No more than he had on the clifftop, would he turn to face Morgiana.

Hasan, freed, pulled himself to his feet and plunged toward her. She caught him before he fell. He wound his fingers in her hair and grinned, deliriously happy. " 'Giana," he said. "Mama. Khalid. Rug, pot, couch, water, sky!"

She heard him in amazement. "He's learning to talk!" And when his mother nodded, proud even through her tension: "He has an Aleppan accent."

Aidan's back was rigid. The lamp caught blue lights in his hair. She wanted to stroke it, to smooth the tangles out of it, to slip her hand beneath and ease the tautness from his shoulders.

I would rather die, he said within, low and bitter cold.

She was, when it came to it, a coward. Or why had she left it to Sayyida for so long, to begin his taming? She shrank from the implacability of his hate. She flickered from the cavern, otherwhere.

And flickered back. No more hiding; no more running away. This was her place. Let him see that she did not intend to leave it, or him, until she had won him.

"Then we will be here until the stars fall," he said, tightly, through clenched teeth.

"Not so long, I think." She came round to face him. He refused to play the child: he held still. His eyes were burning pale. Yet for all of that, he did not have the look of one who gnaws himself in captivity. While she had him to toy with, his kin were safe from her.

She nodded, unsmiling. "Your eye is clear enough. What would it take to convince you that I never willingly worked harm to you or yours?"

"Don't lie to me. You were glad to murder Gereint. You took Thibaut without a qualm. My warriors of Allah are all gone. Joanna—Joanna you would happily have rent limb from limb."

Her breath caught in her throat. "That great cow. What in Allah's name do you see in her?"

He uncoiled. It was splendid, how tall he was, how panther-supple; how oblivious he was to it. His anger rocked her. He would have struck her, but for Hasan; or so it pleased him to think. "What do I see in her? What can you know, you demon, you murderer of children? What do you see in me but what any bitch sees when she is in heat?"

It was brutal, that directness, and so he meant it to be. She told herself that. She said, "Very well. So it is jealousy, and the fire of the body. That was hardly a monk's cell in which I found you, or a monk's abstinence."

His skin was whiter even than her own; a blush was all the brighter for it. "And you think that I can possibly want you, after that? Or forgive you?"

"I didn't kill her."

"Not for lack of trying."

"But for you, I would never have tried at all." That stopped his tongue. Sayyida came quietly, relieved her of Hasan, crept away. Neither paused to notice. Morgiana lifted her chin, glaring up at him. The blood drained from his face. "I was commanded on my sacred oath and bound with words of great power to take her life. I had determined to break that oath; to find her, only, to see her face, perhaps to wound her lightly for my master's sake, then to go away. And how did I find her? That she took pleasure where she could—I could hardly fault her for that. Until I saw with whom she did it."

He knew madness, and jealousy. He had to acknowledge the truth of it. But he would not soften for that. "You regret that you did it; but not for her sake. Because by it you lost me."

"She is human," said Morgiana.

His body snapped erect; his eyes glittered. "Then you'll never grieve if I break yon cubling's neck."

"You would not dare."

"He is human," Aidan said. The exact tone; the exact, subtle air of contempt.

Her fists clenched. He had her there; too well he knew it. There were humans, and there were one's own humans. But that that great lumbering creature should be his . . . it was unbearable.

"You think that you would stop at murdering infants," he said. "And yet that is what you nearly did. She carries my child."

The words refused to make sense. Of course a mortal woman would not . . . how could he . . .

He advanced on her, striking again, deeper, twisting the blade in the wound. "She was afraid to tell me; she feared that I would cast her off. And when she knew that I would not, that after the shock of it I was glad, that I welcomed her, and the child, and anything that might come of it, she was so happy, the air itself seemed to sing.

"Then," he said. "Then you came. You saw, and you struck. You killed any hope of winning me."

She would not weep or rage or cry denial. She was too proud. "Mortal women grow old," she said. "They die."

His face twisted. "Oh, you are cruel, and you are cold. You are nothing that human warmth can touch."

"No more than you," she said.

That struck home. He flinched; his lips set tight.

"I cannot help what the years have made me," she said. "I was alone; I made myself a slave, to lend some purpose to the long days. My folly, and my grief. How could I know what Allah had written for me and for you?"

He had heard all that he could bear to hear. He turned away from her without a word, and strode out of the cave.

She let him go. He could not escape, he knew it as well as she. He did not know, perhaps, that he did not want to. Much of his resistance was rebellion against its opposite.

How well you lie to yourself. His voice in her mind, bitter with scorn. She sent it back to him without the scorn. His mind closed like a gate shutting.

The three of them had made a world for themselves, small but complete. This most unwelcome fourth had burst it asunder.

The girl and the child never minded. He was the interloper, after all, the grown male, the stranger. He had to see how Hasan delighted in Morgiana's simple presence, and how Sayyida opened to her, close and warm as kin. What he had not chosen to see, was now painfully obvious. He had been accepted not as himself, but as Morgiana's.

He took to going out and staying there until hunger drove him in; and sometimes not even then. There was a little hunting, if he was patient. He began to test the edges of the ban, as he had in moving on Masyaf; but this would not yield at all. Its maker was within it, to sustain it, and she knew him now. Better by far, he suspected, than he knew her.

She was always aware of him, as he was of her. Often she followed him. She never tried to catch him. He was being hunted, but the hunter was patient. She seemed content simply to watch him; to know that she had him in her power.

Her mind was open to him. It was trust, implicit and complete. It drove him wild. But not mad, not that. That refuge was lost to him. He had to know how she loved him and wanted him; how deep the wound was, that he would not return the love and the wanting.

Could not.

Would not. She was certain. Damn that certainty. Damn her years and her strength and her obstinacy.

Stubborn, she said to him. *Fool.*

Murderer, he thought at her.

She showed him the first man he had ever killed, when he was twelve years old. She showed him the second, the third, the fourth. She showed him years of errantry, battles fought, cities sacked, foemen cut down without mercy in the blood-red exultation of war. The city—the name he had forgotten, had willed to forget—the city hammered down in siege, the gaunt starved women with weapons cobbled out of anything that would strike and kill, the one who charged shrieking upon him, he in his armor, she in filthy rags, and the baby on her back, but he never saw it until he had cloven her, and it, in two. And for a moment he was appalled, but then he shrugged and wiped his blade and went back to what was, after all, war.

She showed him himself crouched over the gazelle which he had hunted and killed as the cheetah does, by running it down, breaking its neck. Great graceful beast of prey with the taste of blood in his mouth, pale cat-eyes narrowed against the light.

"So has God made us," she said, cross-legged on a jut of stone, gazing down at him. "You no less than I. If you will hate me, then you must hate yourself. We are of the same blood and kind."

Bile burned his throat. "Would to God that you had never been born!"

"Why? Because I teach you to see the truth?"

"Clever lies. Twisting of what is so, to what you would wish to be so. I'm not your dog, Assassin. Let me go!"

Her head shook. "I am no Assassin now. I have forsaken it. I have no faith left to kill for."

It sickened him, that one would kill at all, for such a cause.

Something fluttered out of the air. A bit of cloth with a cross sewn on it, scarlet on black.

The silence stretched. She seemed to have turned her mind from him to ponder the ground of his hunt: the city which Alexander had built to the memory of a hound. He left the cloth where the wind had dropped it, and though his gorge rose, set to gutting and cleaning his kill. He had a knife for it, a rough common blade with a middling fair edge. Her presence was a fire on his skin, her inattention a rankling in his middle.

She had an answer for everything. She would not, could not see the difference between cold murder and clean war.

Clean?

He saw Thibaut's body, serene as if in sleep; and the aftermath of bloody battle.

Not hers, that. His mind was locked shut. She had twisted him within as without.

"I make no apology for what I am," she said. "I only ask that you see it clear, and not as your whim would have it."

"I see clear enough. I see that it is your time for mating, and I am here, and male, and of the proper kind. There is no more to it than that."

"In the beginning," she said, "it was so."

She was before him in cold and enveloping white, like the Angel of Death. No maiden saint could have been less alluring. There was no seduction in her. She had never known what it was.

She reached. He shied, caught himself. He saw the swift wince of pain, the swifter flicker of a smile. Her hand was warm on his cheek. For defiance, for bitter mockery, he matched the gesture. Smooth; wondrous soft. Flesh of his own kind, subtly yet deeply different from the human. With one breath-light finger he traced the shape of her face. Not cold, her beauty, behind the mask she wore. Oh, no. Not cold at all.

He recoiled. She betrayed no hint of triumph. She turned and went away. Walking, as any creature would. Any female creature. No male had that grace, that suggestion of a sway, even scrambling over stones.

His face burned where she had touched it. He bent back to his fresh-blooded kill, shouldered it. The best way back was the way she took. He was not, he told himself, taking it because she had.

For all her boldness and her wild ways, Morgiana shared Sayyida's prudery in the matter of sleeping places. The women spread mats in the kitchen; nor would they hear of an exchange. More often than not, Aidan had Hasan for a companion. Even so young, he seemed to recognize that they were males together; and he loved all the cushions and coverlets. "He's turning into a little prince," his mother said.

"Then he is in proper company," said Morgiana.

Aidan, picking without appetite at a bit of roast gazelle, looked up in time to catch Sayyida's look of comic dismay. "Ya Allah! I'd completely forgotten."

His smile was wry. "Don't bow. You'll fall in the pot."

"I had no intention of—I mean—I—" Sayyida stopped in confusion.

"It's not as if I were real royalty," he said. She opened her mouth, indignant. He laughed. "I know I'm not. I've been told it on excellent authority. How can I be insulted by the truth?"

"That's nonsense," said Sayyida. "Royal is royal. And I never even thought. Ishak told me once—he was full of it. I didn't trouble to remember. What was a prince to me? I'd never come any closer to one than I already had."

"Strange things, your Allah writes, when he has a mind." Aidan gave up the meat and settled for cheese. Morgiana's glance was keen. He refused to see it.

He set down the half-nibbled cheese. "Go on, eat. I'm finished."

They tried to argue with that, but he had no appetite, and they did. While they ate, he withdrew to the bath. It was a wonder to him, to have it there, always, for the taking. And wide enough to swim in.

He dropped his clothes, but he did not go into the pool. Where the stone poured down in a curtain like ice, blue and palest green, he settled on his stomach, chin on folded arms, watching the play of water in the light of the lamp. Idly he made a light that was his own, and shattered it into embers, setting them to dance atop the water.

He yawned, rubbed his cheek against his arm. He was for-

getting how it felt to be clean-shaven. Maybe he would go
back to it. It would shock the women; it would prove that he
was a Frank and a barbarian. And, in body, monstrously
young.

Time left no mark on him. Even scars faded and vanished.
He had taken a blow to the mouth once, long after he was
grown. The stumps of teeth had loosened and fallen; he
learned to smile close-mouthed, and contemplated long ages
of beauty marred. It was illuminating, and humbling, to know
how much it mattered. But a day came when he ran his
tongue along the broad ugly gap, and felt a strangeness. In a
few months' time they had all grown back, all the shattered
teeth, sharper and whiter than ever. Sometimes in his wilder
moods he was tempted to sacrifice a finger, to see if it would
grow again without a scar.

He would never do it. He was too tender of his vanity. He
troubled little with mirrors, but he liked to know what he
would see there. He liked the way people, meeting him, drew
back a little and stared, and doubted their eyes. Even the way
they judged him, mere empty beauty, with no need to be
more. It was always amusing to prove them wrong.

He always knew, now, where Morgiana was, as he knew the
whereabouts of his own hand. He said to the water, but in
part to her, "I'm a very shallow creature, when it comes to the
crux."

She dropped something over him: a robe of heavy silk,
glowingly scarlet. "But very good to look at," she said, "and
no more modest than an animal."

"Why not? I've nothing to hide."

"The Prophet, on his name be blessing and peace, was a
modest man. We follow his example."

Aidan sat up, wrapping the robe about him. It was lined
with lighter silk, pale gold; it was embroidered with dragons.
It was perfectly suited to his taste. "Was he ugly, then?"

"Oh, no!" She seemed shocked at the thought. "He was

very handsome. He looked a little like you: being noble, and Arab, and slow to show his age."

"You knew him."

"I was never so blessed." She was in green tonight. She looked much better in it than in white. Much warmer; much less inhuman.

She had not denied that she was old enough to have known Muhammad.

"I may be," she said. "I don't remember. I was little more than a wind in the desert, until my master found me and made me his own. I remember nothing of being a child. Who knows? Maybe I never was one."

"My mother was like that," said Aidan. "A wild thing, nearly empty of self, until a mortal man gave her a reason to live in mortal time."

"Did she die with him?"

"No. She . . . faded. She went back into the wood. Us— my brother and me—she left. We were half mortal, and raised mortal, though we knew early enough that we were not. As our sister is."

"You have a sister?"

It twisted in him, with pain. "Gwenllian. Yes. Ten years younger than I, and growing old. You killed her son."

"I was oathbound," she said. "Surely you know what that is."

He drew up his knees and laid his forehead on them. He was tired. Of fighting. Of hating. Of grieving for human dead.

"It is what humans are. They give us pain."

"And joy," he said. "That, too. Surely that is what it is to be alive?"

"I don't know. I don't think I've ever lived. Empty of self— yes, that is I. I was a dagger and a vow. Now I am less even than that."

His head flew up. His anger flared, sudden and searing. "You are not!"

He had astonished her. It soured quickly; her mouth twisted. "No. I am something, still. A thing to hate."

"I don't—" He broke off. He could not say it. It would be a lie.

Except . . .

He shook himself. "You *are* more than that! Look about you. Look at your friend; look at Hasan. Aren't they worth something?"

"One friend," she said, "in a hundred years."

"A hundred years of what? Being a dagger and a vow. Serving masters who never saw you as anything else. But you are more; your heart knows it. It found Sayyida, and she had the wits, and the quality, to know you for what you are."

"A murderer of children."

It hurt, to have those words cast back in his face. It was not supposed to hurt. It was supposed to be a triumph. "Yes, damn you. And more than that. None of us is simple, my lady."

"You can say that?"

"You wanted me to see you clearly."

She stood. She shook; it had the heat of rage. "I wanted you to love me."

He cut his beard short, but he did not get rid of it. It was not worth a battle; and his vow was not kept. Not yet.

He decided that he rather liked it, once it was short enough to show the shape of his face. It added years and dignity, both of which he could well use. Besides, as the women said, he was a man, and a man's beauty could not be perfect without it.

Sometimes Muslim customs made surprising sense.

Morgiana left them on occasion, walking her paths that no one else could follow, to fetch food, and drink other than water of the spring, and the odd treasure. Once she brought back a jar of wine, and a lute.

Aidan regarded the lute when she laid it in his lap, and

gently, most gently, caressed the inlay of its sounding board. "Where did you get this?" he asked her.

Steal, he meant. She refused to be baited. "I went to a place where such things are known, and asked where I might find the best maker of lutes. I went where I was shown. I paid," she said, "in gold. My own. Fairly and honestly gained."

He looked down. He had the grace to be ashamed. Lightly, almost diffidently, he plucked a string. The lute was in tune.

"I can't accept this," he said.

"Did I say it was a gift?"

He flushed.

"Play for me," she commanded him.

He was angry enough to obey her, defiant enough to choose a tune from his own country. But she had traveled far; she had learned to find pleasure in modes which were alien to those of the east. This was properly harp-music, bard-music, but he fitted it well to the supple tones of the lute.

She watched him in silence. He was out of practice: he slipped more than once. But he played very well, with the concentration of the born musician, head bending further as the music possessed him, mouth setting in a line, fingers growing supple, remembering the way of it.

When he began to sing, she was almost startled. She did not know why she had expected a clear tenor: his voice in speech was low enough, with the merest suggestion of a purr. In song the roughness vanished, but that new clarity resounded in a timbre just short of the bass. A man's voice beyond doubt, dark and sweet.

It took all her strength to keep from touching him. He resisted her abominably easily; he had only to remember his Frankish woman, and what she carried. He was not like a human man, to be led about by his privates.

But he watched her. She knew that. He found her good to look at. He was beginning, not at all willingly, to forget how to hate her, if never to love her. And he wanted the power she had, to walk in an eyeblink from the wastes of Persia to the markets of Damascus.

She was pleased to teach him lesser arts, to hone the power he had never thought of as more than a child's toy, but that single great art, she would not give him. She knew what he would do with it.

Just this morning, he had tried to trick her out of it. Then when she vanished, she felt the dart of his will, seeking her secret. It was not as easy to elude him as it had been. He was a clever youngling, and he was growing strong.

The lutestrings stilled. He raised his head. His eyes were dark, the color of his northern sea. "Why?" he asked her. "Why teach me at all?"

"Why not?"

"What if I grow stronger than you?"

She laughed, which pricked his pride terribly. "I don't think I need to fear that. But that we may be equals . . . that, I think very possible. I would welcome it."

"Even knowing what I would do then?"

"Ah, but would you do it?"

He was mute, furious.

"My sweet friend," she said, "if you were half as wise as you like to imagine, you would know what it means, that we move so easily in one another's thoughts."

"It means that you will it, and I have no skill to keep you out."

She shook her head and smiled. "You know better than I what it is. Remember your brother and his queen."

He surged to his feet. "We are not so mated!"

He took care to lay the lute where it would be safe, before he flung himself away from her. She saw that; she saw quite enough apart from it. She allowed herself a long, slow smile.

32

He had to get out. He had been holding up well; he had learned to live in his cage. But four of them were too many. And she—she pressed on him from all sides. Wherever he turned, she was there, not even watching, simply and inescapably present.

The worst of it was that he could not loathe the sight of her. Flatly, utterly, could not. When she was gone about her marketing—improbable domesticity, flitting about the world in search of a dainty or a bauble—he was restless; he could sit even less still than he usually did. And he was like that until she came back, when the knot in him loosened, and the world was in its proper place again.

He was like a man enslaved to a drug. He hated it, and he could not live without it.

She had done it to him. She, the witch, the spirit of air. Murderer, he could no longer call her. The word filled his hands with blood and his mind with memories it had long since buried.

He tried to turn her against him. He honed the memories; he gave them to her in hideous detail, heedless of what they did to his sanity. He taunted her with his body. He used her teaching, transparently, to seek out paths of escape.

Sometimes, to be sure, he made her angry, but never angry enough. Mostly, she only smiled.

He did not know what that smile cost her. She knew as well as he, that she could not keep him so. He was not to be tamed in a cage. It was a hard lesson to learn, and bitter to face.

Sayyida understood. "Ishak told me about falcons," she said. "The taming is never complete until the falconer flies his bird free, and it comes back. You've caught this one, you've taught him to endure the jesses and the hood. You've been letting him fly a little, on the line."

"The creance," said Morgiana, but abstractedly, listening hard. "How can I let him fly? I *know* he won't come back."

"Then you'll have to find a lure for him, won't you? What will win him for you?"

"I don't know!" Morgiana cried.

Sayyida's eyes narrowed. "Do you remember when you told me about him, and we talked about how a woman wins a man?"

"What good is that? I'm not a woman."

"But you are! Isn't that the whole of your trouble? What have you done to show him that you're worth desiring?"

Morgiana shrugged angrily. "What can I do? He can see me. He can hear me. He knows what I want of him."

"Of course he does. Do you think he likes to feel like a stud bull?"

Morgiana gasped at the coarseness of it. Sayyida went on unruffled. "If that's all you want, there are other and easier people to get it from. If you want more—if you want him—you're going to have to let him know that you're a woman."

Morgiana looked down at herself. "It isn't obvious?"

Sayyida laughed, but she was a little annoyed. "Morgiana, you are so dense! Come with me."

They went into the bath, drawing the curtain that would warn Aidan not to intrude if he came back from prowling the limits of his cage. Sayyida was ruthless. She made Morgiana strip, to the skin, and no pauses for modesty. No one had ever seen Morgiana naked, except the attendants in the baths, who were trained to see only what needed cleaning or stripping.

Sayyida examined her with a hard clear eye. "You're not as shapely as Laila," she said, "but you'll do. Yes, the way Franks are made, and the way they admire thinness, you'll definitely do. Laila would kill for your skin. And your hair. Do you have any idea how beautiful you are?"

"I look like a starved cat."

"Does he think so?"

Her teeth clicked together. "He never even looks."

"I think he does." Sayyida plumped Hasan at her feet. "Watch him. I'll be back directly."

It was rather longer than that. Morgiana rubbed her arms, not for the chill—the cavern was richly warm—but for the feel of air on her bare skin.

Small arms circled her leg. Hasan grinned up at her. He liked her this way.

"You are certainly male," she said to him, sweeping him up. He did not want to be held; he wanted to try this new art of walking. She mounted guard over the pool, lest he fall in, and let him try his legs among the shimmering pillars.

She sat by the pool and, for something to do, combed out her hair. Once in a great while she cut it, to get it out of the way, but it seemed most comfortable when it was knee-long. Its color always made people stare. She would have been happier if it were black. Like his, thick and glossy, with blue lights. But she liked her skin well enough, purest ivory to his moon-pallor. Her lips were redder than his, her nipples a tender pink like light through a shell. Were her breasts small? They were large enough to fill her hands. And shapely. Not like the Frank's heavy swaying udders, with the blue veins thick in them, and their broad dark nipples, and the weight of milk dragging them down.

"Cow," she said.

"Cow," said Hasan, obligingly.

She laughed in spite of herself. There was little merriment in her, and a great burden of jealousy. That he could love that, and not this. That it should carry his child.

She could not bind him so. She knew it starkly, beyond hope of denial. They had not the human fragility, her kind, but neither had they human fecundity.

And could she wait until the woman died of her own humanity?

Or kill her.

No. That would lose him surely and eternally.

Sayyida came back laden with brightness: the sheerest of all the silks which Morgiana's fancy had gathered.

"No," said Morgiana, growing alarmed. "I won't."

"Do you want him or don't you?"

Morgiana bit her tongue. "But *this*—"

"This is how to let him know that you're a woman. Men don't take to telling, haven't you noticed? You have to show them."

"If he cares enough to notice," she muttered.

"When I'm done with you, he will. Now stand still."

The women were up to something. When Aidan came back from a long day's prowl among the ruins, Morgiana was nowhere to be seen or sensed, and Sayyida labored in the kitchen over what smelled and, from what he was allowed to see, looked like a feast. She came out only to thrust Hasan into his arms and command, "Play with him."

He was glad enough to obey her. He went to wash, reconsidered, bathed all over, and Hasan too. Somewhere in the middle, his power twitched, too quick to catch, too light to be sure of. But he came out to find his Bedu rags gone, and in their place the silks and linen and fine muslin of a Saracen prince, with the dragon robe folded and laid under them all.

He could have demanded his own clothes back, but he chose to play their game. He put on what he was expected to put on, with Hasan for a small but highly appreciative audience. It was all white and gold but the long loose coat; there were rubies sewn with gold thread in the slippers and the cap.

A box appeared next to his hand as he reached for the cap. He stifled a start. Cautiously, though he sensed no danger, he lifted the lid. Jewels—a prince's ransom, at least, in rubies and pearls, gold and diamond.

"This is too much," he said to the air.

It did not answer.

He hesitated, but the glow of the stones was more than he could resist. He chose a ring, ruby set in gold, and an armlet with a pattern of horses and trousered riders. The rest, he let be. He was gaudy enough as he was.

He came out warily. The lamps were lit in the hall, a cloth spread, dishes of silver laid out on it. Still there was no sign of Morgiana. Sayyida claimed Hasan and bore him away; not without a moment's pause to admire Aidan's splendor. It warmed him, the halt, the half-turn, the widening of the round brown eyes.

He sat on the cushion that had been set for him. He did not know what he was supposed to think, or do.

Except eat. He did that willingly, if not entirely happily. Sayyida waited on him; her mind was silent. Veiled from him; as was, always, her face.

"You would think," he said to her, "that by now I'd count as family."

She continued calmly to fill his cup with honeyed wine. When she laid down the pitcher, she seemed to come to a decision. She let her veil fall.

She looked like Ishak. She had his profile, his slightly curved nose; even, suddenly, his smile. Aidan supposed that a Saracen would call her plain. He found her quite handsome.

He said so; she blushed furiously.

He never ate enough to make a human happy, although tonight he tried. He helped her afterward to clear it all away: she disliked it when he did that, especially now that she remembered his rank, but she had learned to put up with it. She all but dragged him out of the kitchen before he could begin the washing—"In those clothes!" She was horrified. She was also determined to stay with him, to keep him sensible.

Even through the veils about her mind, he could sense the swelling of excitement. She filled his cup again.

"You can't get me drunk, you know," he said.

"I didn't think I could," she said calmly.

It was true that wine could not intoxicate him, but it could warm him, and ease the knots out of his muscles. He drained the cup, began another. It was good wine.

The lamps dimmed. Sayyida produced a pipe from somewhere in her swathings of garments. She set it to her lips and began to play. After a measure or two, a drum joined it, beating light and swift.

He knew no fear, not even apprehension, only a kind of lazy anticipation. The wine's doing. He stretched out, propped himself on his elbow, settled to enjoy whatever the conspirators had prepared for him.

Only the music, at first, in a very old mode. Persian, perhaps, and older than Islam. The lamps had all gone out, but for the cluster nearest where he lay. The shadows were black, impenetrable even to such eyes as his.

She came out of the blackest of them, not dancing, not quite: setting her feet down with delicate precision. They were bare, touched with henna over their whiteness. There were jewels above them, and the chiming of tiny bells. Her trousers were of silk as green as her eyes, as sheer as gossamer. Her broad girdle dangled a hundred bells, each hung on a thread of gold. Her bodice was green and gold. Her arms were bare, and jeweled. Her hair was hidden in a veil of sea-green silk. Her brows were bound with gold and silk, and coins of gold set in the bands. Emeralds swung glittering from her ears, but her eyes were more brilliant than they. A dagger hung from her girdle.

If he must die now, he would be glad. He smiled. She seemed not to see him at all. She poised; her head fell back. The music quickened. She began to dance.

"There is a tale," a soft voice said. Sayyida's; and yet the piping went on without pausing. "They tell it in the souks of Cairo and of Damascus; they sing it in the courts of Baghdad. How once there was a man who learned a great secret, a cavern of treasure in the hands of forty thieves; and he tricked them and won their wealth, and one of their number died for it. And that is a fine tale and a true one, as Allah may witness it, but we shall not hear it here.

"No; my tale is the tale of the poor man, grown now into a prince, and the most deadly of the thieves, who was their captain. By sleights and slyness and magic, in the heat of his vengeful hate, he learned the name of the man who had robbed him and slain his fellow, and swore to destroy him in return.

"Thus, upon a day, one came to the house of the pauper who was become a prince: a merchant from far away, a stranger to the city, a trader in olives and fine oils; and he had with him a caravan of mules bearing great laden jars. Our prince was pleased to give him lodging, for is it not written that every man should extend charity to his brother? And being a generous host, he offered his guest all that his house could offer. The merchant was gracious in acceptance, but that he declined a single thing: the mingling of bread and salt. He had taken a vow, he said; he begged pardon, but he dared not break it. His host was more than pleased to indulge him, for he was a pleasant companion, both witty and wise.

"Now, our prince had a slave whom he trusted well, a Circassian whom he had raised from a child and whom he regarded almost as a daughter. She was as wise as she was beautiful, and she was learned, because even as a pauper, our prince had believed devoutly in the power of the Book. It was her duty to prepare the feast; in the midst of her preparations, she discovered that she had omitted to provide oil for the dish which she was making—the delicacy which they call *the imam swooned*, because when his wife made it for him, it consumed in a night the oil which he had meant to suffice for a year.

"The slave was, not unnaturally, distraught, until she bethought herself of the merchant's wares. Surely he would not begrudge a dipper of oil out of so many. She took her dipper and crept out into the courtyard."

Sayyida paused. Morgiana's dance had matched her words. For the prince, a lordly gait, weighty with good feeding; for his guest, a merchant's self-important stride; with a gesture, a curve of the body, she envisioned the whole of the feast. And then she was the slave, the clever, the learned, the beautiful; but young, and quite human enough in her predicament, battling her conscience to a standstill. Boldly but softly, with dipper in hand, she passed from the lights and steams of the kitchen into the dimness of evening in Baghdad, last night or a thousand nights ago.

The tale went on, but the words seemed now but shadows, the cavern a dream. Reality was the slender gliding figure, the lamp in her hand, the dipper, the jars standing woman-high against the wall.

"She lifted the lid of the first, and lo! there was no oil in it at all, but under a mat of palm-leaves, a man, and the glitter of weapons deep within. When he saw that the jar was opened, he hissed up, 'Is it time? Shall we rise and kill the thief?'

"But the slave was quick of wit, and she had not liked the look of her master's guest. She hissed back swiftly, 'Not yet. Wait, and have patience.'

"And so she found in each jar, and so she spoke, until the last, and that, indeed, was full of oil. She drew not a dipper but a whole great pot, and set it to simmering over the kitchen fire. And when it was bubbling handsomely—it was excellent oil, and *the imam swooned* had won much praise from the men at their dinner—she brought it back into the courtyard, and filling her dipper, poured the boiling oil down upon the head of each man in his jar. And so they died, and their master never knew, dining at his ease with the man whom he intended to slay.

"But the slave, whose name was Morgiana, contrived an ambush of her own. It was her custom, when her master entertained guests, to dance for them after they had eaten. One dance in particular was a favorite of her master's, a dance of edged blades, with a dagger in her hand.

"This is the dance which she danced."

Now there was only the music, and the dancer in the light

and the shadow. He had seen that dance before in the markets of the east, in the courtyards of the caravanserais, in the aftermath of banquets in Damascus and Aleppo. In its way it was like the sword-dance of his own people, but that was a man's dance, swift and thrusting-fierce, with a harsh, angular grace. This was made for woman's strength: curving, sinuous, the she-cat hunting, the serpent closing on its prey. The music wound about her; or was it she who was the music? The dagger flashed as she whirled, a wicked, living brightness. The bells sang high and sweet; the coins chimed in her headdress. Her body was an arc of ivory in a mist of green and gold.

His heart beat to the music, swifter, swifter. She spun closer. He could see the sheen of sweat on her cheek, her throat, her breast beneath the bodice. Her scent dizzied him. Her hair whipped free of its bindings, wound with silk and gold, lashing like a panther's tail.

The music swelled. She swooped over him. He lay still, head back to meet her eyes. His throat lay bare to her blade.

Silence.

Her dagger rested, lightly, lightly, where the great vein pulsed with his life's blood.

"And thus," said the voice of the tale, "was the false guest slain, who was neither merchant nor stranger, but the captain of the thieves."

There should have been more of it. Perhaps there was. He saw only the face above him, and the death in it, inexpressibly beautiful. It came down and down. Her lips were burning sweet.

His arms wound themselves about her neck. She gasped and stiffened.

She was afraid of him.

He dared not laugh. She? Afraid of him? She was infinitely older than he, infinitely more powerful. She held him inescapably prisoner. She was as beautiful as she was deadly. She could dance the stars out of the sky.

"Or a witch-prince out of his coldness?"

His hand had a will of its own. It stroked the length of her back, gently. Her skin was child-soft. "God and my dead forgive me, I can't hate you."

Her face was buried in his shoulder. Tautly; as if she wanted it to desperation, but she had to think about it, hard, as a lesson learned but never practiced.

"Never?"

She struck him hard enough to snap his head back. His arms dropped; he sat still. His jaw throbbed.

"*Never!*" she spat at him.

She wanted him to laugh, doubt, call her liar and whore. Then she could hit him again, and drive him away; and he could not touch her where she wanted, and dreaded, to be touched.

He nodded, somber. "It's hard, when one is what we are. The wanting comes so seldom, and when it does, so all-encompassing. And when the other is of our blood . . ."

She tore off her headdress, flung it jangling into the dark. "It's easy for you. You have lovers."

"Not so many. Not so often."

Her lip curled. "Only once in a season."

"Twice in a score of years, and by God's mockery, twice at once."

She started, stilled. "I've seen the Frank. Who is the other?"

"You."

Her head shook hard enough to rock her on her feet. "Don't lie. I can't stand it. I promise I won't kill her. I'm done with killing."

He laid his palm against her cheek. It was wet.

She did not pull away. "I wanted to make you want me," she said. "When you did . . . O Allah, I am a coward!"

"Not that, I think. After all. Only new to it."

"And nothing proper or maidenly in me at all."

"I doubt I would find you so fascinating if you were either."

She scowled. "Fascinating? I?"

"Utterly."

"That," she said. "That is coquetry."

"Gallantry, I beg you. But truth, too. You madden me. I've hated you beyond reason. But I've never found you dull."

She was like Aidan when he came to Masyaf. She stood within reach of what she had wanted for so long, and she could not imagine what to do with it.

Her eyes were wide, a little wild. He bent; he kissed her. She shivered.

No less than he. He retreated a step, two. He bowed with careful correctness. "For the dance, my thanks."

He was half afraid that she would follow him to his bed; half eager for it. But she did not.

33

Aidan woke to the scent of spices steeped in wine. He drew a deep breath, and sneezed violently.

Morgiana thrust the cup back under his nose. "I have a bargain for you," she said.

He drank, because if he did not, the hot wine would pour itself down his front. Memory came back, hard-edged yet dreamlike.

There was nothing in her now of the dancer or the maiden. She was all Assassin again, her hair tightly and repressively braided under the turban.

"Not Assassin," she said, sharp with impatience. "Assassins do not wear green."

He snatched the cup out of her hand and drained it. "You drag me out of a sound sleep, and you expect me to make sense?"

"The sun rose an hour ago. I grew tired of waiting." She folded her arms. "I wish to bargain with you."

"May I—"

"No."

He rose in spite of her. He pulled on a garment or two, ran his fingers through his hair. He considered going in search of breakfast, but Morgiana's mood was dangerous. He sat on a cushion, tucked up his feet, and raised a brow. "Well?"

"A bargain," she said. "I will free you from this place, intercede for you with Sinan, set you thereafter on any path you may choose."

The breath rushed out of him. "What—why—"

"Sayyida reminded me of a tenet of falconry."

She had gone mad. Or— "This is a trick."

"I do not play tricks."

"Neither do you give up. Just like that. And offer to win me the whole of my revenge."

"Why not?"

He clasped his arms tight about his middle. The wine churned there. He could not catch fever, his kind did not, but his head was light; his face burned. "There is a price. Isn't there?"

"Yes."

His arms loosened a fraction. At last; a glimmer of sense. "What is it?"

"You."

He stared at her.

"You," she said again. "In my bed. Until you satisfy me."

He laughed. She did not. The silence lengthened. He leaned forward. "Until I satisfy you? That's all?"

"It is enough."

"What . . . if . . . I won't?"

"Do you mean that you cannot?"

He stiffened, outraged.

"Is it so high a price?" she asked him. "I give you what you most desire. In return, you give me what I have wanted since I saw you in Jerusalem."

"And if I don't want it? If I'm not to be bought and sold?"

"Then you are a fool."

He struck the floor with his fists. *"Damn it, woman! Do you want me to court you or kill you?"*

"I know nothing of courting," she said. "I can only be what I am. Will you bargain?"

"What will a refusal cost me?"

"Imprisonment until you yield. And Sinan goes on with his persecution of your kin."

He rubbed his jaw. She watched him. He lowered his hand. "Would you give me time to think?"

"Until the sunset prayer."

She did not grant it gladly, but she granted it, and generously. He could not bring himself to thank her. He finished dressing while she sat there, and left her sitting, eyes fixed on nothing at all.

He went only as far as the clifftop. She was wise enough not to follow, in body or in mind. He set his chin on his knees. He was aware of Sayyida going about her tasks below, Hasan teaching himself to run. Morgiana was gone. Her absence was an ache behind his eyes.

What in God's name had driven her to offer this bargain? One night of him, in return for so much: his freedom, his vengeance.

Last night she had set out to seduce him. She had gone about it admirably well, until she succeeded. And now, in the morning, this.

She would have been a scandal in Carcassonne.

He was smiling. He bit his lip. He ought to be raging. Was he a Damascus whore, to sell his body for any price?

Even this.

The Church would call it mortal sin.

The Church called him a witch and a child of the devil.

In Islam, even the devil's brood could come to Paradise.

He clutched his head in his hands. Thinking was an art which he had never mastered. He was too much better at doing.

His head tossed. No. He must think. Joanna—Joanna whom he loved, who bore his child—

Joanna who was another man's wife.

Was there nothing in this world that was either clean or simple?

He summoned up her face, the feel of her flesh under his hands, the scent of her as she took him to her bed; the brightness of her blood that sprang beneath Morgiana's blade. Human, all of it. Beloved, and human.

As he was not. Not even half of him. Here in this desert place, in his enchanted captivity, he knew that beyond hope or help. A human man would take what was offered, and turn it to his own ends, and never trouble that he had betrayed his lover. Had she not already betrayed her husband?

She would understand. Not forgive, maybe; she was not as much a saint as that. But she would see the logic in this bargain that Morgiana proposed. Women were appallingly logical creatures; even women who were human.

And he—what he wanted—

He wanted them both.

Yes. Even Morgiana. Beautiful, deadly, implacable Morgiana, whom he had forgotten how to hate.

But to take her as she commanded; to let her take him . . .

He flung himself into the sky.

As the sun sank, he came walking back to the cave. There were a few more tatters in his robe; the wind had made elflocks of his hair. He limped a little. He paused to drink at the spring, matching glares with a desert hawk that rested in the fig tree.

There was food waiting for him as always, but Sayyida laired in the kitchen with Hasan and would not come out. What she thought of matters, he did not want to know. He bathed as always, tugged and cursed the tangles out of his hair, deliberately put the torn and dusty robes back on again. He had no desire to eat, but he drank a cup of wine. He filled it again, and once again.

Just when the sunset prayer should have been finished, he looked up, and she was there.

He had resolved to make her wait; to let her suffer for the suffering she had cost him. Then, sharp and final, the blow. *No,* he would say. *No, I will not. I am not your whore.*

"Yes," he said.

Her expression did not change.

"For my freedom," he said. He was dizzy, but not with wine. "For Sinan's ceasing his assaults against the House of Ibrahim. And one thing more."

She waited.

"You will not again or in any way harm the Lady Joanna or the child she carries."

Her eyes glittered. For an instant he knew. She would do it for him. She would refuse.

She bowed her head. "As you will," she said.

There was a silence. He raised the cup to his lips, hesitated, set it down. Her head was bowed still. He could, if he peered closely, see that she trembled.

She was weeping, and not with joy. Her desolation blew cold in him. She had wanted it so much, and now she would have it, but it was an empty thing, a merchant's bargain, bleak and loveless.

She raised her head. "But I will have it! If this is the only way, then so be it. Allah has written it."

He swallowed painfully. Her face was stark. He leaned forward, took it in his hands. She shivered at his touch. "Lady," he said. "Morgiana. I don't hate you." Her lips tightened; she tried to pull away. He held her. "I don't know . . . I'm afraid . . . I think that I could love you."

She did escape him then; she seared him with her anger. "I told you not to lie. Even to comfort me. Especially to comfort me."

He shook his aching head. "I'm not lying. I wish I were."

He caught her again, by the hands. They were cold. "Don't you think it would be better for us all if I could come to this coldly, as a man to a marriage of state? Dear God! You are infidel and Assassin, and I have taken the cross. Our faiths and our people are at war. Even Joanna with her husband and her kin and her inescapable mortality, is a better match for me than you."

"We do," she said, "agree on very little."

If there was irony in that, it was too subtle for his senses.

She drew a deep, shaking breath. "But it doesn't matter, does it? We've begun to live in one another's skin. I, and an infidel. A Frank. Enemy of enemies. You eat of unclean meats; you drink wine. You pray to three gods when there is only the One. You know nothing of holy Koran." She reached up to trace the sweep of the brow over his eye. "Barbarian. Unbeliever. Worshipper of devils."

Her voice was tender. Her hand was light, unwontedly awkward. He sat still, barely breathing. Her beauty caught at his throat.

But she could have had none, and still been Morgiana. The feel of her hand on his brow was perfectly, ineffably right. Those bones, that flesh against his bones and flesh; the fire of life and power within, meeting his own, matching it.

She lowered her hand, knotted it with the other in her lap. "I don't know . . . how . . ."

"May I teach you?"

The shivering came and went in her. She tried to laugh. "Do you think I can learn?"

"I think you hardly need to be taught."

Her head shook hard. "You don't understand. When I—when a feeling is too strong, my power masters me. I think—I think when I was born, the shock cast me from my mother's body, and sent me otherwhere. What if—"

That gave him pause. But he said, "If it happens, then you can simply come back. I'll be here. See, I'll open my mind, so, like a hand, to hold you."

Her own was like a hand, creeping out slowly, a bare touch at first, then clasping tight. It was as if he had been all his life without one of his senses, and he had never known it, until suddenly, wondrously, it was there.

They reeled. They caught at one another. Was his face as whitely shocked as hers?

"You didn't know?"

Her voice, her incredulity. They were still separate enough for that. "It's nothing one can know," he said, "until it comes. My brother said that. I thought that he was taunting me, because he was chosen and I was not."

"Did you hit him?"

"Of course I did. He, the mooncalf, only smiled with nauseating sweetness and drifted back to his bed."

"I can't imagine you drifting anywhere, for anything."

He laughed. "No. I'm not the sort of lover who drifts. Or smiles. Or warbles by moonlight."

"Good. I don't want to be warbled to. Though a song or two, a real song, with sparks in it . . ."

"Shall I sing for you?"

She paused, tempted, but shook her head. "Later. Maybe. I think—I want to begin my lessons now."

He knew how much courage she needed to say that. Slowly, carefully, he took her hand and kissed the palm, and closed her fingers over it. She looked from it to him. "To keep," he said, "for remembrance, and for a promise. It's not easy, the first time. There will be pain. There may not be overmuch pleasure. But I will give you as much as I know to give."

"You've done this before."

"No," he said. "Not with a maiden."

She flushed. "I wish I had something of my own to give you. Instead of this—this course of study in a *madrasa.*"

"Hardly there," he said, biting down on laughter. There was a sweet, headlong joy in this, now that he had embarked on it; now that he could not, for pride, put a stop to it. "As for giving, you will see what you can give me. Come, now, your turban; and your hair—you should never hide it. It's too beautiful."

She stood frozen as he stroked it out of its plait, braced against the blind animal pleasure of his touch.

"Don't," he said softly. "Don't fight. Think of the dance, how one gives oneself to it. This is the oldest of all dances, and by far the best of them."

She neither moved nor spoke. He kept on speaking, it little mattered what, letting the rhythm of his words now touch the edge of song, now pass over into it. He began, one by one and slowly, to loosen the garments that swathed her. So many of them, like armor. She suffered him, but she had no pleasure in it, no warming to his touch. She was stiff with terror.

When he came to her chemise and drawers, he paused. "It is usual," he said, "for the woman to undress the man."

She started, snatched. For a moment her fingers convulsed in the fabric of his *djellaba*. He felt the coiling of her power.

She thrust it down. Stiffly, as if by rote, she did as he had done. At shirt and drawers she stopped, hands falling to her sides.

"The rest of it," he said.

She shook her head once, tightly.

He said it again, gentle but firm. "The rest of it." And when she would not: "It's not as if you haven't seen it before."

Her power lashed, fierce with temper. He was, quite abruptly and quite without her hands' touching him, naked. Her eyes slid over and round and about, and locked on her feet.

"You stared hard enough," he said, "when I wasn't awake to know it."

Her glare leaped from her feet to his face. He smiled. Lightly, quickly, he slipped off her chemise. Her hands sprang to cover her breasts. He let them. While they were so occupied, he loosened the cord that held up her drawers. She clutched, too late.

She kept the custom of her people. She was all whitely

smooth, like an image carved in ivory. He had been cool, centered on his teaching; but his body remembered, all at once, why it was here.

The catch of her breath was loud in the silence. She had, of course, seen it before. But not truly seen it, as anything that had to do with her.

She was perilously close to flight. He took her hand, touched the palm. "Remember," he said.

"I can't." She was not answering him. "I can't!"

"Beloved, you can."

She shuddered, and leaped. Not away. Full upon him, pressed as close as body could press, gripping him with bone-bruising strength. Her skin was cold to burning.

He struggled to breathe, to speak. "Gently, love. Gently."

She loosened her grip. Her hand moved, up his back to the flex of his shoulders, down to his buttocks. She was just as tall as his shoulder. He was keenly, almost painfully aware of her breasts against his ribs.

She tipped her head back. She had no power to smile, but that was triumph, that light in her face. "Your skin is soft," she said. "And your hair"—tangling her fingers in it. "I thought a man would be all rough."

"Some are."

"Not you." She found the pleasure-places in his back; she started at his shiver of delight, and came back slowly, half fascinated, half afraid. "You are all beautiful, every bit of you." She was determined to prove it with her hands: bold now with desperation, growing bolder as she learned the shape and the size of him. Where he flexed and purred; where he flinched. How the skin fit over muscle and bone. What sparked in him when she closed her hands about his center, gentle with it as with a captive bird.

She let go abruptly, stepped back. Her cheeks were scarlet.

He brushed them with a finger. "Ladylove, there's no shame here."

"Not shame," she muttered. "Not— Allah! All that to carry, and you can walk, too?"

He nodded stiffly, determined to be amused, struggling not to be indignant.

"By the Hundredth Name, how?"

"I manage."

She shook her head. "Incalculable are the ways of God."

"But wonderful. And in you, beautiful." He had her in his arms before she knew what he did, and laid her among the cushions of the bed. She glowed against the silk. He traced the shape of her with lips and hands. She was all new, each spark of pleasure as fresh to her as to him, each secret a revelation to them both. He made her a gift of his wonder. Every lover was different, every night a new pleasure, but the rarest of rarities was this, to be the first who ever woke a maiden's body to the splendor that was in it.

She was losing her fear, warming and easing under his hands. There was fire in her. It kindled his own, almost too well. When she was fully a woman, her fears all put to flight, she would be a lover to make songs of.

All the more cause to go gently with her, although it cost him most of his strength to do it. What was desire with and for a human woman, was nigh a madness now.

Now, she willed him. *Now!*

There was pain, echoing and reechoing in him as in her, but through it, the fierce and utter rightness of it. He, and she, so. Mind to mind and body to body; hearts beating to one measure. For a long moment he wore a different flesh, knew a different turning of the dance. A deeper, inward pleasure; a subtler urgency.

She rode with him, borne at first on his strength, but finding strength of her own. The end was—improbably—laughter, a great, exultant shout of it.

He dropped down beside her, laughing himself, helplessly.

She swept him onto his back and sat on him, covering his face with kisses. "My lord. Oh, my lord! Love me again."

He groaned. "Lady, have mercy! My flesh is immortal, but hardly infinite."

She ascertained as much for herself, to her great disappointment. "That is not how it is in tales."

"Tales lie."

She made a most indelicate noise. But there was no denying the truth. She lay beside him, raised on her elbow, and smoothed the damp hair back from his face. He kissed her hand as it passed. She smiled and laid it against his cheek, smoothing his beard. "The tales also have men falling asleep directly, and leaving their poor lovers alone."

"Human men," he said.

"Ah." She arched her back, stretching like a cat. Desire stirred in him, faint as yet, but promising a resurrection.

Her own eagerness was fading. She ached, if pleasurably. Her body, left to itself, eased into languor. He opened his arms. She came with only a moment's hesitation, and laid her head on his shoulder. She tensed as he folded his arms about her, but again, only for a moment. She shifted closer and sighed. "So," she said. "This is what it is."

"Yes."

She ran her hand idly down his side to his hip. Her pleasure was sharp in him. So different, so wonderful, no curve in it at all. But not so wonderful as what flowered where his legs met.

He shivered lightly under her touch, and gave her back what she had given. The marvel that was woman, and the marvel that was she, alone, of all the women in the world. The silk of her hair, royal crimson; the long subtle curve of her back; the swell of hip and thigh. The scent of her working in him like strong wine. The swift, flaring heat of desire returning fullfold. She met it with startlement that swelled into pleasure.

34

Morning found them tangled in the heaped cushions. He had slid into a warm half-drowse; he woke as she moved, slipping out of his arms, rising for the dawn prayer. Although they had bathed all over only a little while before, she washed as her Prophet prescribed, and dressed fully, before she began her devotions.

He watched under lowered lids, as if he spied on a secret. Both warmth and sleep fled. She who all that night had been the half of his heart, was separate again, alien and infidel, with the dagger of an Assassin at her side. Only her hair was still her own, tumbling over the shoulders of her coat, rippling down her back as she stood and knelt and bowed toward Mecca.

He could never be to her what her Allah was. It was pain, that knowledge. He had his God, but never so close to his center. That was full of what he loved. His brother; his kin; his lover in Aleppo; his far green country. And Morgiana.

He had given her what she wanted of him, and she was content. The edge of her obsession was blunted, the heat of her passion cooled. But he who had been the lesser in desire, more the beloved than the lover, now paid for what was, after all, his sin. He looked at her and knew that hereafter, no mortal woman would be enough.

She rose from her prayer and smiled at him, wide and wicked, almost a grin. He had never thought before this night, that there could be mischief in her. She dived into the cushions and kissed him until he was like to drown.

She pulled back abruptly. He lay and tried to breathe. Her bright mood dimmed. She laid her hand over his heart as if to convince herself that it was there, beating strongly where a human man's could not be. Her eyes took in his body, slowly, flinching from no part of it. "So beautiful," she murmured.

She tugged him to his feet, thrust a bundle into his arms. His clothes. While he dressed, she fetched food in which she forced him to take interest: the eternal bread and dates and cheese of the desert, and for him watered wine, for herself plain water from the spring. "You need your strength," she said, "to face Sinan."

He choked on a mouthful of wine. She did not notice. She ate like a soldier before a battle, grimly, scowling at the air.

"But," he said. "So soon—we've hardly—we can't do it now!"

"We can."

It should have struck him long before it did. She was the Slave of Alamut. For the keeping of a Frank's oath, she would break the vows which she had sworn to a hundred years of masters. No matter that she had gone willingly into servitude, and freed herself more than willingly from it. What this was to him after months of striving, to her was infinitely more.

"Never delude yourself," she said. "Long before I saw you, I wearied of my enslavement. You see merely the end of it, a rebellion to which I have been coming since I left Alamut."

"But," he said, "to do it for me, an infidel—"

"For a creature of my own kind, with whom I have made a bargain."

Cold, all of her, and hard. He set aside the emptied bowl, and stood.

She set something in his hands. A belt which he knew well, and a sword hung on it, and a pair of daggers. He donned them slowly. His finger brushed the hilt of the sword that, returned, was like a part of his body; and, less joyfully, the dagger which he had taken out of Joanna's heart. "This is yours," he said.

Her head shook once. "No. You won it. Let him see it and know that even I am not infallible."

Aidan's fist clenched about the dagger's hilt. He willed his fingers to unlock. Morgiana waited. He drew a deep breath and stepped to her side. Her hand caught his, not for tenderness; but as his fingers laced with hers, for an instant her clasp tightened.

Her power unfolded. There was a flicker of will, a pause at the center; a step, a turn, a shift of flesh and spirit, round and inabout.

Almost before it was begun, it ended. He gasped and nearly fell. Morgiana caught him, held him with effortless strength.

The Old Man of the Mountain sat in his barren garden, serene as if he had been waiting for them. His *fidaïs* stood guard about him: an arc of youths in white with eyes that saw only Paradise; and the gate to it was death.

She granted him no obeisance, no mark of honor or respect. He looked at her and, almost, smiled. "You did well," he said, "to keep my captive for me."

Aidan started forward, but her hand stopped him. He stood in clenched-fist stillness. "He was mine," she said, "before he was yours."

"What is the servant's, is the master's property."

"I am not your servant."

"My slave, then. As you have long seen fit to call yourself."

"I abjure it. A Muslim may not enslave a Muslim."

"As I remember," he said, "you all but compelled me to accept you."

"Such compulsion: I set all my power in your hands, and called you master, if you would wield me for the Mission as those in Alamut no longer knew how to do. They," she said, harsh with scorn, "were much too deeply engrossed in hailing the advent of the Millennium. In wine and coupling and madness they did it, in mockery of all that our order should be."

"And have I so mocked what we hold sacred?"

"No," she said. "Not so openly. Not until you loosed me against the Frankish woman. That she had an ifrit of her own, you discovered soon enough; and he was so obliging as to

come to you. I see your mind, Sinan ibn Salman. If I escape
you, the other must remain, infidel to be sure, but male, and
amenable to your persuasion."

"He has kin," said Sinan.

She clapped her hands. "Spoken like a true bandit! What
will his ransom be?"

"His life in my service."

"Of course." She slanted a glance at Aidan. "You may not
find him as useful a slave as I. His kind serve badly, if they will
serve at all."

"As to the matter of his will, that has been seen to."

Aidan could keep silent no longer. "With words and iron?
Old man, that was never more than mummery."

Sinan did not believe him. The Seal of Solomon gleamed in
his hand. Aidan laughed and woke the fire in it.

Sinan cursed shockingly and cast away the smoldering
thing. It melted as it fell, spattering the earth with molten
iron.

But he was never so easily defeated. "You have kin," he said
again, through teeth clenched with pain. "Will you consider
them?"

Aidan went cold.

Morgiana spoke beside him. "Indeed, he has kin. What
have you?"

"Your name in the Seal of power. This one is protected by
his unfaith. You are not."

A second Seal lay in Sinan's lap. Aidan's power, tensed to
destroy it, froze. She was in it, entwined with it: her oath, her
long years of slavery, the core of her belief. Morgiana had
given it power. Now none but Morgiana could take it away.
And if it burned, so too would she.

Her brow was damp. Her eyes were too wide, too pale. He
willed her to see what he saw. That the bonds were none but
her own. That she could break them; that she had the will,
and the strength. If only she would see. If only she would
believe.

But to believe that, she must deny all that she had done and sworn and held to. She must sunder herself from herself. She must be other than Morgiana.

No, he thought at her. *Morgiana is always Morgiana. Is the serpent less the serpent, because he sheds his outworn skin?*

She clenched against him; but she could not be free of him. Not any longer. He stood in the heart of her and showed her herself. Morgiana. Free and strong and glad. No slave to any mortal man, never again.

She wanted to see it. And yet she wanted to cling to what she knew, whatever its pain, whatever its cost to life and sanity.

Sinan spoke in their silence, softly, each word the link of a chain. "You are mine. Your will is my will, your life my life, unless I choose to let them go. Serve me, and I may set you free. Defy me, and I bind you for all eternity."

"Are you Allah Himself," she demanded of him, gasping it, struggling against bonds and oaths and geas, "that you should so compel me?"

"I am Allah's servant; I wield the power of Suleiman."

Her body shook; her fists clenched convulsively. "I—do—defy you. I *can.*" She sucked in her breath, battling. "I can. I can!"

Freer, each word; stronger. He saw it. "Can you," he asked her, "defend all that is dear to you, for every moment of every day, until you yield or they are all lost?"

She smiled. Not triumphant, not yet. But she had seen the chains about her, and they were chains of air. She was beginning to comprehend it; to believe it. "Can you," she asked her master, "hope to rule a realm under such persecution as I will visit upon it, if you touch anything that is mine?"

"You are powerless. You can only threaten."

She faltered. He was her master. His words tangled about her, dulled her wits, sapped her strength.

"No!" Aidan cried, not caring who heard. "It's he who is

powerless; it's he who has nothing left but threats. Open your mind and your senses. Look at him!"

She looked. She saw power, terror.

Mortality.

Fear.

Fear?

"Fear!" Aidan said, loud in Sinan's silence. "He's afraid of you. He knows what you can do—what we can both do, if he presses us too far."

She was whiter than he had ever seen her, white as death. She would die; she could die, if she willed it, if she clenched her power about her heart, like a fist, just so. Just—

Will and body convulsed together. A sound escaped her, raw animal noise; but strength in it, and will, and—at last— understanding. Her hand swept up, out.

Sinan sat uncomprehending; but slowly he saw what he must see. More slowly still, he began to understand it. His *fidaï*s were gone. All but one, who stood bewildered and alone. And Morgiana was smiling, a white wild smile, the joy of the falcon that flings itself free into the sky.

She turned that smile on the lone *fidaï*; she beckoned. He came, eyes locked in hers. "Child," she purred, "are you a faithful follower of our way?"

He nodded vigorously.

"Do you see that man?" Her finger stabbed at Sinan.

The boy nodded again.

"He has betrayed our Mission. He lusts after a woman of the infidels; he takes an infidel for his servant. Who is to say that he will not command us all to worship the three false gods of the Franks?"

The boy's lips drew back from his teeth.

"Just so," she said, all but crooning it. "Take him now, *fidaï*, warrior of the Faith. Hold him until I bid you slay him."

Sinan struggled in a grip too strong to break. His captor wore an expression of perfect and implacable determination. It would not yield for any word of his, any threat or command or pleading.

"Now," said Morgiana, and her voice was deadly gentle. "Are you prepared to hear us?"

Sinan would not bend; he did not seem inclined to break. He eased in the *fidai*'s hands. "I will hear you," he said.

She nodded, eyes steady on him. She was half-drunk with freedom, with the first sweet taste of victory. That drunkenness could be deadly; could lose them all that they had gained.

But her voice was as steady as her eyes, no hint in it of weakness. "I recall that you have wrought well for the Mission. I expect that you will continue to do so. But that must be accomplished without the aid of either a Frankish baroness or an Aleppan merchant house. They gain nothing for the Mission; they only feed your avarice."

"And my pride," he said calmly. "Be so kind as to remember that. But even I am wise enough to know when I have failed."

"Which wisdom did not wake in you until you saw a greater profit in yon captive Frank."

"That is no less than you have done yourself."

"I make no pretense of sanctity."

The black eyes glanced from Morgiana to Aidan and back again. They understood much too much. "He is of your race," said Sinan, as if he had only begun to perceive its meaning. "Yet for him you would turn against us? For an infidel you would betray the Mission?"

Morgiana's eyes began to glitter. "I turn you back to the way of Hasan-i-Sabbah, on his name be peace, and remove the temptation to stray. In earnest of it, I ask more than your bare word. The blood-price of a baron and an heir to a barony, and the price for the wounding of a baroness—"

Sinan went pale. Now at last she had struck him, and struck deep.

"You will pay," said Morgiana, "as we decree."

He could not speak: the dagger pricked too close. She summoned his servants. They came to her bidding. They heaped gold into the great chest which she bade them set at Aidan's feet; atop the gold they poured a glittering stream of jewels. It was pleasure, that warmth under his breastbone, under even the anger. It was honey-sweet to watch the Master of Masyaf bleed wealth that was more precious to him than blood, and to know that he knew all that he lost with it: his slave who was, his slave who might have been, his certainty that no man in the world was feared as greatly as he. He was master of Syria, more truly than the man who ruled in Damascus, but he could not master the Slave of Alamut. He sat in his own garden, with the dagger of his own *fidaï* at his throat, and paid as he was bidden to pay.

She knew to the last dirham how much he could spare, and how much would cause him pain. He had to see Aidan claim it, and their bargain written and signed and sealed with immortal fire.

When it was done, the dagger lowered from his throat. "So, then, sir Frank," he said. His voice was calm; his eyes were terrible. "Are you content?"

"No," Aidan said.

Sinan smiled. That was the power of the man: even defeated, even humiliated, to lose none of his faith in himself. "Slay me, then," he said. "Shed my blood as your heart longs to do. Rid the world of me."

It was mockery, and it was not. Sinan had no fear of death. Life to him was sweet, with the savor of power in it, the web of spies and servants through whom he worked his will in the east. But he would die content, knowing that his death had made his people stronger.

"Therefore," said Aidan, "I let you live."

"Cruel," said Sinan. "Just, in its fashion. You would have made a passable *fidaï.*" He paused. "Would you, perhaps, consider . . . ?"

"No!" Too loud, too quick. Aidan struggled to recover himself. "I am no man's tame murderer."

"A pity. You would be welcome here, your talents known

and used to their fullest. Where you go, you may find that neither is so."

"I have promises to keep."

"Indeed? And what will you receive in return? I am told," said Sinan, "that Jerusalem stops just short of denouncing you for the deaths of your kin; and that rumor credits you with worse."

"Then the sooner I keep my promises, the sooner I clear my name."

"Or burn for it."

"I am a spirit of fire. What harm can I take in my element?"

"Even in the fires of hell?"

"If I can know them, then I have a soul and can hope also for Paradise. If I have no soul, then death for me is only oblivion; and mortal fire cannot touch me."

"Ah," said Sinan. "A theologian."

"A madman," said Morgiana. "He will not serve you, Sinan ibn Salman, nor can you lure him into your trap. Let him go; surrender him."

"As I am to surrender you?"

"Even so," she said.

He looked long at her. She stood still, enduring it. "What is there for you without us?" he asked her. "Will you turn infidel and run at this one's heel? Can you forsake all that you have been and done, and betray your faith and your given word, and turn against those whom you have served for so long? Will you not reconsider? Will you not come back to me? Free, now; freed from the order of the dagger, set above it as its commander, with no other above you, save only myself."

They were not empty words. He meant them. He was subtler than any serpent. Even truth was his to wield, to twist to his own ends.

"I did ill to keep you so long enslaved," he said. "Now I would amend it. Will you accept what I offer?"

She was silent. Her face was still. So quenched, it lost its vivid beauty; it was only alien.

When she spoke, she spoke slowly, as if to weigh each word before she let it go. "I who have been a slave in defiance of my will, do not trust easily any man's promises, still less those of the one who enslaved me. Yet that you are a man of honor, as you see it, I cannot deny. Is there a price on this freedom which you offer?"

"None but what you have already paid."

She drew a careful breath. "And this that we have settled here—the blood-price, the freeing of the Frank—is it to hold firm?"

"Before Allah I swear it."

"So." She straightened, as if a great weight had fallen from her; the breath which she drew now was deep. Free. "No. No, I will not serve you. Even free; even in a place of power. I am done with servitude."

Even yet Sinan would not concede defeat. "Are you therefore done with Islam? For what is that but perfect submission to God?"

"God," she said very gently, "is not Sinan ibn Salman." And as he stiffened, enraged: "There is no god but God. It is time I learned to serve Him alone, and not at the whim of a mortal man." She bowed, low and low, as a slave might; but it was never submission. "May God keep you, O my master who was, and may He grant you wisdom."

"I should have taken what he offered," Morgiana said.

Aidan did not know where they were. The wealth of Masyaf was with them; the light was dim about them, wan and grey. The air smelled strange. He saw sand and stone, the bulk of a tree, a glint of water. For all he knew, they were in the land of the jinn.

Suddenly he knew it. They were by the spring in Persia; the cave was behind them. Clouds lowered above them. The strangeness in the air was the scent of rain.

Morgiana swayed. He caught her. She was conscious, but

grievously weak, and furious with it. "Too much," she said. "I stretched too far. I was no better than you."

His lips twitched at that. "What did you do with the *fidaïs*?"

"I sent them all away. To a place I know, in a city far from any that they would have heard of. The women there are beautiful and wanton, and each has many husbands. My master's servants may decide for themselves whether to call it hell or Paradise."

Aidan laughed. "And the old man never asked for them back."

"He, like them, believes them dead. He will not find it easy to fill their places."

"Or yours."

"Or mine." Her head rolled on his shoulder. "Allah! What a fool I am!"

"A splendid fool." He turned toward the cavemouth. She lay limp in his arms, fighting the dark, but losing the battle.

Sayyida sprang out of the cave's shadow, wild with fear as she saw what Aidan carried. "She's alive," he said, little comfort as that was. "She pushed too hard, that's all, to win everything for both of us. She'll be well, once she's slept."

Sayyida wanted transparently to believe it. She watched Aidan lay Morgiana on the divan, was there in an instant with a blanket and a scowl. "How could you let her do this to herself?"

"How could I stop her?"

"You should have tried," Sayyida said.

There was no sensible answer to that. Aidan hovered, but he was not wanted. He withdrew to the cavemouth.

It had begun to rain. He had not felt rain on his face since he came to this sun-blasted country. Cold though it was, with an edge of sleet, he welcomed it.

Morgiana was deep in sleep, Sayyida engrossed in fretting over her. He was free. Truly, finally free. Sinan had paid with his own hand for all that he had taken; and he had lost the most useful of his slaves. He would not recover quickly from that blow. Nor would he turn again upon the House of Ibrahim.

Aidan knew what taste was in his mouth. It was ashes. So long a hunt, so bitter a battle, and all that it came to was this. A chest bound with iron, a grey rain falling, and a rending in the heart of him. To stay and be this woman's lover. To go and keep his promises: to Aleppo, to conclude his bargain with the Lady Khadijah; to find Joanna.

He did not even know how long he had been away. A month? He had never gone a day without thinking of her, and being soul-glad that she had not come with him. She would surely have died, and the baby with her.

Maybe she would forgive him for leaving her. Maybe she would even forgive what he had done to win his war with the Assassins. They would find a way out of their coil. His child would not be branded a bastard; his lady would have the honor she deserved.

And Morgiana?

She had what she wanted. He had older ties, and stronger.

Coward. The voice of his deep self.

He thrust it deeper and set his foot on it. What more could there be between a knight of the cross and a devout Muslim, but what there had been? It was over. They had their own worlds to live in, their own and separate destinies.

Still, the small, needling voice. *Craven. Honorless fool.*

"What would you have me do?" he cried to the rain. "Turn apostate? Marry her?" He stopped. "Yes, why don't I go Muslim? Then I can have both of them."

The voice was silent.

He tossed his rain-wet head. "My way is chosen. My mother chose it the day she brought us to Caer Gwent and told our father that we were his."

Silence, still; silence that was reproach.

He went back into the cave that was more splendid than many a lord's hall in the west, and found nothing changed.

Morgiana looked like a child, asleep. He wanted to bend and kiss her. He wanted her, starkly and simply.

He firmed his will. It took more strength than he had expected; almost more than he had.

Sayyida took no notice of him, except to rebuke him for dripping on the carpet. Hasan was asleep.

Signs enough, and farewell enough. He remembered the way of Morgiana's magic, that she had given him after all, as if she wanted him to know it, to do what he did now: the fixing of the mind, the gathering of power, the indescribable inward turn and flex. He paused on the very edge of it, not quite afraid. No one moved. No one called him back. He let himself go.

35

While Morgiana pursued her Frank, and after she had caught him, Sayyida had time to think. Watching them was peculiarly painful: a dance of advance and retreat; a glitter on the edges of their meetings, like the flash of honed steel. They seemed barely to know how their bodies yearned toward one another —even Morgiana, who knew that she wanted him, but went about winning him with the deadly simplicity of a child. When they were together, even quarreling as they mostly were, something in the way they sat or stood or moved, was like the notes of the lute that underlie the song.

Sayyida had that with Maimoun. Not as these two did, all fire and passion, but in their quiet, ordinary way, they went well together.

If only Maimoun could learn a little sense. A man who kept his wife in a cage, had only himself to blame if she tried to fly from it.

"A woman should always be humble," she said to Hasan

when Morgiana had gone with Aidan to face the Old Man of the Mountain. Sayyida did not want to wear herself to rags in fretting over them; therefore she fretted over herself. "A woman should be conciliatory. A woman should never oppose the will of her man, whom Allah has set over her."

She was making bread, kneading it on the hearthstone. She set her teeth and attacked it until her arms cried protest. "Never," she said, "except when she can be subtle, and suborn him, and play him into her hands. Which is almost always. Unless she is caught in the act. As I was." With each pause, she pummeled the yielding dough, beating tenderness into it.

She looked at her thickly floured fists. Tears pricked her eyes; laughter bubbled in her throat. "Oh, Hasan! I miss your father."

Morgiana came back half-dead, in Aidan's arms. He seemed unworried; Sayyida supposed that he would know, being what he was. But he was a man, when it came down to it: a very large and very willful child, who, having dropped his burden in Sayyida's lap, went off and left her to it. She suspected that he might be sulking. Men hated it when women ignored them for other women.

She shook her head and sighed. It was not anger that stirred in her, not anymore: only a kind of fond exasperation. That was the way men were. The way Maimoun was.

Would he take her back?

She stopped. She could not go back. He had struck her; he had called her a liar. She could not forgive him.

Could not, or would not?

So, then. If she would go back, if she would have sense, and stop being a burden on her friend—would he take her?

He would have to. She would not let him do anything else.

Morgiana was a long time waking. Well before she did, Sayyida knew that the Frank was gone. He always came back for the sunset meal, and he always slept in the hall. Tonight, he did neither.

He had found a way out of his cage. She could hardly blame him for taking it. Or, she supposed, for abandoning Morgiana. That was what came of turning love into merchant's bargain.

Still, she was sorry. She had thought better of him than that.

She was ready when Morgiana woke, and braced for the storm. When it did not break at once, she was by no means comforted. "When did he go?" Morgiana asked quite calmly.

"Last night," Sayyida said. "As soon as he brought you back."

Morgiana closed her eyes. Her face wore no expression. For a moment she seemed not to be there at all.

Her eyes opened. She was smiling. "So he did," she said. And, more slowly, almost tenderly: "So he did."

"Morgiana," said Sayyida. "Don't do something you'll regret."

"I already have." Morgiana sat up, frowning. "I didn't win him at all. I bought him."

"You're not going to drag him back, are you?"

"No," said Morgiana. "No, I'm not going to drag him back. He gave me what I paid for." She paused. "As he sees it. I might have begged to differ."

Sayyida wondered at the power of a night's loving, to reduce Morgiana to mere and acquiescent womanhood.

Morgiana laughed, fierce and high. "Do you think so? Will I make a proper female after all?"

"Do you want to?"

"I don't know." Morgiana stood, took a moment to steady herself, walked in a slow circle. There were signs of Aidan here and there: a cushion he had liked, in the corner he had often retreated to; the cup he had used, beside the flagon of wine; the robe he looked so well in, folded at the foot of his bed.

The lute in its wrappings, silent now, bereft. She paused by none of these, barely glanced at them.

She came back to Sayyida. Something lay on the divan where she had been sleeping; as her shadow shifted, for an instant it caught the light. Sayyida reached for it, curious. It was a knife, simply but rather elegantly made, with a plain silver hilt.

"He made it," said Morgiana. "It's not bad, for 'prentice work."

She was a little too calm. Sayyida let her take the knife; saw the way her fingers tightened on it. "He left it for you."

"Idiot," said Morgiana. She did not say which of them she meant. The blade had cut her fingers lightly; she stared at the thin line of scarlet as if she had never seen blood before.

She drew herself up, thrust the dagger in her sash. "Did you save any breakfast for me?"

Her eyes warned Sayyida not to press. Sayyida made herself nod. "I'll fetch it."

Morgiana followed her to the kitchen. They ate there, squatting like servants by the hearth, since neither of them was minded to spread a cloth in the hall.

Hasan woke in the middle, and needed bathing and feeding. "He'll be wanting weaning soon," said Sayyida, wincing as he brought his teeth to bear. "Ah! Cruel. Have a bit of bread, if it's chewing you're after."

He transferred his affections quite happily to a crust dipped in honey. His mother began to tidy the kitchen, while Morgiana watched, silent. Morgiana would never make a plain man's wife. She knew too little of the womanly arts, and she did not seem inclined to learn more.

"They're dull," she said.

"Necessities often are." Sayyida tested the washwater in its cauldron over the hearth, dipped out enough to fill the basin. "It's pride that makes them shine: doing them well, and knowing it."

"You like them?"

"They're what I do. Fahimah says I'm good at them."

"So does he."

"Khalid?"

"Aidan." Morgiana sounded almost angry. "As if he could know."

"He notices things. It's his way. I suppose because he's a Frank. They're odd when it comes to women's matters."

"He is purely odd." She set herself in front of Sayyida, blocking her path to the basin. "Show me how."

"Why on earth would you want to—" Sayyida broke off. "Well, then. Watch, and see."

By the time they were done, they had turned out the kitchen and the hall, and scoured them from end to end. Morgiana flung herself into it with rare passion; what she lacked in skill, she more than made up for in enthusiasm.

When every inch was scrubbed and spotlessly tidy, Sayyida leaned against the wall and mopped her brow. Morgiana handed her a cup. Sherbet bubbled in it, rich and sour-sweet, exactly as she liked it. She stared at it. "We could have used magic," she said.

"Muscles are better." Morgiana propped Hasan on her hip. She looked flushed, disheveled, and almost happy. "You want to go home, don't you?"

Of course she would know. Sayyida was a little disappointed: she had been working hard to find a way to say it. It was like Morgiana to go straight to it, as soon as it came into her head.

"Yes," Sayyida said. "I want to go home." Now it was out. She felt oddly empty; oddly excited.

Morgiana reached for her; she pulled away. They stared at one another. "You should go now," Morgiana said, "if you're going to go at all."

Sayyida shook her head. "I can't." She brushed at her gown; at her hair. "I can't go like this."

"A bath, then," said the ifritah. "Then we go."

Sayyida swallowed. This was more than she had bargained for. Though she should have known. She knew Morgiana. "Will you come with me?"

"Do you want me?"

She nodded. Her hands were cold, but her face was burning. "He has to know how it was. So—so that he can decide."

"To divorce you?"

"Or to take me back."

"It seems to me," said Morgiana, "that the taking should be on your side."

Sayyida smiled, not too shakily after all; now that there was no escaping it. "I know that. He needn't."

"That's not honest."

"No," said Sayyida. "But it's love."

Morgiana shook her head. She did not understand. Maybe it was a human thing. That a man could give, while seeming to take; that a woman could choose, by letting him choose.

"Not my way," said Morgiana. "Or ours." But she was wise enough not to argue with it.

While Sayyida bathed and made herself presentable, she scraped together her courage. She was going to need all of it. Morgiana had put on women's clothes, she noticed.

Then there was no more delaying it. Hasan was in his new coat. Morgiana was gowned and veiled. Sayyida was ready in every way that she could think of, except one.

That would never come while she waited. She drew a deep breath, and got a good grip on Hasan. "Now," she said.

Home was smaller and darker than she remembered: a little shabby, a little worn about the edges, but comfortable. Her nose twitched. Fahimah had been making *zirbajah* with its pungency of garlic, as only Fahimah could make it. It hurt to smell it again. To be home.

Morgiana's sudden movement brought Sayyida back to herself. They were in a small room on the edge of the women's quarters, where no one ever went except, now and then, a guest for whom there was no room elsewhere. It was close and musty, as if it had not been opened in a long while. The ifritah opened the door, paused.

"Trouble?" Sayyida asked. She could hardly manage a whisper, her throat was so dry, her heart hammering so hard.

"No," said Morgiana. She beckoned. Sayyida stumbled after her.

They were all at dinner. Morgiana's doing, maybe. Once in a great while Laila would wait on her husband, and Fahimah liked to assure herself that her men were eating well, but Mother never stooped to it. Except that, tonight, she had. Maybe it was that Ishak was there. If she had pretended to play the servant, she had been dissuaded quickly enough and set on the best cushions, next to her son.

It was no joyful gathering, even with Ishak in it. Farouk looked almost old. Mother was grim. Laila was muted, quenched. Maimoun ate methodically, but not as if his mind was on it. The line between his brows was etched deep; there were shadows under his eyes.

Sayyida started forward, but Morgiana's arm barred her.

Ishak set down his cup with a thud. The noise was loud, and abrupt. "Ya Allah! A month, you've been at this, and for what? Won't you even begin to look for them?"

"What use?" his father said. "We know who took them."

"And why." It was a growl in Ishak's throat.

Maimoun did not respond to either growl or glare. He chewed the last of his bread, swallowed, reached for his cup.

Ishak caught his wrist. "Iblis take your bones!"

He freed himself, easily, and drank.

"If they've been killed because of you—"

The cup jerked in Maimoun's hand. He set it down. He rose, bowed first to Mother and then to Farouk.

"No, you won't," said Ishak. "You've walked out enough. Now you'll face what you did."

"I know what I did," said Maimoun.

"You tried to keep your wife in chains. What had she ever done to deserve them?"

"She kept company with a demon," Maimoun said.

"And you angered the demon. Which of you was the greater idiot?"

"I did what I thought I had to do."

"*You* thought." Ishak started to spit, caught his mother's eye, grimaced instead. "All you were thinking was that it was a heady thing to be someone's lord and master. Emirs who treat their troops like that, don't go far."

"I didn't say I was right," said Maimoun.

Sayyida could not stand it any longer. "You were as right as you knew how to be," she said.

In stories, the return of the long-lost child was perfectly simple. She—or more often he—came back, her aged mother fell into her arms, her aged father wept on her neck, and everyone lived happily ever after.

Sayyida's father was not one to weep on anyone's neck, and Mother only swooned when she had something to gain from it. There was a very long silence. No one looked particularly surprised; merely nonplussed, and a little disappointed. It was difficult to shift one's mind from the prospect of a kinswoman lost and maybe dead, to one alive and all too evidently thriving. She could not even manage to look as if she had suffered for the lack of them.

Ishak was the first to scramble his wits together, and leap regardless of Morgiana who stood at Sayyida's back, and hug her and Hasan until they gasped for breath. He pulled them into the room, pelting Sayyida with questions. "Where were you? What did you do? You look marvelous—and Hasan, he's grown. Who took care of you? It wasn't—"

" 'Giana," said Hasan clearly. "Mama. Hasan." He waited.

"Ishak," his mother said, trying not to laugh. Her brother's expression was comically shocked.

"Ishak." Hasan grinned at them all.

No one could ever resist a baby; and this one had been

taking lessons with Morgiana's Frank, who could charm a star out of the sky. Fahimah greeted Sayyida gladly enough, but she fell on Hasan, laughing and crying at once.

Without him to fill her arms, Sayyida felt naked. She could feel Morgiana behind her, a shadow in a veil. No one seemed to have noticed her, except Ishak, who was not choosing to speak of it.

The fuss over Hasan gave Sayyida time to bolster her courage. Ishak still had his arm around her, a little too heavy, a little too tight, but blessedly welcome. Everyone else was cooing over Hasan.

All but Maimoun. He watched his son hungrily, but he could not seem to make himself move. He would not look at Sayyida.

Hasan decided his own share of it by wriggling out of Mother's clasp and onto his very capable feet, and clambering into his father's lap. "Papa," he said.

Maimoun lit like a lamp. "Did you hear that? Did you hear what he said?"

They nodded. Even Mother was smiling.

"He's walking, too," said Maimoun. "My son is walking. And talking."

"Talking," said Hasan. "Walking."

After that, no one was much minded to flay Sayyida with questions, though Ishak looked near to death of curiosity. Sayyida was back, safe and whole. Farouk seemed content; the women followed where he led.

They trusted her. She almost broke down, realizing it. Her father at least, Fahimah certainly, maybe even Mother—they were not afraid that she had dishonored the house.

Nor was Ishak, but he would die if he had to wait much longer. "I was in a place Morgiana knows," Sayyida said: "a secret place, far away from any city. I haven't seen a human being since I left here."

"That's horrible," he said.

"It was peaceful." Most of the time. "I took care of Hasan.

I looked after the house. I cooked. I did woman-things. Sometimes I went out. The sky was very wide. I could stretch my mind so far, there was hardly any me left at all."

"Don't tell me it turned you into a mystic."

"When there were dishes to wash? Don't be silly."

"You were really . . . all alone?"

Maimoun said that. He still would not look at her. His voice was rough.

"Morgiana was there," Sayyida said. Light, cool, steady. She was proud of herself.

They saw the ifritah then: she moved out of Sayyida's shadow, into the light. She did not lower her veil.

"I asked her to come," said Sayyida, not so steadily now. "I owe her a debt, for giving me a place to go, and looking after me while I was there. I want her to stay for a while. She's not an Assassin anymore. She wants to learn to be a woman."

They greeted that with varying degrees of incredulity. None of them went so far as to say it. Even Maimoun.

"I will not presume on your hospitality," Morgiana said. She did not sound as haughty as she might have.

"No," said Farouk, thickly. He cleared his throat. "No, you don't presume. You're welcome in my house."

Laila might have had something to say; Mother certainly would. But Farouk had taken it out of their hands. Sayyida could not tell if he regretted it. He did not seem to have done it for fear of what Morgiana could do; he had certainly not done it for liking.

Morgiana bowed as a woman of rank to a benefactor. "You are most generous," she said.

"My daughter owes you a debt. Should I be niggardly in repaying it?"

"Some might," said Morgiana.

Nothing about her singled out Maimoun, but he stiffened. He did not say anything. He did, finally, dart a glance at his wife. She could not read it, except that it was not altogether furious. Maybe, after all, he would forgive her.

Suddenly she was tired of all these crowding kin, their fuss and flutter that never quite settled, their desperate efforts to make it all seem ordinary. Harmless. As if Sayyida's month among the afarit had never happened.

But she knew why she had gone; and Maimoun remembered. She drew herself up. "Thank you, Father," she said. "Mother, Fahimah, Laila: my respects. Ishak, I'm glad to see you again. Maimoun—" She had to stop, take a breath, go on again. "Maimoun, husband, if I may still call you that—"

"You may."

He was having no easier a time of it than she. It helped her, a little, to know that. "Husband," she said. "I'm sorry I went away."

He swallowed visibly. He was blinking too much. "Yes," he said. "I'm sorry, too." He glared at his feet. "I'm . . . sorry . . . I did what I did."

"I, too." She let it dangle for a bit. "Can you forgive me?"

"I . . ." He blinked hard. "Yes. If you'll forgive me."

She nodded.

He had to look up to see it. He was trying not to break down and cry.

That almost broke her. But this was no place for it, for either of them. She lifted her chin. "If everyone will pardon me, it's been a long while since the dawn prayer, and I've been missing my own bed. May I have permission to go to it?"

They did not want her to; Fahimah protested that she could not go to bed without eating first. But she was firm. She felt like a coward, leaving Morgiana to their tender mercies, but their fear of the ifritah would keep them honest. Sayyida needed to talk to Maimoun. And maybe not only talk.

But, once Fahimah and the servant had seen at exhausting length to Sayyida's comfort, Sayyida began to be afraid that she had been too subtle. That he would not come. Or that he refused to, because he could not forgive her so far.

She was ready to go back, at least to retrieve Hasan. She had even started to get up, when Maimoun opened the door.

He did not look as he had the last time he came to her. He was quieter this time; more subdued.

She sank down on the mat. He stood with his back to the door, and looked everywhere but at her.

"Maimoun," she said, suddenly shy.

"Sayyida," he said. He chewed his lip, fidgeting. "You're really well?"

"Really."

"You were—really—where you said?"

"Really. We were somewhere in Persia, I think. In the desert. There was a fig tree, but the birds ate all the fruit."

"You liked it there."

She could not deny it.

"I wasn't trying to shame you," he said. "I wanted to do you honor. Like a lady."

"I know," she said.

"It was just—that—that creature—"

"She's not easy to like," said Sayyida. "At all. I think you have to start when you're a baby."

"She took good care of you."

He was trying to talk himself round. Sayyida gave him what help she could. "She did. She's loyal to her friends. And she loves Hasan."

"I . . . could see that. She almost looks human, when she looks at him."

"She's trying very hard. It's not been easy for her, being an Assassin. She had a bitter time to win her freedom."

He was not ready to talk about that. He pulled at his beard, shy again, wavering as if he wanted to bolt.

Sayyida gave up her thoughts of subtlety. She was on him before he could move, holding him tight. "I missed you, Maimoun."

He mumbled something. At first he was rigid, but she held on. His arms crept stiffly around her. He patted her back.

She was crying. She had not even noticed. Once she did,

she could not stop. She did try. Maimoun hated tears; they made him desperately uncomfortable.

"I'm sorry," she tried to say. "I didn't mean to—"

"I missed you, too."

She tilted her head back. His beard was damp. She brushed at it. "Does that mean you won't divorce me?"

"Should I?"

"I haven't done anything dishonorable."

"So. Why would I want to put you aside?"

She shrugged. "You might not trust me."

"You know what came of that."

"I do want to be a good wife," she said. "I try to obey you."

"I should try to give you orders you can obey."

"You could," she said slowly, "order me to kiss you."

He blushed crimson. But he laughed, which startled her. "Well, then, I will. Kiss me."

She was delighted to obey. He was delighted to command it again.

And he had not even drunk any wine. She drew back in the middle of it, to catch her breath. "I'll have to run away more often," she said, "just for the homecomings."

Her hair was down, and his fingers were tangled in it. They tightened briefly, painfully. "What if I order you not to?"

"I'll try to be obedient."

"But you might not be able to." He was learning. It was hard; he did not like it. Still, he tried. She admired—no, more than that; she loved him for it.

She kissed him yet again, with fervor that left him reeling. "You are my husband. Even when I was most angry, I never wanted to belong to anyone else. I'm glad my father gave me to you. I'm glad you gave me Hasan. I'm glad to be here, with you, being your wife."

He did not answer that, except to hold her a little more tightly, but she could feel the happiness grow. He was only stolid to look at, was Maimoun.

Tomorrow might not be so joyful. They both had much to

forgive, and Morgiana was there to remind them. Maimoun, being human, and male, was not going to find it easy to change his ways. Sayyida, being Sayyida, was sure to do something to aggravate him.

For once, she could not care. They had the night. Tomorrow would look after itself.

VI

ALEPPO

36

Aidan fell out of nothingness, dizzy and reeling. Morgiana had made it seem so simple: as if one stepped through a veil of air. But in that veil was limitless void, and passing it was to chance one's utter dissolution. It sapped the will; it robbed the mind of its vision, the doubled awareness of the place one left and the place one sought, without which one could not master the dark.

For a long while he could not even remember where he had wanted to go. Fear swelled. Had the void taken him after all? Had he gone astray, lost himself with no hope of returning?

The light came back all at once. He crouched in the room that had been his in the House of Ibrahim, and beside him the chest of his kinsfolk's ransom. Both of them seemed intact, except for the bruises where he had fallen.

He drew a sharp breath, levered himself to his feet. God be thanked that no one had seen him. He did not need to be told that he was a fool to have tried it, alone, without teaching.

Not again, by God and all the saints. Henceforward he would travel by plain human means, and slowness be damned.

He left the box where his power had dropped it, and went out into the last light of the sun. It startled him. He had gone so far since morning; surely by now it should be deep night.

The murmur of Muslim prayer ran with him, less in the ear than in the mind. They were like monks in their offices, all these easterners. Time and the desert had changed him: he felt strange, walking upright and unsanctified in the hour of prayer, when everyone around him at least pretended to turn toward heaven. Nor was he minded to cross himself, and so defy them all.

The harem's guards were not Muslims, and not at prayer. They admitted Aidan without question. "As the lady wills," one of them said.

She received him almost directly. The woman with her was not Joanna; with them, as if to guard them, sat Karim. Aidan bowed to them. They greeted him without surprise; even with pleasure. Even Karim, although his pleasure was not so much for Aidan's sake as for what Aidan must inevitably be told. The honor of the House was well on its way to being mended. Joanna was gone.

Perhaps Aidan spoke words of greeting. Perhaps he said nothing at all, but stood motionless, speechless. How could she be gone? She was here, mending, waiting for him to come back.

He must have said it aloud. Khadijah said, "Is she your wife, that she should wait for you?"

"You sent her away," he said.

"Allah bear witness," said Khadijah, "I did not. Nor would I have considered it. Indeed I sought to dissuade her, but she was set on it."

Riding to Acre. Going back to her husband. Cozening him into accepting her child—Aidan's child—as his own.

"She was set on it," Khadijah repeated. "She was wise, if not precisely prudent. I hope that you share somewhat of her wisdom."

Aidan sank down. His knees throbbed; he sat on his heels. So much fear, he had had: for her, for the child. So little thought for what they would do, past Masyaf. She had thought—he had given her time for that. Time alone. And she had taken it.

She had not left even a word of farewell. No message at all, except her absence.

"She was well looked after," said Khadijah, as if that could comfort him. "A troop of guards accompanied her. The physician rode with her, to see that she did not harm herself more than she must. Although she scarcely seemed to need so much: she was most miraculously recovered."

Miraculously. Yes. He began to laugh. For her he had abandoned Morgiana. For her child's sake she had abandoned him.

One woman was not of his faith. One was not of his kind. Now he was alone again. Alone, and victorious.

Despair was perfect, and being perfect, gave him power to do what sanity might never have permitted. Silver and gold rained down out of the air, filling the laps of the queen of merchants and her heir. Their wonder was bittersweet. "Sinan's gold," Aidan said. "Assassin silver. Your share of his blood-payment to the House of Ibrahim."

They were astonished. He laughed again, light and joyless. He laid the scroll of the agreement in Khadijah's hands. "As you see," he said. "Signed, and sealed."

She took her time in reading it. "It is well negotiated," she said, "and not too badly conceived."

He did not see the need to tell her how that could be. But some glimmer of compunction made him say, "I had an ally among the Assassins. That one bargained in my name."

"Not at too great a cost to himself, one can hope."

"No," he said. "Not too great." He could not stop seeing Morgiana as he had left her, unconscious, with her friend for nurse and guard. He seemed to make a habit of leaving women so.

Maybe Morgiana would wake as Joanna had, and find herself alone, and choose anew: go back to Sinan, become his captain, rule among the Assassins.

He raised his eyes to Khadijah. "Have you a horse which I may purchase, against my share in the House?"

"What will you do with it?"

"Does it matter?"

"No," she said. And waited.

"Ride," he answered her. "To Jerusalem, to enter the king's service."

"To Acre, to confront your kinswoman?"

His mouth opened; closed.

"You may do as your heart bids you. I only ask that you allow your mind a moment's grace, and consider. What can you do but hurt her? Bitter enough for her that she was forced to choose as she has, and with such a burden as she bears. Need she endure the grief which your coming would bring?"

He gritted his teeth. "I would not betray her. Or make her betray herself."

"No?"

Joanna was a wretched liar. Aidan knew it as well as Khadijah. He unknotted his fists one by one. "But if she fails to win her husband over—if she needs me—"

"If she needs you, then surely you will know."

He had not even known that she was gone. He raked his fingers through his hair, clawed them against his skull. How could she be gone? How dared she?

The pain brought him to his senses. He wondered if he could ever be truly or simply a wild thing again. Something in him had changed. Grown, maybe. Been tempered with fire.

It would have been easy to run mad. Give himself up to his pain. Kill something. Or someone.

Too easy. And much too imprudent.

"I will not go to Acre," he said. "I give you my word."

But if she was in Jerusalem . . .

Khadijah, mercifully, did not say it. Could it be that she was not omniscient? She only bowed her head, accepting his promise.

He left in the morning. It would not be fair to a horse to ride nightlong as he would have liked to ride; and he surprised himself with sleep, and with waking hungry. There was food for him; his clothes were mended, even made new where the tatters were most hopeless.

When he came out at last into the courtyard, a caravan waited. Mounts; mules and camels; a handful of the cousins who, they said, were being sent to Jerusalem on the business of the House.

And guards. Anonymous in plain armor, like hired soldiers; faces demurely or discreetly lowered, eyes fixed on anything but the one they were to guard. He did not know what it was

that woke in him, whether joy or rage or sheer, blank astonishment.

"But," he said. "They were dead."

"Hardly," said Karim behind him.

He did not turn. His eyes, he knew, were wild. "She did it.
Didn't she? And never told me. Damn her. Damn her to her
own hell."

"Indeed," said Karim dryly. "Did you think that you could
be free of them?"

"They should be free of me. I'm no master for good Muslims."

Aidan barely had time to brace for it before it was upon
him: a tide of armored bodies, a clamor of voices, a flood of
joy and tears and sudden, righteous anger. "No master for us,
are you? Abandon us, would you? Freedom, do you call this?
What do you take us for?"

"Idiots," Aidan answered them, not gently. He rocked like
a stone in a torrent, but he kept his feet.

They were all present and accounted for, and quite exuber-
antly defiant. Having destroyed dignity and discipline by overwhelming him, they remembered both, to drop down in obeisance. Timur spoke out of turn, and Arslan kicked him
soundly for it, but he spoke for them all. "We belong to you.
We don't want to belong to anyone else."

"Even yourselves?"

Their heads came up. "But," said Conrad in his sweet, baffled, singer's voice, "we have to belong to somebody."

"You can belong to—" Aidan broke off. They would never
understand. Karim's mouth was hidden behind his hand, but
his eyes betrayed him. He was laughing.

Aidan turned on him. "You hired them. You keep them."

"Not I," said Karim. "I but kept them for your return, as
honor bade me." And he was more than glad, Aidan could
see, to be relieved of them and honor both.

"She told us," Timur said. "When she sent us away. You

wouldn't want us, and we shouldn't want you. She expected us to listen to her. What does she think she is?"

"A daughter of Iblis," Aidan said.

Ilkhan made a face. "She's a woman. We belong to you. She left us in Damascus; we knew better than to stay there, and she wouldn't let us follow you to Masyaf. So we came here, where we knew you would come. You have to take us back; you have to punish us. We let the Bedouin take you."

They were as perfectly unreasonable as any creatures he had ever seen.

"If you leave us behind," said Arslan, "we will follow you."

Aidan reared up, half in anger, half in perilous mirth. "I'll make you put off your turbans. Shave your beards, if you have any. Bow down to the Church of Rome."

One or two blanched. The rest never wavered. "You won't," Timur said. "It's not in you."

"How do you know what is in me?"

One or two more began to quail. But not Timur. He had never enough wits for that. "I know you want us. Your conscience is in the way. Can't you just accept what is?"

"I know what is. There's the little matter of the Kingdom of Jerusalem, and the Crusade against the infidel."

"Oh," said Timur. "Crusade. That's jihad, no? Jihad is holy. We're enjoined it in holy Koran."

Aidan threw up his hands. "Master Karim! Can't you beat sense into these thick skulls?"

"I doubt that anyone can," Karim said.

"You won't take them?"

Karim was adamant. "I will not. If you care nothing for me, take thought at least for the House; remember whose mamluks these have been, and what city this is."

Aidan bit his tongue.

"You want us," Ilkhan said. "You need us. Didn't you say you were thought ill of in Jerusalem, for coming without an army? Now you have one."

"Such an army," Aidan said. "Sweet saints have mercy, I had

little enough welcome before. But the king . . ." He paused. "The king will be amused."

"The leper?" asked Dildirim.

"The king."

That was fierce enough to cow even the Kipchaks. Small victory: they had still won the war.

"God will judge you for this," Aidan said, growling low. They kept their heads down, but he saw the white flashes of smiles.

Karim spoke before the silence could stretch. "You will find that they are all in order, and their belongings with them. And," he added, "a thing or two of your own, which you might be glad of."

One of which was his robe of honor, packed as it had been in the baggage, and therefore lost. Aidan held it for a moment in his arms, aware of its weight as of its beauty. Like the mamluks who had come with it, it was both a joy and a burden.

It was what he was born to, who was the son of a king. He set it back carefully in its wrappings, and turned to what mattered even more, because it had been Gereint's: his own lost gelding. It waited patiently, but its nostrils flickered, welcoming him.

For all that had befallen him—even with his hellions all safe and restored to him, for whom he had grieved so long—he had not come close to weeping. Now, for this mute beast, he did. He set his teeth against the flood, and swung astride.

As he settled in the saddle, Karim's improbable turban appeared at his knee. "Keep your head down," the merchant said, "until you are well out of the city; and see that your imps do likewise. You are remembered here, and not kindly."

"Your regent can't harm me," Aidan said, "or any who rides with me."

"You, no." Karim shook his head. "We are well rid of you, sir Frank."

"Truly, this time," Aidan said. "I'll not be troubling your peace again."

"Thanks be to Allah." Karim said it devoutly, but without rancor. "You have been of great service to us—that, even I can confess. We owe you a profound debt; we shall repay it as we have agreed."

"And not one dirham more."

Karim smiled. "We are merchants, after all."

"After all," Aidan conceded. He grinned suddenly. "Give my respects to your lady. She's more worthy of the name of queen, than most who have claimed the title."

Karim bowed slightly. "You are the proper image of a prince," he said.

"Aren't I?" Aidan gathered the reins. "God keep you."

"And you," said Karim with unfailing courtesy. But his glance, for an instant, was as wicked as a boy's.

37

Joanna did not leave Aleppo for anger at Aidan, or for anything that touched on courage. Oh, no. She was thoroughly and spinelessly terrified.

But under it her mind was clear. She saw what she had been refusing to see. What she had with Aidan was a true thing, and deep. But it could not go on. She was mortal. He was not. She had a family, which she loved; a world in which she belonged. He was part of it, but not, past these few stolen moments, as her lover. Their dream of going away to have their child in peace, was only that. Words and wishes, and a bitter exile.

He knew it, she thought, perhaps better than she. Neither of them had ever spoken of marriage: of what a royal prince could do, even in the face of holy Church. They had a bond as strong as any in law or sacrament, but it was not a part of either.

The Assassin's blow rent away her self-deceptions. Aidan's absence only gave her time to comprehend them.

It was very simple, when Joanna reduced it to its essence. She did not want her child to be called a bastard. No more did she want Aidan to abandon his rank and his pride and his renown in the world, to become a nameless exile.

Once she had accepted that, she knew what she had to do. It was anything but easy. She healed miraculously, with Aidan's magic burning in her like a steady fire, but the pain was slow to pass: a stitch in her side, a deep ache. And worse than that, the soul's pain. To make her choice. To end it, so, without a word to him. For if she waited, if she saw him again before she began, she knew surely and completely that she could not do it.

She cried at first, in the lonely nights, biting down hard on her pillow. Her throat always seemed to ache, her eyes to sting. But it was a long way to Acre, and she was stubborn. The tears dried. Her heart set hard. Her body, with its new and wonderful strength, took joyfully to the long hours in the saddle, the nights in caravanserais, the danger of storms and brigands. Whatever came of this, she would not again confine herself in the harem's walls.

Ranulf was not in Acre. He was gone, his people said, to Jerusalem, for the Princess Sybilla's wedding.

After a howl of rage, Joanna began to laugh, because she had no tears left. Then she gave her orders. They were obeyed, which surprised her somewhat. She was still his wedded lady. Her sojourn in Aleppo, it seemed, was ascribed to grief for her brother and for her mother's husband, and the necessities of her infidel kin. Ranulf's people—her people— seemed actually glad of her return. She surprised herself with gladness at the sight of them. Homecoming, where she had never thought to find home.

Cowardice begged her to linger in Acre, to wait for him to come back. Obstinacy, and time that would not wait nor diminish the child in her womb, set her in the saddle again and turned her toward Jerusalem.

There where it had begun, now it would end. One way or another.

God was merciful, perhaps. Ranulf had taken up residence in the same house as always, but he was not in it when she came to it. She had time to bathe, eat, shed her travel-stained clothes, even rest if she was minded. She did all but the last. Her body was as comfortable as it would allow itself to be, settled in the solar with a book and a flagon of wine, but her mind bated like a hawk in a cage. She filled a cup. The scent of the wine made her ill; she set it down. Her eyes would not focus on the page. Her hands were icy.

She had rehearsed, over and over, what she had to do. Grovel at Ranulf's feet. Beseech his forgiveness. Seduce him. Give him reason to believe that he was the father of her child.

She did not have to like herself for it. She would never call it folly, what had been between herself and Aidan, but neither did she intend to make their child pay for it. What she did, she did for her baby; and for Aidan's honor and her own. And Ranulf's . . . yes, even his.

It would seem, at best, a six months' baby. But there were ways to hide it, old ways, women's ways. A retreat to a convent, to mourn the deaths of her kin. A pilgrimage on the same pretext, and care taken that her husband did not take it into his head to accompany her. Even return to Aleppo where he could not follow. Ranulf would never know how brief a time had passed between his reunion with his wife and the birth of their son or daughter. And she would pray that it did not take after its father.

As thin a line as she walked, thin as the sword's edge, it was no wonder that she nigh went mad waiting for Ranulf to come back. She refused to think of what would happen if he did not; if he was drowning his sorrows with one of his whores. *He* need do no more than deny his paternity, to escape acknowledging a bastard.

She could not indulge her anger at the unfairness of the world. For her baby's sake, she must not. She made herself bend to her book. Natural philosophy seemed a dry and sapless thing beside what she was suffering, but it offered an escape. She set her teeth and took it.

Ranulf found her so, deeply engrossed in Pliny the Elder. It was a long moment before she knew that he was there. She looked up, blinking, more than half out of the world.

He was thinner. She noticed that first. There were shadows under his eyes. He was clean, shaven, his hair newly and neatly cut, but all of that had the look of a servant's care, not of his own. He had a new scar on his cheek, somewhat swollen still, but beginning to heal. It did not disfigure him too badly. Zoe should look at it, Joanna thought. The Greek was a better doctor than any of the butchers in Jerusalem.

He stood in the door, holding fast to the sides of it, as if to keep himself from falling. He was not drunk, she did not think. His face was perfectly blank.

She lowered the book to her lap. "Good even, my lord," she said.

He moved forward. She had forgotten how big he was; she had never noticed that there was grace in his bulk.

He stared down at her. Very likely he was angry. She could not read him at all.

"I came back this morning," she said. She was trying not to babble, but her tongue had its own opinion in the matter. "It was a good journey, all things considered. I went to Acre, but you were gone. I hoped I'd find you here."

"I didn't think you were coming back," he said.

She laughed shrilly; caught herself. "Of course I came back. You said you'd let me have Aimery."

"You wouldn't take him."

"I've had time to think."

"He turned you away?"

She went hot, and then cold. She had begun to shake. By a miracle, her voice was steady. "If you mean the Prince of Caer Gwent, he left me in Aleppo as he was sworn to do, and rode against the Assassin."

"Did he succeed?"

"I don't know." She knew how that sounded; she hastened to cover it. "I couldn't stay. I was going mad in the harem."

"You were mad to leave it, with an Assassin hunting you."

"Not any longer. I was caught."

The color drained from his face.

"I wasn't hurt badly," she said, praying that he was too distraught to scent the lie. "The Assassin was driven off. That was how—that was why his highness left. To hunt the Assassin."

"So he sent you back here. What made him think you wouldn't be bait?"

"I wasn't," she said.

Ranulf glowered at nothing and everything. "Why did you come back?"

"I told you," she said. "I want Aimery."

"What if you can't have him?"

Her shaking was harder now, almost too hard for speech. "Then you've lost me. I'll—I'll go into a convent. I'll demand sanctuary. I'll never let you near me again."

He stood and stared at her. All her plans and all her strategies, and the moment she saw him, she forgot every one of them.

She struggled to remember what it had been like before Aimery. A hard pregnancy; months of swollen, burdened misery. Before that, not bliss, but something better than this. After her hoyden girlhood, she had decided to become a perfect lady, chatelaine of her own manor, baroness to Ranulf's baron. She had not been very good at it, but trying had kept her amply occupied. She had liked Ranulf then. They had been able to laugh together, sometimes. He was hardly what she would call a good lover, but he gave her pleasure more often than not, and when she tried to give it back, he seemed to be pleased.

He was happy when she told him that she was going to have a baby. He gave her a necklace of blue stones from Persia, and smiled to see her in it. "You're beautiful," he said then. The only time he ever said it.

Then when their son was born, Ranulf took him away from her.

He faced her now, on the other side of that wall, and his scowl was black. "You don't ever forgive anything, do you?"

"Do you ever think of what anyone wants but yourself?"

She wondered if he would hit her. He never had. Even under richest provocation.

He did not now. He raked his hand through his hair, ruffling it into disarray, like a child's. Suddenly he seized her. She was too startled to fight, too startled even to dig in her heels. He dragged her out of the room.

By the time she gathered her wits to do battle, she was moving too fast for anything but keeping her feet. His grip was strong but hardly painful, simply inescapable. He swept her past the servants' regions, through an angle of garden, into the one place she had sworn not to approach. It would have been the nursery.

He let her go so abruptly that she stumbled and fell. She clutched, caught the first prop that presented itself: Ranulf's body.

She was hardly aware of what she clung to. She was being stared at, hard. By a woman somewhat older than she, a dark, round, placid creature. And by what sat in the woman's lap.

He looked like his father. He had Ranulf's wheat-gold hair. But the jaw, even so young, had a stubborn set to it which Joanna knew too well.

She could not move. This was not her baby, this stranger, this solid youngling of half a year's growth. She did not know him at all.

Nor could he know her. He looked her over and debated, visibly, the wisdom of a howling fit.

"Aimery?" It was barely audible.

He frowned. His face began to redden.

"Aimery," she said. "Aimery."

He let her hold him. He stiffened only a little. He seemed to remember something: he nuzzled, seeking. She buried her face in his hair. His scent was warm and milky, a rich, sweet baby-scent, that brought the tears springing.

She shook them away. Ranulf was glowering again. He looked exactly like Aimery.

Something huge that had been in her, swelling, choking her, suddenly burst its bonds and shattered in the air. It left her light and hollow. Except for what burned steadily, down below her heart, where Aimery had begun.

He shifted in her grip, protesting its sudden tightness. She eased as much as she could.

She had dreamed of this, and it was not the way it should have been at all. Aimery had grown while he was kept away from her. And she—she had done things that could never be undone. Only lied about. Only hidden.

"I give you my word," said Ranulf. "If I ever take another baby from you, it will be because you ask it."

Her breath caught on something—laughter, sob. If he knew—if he only knew—

He was trying so hard. To please her. To keep her. To be what she wanted him to be. Poor, clumsy, mortal man.

Why, she thought, looking into his wide blue eyes. *He's terrified of me.*

Because she was a woman. Because he could never know what she would do next. Because—God help him—he loved her.

He did. Maybe it was Aidan's magic, lodged deep in her, or Aidan's loving, that had given her eyes to see.

Aidan was fire. This was earth, plain and solid, no words in it, no grace and no lightness. It would never know what to say; seldom what to do. Except persist.

She gave Aimery back to his nurse. He protested: a stab of grief in her, and a flare of joy, both at once. He remembered her. After all, he remembered his mother.

"Hush," she told him. "Hush, love. I'll come back soon. I promise."

Promises meant nothing to a baby deprived of his mother. His nurse stopped his howls with her breast.

Joanna's heart twisted. She had no milk now; nor would again, for Aimery.

She turned away from the sight of another woman doing what she could not, and faced her husband. Her arms circled his neck. He was only a little taller than she, but much larger, broad and thickset, with none of Aidan's panther-suppleness. His skin was human skin, his scent human scent: strange now; alien. He was rigid. Terrified.

So would she have been, if she had had time to think. He followed her docilely, as if she had bewitched him. Maybe she had. There was a demon in her now, in more ways than she could count.

She brought him past servants and stares and questions, into the bedchamber. She disposed of his squire, and even of his favorite hound. She got him out of his clean new clothes, not without difficulty: he could be as modest as a girl. Though what he had to be ashamed of, she could not see. Under the knots and scars and the mat of wheat-gold hair, he was a well-made man.

She surprised herself. She wanted him. His humanity; his strength and his mortal fragility. He was hers; he belonged to her. Only God could take him away from her.

It was outrageously wanton: to lust after one's own husband. The priests would be shocked.

She laughed, which shocked Ranulf. He had never seen her like this. She tried to explain. "I'm home, don't you see? I've come home."

He could call it hysteria, if he liked. His scowl was not anger, she realized. He was struggling to understand. How much of him had she ever understood?

She dropped her own garments, shocking him further, and led him to the bed. A glint had wakened in his eye. He liked what he saw. A good solid armful of woman, he had called her more than once. Now, again, he made sure of it. She kissed him deep, to his astonishment and sudden pleasure. She felt it all through her skin, like a breath, or the brush of a hand.

He hurt her a little, with his weight, with his ardor. He had no power to know when she was ready, or where; or how to pleasure her. She tried to show him. It was awkward. They were beginning all new, as if they were strangers. He needed more than showing. He needed telling: a nudge, a word, a guiding hand. It made her think of training horses.

This time she buried her laughter in his shoulder. He was too preoccupied to notice. Men seemed to need more of themselves for this. Maybe because this was all they gave. Women had the consequences to face.

He stayed awake long enough to ask her if she was happy. She gave him the answer he wanted to hear. The whore's answer; though it might have been the truth. He went to sleep smiling.

She wept, at first hardly aware of it, then painfully so. Some of it was relief. She was safe now. She had Aimery; she had her husband.

What she had lost . . .

She should hate herself. That was part of why she cried: because she could not. She had sinned mortally, and she repented not a moment of it. A man could go without shame from woman to woman. She had gone to one man. She could not go back to him. Nor would she regret him. He had found her broken, and made her whole. That she had still a few scars, that they ached when the wind blew cold, that was but mortal reality.

Aidan would understand. He lived his own lies, for his

safety's sake. Ranulf never lied; he never needed to. She could never tell him the truth. He would see it all awry. He would hate her.

And that, she knew surely, she could not bear.

She prayed. Maybe she should not; maybe she only damned herself more blackly. Yet she shut her eyes tight and made of her whole self a prayer. For the child that would be; for Aimery; for Ranulf; for Aidan. And for herself. To keep them all safe; to protect them from one another.

VII

JERUSALEM

38

Aidan stood on the Mount of Olives, just where Tancred had stood, a hundred years ago, with his army of soldiers and saints and outrageous sinners, under the banner of the first Crusade. Tancred had wept to see Jerusalem; to know that it lay under the sway of the infidel. He had won it, he and his brother princes: Raymond, Robert, Bohemond, Godfrey of Lorraine. The names rang in the silence of Aidan's skull, like the song of steel on steel.

He turned slowly about. On the summit where he stood was the ruined chapel, the shrine where Christ had left the mark of his foot. Eastward shone the lake of Sodom beyond the march of blue-hazed hills, and the long ridge of Moab like a dragon's back above the silver ribbon of the Jordan. Westward was the deep valley of Kidron, and the walls of Jerusalem.

His mamluks, for once, were both mute and still. One or two of them seemed close to weeping.

He did not know what he felt. Joy, yes; awe of the high and holy city; eagerness to enter it, to pay fealty to its king. But sadness, too, and something very like regret. He had no lover to share this moment with him. Joanna was gone. Morgiana had not come to claim him, though over and over on the long road he caught himself riding with his chin on his shoulder, starting at every sound or shadow, calling her name. She never answered. The air, like his heart, was empty.

His gelding stamped, and snapped at a fly. He gathered the reins. He had paid no heed to the pilgrims who flocked upon the Mount; now they burst upon his consciousness: a babble of voices, a mutter of prayer, a glitter of eyes at the outrage of Saracens in this most Christian of places. He crossed himself with conspicuous devotion, and vaulted into the saddle. The shocked stares lightened his mood miraculously. He wheeled his gelding on its haunches and sent the whole troop of them thundering down the hill.

Jerusalem spread wide before him. He found that he was singing as he had on that first morning on the road to Aqua Bella; but without that giddy lightness which should have warned him of disaster. His victory was won, whatever its price. He had come home.

The cousins and the caravan had gone their own ways even before Aidan turned off to climb the Mount of Olives, promising to deliver his baggage to Lady Margaret's house. The mamluks had not let him send them away then, and would not now. They crowded about Aidan, jostled together in the narrow streets, bristling like hounds in a strange kennel. He welcomed the labor of keeping them in hand. It kept the city from overwhelming him.

Near the crossing of the roads, where they should turn off toward David's Tower, they came to a halt. A baron was passing with retinue enough for a king and clamor enough for an emperor. Aidan's hellions would have pressed on regardless, for their prince's honor; the baron's guardsmen were not inclined to indulge them. Aidan extricated Timur by the scruff of his neck and hauled Conrad back by the belt, before they could begin a war. Timur was frothing with rage. "Did you hear what he said? Did you hear? Filthy Saracen, he called you. *You,* my lord!"

"So he did," said Aidan. "In atrocious Arabic, too."

"And you'll *allow* it?" cried Ilkhan.

Aidan grinned at him. "Why not? He thinks he's telling the truth."

By now they were used to his outrageousness. The Kipchaks subsided. Conrad stopped cursing and blinked at him. The others settled in to watch the procession, since their lord seemed minded to do the same. It did not go on much longer, although it seemed to, as crowded as the street was, and growing more crowded as the side ways added their streams of people to it. Even when the stream began to move again, it advanced sluggishly, with many halts and entanglements.

Aidan, seeking a clearer path, got down and led his horse. His mamluks followed in file, with Arslan last, riding herd on the twins. The horses were uneasy, unused to the press and the tumult. Timur's mare squealed; Aidan heard the boy's curse, and a child's sudden, full-throated howl.

He flung the reins into Conrad's hands and bolted back down the line. It was like swimming upstream in a flood. He thrust through it without mercy. He might have bowled someone over; he hoped that it was one of his own.

Timur's mare had gone quite gleefully berserk, spinning about the center that was her white-faced master, lashing out with her heels. She had caught Ilkhan's gelding, who had since had the sense to stand still, out of her reach, ears flat to his head. The crowd eddied, with an occasional foray past her. Beyond her, flattened against a wall, was the trembling, wailing figure of a woman, clinging desperately to the baby, which had begun to scream in earnest.

The mare had cleared a goodly circle. Aidan walked through it, taking no particular care to elude the restless heels, and set hand to the bridle. The mare jibbed; her eye rolled; her heel trembled, paused, settled to the ground. "Wise," Aidan said to her. "Most wise." He ran a hand down her streaming neck. She settled slowly. He coaxed her toward the wall, into the illusion of safety. The crowd began to move again, tentatively at first, then more strongly.

The baby's howls subsided into hiccoughs. It seemed none the worse for its ordeal, a robust, fair-haired Frankish child in the arms of a nurse who was, all too evidently, indulging in a bout of hysterics. As it caught sight of Aidan, it stopped howling to stare. Its eyes were wide and thunder-colored, dark not with terror but with rage; though that was giving way to curiosity. It wanted to touch the wonderful, terrible animal with the flying heels. Its nurse had all but strangled it, and driven it wild with her crying and carrying on.

A woman thrust past Aidan to snatch the baby out of the nurse's arms. Her eyes were the same thunderous blue as the child's; her face had the same furious scowl. She shifted the baby to her hip and struck the nurse backhanded across the face.

It was brutal, but it was effective. The woman's blubbering stopped abruptly. The newcomer, having dealt with her, turned her glare on Aidan. "Can't you ever do anything quietly?"

He opened his mouth, closed it. It was never the greeting he would have expected. If he had expected one at all.

Joanna set her fist on her hip. The baby on the other hip had to be Aimery. It hurt to see him; to know what he meant. And yet it was sweet to bear even his mother's temper, to see her, to know that she was here, and whole, and utterly herself. "If that one"—her chin stabbed toward Arslan, who looked both bruised and cowed—"had not manhandled me into a corner, I could have stopped this silly nit's hysterics, got the baby out of the way, and saved you no end of explanation. Now. Are you prepared to explain?"

Aidan drew himself up. "Madam, I regret that my servant failed so signally to control his horse, and thereby caused you grief. If you require further satisfaction—"

"You might," snapped Joanna, "explain why it took you so damnably long to come back."

His teeth clicked together. He had forgotten how utterly, maddeningly unreasonable she could be. "Why in God's name should I have to—"

"The king has been waiting for you. They found a husband for Sybilla; she likes him, and he's not displeased with her, or with what comes with her: the counties of Jaffa and Ascalon, and maybe the throne of Jerusalem. Baldwin was hoping that you could be here for the wedding. He was disappointed when you weren't. Do you realize it's past Martinmas? What kept you so long?"

"Assassins."

That silenced her. She went red, and then white. When she spoke again, she spoke much more softly. "You won. We heard. Great-grandmother sent a message."

"You've been living with your mother?"

Her eyes dropped. "No." They came up, suddenly fierce. "What else could I do?"

Aidan could not answer. Dared not. He had expected to grieve that he had lost her. He had not expected to hate Ranulf for winning her back.

She saw, God help her. The color drained from her cheeks. She stood as still as a bird before a snake; she said nothing at all.

Aimery, neglected, began to fret. The nurse reached for him. Joanna clutched him to her.

Aidan almost cried aloud. She was afraid of him. That was why she had babbled so; that was why she held so tightly to her son, shielding with him the life that swelled in her womb.

"You never knew me at all," he said.

She gasped.

"If you can think that I would touch a child . . ." He choked on it. Suddenly he could not bear it, not for one moment more. He spun away from her.

His mamluks had made themselves a wall against the thronging city. She caught him as he reached them. Aimery stared, big-eyed, from her hip.

Her hand was white-knuckled on his arm. She eyed it as if it did not belong to her; opened it, let him go. "I . . ." Her voice was a croak. "Don't go."

"Why? So that you can flay me further? So that I can learn, in detail, exactly how you have taught yourself to despise me?"

"Why should I bother? You know it all already."

"I can hardly help it, with you shouting it in my face."

She flung up her head. "I never said a word!"

"You thought it."

"I did not."

"You did."

She hit him.

There was a long, stunned silence. He did not even think to hit her back. He raised his hand, slowly, to his stinging cheek.

She burst out laughing. "You look—" she gasped. "You look —so—poleaxed!"

He could not move for outrage. He could barely speak. "If you are quite done, my lady," he said, "may I have your leave to go?"

"No." Her laughter was gone. "Will you—please—come with me, to somewhere less public? And start again?"

He tensed to resist, but her eyes held him. He inclined his head the merest fraction of a degree.

There was a church a little distance down the street, small and dim and forgotten by the crowds of pilgrims, with a startling bit of garden, and a trickle of fountain. The water was cool and sweet. Aidan drank a deep draught and laved his face.

Joanna sat on a bit of fallen column. The others had not followed them so far. Even the nurse was occupied without, giving suck to Aimery and telling her troubles shrilly to Aidan's mamluks. It was a fitting punishment, he reckoned, for the trouble they had caused.

Joanna spoke abruptly, rapidly, without preliminary. "I had to do it. For Aimery. For the one who will be born. I don't expect you to understand, or to forgive. I only ask, if there's any mercy in you, that you let us be."

He laughed then, but in pain. "Is that what you've been telling yourself, to make it easier to bear? That after all you've known of me, I'm a mere and soulless monster? That I could ever harm anything that you love?"

"You can't be that perfect a knight."

"Why not?"

"Because," she said, "if you are, I'm going to break down and howl."

He rose and stalked the length of the garden and back. He stood over her; he knotted his fists behind his back, to keep from shaking her. "No. I'm not perfect. I'd like to throttle your husband. I'd like to thrash you until you howl for mercy. But I won't," he said. "I won't stoop to it."

"You hate me," she said.

"Don't I wish I could?" He dropped beside the fountain again, laid his head in his hands. "Joanna, give it up. You won't make anything simpler by quarreling."

He felt her battle to keep from touching him; to stand so close, and come no closer, nor take refuge in flight. Her voice came low and hard. "No. It doesn't work, does it? It will never work."

"It never did. We pretended—sometimes, well enough to deceive ourselves."

Her hand brushed his hair, light as a breath. He sat still. She backed out of his reach, arms clasped about herself, shivering. "I thought I could do it. When I saw you in the street, and that she-demon of Timur's started raising her particular kind of devilment, and Aimery was in the middle of it, and there was no escaping it, or you. Confront you. Catch you off guard. Drive you away. Put an end to it." Her face twisted. "As if it could ever be that easy. Someone will guess. Someone will be able to count."

"I was nigh a year in the womb."

She opened her mouth, closed it. "That's not possible."

"I'm not human."

"Then—"

"Then."

He could forgive her the sudden, incredulous joy. She had been so terribly afraid, locked in her net of deception, knowing it necessary, hating it; and not even the certainty that it would come to anything. She might still have to explain a black-haired child; it would be of his kind. But humans—and Ranulf most of all—would count to nine and be, perforce, content.

"I can help you," he said. "If you will let me."

"Do I dare?"

445

"You don't dare not to. Witch-children are different. They need the touch of power to guide them, lest they guide themselves."

She searched his face, as if she could see through to the mind behind it. "You want this baby, too."

"I won't take it away from you."

Her eyes filled. She rubbed them, angrily. "You are so damnably noble."

"I'm not. I'm devious. I can cast a glamour, if you need one. I can rein in the little one's magic. I can help you where no one else can. I can be everything that a proper royal uncle should be. All to have my share in the only child I'm likely to get in this age of the world."

"How do you know that?"

"I feel it in my bones."

She made an indelicate noise. "We'll see what you feel when you lay eyes on another woman."

He stiffened as if she had struck him.

It was only the fraction of an instant, but she was a woman, and she had a share of his magic. She looked at him and knew. "You have. Haven't you?"

He saw the utter absurdity of it. They could not be lovers again. She had her husband, her son, her whole world. He had one night, little more than a whore's bargain. And he could not say a word.

She leaped into his silence. "Who is she? Couldn't you even wait for—how could you—*who is she?*"

"Morgiana."

That stopped her cold. She could not have expected the truth, even from him. Not so soon. "Morgiana?"

"The Assassin."

She laughed. "You're joking."

"No."

"How in the world . . ." She trailed off. "She's like you. She's . . . like . . . you."

"Yes."

"God," said Joanna. "That hurts." She pressed her hand to her side, below the heart. "That hurts like fire."

"It does, doesn't it?"

She did not flinch. She even tried to laugh. "No wonder you've been so magnanimous."

"I might have managed that by myself."

"You know what I mean," she said. And, after a little: "It's true, then. What people are saying. She turned on her master. She did it for you, didn't she?"

"She said not."

Joanna shook her head. "Of course she would. She'd have her pride. I'd have said the same; and done the same." Again, she paused. "Is she as beautiful as they say?"

"More."

Joanna smiled painfully: almost a grimace. "I never saw her. She was jealous, wasn't she? Or she'd never have missed."

"One would think you knew her."

"I know myself."

"It doesn't change anything," he said.

"No. No, it doesn't, does it? Will you marry her?"

"I left her."

Joanna's teeth clicked together. "You did what?"

"She is a devout Muslim. She loathes everything I stand for."

"I doubt that," Joanna said.

"I can't forgive her for what she did to Gereint and Thibaut. And to you."

"There is that," she said. "If you'd done the killing, it might have been easier. Women learn to live with such things."

He looked narrowly at her. She did not seem to be mocking him. Certainly she had no love for the Assassin; and her heart still stung, that he could have turned to anyone else, so soon, before he could have known that she was leaving him.

He wondered how Muslims did it. Morgiana, who was one, was as fiercely jealous as any creature he had ever heard of.

Joanna was less murderous, but she was not inclined to share him.

Maybe the men did not know, and took care not to ask. Keeping their women in harems would be useful for that; and raising them to be submissive.

What would Sayyida do if Maimoun took another wife?

Questions, again. Maybe he should become a Hospitaller and forswear women altogether.

He had said it aloud. Joanna leaped to protest. "Don't do that! You know how you are about your given word."

He shivered. She had too much sense; she knew him too well. To bind himself to monk's vows, for as long as he had to live—he could not do it. He could hardly endure to think of it.

She touched him again, but differently, as a sister would: clasping his shoulder, shaking him lightly. He knew what it cost her. "It won't stay as hard as this. We won't let it."

"Both of us?"

"All of us," she said. "God, too. I've given Him a talking-to."

"It's time that someone did."

For a moment she wavered. She looked ready to cry. "Oh, God! I wish we didn't have to lie."

"We could tell the truth and take what comes."

She folded her arms about her middle. "No. I won't chance it. What I would pay—I don't care. But not my baby. God witness it: not my baby."

He bent his head. He could not judge it a sin, either, to protect his own child. But—

"We're going to have to be seen together," he said. "Often, if I'm to do the little one any good. We'll never be able to tell the truth; we'll never dare to hint at it. We'll have to pretend, perfectly, that we are no more to one another than kin and, betimes, friends. Have you stopped to think how hard that will be?"

"Constantly," she said. She drew a deep breath, as if to

gather her forces, and clasped him in an embrace as chaste as it was defiant. "You see? It's possible. Give us time, and it will be easy."

He slipped out of her arms before either of them could break, and made himself smile. "Possible," he said, "yes. Easy . . . God grant it."

"He doesn't have a choice," Joanna said.

39

Joanna did not want an escort to her husband's house, but she had one, and a mount into the bargain: Aidan's own grey gelding. It was revenge, of a sort, for the choices which she had forced upon them both. It was the sign of how they meant to go on.

Aidan left her standing in the gate, the hand which he had kissed in farewell clenched at her side, and Aimery raising a new wail. He wanted the horses back again, and the men with their scarlet coats, and the jangle and clatter of their passage through the city. He was his mother's son, that one.

For all that it had done to Aidan's peace of mind, the diversion had cost him a scarce hour. It was still somewhat short of noon. He was hardly farther from his destination than when he began, and by rather less difficult a way. It could almost have been good fortune which sent Joanna in flight from her mother's house at the news of his return, and cast her full in his path.

Almost.

He turned his face away from the gate and the woman in it, toward the Tower of David.

The High Court of the Kingdom of Jerusalem had barely begun to disperse after the princess' wedding. The barons lingered still, pondering new intrigues now that there was a new lord in the realm, watching their king narrowly for signs of either enmity or excessive amity toward his sister's husband. There was little enough to see, as yet: the wedded couple were gone to their new demesne of Jaffa and Ascalon, and Baldwin kept his place in Jerusalem, ruling his realm in what quiet the court would allow.

Aidan gave them something new to talk of: riding in at the head of his troop of Saracens, in his Saracen robe, with his Saracen sword, making truth of all the tales and rumors that had run before him. Even as a lad came to take his horse, the tide broke upon him. His mamluks bristled; he called them to heel, meeting the flurry of questions with a grin and a flourish. "Come now, won't you let me pass the door before I sing for my supper?"

"Pass it, then," someone cried, "and be swift, before we die of curiosity!"

He laughed and strode forward. A way opened for him; his hellions fell into step behind him. He would not, for dignity, glance back, but he knew how they swaggered, hands on hilts, heads held high under their turbans.

The hall was splendid with the new hangings which had graced Sybilla's wedding, thronged with the great ones of the kingdom. They paused for his coming. The murmur of voices quieted. The thud of his feet was distinct, and the clink of his mamluks' finery, and the breath that ran with them, drawn long and slow.

The High Court had seen such a spectacle before, in embassies from the infidel. But never with one of their own at its head. Aidan was that, visibly enough. His robe was Saracen, but he wore it as a Frankish cotte, with the air of one who deigns to set a fashion. His hair was cut in the western manner, but he had kept his beard. He wore no turban, but a cap that could have been of either west or east.

He knew how he looked. He made the most of it as he crossed the field of many battles that was the High Court.

They were all here, all who mattered in the kingdom, not only Baldwin's vassals but the great lords of Antioch and Tripoli, and embassies from both east and west, and the papal legate with his train, and a gathering of knights from over the sea: a portion of those who had sailed with the new count of Jaffa and Ascalon.

He took little notice of them, beyond the most essential courtesies. Lady Margaret was there, with her daughter's husband for escort. Ranulf greeted Aidan with honest pleasure. There was less pain in the sight of him than Aidan had expected, and after all, no hate. He was a good enough man, no great marvel of intellect, but wise enough in his way. He knew what his wife was worth; he loved her. He had the look of a happy man.

Margaret, beside him, was no more beautiful than Aidan remembered, and no less. Perhaps he could see a little more clearly through her serenity to the woman within. He had seen the Lady Khadijah: he knew what she endeavored to be. Would be, he was certain. She was of that quality.

She was glad to see him. That warmed him. When he would have bowed to her, she turned it into an embrace and the kiss of close kin. "Welcome," she said. "Welcome home."

He brushed a tear from her cheek. "As glad as that, my lady?"

She smiled and shook her head. "You were a part of us before we ever saw you. How could I not be glad to see you safe and whole?"

"And I look like him."

"And you look like him," she said. "And I find that I can forgive you. How many men will endure in living memory, for as long as Gereint will?"

Aidan could not answer her.

She gathered herself, firmly, and regarded him with a clear cold eye. "Tell me," she said.

He told her all of it, except what was not wholly his to tell: Joanna; that last night with Morgiana. That he had had a bargain with the ifritah, he did not conceal. He did not judge it proper, in this place, to explain how he had paid it. Nor did Margaret judge it proper to ask. Perhaps she guessed. Perhaps she reckoned that remorse, and atonement for murder, and escape from slavery, had been enough.

When he was finished, there was a long sigh. The great circle of courtiers drew back, as if he had not known very well that they were listening, and pretended interest in one another.

Margaret was silent for a long while. As she pondered, she paced slowly. Aidan and his mamluks followed. Ranulf did not.

Her pacing led them with apparent aimlessness, yet it ended where surely she must have meant: in a broad bay behind a pair of pillars, where they could converse in privacy. "You did well," she said at last. She said it slowly, with her eyes on her clasped hands, where the ring of her betrothal to Gereint glittered still. "You did most well. Not to kill Sinan, after all; to demand a price which would win his respect but not, beyond reasonable measure, his enmity. And that his slave is free—I am glad for her. Such servitude can never have been less than cruel."

It was like Margaret, to forgive even the one who had wielded the dagger. "She is free now," Aidan said, "but no danger to you or yours."

"I never feared that she would be." Margaret looked up. "What will you do now?"

"Keep the last of my promises," Aidan said. "Offer the king my fealty."

"I had thought that you might be weary of us all, and eager to return to your own country."

"Not quite yet," said Aidan.

She smiled faintly. "And I have insulted your fortitude by implying it. Please, pardon me."

"There's nothing to pardon." Aidan forgot for a moment where he was, started to prowl, stopped. Margaret's amusement won from him the flicker of a smile. "I've been too long in desert places. I've forgotten how to be a prince."

"You can never be other than what you are."

He stilled. She was calm, meaning no more than she said, and no less.

"The Hospital speaks for you," she said after a pause.

"Do they?" He did not know why he should be surprised. Maybe she did. She was amused. "They know the difference between a fortune hunter and an honest soldier of God."

"Ah, but am I God's? Methinks I'd be the devil's minion."

"I would hardly call you a saint. But a devil, no. You are too wretchedly poor a liar."

"Have I lied to you?"

"Never. Nor concealed yourself well from any but the blind and the foolish. There is no doubt that you are what you are. Jerusalem can endure it, I think. It needs you badly."

"For my sword-arm? Or for that else I can bring?"

"There is a parable of lamps and bushels. Though your lamp may be too rare a splendor for common eyes to see."

"I do tempt fate, don't I?"

"I call it dicing with death. Since you are not his by right, you gamble. Would you have offered yourself in Gereint's place, if you could?"

His heart was cold, but he smiled. "Yes. I would."

"So," she said, "would I." She lifted her chin. "We master it as we may. I shall not marry again, I think. A woman twice widowed is allowed somewhat of the freedom of a man. The power that goes with it, I have the wherewithal to claim."

His glance took in the court beyond the bay, the eddy and swirl of great powers about no certain center. "You'll be sought after," he said. "You're still young; you have both wealth and lands."

"And I could still bear an heir or three." There was steel in her voice. "No, my lord. I am done with the burdens of my sex. God be thanked, I need not bear those of yours; except as I deem them necessary."

Aidan bowed low, conceding the stroke. He knew what he was doing; as did she. She regarded him with pleasure which was not entirely devoid of desire. He smiled back. "Your grandmother would approve of you," he said.

Margaret laughed. It was a startlingly beautiful sound. "I gather that she approved of you."

"Insofar as she could, of anything both young and male." And so indiscreet as to get Joanna with child.

Margaret did not know of that. He kept his smile and his air of lightness as she said, "You are an ally worth having. I, in return, can aid you in quelling the whispers against you."

"Bargains, madam?"

"Bargains." She matched his wry face. "Let us say that I prefer to settle now all that should be between us hereafter. I consider us to be kin. I know that you intend to be a power in this realm; I believe that we can profit one another."

"I would rather regard it as friendship."

"The folk of Islam," she said, "must have found you refreshing."

"Shocking, more like," he said. He offered his hand. "Friendship?"

She took it. Her clasp was firm. "Friendship," she said.

The barons, deprived of a spectacle, had long since returned to their own concerns. Aidan's return roused barely a ripple. It was the delicacy of courts; and the fickleness of courtiers.

The king came in quietly while Aidan exchanged courtesies with a baron from Tripoli, and sat without fanfare. For a long while no one noticed him.

Aidan knew him the moment he passed the door. The sickness was stronger in him, but he had grown as if to fit it. He was an image of a king, though a king without a face, veiled in the *kaffiyah*. His eyes were all but hidden in it, yet they followed Aidan, bridling impatience, glinting as they reckoned the mood of the court.

Aidan met them across the hall. The gladness in them was

all the more splendid for that it did not diminish itself with words.

A tilt of Aidan's head brought his mamluks to order behind him. They were goggle-eyed at all the brazen, veilless women. The king at least distracted them: a leper, and a king, and no one shrank from him or thought the less of him for what God had inflicted upon him.

Aidan took the straight path to the king. In front of the throne, he halted. The court had stilled anew. The king waited in thrumming silence. As Aidan bowed, his Saracens went down, offering their own reverence to this one whom their master would call master.

The king rose. Aidan straightened. Baldwin had grown indeed: they were almost eye to eye. The king neither asked nor offered, except with his eyes.

Aidan kissed the jeweled glove. The hand within, the good hand, was thinner even than it had been, the fingers drawn into claws with the sickness; but it was steady. The voice was soft, neither deep nor light, simply itself. "My lord. Well met again."

"Well met indeed, sire," Aidan said. "I've come to serve you, if you will have me."

"Have you?" Baldwin's voice went up an octave. "You do wish it, then?"

"With all my heart."

The king's eyes shone. They leaped past Aidan to the row of rumps and turbans, and began to dance. "Would this be your knight's fee?"

"If your majesty will accept it."

"Does it agree to be paid?"

"It will hear of nothing else."

It most certainly would not, from the flash of eyes under the turbans. Aidan's hellions had judged this king, and found him worthy of their notice.

Baldwin sat, not weary, not quite, but careful of his

strength. There was a smile in him, a glint of wickedness. "This is scandalous."

"Isn't it?"

Baldwin laughed. "It's been dull without you, my lord."

"A rather lively tedium, I should think," Aidan said, with a glance at the court.

"Lively," said Baldwin, "but never outrageous."

"Ah. A definite lack. I do like to know I'm useful."

"Always, my lord." The king was grinning, Aidan suspected. He was transparently delighted. "I'm glad you came today. There's nothing interesting happening, now that my sister is wedded and bedded. Shall we turn dinner into a celebration of your victory?"

"My lord is generous," Aidan said.

"You really do mean it, then. You'll enter service in Jerusalem."

"With you, my lord, and no other."

Baldwin was king; he did not protest his unworthiness. But he was glad, and proud, and a little afraid, as one is when one does something irrevocable.

Aidan knew. It was the same with him. He knelt suddenly, and held up his hands palm to palm, offering his homage.

Baldwin looked at them. Aidan gave him gladness, and pride, the free surrender of a vassal to his chosen lord. "You are my king," Aidan said, "my lord and my liege. I serve you of my own will. I grant you the reverence of liege man to liege lord."

"That is high honor," Baldwin said, "and a royal gift." His gloved hands settled lightly over Aidan's bare ones; he drew breath to begin the oath of fealty.

Aidan was aware of little beyond the king; but his senses kept a watch of their own. He knew that the hall had stilled in a long ripple from the center to the walls. The last of his colloquy with the king had fallen in silence.

As Baldwin's hands came together over Aidan's, the quality

of the silence changed. Something had come into it; something unwonted. As the king moved to speak, a clear cold voice forestalled him.

40

"Lord king, if you would take yon knight into your service, will you take also his debts?"

The echoes ran up to the roof and faded. No one said a word.

Aidan knelt immobile. His heart had done an appalling thing: it had leaped up and begun to sing.

He marked her passage in murmurs, and in the gleam of the king's eyes. In a moment he would break, and turn, even knowing what he would see. No escort at all, no mark of station, only the lone slender figure born out of air, swathed in veils and speaking, defiantly, in the *langue d'oeil*. Her accent was enchanting.

Morgiana halted close behind him. Her presence throbbed like pain; her shape was drawn in fire on his skin. To human eyes she was a human woman, a Saracen of rank in gold and silk, wrapped and shrouded in veils.

She bowed to the king: a swelling murmur, as she went down among the mamluks and showed them all both her grace and her foreignness. The murmur followed her back to her feet, but died as she spoke. "My lord of Jerusalem, this man will tell you that he comes unencumbered, freed of all debts and promises. I submit that he does not."

Aidan's hands dropped from the king's clasp. He turned, but slowly.

Her veils were green. They enveloped all of her but one white hand.

"Did you plot this from the beginning?" he asked her.

She took no notice of him. "He owes me a debt, lord king, which he may do well to discharge before you accept his fealty."

"I paid it," Aidan said, "in every particular." *Damn you,* he cursed her where only she could hear. *Damn you for doing this to me.*

He might not have been there at all. She sank to her knees and beseeched the king. "Lord, will you hear me?"

Baldwin glanced at Aidan. Aidan kept his eyes on Morgiana. "I will hear you," the king said.

She bent her head. "You are gracious, lord, to one who was a slave. I am called Morgiana; I served the masters of Alamut, and after them the lord of Masyaf."

The court had been diverted by her presence. Now it was fiercely intent. Aidan tensed. Not, God help him, for himself. Could even Morgiana escape, if the High Court rose up against her?

She was not aware of them at all. "I was the Slave of Alamut," she said. "Now I am free, and in part I owe it to this knight. We struck a bargain. I brought him before my master, and protected him, and won for him all that he sought, and my freedom with it."

"And the prince?" the king asked. "Dare I ask what he gave in return?"

"No," Aidan said.

"Yes," said Morgiana, "lord king. I am but an ignorant Saracen, yet I know somewhat of your knights. Their honor; their loyalty; their prowess in the field. Their mastery of the arts of love."

Aidan's cheeks flamed. God be thanked that he had kept his beard; it hid the worst of it.

She could see. He felt her mockery.

"I thought," she said, "that I would find myself a knight, for surely he would honor me, and serve me in all humility. And lo! Allah sent me not any knight, but a flower of chivalry, a trueborn prince, a moon among the stars of his firmament. I

458

laid my nets for him, I confess it. I took him captive, not in my master's name, but in my own."

"Yet serving your master, surely," Baldwin said.

It was a little uncanny to be caught between them: veiled ifritah and veiled king, voices without faces, masks about the glitter of eyes. Morgiana answered strongly, with a toss of her shrouded head. "By then I had no master, except in name. What I had done for the one who held my oath, I now repented. But my knight would not believe me, nor forgive me, on my simple word. I undertook to prove it to him. I offered to give him his vengeance on my master, but for a price."

"Was that honorable, to ask for payment?"

"It was necessary," she said. "I loved him, you see. I had loved him since first I saw him. He would not permit himself to love me. I saw that he never would, unless I bound him to it."

"Therefore you bargained," said the king.

"Therefore I bargained. He would have his revenge. I would have him."

"Until I satisfied you," said Aidan. "No longer."

"And no shorter," she said.

No one laughed, or even smiled. No one dared.

"I gave you what I had to give," Aidan said. "I took the freedom which I had won. There is no debt owing."

"You never asked if that were so."

He swallowed, dry-throated. His voice came hard and harsh. "I had reason to believe that it was."

She shook her head. "You never listened, did you? Or thought. Or did anything but run, and pray that I would not follow."

"Are you calling me a coward?"

"No," she said. Simply, as she always did. She had no artifice at all. "I call you thoughtless. Obstinate. Cruel, perhaps. A man can be cruel, when his selfishness is threatened."

He drew a deep, steadying breath, and made himself speak

calmly. "My lady, part of our bargain was my freedom. From you, as from your master. Have you forgotten?"

"Cruel," she said, as if to herself.

"Are you any less? To come to me now, to shame me before the chivalry of Outremer—are you content? Will you let me go?"

She swayed a little under the force of his temper. She said, "I am not content."

He flung up his hands. "Then what will satisfy you?"

"You."

His hands clenched into fists.

He was not dismayed. He was not angry—not any more than he should be, in such a time and such a place as she had chosen to call him to account. What was welling up in him was shockingly close to joy. The hawk, netted at last, found himself longing for the jesses.

But he was a wild thing still. He would not submit, even to Morgiana. "You have had me," he said, and no matter what their avid audience made of that. "Did I fail to please you?"

"You pleased me," she said. "Too well. Did you truly believe that fire could quench fire?"

"I was a greater fool than that. I thought that a woman could be satisfied."

She laughed, light and piercingly sweet. "Oh, my lord! You are growing wise."

His temper snapped. He sprang. He meant to rend her veil, to do to her precious modesty what she had done to his pride, but his hand would not obey him. The silk was cool; her eyes were burning. Veil and headdress slipped free and fell. He heard the long sigh as her hair tumbled down; and, behind him, the catch of the king's breath. Aidan was not breathing at all. His only thought was a dim surprise. She was eerily, improbably beautiful.

His hand knew where it belonged: fitted to the curve of her cheek. He stared at it, willed it to fall. "We don't even believe in the same God," he said.

"There is no god but God." Soft, pure, and absolute.

He sucked in a breath, filling his emptied lungs. "There is blood between us."

"Does not your faith preach forgiveness of one's enemies?" She tossed her hair out of her face, and turned the fire of her eyes on Baldwin. "Lord, you are king here. I bid you judge. This man promised himself to me. He fulfilled only the barest beginning of that promise. Shall he then go free? Must I surrender my claim to him?"

Aidan wheeled to face the king. "Must I surrender my freedom again? Must I pay a price which I have long since paid?"

The king looked from one to the other. Without even knowing it, Aidan had stopped shoulder to shoulder with Morgiana, as if they were together in this battle, and not bitterly opposed.

Baldwin's glance acknowledged the irony. After a moment he said, "A bargain is a weighty thing; the more so when the principals cannot agree on its completion. Tell me honestly, my lady. Do you desire this man? Will you do anything to win him?"

"Within the bonds of faith and reason," she said, "yes."

The king nodded slightly. "And you, my lord. Does this woman revolt you? Do you despise her?"

"No." Aidan bit off the word.

"Then your objections are entirely religious?"

"No."

Baldwin waited. Would wait, it was clear, until Aidan spoke again. Aidan gave him what he wanted. "Do you think I have no pride?"

"Quite the opposite," said the king. He was enjoying himself, Aidan could see. Damn the boy. Had he and the Assassin plotted it between them?

Aidan reined himself in. He needed his wits about him: more, maybe, than he ever had in his life. "I have my pride," he said, "and, yes, my faith. And my certainty that I owe this lady nothing, except my forgiveness. I give it. I absolve her of all that she has done to me and mine."

"And what you have done to me?" she asked. "Will you absolve yourself of that, too?"

"Do I need to be forgiven for loving you?"

"No," she said. "Only for leaving me."

"You might also," said Baldwin, "consider the sin."

Morgiana's stare was blank. Aidan could not make himself do as the king bade, although he knew well enough why Baldwin did it. The Church was listening, and its own judgment was never in doubt. Aidan should have been more sanguine than he was. A proper confession, a fitting penance, and he could be free. He had only to call on the prelates who were there. They would even exorcise the demon for him, if he gave them leave.

Baldwin was a devout Christian, but he was also king, and he was young. How young, Aidan tended to forget. This that he must judge was nothing that he could know for himself, or with his sickness would ever know. It set him apart; it gave him distance, such as even a priest could not truly understand. A priest was a man beneath his tonsure, and bound by vows to one path and no other.

"Is it a sin," Morgiana asked, "to embrace one's husband?"

Her blankness had not been shock. It was the pause before the kill.

Baldwin sat bolt upright. "He married you?"

"No!" cried Aidan.

"No," Morgiana said. "Not strictly in law. But the deed is enough, if one can prove the intent."

"I intended nothing but the execution of our bargain."

"Exactly," she said.

Baldwin propped his chin on his hand. "It would," he mused, "be remarkably tidy."

Aidan hardly heard him. "Is that what you want?" he demanded of Morgiana. "To marry me?"

She blushed not at all. She did not even lower her eyes. "Yes," she said.

"That was what you bargained for?"

She nodded.

He laughed. It was half a howl. "You never told me."

"You didn't listen."

"Where are the go-betweens? Where is the dowry, the land, the promise of alliance? What can you offer me, my lady?"

"Myself."

He had heard a song once; or maybe it was he who had made it. Her eyes were her dowry. Her eyes, and the witchery behind them.

She took his hands. Her fingers were thin and cold and inhumanly strong. "Is it knightly, my lord, to spurn a lady?"

And he had been thinking that she had no artifice. She was as devious as any woman born.

The king spoke in their silence. "Answer me this, my lord. Tell me truly. Would you find it unbearable, to take this lady as your wife?"

Aidan's mouth opened. No words came. He closed it. His hands were still in hers, the fingers woven almost beyond untangling. His mind beat against its walls, yearning for her. All that stood between was a small, cold core of resistance. Of fear. What humans called love was a feeble thing; a word, a gesture, could end it. This was stronger by far. And if he took it, he could never let it go.

"You don't take it," Morgiana said, reading him as she always did, with perfect clarity. "It takes you. Look about you. Is that free air? Or don't you recognize the dragon's maw?"

"I don't," he said, struggling. "I don't hate you. I don't— want— How can I marry you?"

"Easily," she said. "You say the words. You mean them."

"But which words?"

"Ours," said the king. And as they spun to face him: "I am the Defender of the Holy Sepulcher. I have my own vows, and my own obligations. You ask me to judge you, lady. So I do. I grant the merit of your petition. I acknowledge that there is a debt, and that it has yet to be discharged. Are you willing to give up your faith for it?"

"No!" Aidan said it before she could move. "That's not part of any bargain, for her or for me. I am the stake in this game. I say that I will yield—if my lady will wed me by the Christian rite."

His heart was hammering. The dragon's maw, was this? It was sheer, stark terror. And mad joy. And Morgiana, hand-locked with him, astonished that he should have defended her faith. As if he did not know what it was to her. As if he could not care if he destroyed her.

She searched his face and his mind, fiercely, not daring even yet to trust him. "You love me as much as that?"

"Yes," he said.

Her joy was almost more than he could bear. "I will marry you," she said. "I will say the Christian words." They were only words. It was the spirit that mattered.

He heard the whole of it. His heart was singing; all its walls were fallen. She was in his mind, filling its empty places, heal-ing its scars. Yet she was no sweet, placid presence. She would defy him more often than she yielded to him; she would match him temper for temper. And when the war came at last, when jihad met Crusade, and God chose between them—

"Then God will choose," she said, "as He has written, and we will do as we must."

"So says the infidel."

"Only a Frank would make a mock of fate."

They glared at one another. "I'll serve my king in spite of you," he said.

"Why would I object? He's worthy of it."

"Ah, but am I?"

"You," she said with a lift of her chin, "are the best knight in the world."

The best knight in the world looked at the fairest lady in the world, and considered the wisdom of a reply. The court waited breathlessly for him to choose. The lady dared him to contradict her, or to agree with her.

A knight knew when to speak. He also knew when to be silent. Aidan bowed low and offered her a smile.

She considered it with care. She weighed it, measured it, assayed it. She tilted a brow.

He broadened the smile by a little.

The other brow went up.

Merchants all, these easterners. He would have to watch her when it came to the marriage vows, that she did not try to haggle with the priest.

She sparked at that. He caught her before she could burst into speech, and kissed her soundly.

Frankish directness, he reflected, could be useful in taming Saracens.

She laughed. Cruel, she; no mercy in her for his poor battered pride. But he forgave her. He was, after all, the best knight in the world.

AUTHOR'S NOTE

The events of *Alamut* are fairly equally divided between history and fantasy. Prince Aidan and his Assassin are, of course, imaginary, as is the kingdom of Rhiyana; likewise the House of Ibrahim and its dependents, and the family of the swordsmith in Damascus. The rest of the *dramatis personae,* however, are quite solidly historical, including the emir Usamah ibn Munqidh and his son Murhaf. The tales which Usamah tells are authentic, taken from his memoirs; these are available in English, in *An Arab-Syrian Gentleman and Warrior in the Period of the Crusades,* tr. P. K. Hitti (New York, 1929). Likewise the tale told by King Baldwin's tutor, Archdeacon (later Archbishop) William of Tyre, of his discovery of Baldwin's leprosy, is William's own; it can be found in volume two of his *A History of Deeds Done Beyond the Sea,* tr. Emily Babcock and A. C. Krey (New York, 1943).

I have built a castle in place of the ruined manor house at Aqua Bella, and given it to the fictitious family of the Hautecourts. The original manor, it may be noted, was a holding of the Knights Hospitaller, who also held the great castle of Krak des Chevaliers. Krak was restored earlier in this century by the French, and has served, most recently and most ironically, as one of the chief strongholds of the Palestinian Liberation Organization.

King Baldwin IV of Jerusalem was indeed a leper, and his sickness was indeed accepted by those whom he ruled as king; there was never any question of his right to the throne of his uncle, Baldwin III, and of his father, Amaury I. At the time of the novel (summer and autumn, A.D. 1176) he was about sixteen years old, and had been king since the age of thirteen. He was a military strategist of no small ability, and while his health allowed, he ruled firmly and well. The next year, at seventeen, he would deal Saladin his single worst defeat, at the battle of Montgisard. He died in 1185, blind, faceless, his hands and feet eaten away by his sickness, but even in the last year of his life he led his armies against the Saracen sultan, borne to the field in a litter. He died in his bed, of a fever, and was buried in Jerusalem in the Church of the Holy Sepulcher.

Baldwin's sister, the Princess Sybilla, had neither his intelligence nor his sense of proportion. The husband who had been found for her, William Longsword, Marquis of Montferrat, was an admirable choice: young, attractive, a good soldier and a skillful politician. Tragically, he fell ill of a fever and died the following year; his son and heir, named Baldwin after the king and called Baudouinet, "Little Baldwin," was born some months after William's death. Sybilla seems to have mourned him sincerely, but she soon found consolation: a French knight of no particular distinction, but strikingly handsome and adept with the ladies, Guy de Lusignan, whom she married in 1179 over the objections of the magnates of the kingdom. Her brother, enfeebled with his illness, permitted the marriage; he soon regretted it, however. Guy was more weak than truly treacherous, but Baldwin knew that the throne of the embattled kingdom should never be allowed to pass into the hands of a man who was constitutionally incapable of making a decision. When the leper king died, his nephew, the child Baldwin V, was crowned in his place, under the regency of Count Raymond of Tripoli. This was a direct slight to Guy, and Guy treated it as such; he rebelled against the regency and, when Baldwin V died after a year of kingship, seized the throne for himself. A year later, on 4 July 1187, Guy lost the greater part of his kingdom to Saladin in the battle of the Horns of Hattin. By the autumn of 1187, Saladin ruled as lord in Jerusalem. The Crusader Kingdom of Jerusalem, founded in 1099 after the capture of Jerusalem by a western army under the command of, among others, Count Godfrey of Bouillon, had fallen; it would never recover. Nor would any subsequent Crusade succeed in winning back Jerusalem from the infidel.

The Sultan Saladin (Salah al-Din Yusuf ibn Ayyub) was indeed in Damascus in the late summer of 1176, after his abortive attack on Masyaf; he married the Lady Ismat, widow of the Seljuk sultan Nur al-Din, somewhat later than I have indicated, in the autumn before returning to his second sultanate in Cairo. His elder brother, Turan-Shah, remained as regent in Damascus. He would return some years later, to strengthen his power in Syria and to extend it to Aleppo. The Prince al-Salih Ismail, son of Nur al-Din by another wife than Ismat, died in 1181, at the age of nineteen; in 1182, the city fell to Saladin. For an excellent and highly detailed biography of the sultan, see M. C. Lyons and D. E. P. Jackson, *Saladin: The Politics of the Holy War* (Cambridge, 1982).

The Islamic sect of the Assassins (more accurately, the Ismailis), founded in the late eleventh century by the warrior and mystic Hasan-i-Sabbah, was an extremist form of Shiite Islam, devoted to the principle of domination by means of assassination. Its central stronghold was in Alamut, the Nest of Eagles, in the Elburz Mountains in what is now Iran; Aleppo was a strong supporter of its policies. Sinan ibn Salman, the Old Man of the Mountain, was the greatest of the Assassins in Syria; born the son (he said) of a nobleman in Basra, he made his way to Alamut and swore fidelity to its master, Kiya Muhammad, and was raised and educated with the master's heirs. In 1162 Sinan was sent to propagate the faith in Syria. In 1164 Kiya Muhammad's son and heir, Hasan, declared the Resurrection of the Lost Imam and the advent of the Millennium; Sinan allegedly supported the violence done to the ascetic law of the sect, but then repudiated it. For the next thirty years he ruled all but absolutely in Syria; his final accomplishment was the murder of the would-be claimant to the throne of Jerusalem, Conrad of Montferrat—perhaps with the collusion of King Richard the Lionheart of England. Bernard Lewis provides a brief but thorough history of the sect in *The Assassins: A Radical Sect in Islam* (New York, 1967).

Although Alamut was destroyed by the Mongols in the thirteenth century and the Assassins themselves reduced to a minor sect of Islam, the line of the last Master has survived into the twentieth century. His direct lineal descendant is the Aga Khan.

The writing of a historical novel can, and does, involve as much sheer slog through the library as a doctoral dissertation; it is a considerable challenge to distill the mountain of research into a seamless story. My story could not have been what it is without the help of the books listed above. In addition, I am indebted for drama and for local color to Robert Payne, *The Dream and the Tomb: A History of the Crusades* (New York, 1984)—it was his section heading, "The Young King's Valor and the Fall of Jerusalem," which brought me first to the leper king; to C. R. Conder, *The Latin Kingdom of Jerusalem: 1099–1291 A.D.* (London, 1897), despite some errors of fact; and to Colin Thubron, whose *Mirror to Damascus* (Boston, 1967) guided me through the oldest continuously inhabited city in the world, and gave me the setting for the Damascene portion of the novel.

The song which Prince Aidan sings at the beginning of Chapter 1 is an authentic song of the Crusades, a rallying cry for the Second Crusade of 1147. The Old French text and music are taken from Joseph Bédier and Pierre Aubry, *Les Chansons de Croisade* (Paris, 1909); the English translation is my own. A good modern recording of the song as sung by baritone solo and chorus is that of David Munrow and the Early Music Consort of London in *Songs of Love and War: Music of the Crusades* (Argo).

Judith Tarr

Chevalier, mult estes guariz

Knight, you are most fortunate,
For God has set before you His complaint
Against the Turks and the Almoravids,
Who have done Him such great dishonor.
For by deception have they seized His faithful;
Well may we grieve for this,
For in that land was God first worshipped,
And known as Lord.

He who will go with Louis
Need have no fear of hell,
For his soul will go to Paradise
With the angels of our Lord.

 •   •   •   •   •   •   •   •   •   •

Let us go and conquer Moses,
Who sleeps on Mount Sinai;
Let us leave him no longer among the Saracens,
Nor the rod with which with a single blow
He parted the Red Sea,
And the great throng followed him;
And Pharaoh came after them:
He and all his people perished.

Che- va- lier, mult es- tes gua- riz, Quant Deu a
vus fait sa cla- mur Des Turs e des A- mo- ra-
viz, Ki li unt fait tels des- he- nors. Cher a tort
unt ses fieuz sai- siz; Bien en de- vums a- veir do-
lur, Cher la fud Dieu pri- mes ser- vi Et
re- co- nu- u pur se- gnuur. Ki ore i-
rat od Lo- o- ïs Ja mar d'en- fern a-
vrat pou- ur, Char s'alme en iert en pa- re-
ïs Od les an- gles nos- tre Sei- gnor.

Judith Tarr

Judith Tarr is the author of a number of novels of high and historical fantasy, including the award-winning *The Hound and the Falcon* trilogy, which is set in the same world and with some of the same characters as *Alamut;* and, from Bantam Spectra, *A Wind in Cairo* (also a novel of Saladin and the Crusades) and *Ars Magica*. She holds a Ph.D. in Medieval Studies from Yale University, as well as degrees from Mount Holyoke College and Cambridge University, and is a frequent lecturer and panelist on topics medieval and fantastical. She lives in New Haven, Connecticut, and is completing *The Horns of Hattin*, a new novel for Doubleday and Bantam.

BOOK MARK

The text of this book was set in the typeface Galliard by
Berryville Graphics, Berryville, Virginia.

The display was set in Abbott Old Style
by All-American Photolettering, New York, New York.

It was printed and bound by
R. R. Donnelley & Sons, Crawfordsville, Indiana.

Designed by Patrice Fodero

FLYING FOR FREEDOM